D0961870

PRAISE FOR ONE POTATO

"This novel is deranged, in the best way. If Aimee Bender and Charlie Kaufman wrote a book together, this is what it would sound like. McMahon has written a perfect novel satirizing our imperfect time."

—Joshua Mohr, author of *Sirens* and *Model Citizen*

"You're going to want more than a helping of *One Potato*, which humorously weaves together such disparate topics as American intervention in South America, the dangers of botanical monoculture, violent revolution, population bottlenecks, and a good, old-fashioned love affair. It is a sign of a truly accomplished writer that this novel entertains as it elucidates. You'll never see a spud the same way again."

—Allison Amend, author of *Enchanted Islands, A Nearly Perfect Copy, Stations West* and *Things That Pass for Love*

"With urgency, wit, and vivid imagination, Tyler McMahon's *One Potato* engagingly explores the dangers of monoculture, a ruthless dictatorship, GMO controversies, corporate greed and corruption, and the necessity and power of a free press. Packed with absurdist humor and a vibrant sense of place, a fast-paced and suspenseful plot and a layered rendering of its often hapless characters, *One Potato* is a memorable novel with an impressive scope. I was wonderfully entertained by this book, but I also learned so much from it."

—Joanna Luloff, author *Remind Me Again What Happened*

"Fast-paced, comedic, with significant social undercurrents—Tyler McMahon's latest novel *One Potato* is a wild ride with real heart. [McMahon] pairs hilarious antics and a sweet romance with very real research into GMO plants and products. If you've always wondered how Michael Pollan's nonfiction would look in the hands of Tom Robbins or TC Boyle, then this is the novel for you."

—Kristiana Kahakauwila, author of *This is Paradise: Stories*

"*One Potato* blends cauterizing satire with a deeply humane worldview. It manages to be—all at once—fast-paced and thoughtful, hilarious and consequential, disturbing and delightful."

—Elise Blackwell, author of *Hunger* and *The Lower Quarter*

"Like the diaries of Ché Guevara seen through an Ore Ida lens, this deeply funny yet pointed novel juggles the acknowledgement of a future we should all be terrified by, and the hope that our shared but loveably flawed humanity will win out in the end. Buy two copies, read one, and use the other as compost for your new organic backyard potato patch."

—Sean Beaudoin, author of *Welcome Thieves*

"Reminiscent of Vonnegut in his prime, *One Potato* drives the tantalizing line between satire and global reality, using quick, vivid chapters to create a captivating read. Eddie Morales and his game sidekick Raven Callahan are in over their heads in the most wonder-filled ways as they venture into the unknown world of Puerto Malogrado and the mysteries of genetics. Their story is both insightful and poignant, their trail of discovery one you can't help but follow."

—David Bajo, author of *The 351 Books of Irma Arcuri* and *The Ensenada Public Library*

"*One Potato* is a brutal, hilarious, and perfectly-timed interrogation of Big Agriculture's colonization of the human food supply—And McMahon's landscape of "third world conflict porn" is brilliantly pollinated by unforgettable characters either longing for connection, painfully suffering their genetics, or absurdist and malignant in their dedication to the regime of Capitalism crop-dusting our minds and hearts."

—J. Reuben Appelman, author of *The Kill Jar*

ONE POTATO

ONE POTATO

A NOVEL BY

TYLER McMAHON

KEYLIGHT
BOOKS

Keylight Books
a division of Turner Publishing Company
Nashville, Tennessee

www.turnerpublishing.com

One Potato

Cover design by Lucy Kim
Book design by Mallory Collins

Library of Congress Cataloging-in-Publication Data

Names: McMahon, Tyler, 1976- author.
Title: One potato / Tyler McMahon.
Description: First edition. | Nashville, Tennessee : Keylight Books, [2022]
  Identifiers: LCCN 2021030552 (print) | LCCN 2021030553 (ebook) | ISBN
  9781684427833 (hardcover) | ISBN 9781684427826 (paperback) | ISBN
  9781684427840 (ebook)
Subjects: LCSH: Transgenic plants--Fiction. | Genetically modified
  foods--Fiction. | LCGFT: Thrillers (Fiction)
Classification: LCC PS3613.C5846 O54 2022 (print) | LCC PS3613.C5846
  (ebook) | DDC 813/.6--dc23
LC record available at https://lccn.loc.gov/2021030552
LC ebook record available at https://lccn.loc.gov/2021030553

Printed in the United States of America

For Paul Diamond

ONE POTATO

B efore the ordeal, all I cared about was my assistant Jill and the perfect vending-machine French fry. I finally had my own lab on the second floor. Our latest round of prototypes had brought us so near to a breakthrough that I could almost taste it.

"We're getting close," Jill said over the bubbling oil. Her chestnut hair was pulled back into a tight ponytail just below the strap of her safety goggles. Even under the fluorescent lights, the skin of her face looked dewy and round.

"Very close." Indeed, after months of hard work, the reconstituted potato flakes had finally formed into convincing batons. We'd worked out a particular blend of oils, the perfect temperature, and a viscosity that wouldn't clog any of the machine's parts. The only aspect that still eluded us was aesthetic: a crispy, golden-hued outermost layer. The samples we'd produced thus far all had a mealy texture and a pale color—never quite brown enough.

I was convinced that one more step, some sort of coating or varnish, would take our product to the next level.

We spread a batch of samples across the stainless-steel counter, along with a dozen potential browning agents. I painted the latter onto the fries, while Jill labeled the grid.

"Seriously, Eddie. This could be a game-changer." Jill's voice grew throaty with excitement. The smell of her shampoo was still faintly pleasant over the aroma of hot oil.

"I'm just the R & D guy." I shrugged.

"Don't be so modest!" She gave me a playful hip-check. "Warren changed the world with frozen fries, half a century ago. If you figure this out, no teenager will have to stand over a fryer getting acne ever again."

I nodded.

"Imagine it," she said. "They might as well put a fry dispenser beside the soda dispenser in McDonald's."

"Self-serve." I said it as though the concept hadn't occurred to me. "It's possible." In truth, I preferred to imagine these machines at lonesome truck stops and rest areas, the waiting rooms of hospitals and bus stations. What motivated me most about this project was the notion that any American anywhere might be able to buy real, warm fries—the world's greatest comfort food—at any hour of the day or night, with one unwrinkled dollar bill. No prep and no mess.

"It's more than possible." Jill's elbow brushed mine. We exchanged a mutual embarrassed glance.

"Once we get our part sorted out," I said, "the engineers will have to finish up the machine."

"Then we can finally celebrate." Jill looked up from the grid and cocked an eyebrow at me.

I felt my face start to blush and turned back to the varnish.

"Morales!" The door to the laboratory burst open. "Is Doctor Morales around?"

"We're in the middle of an experiment here," Jill shouted.

The intruder was a big-shouldered lump of a man with a dark suit and a shaved head. I could tell by his red badge that he was from Operations.

"What can I do for you?" I snapped off a rubber glove. "I'm Doctor Morales. And you are?"

"Lutz." His big hand gave mine one hard squeeze, then released. "You're needed on the eighth floor. Immediately."

"That's Warren's floor!" Jill stage-whispered.

"There must be a mistake," I insisted. The oil inside the beaker let out a spatter. "I don't have any business up there."

"Smells like fries in here," the Ops man said. "You coming, or what?"

"Go!" Jill said. "I'll handle this."

I nodded and took off the goggles and lab coat. Jill straightened my collar, tucked my hair behind my ear, and gave me a thumbs-up. I followed Lutz to the elevator. His thick finger nearly covered the Up button as he pressed it.

"The eighth floor?" I asked.

"That's correct," he said.

"I've never even been up there before."

Lutz sighed. "The elevator does most of the work."

Warren Shepherd had started this company when he was fourteen years old with a few potato seeds and an acre of southern Idaho soil. Now, Tuberware was the world leader in all potato-related products, taking *Solanum tuberosum* into areas of science not previously considered possible: improved foodstuffs, many of them frozen or shelf-stable; starches and fillers for use in other processed foods; non-edible goods like potato-based insulation and packing materials; as well as a whole new array of plants and seeds. This building, One Potato Way, functioned both as an executive headquarters and an innovation laboratory for new products and technologies.

I'd shaken Warren's hand at the Christmas party a couple of times, but I'd never had a full-blown face-to-face conversation with the man. He kept a private office on the eighth floor. When I'd first started here, a sign in the elevator had explained that no employee was allowed to enter without an invitation or an escort. Now the sign was gone and the fact was simply understood.

"Is this about the machine?" I asked Lutz as we slowly climbed.

"The what?"

"The French-fry vending-machine prototype."

"I doubt that Warren is aware of that project's existence," Lutz said.

"So it *is* Warren I'm going to see up there? Mister Shepherd, I mean."

"Nobody else has an office on that floor."

The doors slid apart. Lutz held them open with one hand and gestured for me to exit with the other. Once I was out of the metal box, I turned back to him.

He didn't say goodbye—only used his eyes to gesture toward the opposite side of the floor—as the elevator doors slid closed.

Upon first glance, this wasn't so different from the other levels of One Potato Way. I stepped out onto the same gray tile as my lab, surrounded by similar off-white walls—the only light coming from fluorescent tubes along the ceiling. But at the far end stood a different sort of wall, this one of rough-hewn timber, like an old ski lodge or a Western saloon. In front of that was a small desk with a woman seated behind it.

"Eduardo?" she asked.

"Eddie is fine," I said.

"He's ready for you." She smiled: white teeth through dark lipstick, her hair pulled back in a tight bun.

"Mister Shepherd is ready for me?" I asked.

She nodded and stood to open the wooden door.

I met her eyes and saw my confusion reflected there. Was nobody going to tell me what Warren wanted before I went into his office?

The woman extended a hand, as if to show me the way.

Once inside the office, I had to squint. The north-facing wall was entirely floor-to-ceiling windows, looking out toward the foothills. In the distance, the tallest peaks of the Boise Mountains were capped with snow and reflected the afternoon sun. Once my eyes adjusted to the brightness, I made out a long executive desk—built from a blonder strain of timber and coated in an inch of varnish. The interior wall, even the flooring, was all knotty wood. It was a charming log cabin suspended eight stories up in the sky.

Sitting behind the desk, Warren Shepherd stared out the window, the back of his head shining with thick silver hair.

"It's beautiful country, isn't it?" He didn't turn around.

"Idaho?" I said sheepishly. "It certainly is."

"America." The chair spun, and Warren sat there facing me. His expression was more somber than in the photographs that hung throughout the hallways.

"Right," I said. "They're both beautiful countries. States. Sorry. They're both very nice."

"Have a seat," he said.

I sat down in a stiff wooden chair—the lone piece of furniture on this side of his desk.

"You're Cuban; isn't that right, Eduardo?"

"'Eddie' is fine, sir. No, I'm from Florida, actually. My parents left Cuba after the Revolution. Cuban-American, I suppose."

"A hell of a thing." He looked down at the desk, tapped at it with a long fingernail. "Losing your country right out from under you like that."

"Yes, sir. I wouldn't really know, sir. I've never been to Cuba."

"I meant your family."

"My family! Yes. Hell of a thing for them, sir."

"Speak Spanish, is that correct?"

"Me or my family?" I asked.

"*Tú hablas español?*"

"Oh, right. We spoke it in my home, growing up. I'm rusty now, sir."

"Rusty?" he said.

"Yes."

"Do you enjoy working here, Eduardo?"

I paused and took a breath. "It's my dream job, sir. I love it." That was true. I'd worked with potatoes even as a college student. Before my graduate study was finished, it was clear that Tuberware would be the perfect place for me.

"Outstanding." Warren opened a drawer and produced a thick manila folder. "You've heard of Puerto Malogrado?" He dropped the folder onto the desktop with a thud.

"The country?" I asked. "In South America?"

He grunted. "A landlocked nation named for a port. How do you like that?"

"Some consider it the birthplace of the potato," I said.

Warren looked up from his documents and held my stare for a second. "Is that so?"

I shrugged. "It's contested, but yes. That's one theory."

"Well, they get them from us now."

"I heard about that. They're buying the DS 400s, correct?"

Warren leaned back, his interest in the documents appearing to wane. "Do you know what that 'DS' stands for, Eduardo?"

"No, sir. Genetics isn't really my field." I touched my yellow Processed Foods badge, a subtle reminder of my actual role in his company.

"Dog slobber," he said.

An awkward second of silence passed. Outside, a crow flew danger-ously close to the window behind Warren, but pulled up at the last minute. I flinched in my chair.

"Is that a joke, sir?"

"The 'S' started off as 'saliva.' Maybe you could say that 'slobber' is a joke. It does roll off the tongue a little better."

"That's funny: that last part." I grinned. "Slobber. Off the tongue."

Warren didn't appear to get it. "Here's the deal. We'd been selling Puerto Malogrado our Idaho Bombs for years. They're a bigger and much more calorie-dense product than those scrawny blue ones they got down there. Problem is, at certain elevations, they get attacked by some odd unidentified bacteria."

"So you got Gen-Mod on it?" I asked. The Genetic Modification unit specialized in creating strains of tubers that were resistant to pests—and pesticides.

He nodded. "And do you know where you find a wealth of robust, broad-spectrum, bacteria-fighting enzymes, Eduardo?"

"Ed. Or Eddie's fine. No, sir."

"Dog saliva." Warren smiled. "Why do you think they're always licking their wounds?"

"Sorry, sir. Vertebrates are not a specialty of mine either." It did make a bit of sense, I supposed. "Does it work?"

"Like gangbusters." He slammed his fist onto the desk. "Not a single case of infection on the plant since we started testing those seeds down there, over a dozen years ago now. The FDA approval is still in process. But we could be talking about a potato variety for all seasons and all climates here." He grew short of breath.

"So, what's the problem?" I asked.

"The problem is," Warren pushed around the papers from the file, "in one of the farming villages where they're growing DS 400, three children have been born who allegedly cannot walk upright on two legs."

I waited for him to erupt in laughter or scream "gotcha!" at me. Only silence.

"You're not serious," I said.

He took one piece of paper out from under the others, turned it around, then passed it to my side. I pulled my chair up closer to his desk and had a look. The page was a printout of a low-quality photograph showing three children crawling across the ground on the balls of their feet and the heels of their hands. They looked to be just outside a humble adobe house, some chairs and a clothesline in the background.

"But this," I couldn't look away from the picture. "This is ridiculous. It doesn't make any—"

"It's *beyond* ridiculous." Warren raised his voice. "It's complete horseshit. There's no relationship to our potatoes at all. But now we've got all the makings of a full-blown media circus on our hands."

"Are they faking it?" My eyes stayed on the photo.

Warren blew a puff of air out one side of his mouth. "Most likely. There certainly are people who'd love to see our GMOs linked to something like this. There's a very small chance it could be a legitimate genetic anomaly. It happens a couple times a century, or so I'm told. Either way, now there's not much stopping every family in Puerto Malogrado from making their kids walk on all fours and bark out loud."

"Can I ask a question, sir?"

"What's that, Eduardo?"

"Why are you telling me all this? I don't do genetics. I have no background in it. I'm a Processed Foods man, an R & D guy—fries mostly, oil-starch interface. This is way out of my area." Again, I tried to lift my badge and demonstrate its color.

A grin grew wide across Warren's face. "But you do speak the language."

"Excuse me?" I said.

"You're going to Malogrado."

"Sir, I'm sure I wouldn't know the first thing about—"

"There won't be any actual science going on, son. It's all smoke and mirrors. We send down some bodies with white coats and clipboards—PhDs after their names. Take some samples. Talk a little jargon. Invite the media. It's a good-faith effort to look concerned. Then it all blows over. Think of it as a vacation."

"Isn't there some kind of a revolution going on in Puerto Malogrado?" I asked.

Warren sighed. "The answer to that question has technically been 'yes' for at least two decades now. Revolution is a tradition in that country. They hold them the way we hold baseball season. Why do you think we're able to test so many varietals down there without the red tape?"

"This is all very flattering, sir. But there's zero chance that I'm the right man for this. Wouldn't it be better to send someone with a public relations background?"

Warren held up a palm and made a gentle "sit-back" gesture. I leaned against the stiff chair. He turned toward the landscape of his beautiful city, this state of his, him the closest thing there was to a king of all Idaho.

"First, there's the language." Warren held his hands together at the small of his back.

"Surely I'm not the only one in this company who can speak a little Spanish." I let out a small, nervous chuckle—then realized that I probably was.

"You mentioned public relations," he said. "There's also a certain optical aspect. It would be nice if we sent somebody down there who wasn't so . . . wasn't quite so lily-white as most of our scientists."

"Sir." That stupid chuckle escaped my mouth again. "I'm not sure if you've noticed, but I'm not all that brown."

Warren turned away from the window. His bottom lip stuck forward a bit. He looked me up and down where I sat in the chair. "Mmm," he said. "You're brown enough."

Lutz waited outside Warren's office and escorted me down to the seventh floor—another place I'd never been, but which lacked the mythology of Eight. There, outside the elevator, I was met by a doughy young man with spiky blond hair.

"Doctor Morales." He grabbed my hand and shook it like an aerosol can. "I'm Mitch. International Strategy."

"Pleased to meet you," I said.

Our two hands bounced up and down between us for another second.

"You wouldn't happen to have a vaccination card, by any chance?" Mitch asked.

"I do not."

"What about foreign travel? What regions have you visited recently?"

"I went to a conference in Vancouver last year. Other than that, I've never left the United States." Nor did I have much desire to start now.

Mitch made a sinister grin and patted my upper arm. "A blank slate! We'll start from scratch."

"You know, downstairs I have a—"

"Roll up your sleeves, partner. Both of them. I hope you don't mind needles."

"Actually, I—"

"'Cause there's no other way to get these vaccines!"

Mitch led me to a smaller room—this one with anatomy charts on the wall—and had me sit on a medical examination table. White paper crumpled under my thighs. A female assistant, wearing rubber gloves and surgical scrubs, carried in an enormous needle. She swabbed my arm with alcohol.

"Are you a nurse or something?" I asked. "Do we have those here?"

"Relax," she said. "Breathe out."

"Could we slow down? I'd like to know what sorts of shots I truly need."

"They've got a little bit of everything down there." She stuck her syringe inside a vial. "Rabies, TB, yellow fever, some things I've never even heard of."

In my peripheral vision, I saw grainy static—like a television losing a signal. "Are you sure?" My mouth suddenly felt so dry I could barely speak.

Then the prick. The sharpened length of steel felt like a kabob skewer scraping around underneath the skin of my arm. The blur at the sides of my eyes spread across the whole of my vision. The last thing I remembered was a strong smell in my nostrils; I couldn't decide whether it was perfume or antiseptic.

——

When I awoke, my body lay prone across the examination table. Both my sleeves were rolled up. My biceps throbbed as though they'd been attacked by a swarm of bees. A white flower—a small orchid, perhaps—had been placed on my sternum.

"Am I done?" I asked, not sure if anyone was around to hear me.

I picked up the flower from my chest, sat up, and took a look at my arms. They were a sickly shade of greenish yellow, bruised as if by repeated punching.

"Morales!" Mitch came into the room, his face pink and giddy. "You were out cold, dude."

"I noticed."

"Seriously: you turned white. It was hilarious."

"Can I go?" I asked.

"You're done with the shots but not the other stuff. Here." He handed me a small dossier of documents. "We got your official scientific visa in there, plus a letter in both English and Spanish explaining your mission. There's also a State Department report on the situation in Puerto Malogrado. I'd skip the sections on disease and crime if I were you. They're scary as fuck."

Still dazed, I flipped through the documents without actually reading a word. The photo Warren had shown me upstairs was also included.

"You've still got the passport from your Vancouver trip, I presume? Those are the phone numbers of the nearest consulate. Call them if you have any problems. Those numbers are also in your belt."

"My belt?" I looked down at my pants and noticed an unfamiliar leather strap through the loops. This one was thick and black and didn't match my shoes. "You changed my belt?"

"That's right. What you got on now is state of the art. There's a zippable compartment on the inside with photocopies of your identification, the embassy contact numbers, plus ten one-hundred-dollar bills. Everything you need in case of an emergency. Plus," Mitch undid my belt buckle, removed the belt, and held the underside up to me. "The panic button."

Behind the buckle, there was a plastic cover, which hid a bright red button and a tiny digital readout.

"Hit this if things get really hairy."

"What happens then?" I asked.

Mitch's expression changed. "I don't know, actually." He cocked an eyebrow. "Why don't we try it?"

"But—"

"Just kidding! Lighten up, dude." He handed it back to me. "There's a homing beacon in the buckle. It'll alert us to your location. We'll send in private security and call the local law enforcement."

"This trip that Warren wants me to take, whatever he thinks I should be doing down there, is it really all that dangerous?"

"I wouldn't worry about it. You'll probably never need that thing. But still . . ."

14

"Better safe than sorry?" I offered.

"Well, yeah. And, it's just awesome! I mean: any excuse to wear it is worth the trip, in my opinion."

"When, exactly, does Warren think I should leave?" I stood and passed the belt through the loops on my pants.

"Tomorrow. This shit is time-sensitive, is my understanding."

"Tomorrow? That's completely impossible." I went to fasten the belt and noticed that its tightest hole was still too loose for my waist. "You're going to have to find somebody else for this. Hopefully someone a bit thicker."

"Sorry, bro." Mitch picked up a clipboard and checked off a series of boxes. "Those kinds of decisions are way above my pay grade. I'm just following orders here."

I pulled against the belt and produced two inches of slack between it and my waist.

"Sign here, Eduardo." Mitch passed me his clipboard. "It shows that you got your shots and your files and stuff."

"Don't you have this belt in a smaller size?"

"Sorry." Mitch shrugged. "We'll send a car for you in the morning."

—

It was nearly five p.m. once I got back down to the lab, the dossier tucked under one of my throbbing arms.

"Eddie!" Jill dropped her tongs and lifted her goggles to the top of her head. "How did it go? What did Warren want?"

I walked over to our worktable and put the dossier on the counter. "He wants to send me to South America."

"What?"

"Puerto Malogrado. There's some kind of situation there."

"You mean the revolution?"

"Besides that. A problem with the DS 400s."

"Isn't that more of a Gen-Mod issue?"

I nodded.

"Why you?"

"Because I speak the language, I guess." I left off the being brown part.

"What did you say?"

I shrugged. "It wasn't really a question, you know."

"This is great news, Eddie!" Jill squeezed my arm.

"Ouch," I said. "I just got some shots."

"He must think so highly of your work."

I looked down at the tray by the burner, the grid with labels written in Jill's delicate, rounded script. Nearly every fry from the new batch was burnt black. Must be too much sugar in the varnish. "I'm sure that's not the case."

"It isn't so strange." Jill's excitement wouldn't cease. "Warren was just a farmer before he started running this company. Maybe he sees leadership potential in you."

I was quite certain he'd never seen anything of me—except for a personnel file, perhaps—before I'd walked into his office today.

"When are you supposed to leave?"

"Tomorrow."

"Tomorrow?" Jill's grin widened. "Let's celebrate!"

The bar was lit only by a series of televisions fixed to each corner. Boise State football fans—dressed in orange and blue gear—crowded the place. Jill found us a high table in the middle, the point farthest from the screens.

"Wow. What's all this?" Jill asked, nodding at the load I was carrying in my hands.

"Some kind of special for the game." I dropped a pitcher onto the polished wood of the table, then struggled with a platter of thick-cut potato wedges and stuffed potato skins. "It came with the beer."

Jill helped make space, then poured me a glass.

I managed to fit the food onto the table and accepted the beer from Jill. The other patrons clapped at the television.

"So, is Warren's office everything they say it is?" Jill seemed more interested in my trip to the eighth floor than the one to the Southern Hemisphere.

"It's definitely got a certain log-cabin aesthetic." I wasn't sure what rumors she'd heard. "Apart from all the glass and the fact that it's eight stories up in the air."

"He built that thing himself." Jill filled her own beer mug. "Can you believe that?"

"Warren did?" I reached for a potato skin and tried to picture the old man with a saw and hammer, shouldering logs while the concrete building was finished around him. "Are you sure?"

"Not the eighth floor, but the original. Once he moved into his office at One Potato Way, he felt something was wrong. So he ordered the cabin from his very first farm—the one he'd built by hand—to be taken apart and reconstructed up there, as his office. He says it keeps him grounded."

That made a little more sense. "Where did you hear all this?"

Jill took a sip of her beer. "The grapevine. So, tell me about these kids," Jill said. "They crawl but they can't walk? Like babies?"

"Not exactly." I shook my head. "In the photo I saw, they didn't use their knees, only their feet and hands. It's known as a bear crawl."

"What might cause that?" Jill asked.

"Most likely they're faking it." I finished off the potato skin. "Some whack-job greenie group probably heard about the DS 400s and cooked this all up—threw some cash at a *campesino* family and leaked it to the press."

"Of course." Jill held a wedge at her mouth level but paused before taking a bite. "But say it was real, hypothetically; what would explain something like that?"

I shrugged. "In theory, maybe a small mutation, something in the lower brain or the inner ear related to walking upright. A forgotten synapse that helps with balance."

"It's amazing." She finally took a bite from her potato wedge and returned the rest of it to the platter. "All the things we take for granted. How many tiny little mechanisms that need to come together in order for something like bipedalism to work."

"Apparently, this wouldn't be the first case that's ever been observed. I guess it happens once a century or so. The last documented case was in rural Turkey, several years ago."

"That should help, right? Some precedent? Occurrences that have nothing to do with our crops?" She picked up her beer and took a sip.

"Maybe," I admitted. "Thing is: even in those other cases, nobody has a clue as to the cause."

Jill nodded, then turned to look at the televised game. "But you're right: they're probably just faking."

An incomplete pass replayed over and over—slow motion and reverse—the ball passing right through the hands of the open receiver.

"I've got to find a way out of this trip," I said.

"A way out?" Jill slammed her glass onto the tabletop. "Are you kidding? This is great news."

"It's going to put us so far behind on the machine fries."

"Eddie." She reached out and touched my hand. "Forget the machine fries for a second, would you?"

"Forget it?" I looked down at her fingers on mine.

"This is a bigger deal. This is a chance for you to shine. You're going to be the face of this company to the world."

I knew she was right. But the truth was, I had no interest in shining. I liked my role in the company. I ran my own lab now, with the perfect assistant. I'd even worked my way up to a decent parking space. Behind-the-scenes suited me. I never got any glory and never asked for it. It was hard work and humility that had brought me to Idaho, to my work with potatoes.

"It's not my area." On television, a wide shot of the blue football field.

"You'll do great," Jill insisted. "Will they send you down on Warren's jet?"

"Potato One? I'm not sure. A car is coming for me in the morning."

"I saw it at the airport once, but I've never been inside."

"That would be something," I agreed.

The bar erupted in cheers. A BSU player spiked the ball in the end zone, did a well-rehearsed dance.

"Eddie," Jill said. "Why don't we get out of here?"

"Already? We've barely touched the food." I gestured toward the appetizers on the table.

"Leave it." She leaned toward me and met my eyes, put her hand back over mine. "It's your last night in town until who knows when. Let's get out of here, shall we?"

"Oh." I wiped my mouth with a napkin and stood up from my barstool. "After you."

We abandoned the beer and the food and headed out into the now-cool Boise night. Though neither of us mentioned a destination, Jill led the way toward my building.

The door burst open to my downtown condo. The two of us fell all over each other—kissing and groping our way straight to the sofa. At first I was ecstatic. She pinned my shoulders against the back of the couch and sat astride me, her lips at my ear, her chestnut hair—so straight and shiny—tickling my collarbones. There had always been chemistry between Jill and me; it was past time we acted upon it. But as the minutes of making-out continued, something seemed off. We hadn't removed any clothes besides our jackets. Instead, Jill's energy was devoted to rubbing against me—hard, right through our pants.

Like many of my friends and neighbors in Idaho, Jill had been brought up in the Church of Latter-Day Saints. I've often heard that, among lapsed Mormons, certain lifestyle quirks persist long after the religion is abandoned. These were said to include distaste for coffee, fondness for board games, and—as seemed to be the case with Jill—affinity for dry-humping.

We went at it, pants on, for what felt like hours. I was wearing a stiff pair of chinos, and soon—between the swelling and the chafing—was in no small amount of pain.

"Um, Jill. . . ."

"Oh, Eddie!" she grunted.

"Do you think . . . maybe we could. . . ."

But it was no use. Her teeth were clenched tight and her eyes turned upward, her body grinding on my lap like a mechanical bull.

Finally, mercifully, Jill rolled off me and said "I can't do this anymore."

"Okay!" I figured she meant it was time for the pants to come off, and I reached for my fly.

"You're technically my superior," she went on.

"Oh . . . right."

"I like you, Eddie. I love working with you. But I want a long career at Tuberware. I can't be the girl who screwed her way to the top."

"Of course." I pulled my hand back from my waistline. "I mean, technically, this isn't . . . screwing is more like. . . . No, I get it." My face felt flushed, and my crotch ached. I did my best to smile. "Plus, we wouldn't want it to get weird, at work."

Jill gathered up her coat. "I would hate for it to get weird."

"You know." I felt my eyes water. "Chances are we'll be moved to different projects after the machine fries are finished."

"That's true." Jill turned back to face me. "We could even put in a request."

"And if this trip goes well, maybe I'll get promoted." I rose to my feet, found a comfortable stance, and tried to lighten the mood with a little sarcasm. "Hell, if it's like you say—leadership potential and all—I might be put in charge of my own division!" I grinned wide, expecting to share a laugh.

"You're right, Eddie." She sat up on the couch. "You could have your pick. If we move to different areas, there'd be no conflict of interest."

"Um, yeah," I said. She hadn't taken it as the joke I'd intended. "No conflict whatsoever. But seriously, Jill, maybe we shouldn't put too much faith in this little trip of mine. Anything could. . . ."

Her stare still squarely fixed on my eyes, she reached under my emergency belt and undid the top button of my chinos.

". . . happen," I said.

A firm knock at my door jolted me awake. Some piece of clothing must've landed over my alarm clock's digital display. The sun's first soft rays struck my curtains. Another knock. I rose, found a pair of pants, and managed to pull them on. On the far side of the bed, Jill's tiny breaths whispered in and out of her mouth.

"Yes?" I opened the door a crack and pressed my face toward it.

"Doctor Morales. It's time to go."

Still squinting with sleep, I barely recognized Lutz. Bluish bags hung under his eyes. The stubble along his scalp had grown out since I'd last seen him. He appeared to still be wearing yesterday's suit.

"I haven't finished packing yet." I hadn't started either—hadn't even thought about packing, in fact.

Lutz lifted a cell phone and looked at its screen. "Five minutes. That's it. I'll wait out here."

I nodded and eased the door shut. First I put on a clean shirt and the too-big, money-stuffed belt that was supposed to keep me safe. Next, I found my once-used passport in the drawer of my desk. Hangers and all, I pulled clothes straight from my closet and stuffed them into my suitcase. In a back corner of the closet, an old lab coat gathered dust. I recalled Warren's description of my duties in Puerto Malogrado and tucked that in as well. From the bathroom I grabbed my toothbrush, a razor, and a small bottle of hand sanitizer.

Jill stirred and looked around. "What time is it?" she asked.

"I'm not sure. The Ops man is outside. I'm about to leave."

She sat up on the bed. "Already?"

"Afraid so. Do you think you can let yourself out?"

She rose from the bed and stroked my back. I zipped up the rolling suitcase.

"Do they have beaches down there?" she asked.

"No coast," I answered. "In spite of the name."

She put her arms around my middle and leaned her head into my shoulder. "You'll do great down there, Eddie. I know you will."

I stopped packing and returned her embrace.

"And once you get back, the sky's the limit."

I suppose she was speaking about my career. But in my mind's eye, I thought only of our future, of the relationship that we might have, now that the ice was broken. Jill was a catch: beautiful, smart, with a good career, very little debt, no children or previous marriages. We could have a nice life together. This condo would probably be too small for our needs; perhaps we'd find a single-family home on the Bench or in the ragged edge of the North End. Heck, if I did come back to the kind of advancement opportunities she had in mind, maybe even Warm Springs or Hyde Park. A real house, wood siding, a big yard, gables and dormers, Sunday dinners—all I'd ever wanted.

She was right: things would turn out fine. The only thing standing between me and my dreams was a small misunderstanding in South America.

"I have to go." I kissed her on the lips. "But I'll be back soon."

———

Lutz led the way to a car parked outside. He put my bag in the trunk, opened a back door for me, then got behind the wheel.

"Mister Lutz, can I ask a question? Do you happen to know the nature of the flight I'm about to take? Of the . . . the aircraft?"

"You're on Warren's jet for the first leg." He barely looked away from the road.

"Potato One!" I did my best to sound nonchalant.

"Just to Miami."

"Miami?" A sour note rang out in my voice. "We're stopping in Miami?" I hadn't anticipated going through my home city—a place that I avoided, had spent my whole life escaping from.

"Just a layover. An hour or so. You're on commercial the rest of the way."

"Right. Of course."

"You can't fly a little private jet all that distance." He then let out an uncharacteristically emotive sound—a scoff that bordered on a laugh. "And we sure as hell don't have any flights to South America from here in Boise."

"One more thing I like about this place," I said under my breath.

otato One was everything I'd hoped. We drove right up to the charter terminal—no parking hassles or waiting in lines. I settled into a luxurious leather seat. There was even a stewardess on board, offering me juice and coffee. This was the sort of travel I could get used to. Perhaps Jill was right: maybe it *was* time to take an executive turn. I opened the dossier and had another look at the photos. The coffee woke some sleeping ambition within me. More than ever, I felt ready for this—felt I was the right man, after all. What was called for here was some sort of actionable plan, a set of tests or procedures defined by Tuberware. Something with the appearance of rigor, of objectivity—and, most importantly—of closure.

"Excuse me! Wait just a second!" I heard a female voice call out. "I'm supposed to be on this plane!"

Then she appeared.

The young woman who stepped aboard looked as if she'd gotten dressed in a safari-supply store with the lights off. Her clothes were all baggy synthetic khaki, and covered in pockets. She wore an overflowing backpack and a floppy wide-brimmed hat.

Out of breath, she set down the pack and said: "Thank goodness. I thought I'd missed this flight."

"I'm sure you're not supposed to be here," I said.

"This is the potato flight?" she asked. "Heading to Puerto Malogrado? I'm a journalist. I'm coming to cover this case."

I immediately closed up my dossier with the photo of the children.

"Raven Callahan." She held out her hand.

"Raven? That's your name?"

"Yes."

"Is there something else that your friends call you?"

"My friends call me Raven."

"That's unfortunate." I shook her hand. "I'm Doctor Morales."

"Ma'am," the stewardess interrupted. "Would you mind sitting down and fastening your seat belt? We're almost ready for takeoff."

"Of course."

The stewardess struggled to fit the giant bag into one of the few storage compartments, then finally gave up and left it near the door. Raven sat in the chair next to mine. She removed her hat and revealed a cascade of long, wavy red hair, loosely tied together in the back. Her face was without makeup, her cheeks densely freckled. From a few of her many pockets she produced an odd assemblage of charms and trinkets: what looked to be a St. Christopher's medal, one of those feather-and-twine dream catchers, a crystal of some kind, a string of beads, and a tiny doll with tassels.

"Don't take this the wrong way," I said. "But you might be offending more gods than you're invoking with that hodgepodge."

She turned to face me, genuine concern in her eyes. "Sorry. I'm not a good flyer."

"Despite the Raven thing?" I asked.

The plane taxied down the runway.

"The takeoffs get to me." She took a prescription jar from another pocket on her vest and swallowed two pills from it.

"It's the safest form of travel," I said. "You're in much more danger on the cab ride to the airport."

"I rode my bike here," she said.

"With that backpack? You're lucky to be alive. This flight will be the safest thing you've done so far today."

The jet's engines kicked into high gear. I buckled my seat belt and checked my phone one last time.

"Doctor Morales," Raven said. "This might sound a little weird. But do you think you could hold my hand?"

"Excuse me?"

"Just for the takeoff. I always ask the person sitting next to me on a normal flight. I've never been on a plane like this before."

"You know, I'm not really a touchy sort of—"

"Please."

"Sure. Fine." I reached into my pocket and took out the bottle of hand sanitizer. "Just one second." I squeezed a tiny bead into my palm, then rubbed it around with my fingers.

"Jesus, Doc!" Raven frowned at me. "It's not like the fear of flying is contagious."

"Sorry," I said. "It's important that I stay healthy on this trip."

"We're almost in the air already."

"Okay." I set my hand on the armrest between us.

She grabbed hold of it in her sweaty palm, pulled it toward her abdomen, and wrapped it up inside her other arm. The jet's wheels lifted off from the runway. Raven's eyes shut tight, she squeezed hard at my hand—as though the doors of the plane were still open and she'd be thrown out if she didn't cling to something.

I turned away from her—to the extent that I could, while still in her clutches—and had another look out my window. The plane made a wide, arcing turn. For a brief moment I saw the Owyhee Mountains to the south—their dry, rugged severity against the clear blue of the sky. The plane banked, then straightened out, and suddenly I had a glorious view of the Boise Range, the towers of Bogus Basin, the Lucky Peak Reservoir reflecting the sun.

"Open your eyes," I said to Raven. "It's a beautiful day."

She let out a breath and appeared to relax, finally letting go of my hand.

I pointed to the view out the window.

But by now we were over the dry-land potato farms of southern Idaho. Enormous green circles—formed by the radii of irrigation pivots—covered the ground. From above, the landscape resembled a massive tray of Christmas cookies, all with bright green sprinkles, all impossibly round. The un-irrigated corners were as black and dead as the patina on an old baking sheet. I could tell that these were "clean fields": recently sprayed, devoid of all insects or fungi—of any life-form other than potatoes.

"Well." She sighed. "It's nice to be leaving Idaho, at least."

"I love Idaho," I said softly.

We reached our cruising altitude, and Raven let go of my hand.

The flight attendant rose and approached our seats. "More coffee or juice?"

"I'll take some more coffee," I answered.

"Juice would be great," Raven said. "And if you have anything stronger, I'd appreciate some of that as well." She let out an awkward laugh. "Nervous flyer."

The stewardess nodded. She came back a second later with a coffee for me and a glass of juice and two small bottles of vodka for Raven.

From one of her largest pockets, Raven removed a guidebook on South America, spread it across her lap, and eagerly dog-eared the pages. I wasn't sure what she knew about the case so far, but I wasn't about to share my documents.

Once certain that she was engrossed in her book, I took out my dossier and had a discreet look at the written materials that accompanied that one grainy photo.

They were three siblings—one male and two females—all born to the same parents, in a small town called Huanchillo, a hundred miles from the capital city. The oldest boy was capable of walking nearly upright if he held on to a wall or a table. Other than that, they got around on all fours—feet and hands. In the photo, two of them had their hips stuck high in the air, their legs and spines fairly straight. The daughter in the back looked to be taking a break, her neck craned upward and the weight of her torso resting on her knuckles rather than her palms. There was a resemblance to the posture and stride of large apes. I wondered if the children—or whoever had put them up to this—had studied wildlife films.

The timeline appeared to work out. The oldest was born roughly a year after the DS 400s first went into the ground. Though who's to say that they weren't lying about their ages as well? I made a note to look into any sort of birth records—if they existed—for the children. That might be one way to debunk this mess.

"Do you think it's true, about the dog slobber?" Raven leaned over toward me.

I snapped shut the dossier.

"Do you think that's why the kids walk funny?"

"Absolutely not."

"It makes sense, though, right?" Her voice was thick and sluggish with the pills and booze. "I mean, there's dog genes in the potatoes."

"So what?" I moved the dossier to the far side of my seat. "There are potato genes in the potatoes also. Does that make children express potato-like characteristics? You could eat a whole dog—people probably do that where we're going—and it wouldn't affect the way you walked." I took a deep breath. "When you eat chicken—which is full of chicken genes—do you start clucking or growing feathers?"

"I'm vegetarian, actually."

"I'm so shocked to hear that," I said.

She rolled her eyes. "But nobody knows anything about these GMO crops, right? I mean, these folks down in Puerto Malogrado, they're the guinea pigs."

"I work with some scientists who know a hell of a lot about GMO crops. They know all there is to know about them. Look, whenever a technology is new—and effective—people blame it for unexpected problems. That might make for good headlines, but it doesn't do much for progress."

"Progress!" she scoffed. "These people were feeding themselves pota-toes for centuries and doing a lot better than they are now."

The plane hit a patch of bumpy air and bucked below us. That big backpack slid across the cabin floor. I put my hand over my coffee. Raven let out a tiny squeal, then applied a death grip to each of her armrests. The pilot came over the intercom and apologized for the turbulence.

"It's all right," I said. "Just a few bumps."

She nodded, then drained her drink in a single gulp. "I'm not a big fan of that part, either."

"I noticed."

A few slow seconds slipped by, and the air grew smoother.

"Listen," Raven said. "Could I quote you on that 'eat a whole dog' thing? My readers would love that."

"Quote me?" I wished Warren and the team had prepped me on how to speak to the press. "I suppose. To clarify: I'm not sure that they do eat dogs in Puerto Malogrado. That was just a joke."

"Of course." She took a small ledger-style notebook—probably brand-new—from one of her pockets and scribbled away.

"What newspaper are you with, exactly?" I asked. "The *Statesman*?"

"No." She coughed into her hand. "I've moved away from the print, old-media venues. I'm trying to look to the future. Online reaches more people. Plus it's greener, more consistent with my values."

"I see. So what website or online magazine do you write for?"

"Different places. Whatever suits the story. I have my own site as well: *The Raven Report*." She turned her head toward her lap. "Most of my stuff has ended up there."

"So you're a blogger," I said.

She looked up at me, eyes suddenly red. "Among other things."

"How did you get chosen for this assignment?" I did my best to ask the question without judgment.

She shrugged. "Your company's Public Relations department. I wanted to do an interview with Warren—"

"Mister Shepherd," I corrected her.

"Right. Then this came up." She paused. "Also, it's true that I did go to high school with the PR director at Tuberware."

"I see." I fumbled through my briefcase and found my sleeping mask and neck pillow. Best to catch up on a little sleep in this airplane, rather than the cramped commercial leg.

"We weren't close or anything," Raven went on. "He knew I was up to it, is all."

"Of course." I put the pillow around my neck and pulled down the shade on the nearest window.

"I'm serious; I can do this."

I wasn't sure how to react. She obviously felt defensive. It's true that her credentials didn't impress me. But from my perspective it was perhaps better to have an amateur journalist along. A competent one might be even more trouble.

"Don't worry about it." I put the mask up around my forehead. "This won't be much of a story."

"Don't be so sure." She raised an eyebrow.

"Trust me: It's a hoax." I pulled the mask down over my eyes. "There's nothing to this."

managed to get a few hours' sleep and woke as the plane descended. Raven snored loudly in the seat beside mine. I opened the window shade and saw the swampy, flat, overdeveloped landscape of south Florida. If only we could've connected someplace else.

The stewardess came by and presented me with my ticket and documents for the next leg of the trip, offering instructions on how to find the terminal.

The plane touched down with a bump and squeak. Raven's head bolted upright. She looked around, confused, then peered out the window.

"We're here already?"

"You sound disappointed," I said. "Were you hoping for a chance to panic about the landing?"

She turned to the window again. "This is Puerto Malogrado?"

I laughed. "No. Just Miami. We're on commercial the rest of the way. She's got your ticket." I tilted my head toward the stewardess.

Raven nodded, blinking the sleep from her eyes.

———

We must've cut quite a figure walking through the airport: me in the lead, dragging a sensible rolling bag and briefcase; Raven in her Indiana Jones outfit, hunched like a Sherpa under that lopsided backpack. I'd been through this terminal many times, so I found the gate without incident. I took a seat near the Jetway and tucked my luggage beneath my chair.

Raven groaned as she de-shouldered her giant pack. "I'm starving."

I nodded. "We have about thirty minutes."

She smiled and headed off to the food vendors.

I took a reluctant look around the city of my birth: the capital of Latin America, as it was called. I'd heard no English spoken thus far, not even over the intercom. Everyone in sight—the old men in *guayaberas*, teenage girls in their dark eye makeup and high-cut shorts, the Haitian guys with dreadlocks—all performed their given roles in Miami's ongoing circus. It was as if they'd come straight from central casting, styled and costumed by some producer who was determined to maintain this city's identity and conform to all its stereotypes. I worried that some friend of my parents might see me and report back that I was in town.

My phone buzzed with a new message. It was from Jill: *Have a safe trip, Eddie :) Miss you already :(*

Raven returned with a white paper bag and sat down in the chair next to mine.

I moved my phone to the other side of my lap and wrote: *Miss you too!*

"Doctor?" Raven took out an item wrapped in foil and handed it to me. "One sandwich *cubano*? You must be hungry. Last stateside meal right here."

"Thanks. That's very kind of you." I took the sandwich. "You can call me Eddie, by the way."

We both took our first bites.

"Wouldn't it be great if we could get out and walk around a little?" Raven asked.

"Not really," I said.

"Don't you just love Miami?"

"I do not."

"No? But it's so . . ." She put one hand in front of her face, fingers fluttering, as if grabbing at the right word somewhere in the air before her. ". . . so real."

"It's not that real," I said.

"Have you been here before?"

"I grew up here," I said. "I hate the place."

"What could you possibly hate about it?"

"The humidity, the bugs, the loud dance music all the damn time. That hideous architecture that everybody's so proud of. Cocaine . . . there's plenty of reasons to dislike it."

She shrugged and went back to her sandwich.

"The food is delicious," I admitted. "So there's that."

Raven said nothing for a string of minutes, and I couldn't help but feel bad for all my negativity.

"Look." I sighed. "When you're a Cuban-American kid growing up in Dade County, people expect you to act a certain way, talk a certain way. There's a pre-made set of assumptions. Everyone thinks you're obsessed with baseball and cars. You're not supposed to be shy or studious, or like science. Childhood wasn't the best time for me."

Raven looked up from her food, as interested in this as in anything I'd said all day.

"I like Idaho," I said. "I love it. The extremes: the desert and the mountains pressed up against each other. The seasons: cold winters and hot summers. No bugs. Even the river that goes through town is clean. I like the austerity and the breathing room. It's a place where they let you start fresh."

"I suppose." Raven covered her mouth with a fist. "Though I doubt you'd find Boise so open to change if you'd grown up there."

I finished the sandwich.

—

Our seats were in what passed for business class in the only commercial airline still operating in Puerto Malogrado. Fortunately, Raven fell asleep before takeoff; I was excused from hand-holding duties. Once we reached cruising altitude, I put my mask on and hoped for a little rest of my own. Hours later, I felt a small spot of dribble along my cheek. I woke, lifted the mask, and wiped at my face.

Out the window, I caught a glimpse of tall mountains at dusk. They were green, covered in foliage, rounded at the tops, their verticality made even more dramatic by the long shadows of the setting sun. They seemed only a few feet below the plane. In the distance stood an even taller set of peaks—far above the tree line, the snow at their summits glowing orange in the dusky light.

"They're beautiful, huh?" It was Raven's voice over my shoulder. "The Andes."

"I've never seen anything like that," I agreed.

"They put the Owyhees to shame, that's for sure," Raven said. "Have you been here before?"

"No. I've only left the US once, for a conference in Canada."

Over the intercom, a crackling, barely intelligible announcement was made in Spanish.

"What did they say?" Raven asked.

"I'm not sure," I said. "Probably that we're about to land. I'd fasten your seat belt, at any rate."

The plane did indeed seem to be descending. We banked for a couple of hard turns, and I was allowed a view of the narrow valley that contained the country's capital city. A few modest skyscrapers in the downtown, several plazas with Spanish colonial buildings: palaces and cathedrals—all lit from below. Higher up along the hillside, I could make out a shantytown, pieced together from colored scraps of metal and cardboard, barely recognizable by the smoky light of cookfires.

We went straight over a run-down stadium, a soccer field at its center. A group of barefoot children took a break from their penalty kicks and looked up at our fuselage.

The landing itself seemed unnecessarily violent—as if the runway were too short or the angle the pilot had taken too severe. Our wheels bounced once, then twice, while the seat below me trembled. Raven put her head down between her knees. Soon, we slowed down, and we eventually came to a stop without any taxiing.

The flight attendant opened the door, and a set of stairs was rolled up for us. Another crackling announcement was made, but I couldn't understand a word of it.

Raven gave me an inquisitive look.

"We're here," I said.

We walked down the stairs and onto the rutted tarmac of the runway. The sun had fully disappeared behind the hills. We followed the other passengers toward a low building attached to a tower. Two men in stocking caps loaded our luggage into a flatbed pickup truck pulled alongside our airplane.

"What does it say?" Raven pointed at lettering along the wall.

"International Airport of Puerto Malogrado."

"I didn't expect it to be this cold here." She rubbed her bare arms. "It's the tropics, right? I packed for heat."

"You'll get that too," I said. "It's tropical mountains. The sun will be strong, when it's out."

"My head is killing me." Raven put a finger to her temple.

"That's the elevation," I explained. "We're above eleven thousand feet."

"What is that, like Denver?" Her breathing quickened, now that she had an explanation.

"We're twice as high as Denver."

By the time we reached the building, the truck with our luggage was ready to drop off its first load. We found our bags and headed for a single immigration line. Raven was obviously affected by the altitude: she couldn't even hoist her pack all the way up. It hung off one shoulder, balanced on her hip.

"Welcome! Welcome!" The immigration agent was a thin man with a narrow mustache, wearing a navy blue windbreaker over shirt and tie.

"*Buenas noches*." I dusted off the language skills that had gotten me into this mess. "I'm here on official business. This is my passport, scientific visa, and a letter from my company."

"Ahhh," the man touched the sides of my documents gently with the tips of his fingers. "Business . . . I see. Your letter, indeed."

"What's he saying?" Raven asked.

"Nothing," I said. "He's just repeating a couple of the words I said to him."

The agent looked up from the papers and smiled. "How long would you like to stay?"

"Not long, I hope."

He frowned abruptly.

"Sorry. I mean: it shouldn't take long, my business here."

The smile returned. "I give you thirty days." He inked up a rubber stamp that was nearly the size of my passport, and slammed it onto an empty page.

I nodded. "*Gracias.*"

"For your wife, as well?" He pointed at Raven.

"She is not my wife," I explained.

That got a chuckle and a raised eyebrow from the agent, who inked up the stamp again. "No problem!" He grinned. "None of my concern, what you do on your 'business trips,' no?"

Raven handed him her passport.

"No, it's not like that—" I said.

The big stamp slammed down again.

"*Gracias,*" Raven offered.

The man grinned at her, said that he was pleased to make her acquaintance.

I opened up my own passport and studied the stamp. It was a picture of a Harley-Davidson motorcycle, with no text or numbers whatsoever.

"*Perdón, señor.*" I held it up. "This is our visa?"

He turned away from Raven. "Thirty-day visa, yes. If you prefer ninety-day," he held up another stamp, this one with a hula girl in a grass skirt playing the ukulele, "then you must bring two English letters."

39

"Fine," I said. "This will do."

"Customs is right over there." He pointed around the corner.

We continued down the hall and found a chubby boy of about twelve wearing what looked to be a bellhop's uniform, *ADUANAS* written on the cap. He stood beside a dusty machine that consisted of a short, still conveyor belt and a big metal box with red and green light bulbs at the top.

"Anything to declare?" the kid asked.

"No," I said.

"Put your things on the conveyor belt, press the button, wait for the green light."

We piled everything up, then paused at a yellow line on the floor beside the button.

"What happens if the light turns red?" I asked.

The kid shook his head. "It won't turn red."

I pressed the button, and the belt came alive with a grinding of gears and jerking of wheels. Our mass of luggage slowly crept toward the metal box and finally paused when it was halfway through. The green light came on and everything continued to the other side.

"Have a nice trip," the kid said.

We collected our bags at the far end.

"That was easy," Raven said.

"Among other things."

Outside the gates of the airport, we were swarmed by men shouting "Taxi! Taxi!" and physically attempting to wrest our bags from us. Their ID badges dangled as they went after our luggage and stood in our path. Raven had to pivot her backpack away from their clutches, boxing them out like a power forward. I lifted my briefcase to chest level, ready to swing it if necessary.

"Leave us alone!" Raven slapped a hand away from my rolling bag.

Up ahead, I spotted one man in the parking lot holding up a cardboard sign that read "Tuberware."

"This way." I took Raven's arm and pulled her free of the scrum.

The man with the sign made eye contact with me. Short, with wavy hair and a thick goatee, he took a few steps toward us, then shooed away the other drivers. "Go on, *cabrónes*! They're with me." He used his cardboard sign to whack one stubborn *taxista* on the head.

The pack of them turned back to the airport, sadly muttering "taxi, taxi" to themselves, waiting to serve tourists who were not coming.

The man with the sign managed to sling all our luggage over his shoulder and keep one arm free to shake our hands.

"I am Oscar," he said. "Sent to do your driving." He had a mischievous smile, one of his front teeth crooked in such a way that it appeared sharpened.

"Excellent," I said. "Your car is . . . ?"

"This way." He began walking.

"He seems nice," Raven whispered to me.

I nodded.

We walked to the far end of the parking lot and came to a vehicle that—while certainly not a car—didn't clearly fit into any other category. The front was an off-road motorcycle with a beach umbrella propped up over the driver's seat. The back had two wheels, with a covered bench seat like that of a horse-drawn carriage. The outer covering was made of canvas. Across the back window—if you can call a piece of clear plastic sheeting a window—"*Milagrosa*" was written in blocky script.

"Here we are," Oscar said. Straightaway, he went about strapping our luggage to the top of the back carriage. The ceiling dipped downward toward the bench like a hammock.

"After you," I said to Raven.

She climbed aboard, and I followed. Our heads rubbed against the cloth-covered outlines of our luggage, pushing down from above.

"Those taxi drivers don't seem like such a bad idea now, do they?" I said to Raven.

She shifted her head to support the weight of her backpack.

"Very good!" Oscar said, as if surprised that the roof hadn't caved in on us.

He climbed onto the motorcycle saddle. "To the hotel." With a swift kick from his boot, the engine fired up, and we were off.

The streets of Puerto Malogrado looked as if they had recently seen rain. Once out of the airport, we crested a hill and saw the yellowish lights of the city further down the valley below, the dull red-orange of cookfires shining brighter in the hillside slums above. Oscar drove fast, weaving in and out between buses and taxis and a few official-looking SUVs.

With each pothole, our little rickshaw bucked hard, bouncing our heads against our luggage above, and our tailbones against the thin upholstery of the bench.

"We almost arrive!" Oscar called back over his shoulder.

"Keep your eyes on the road!" I hollered back.

"This is fun!" Raven squealed as we got up to speed. "I've never been on a ride like this before."

"You're afraid of the safest form of travel ever invented, but you're enjoying this?"

Oscar came to a stop at a building fronted by a large iron cage. He pressed on a buzzer outside. A teenager walked past carrying a semi-automatic rifle, wearing a mismatched cap and uniform shirt. He looked us up and down. Oscar gave him a nod. He kept walking.

"What's that all about?" I asked.

"Him?" Oscar said. "Private security. Paid for by the neighbors."

Finally, a woman wearing a house-frock emerged from the gate and let us in. She spoke so quickly that I could barely understand. I gathered that her name was Doña Ana, and this was her hotel.

"It says here two rooms." She looked up from a scribbled-upon piece of paper.

Oscar carried our luggage over from off the canopy of his cycle-car.

"That's correct," I said.

"You and your wife, you don't share the bed?" Doña Ana gestured toward Raven.

"She's not my wife."

"No?" Doña Ana perked up a little. "Your girlfriend?"

"No!" I said.

"Coworkers?" She raised her eyebrows.

"Something like that, unfortunately."

"Aha," she said. "Right this way."

Oscar had once again managed to shoulder all our luggage at one time. Doña Ana led us first to a small room with a single bed and a high window that let in headlights and traffic noise from the outside.

"This one is for her," Doña Ana gestured toward Raven.

"*Sí, señora.*" Oscar lowered the baggage and dropped Raven's over-stuffed backpack onto the bed.

"This is your bedroom," I explained to Raven.

"Oh," she said. "It's . . . nice."

"And for you, sir." Doña Ana led Oscar and me down the hallway. At the far corner of the building, she opened the door to another room. This one had a queen-sized bed, a television, and a glass door that opened up to a solarium in the hotel's core.

"Our finest room." Doña Ana smiled.

"Thank you very much," I said.

"Breakfast is at seven." She dropped the key into my palm.

Oscar piled my things on the bed. "Okay, boss. I'll come for you at eight in the morning."

"Perfect." They left me alone. I turned on the television and flipped through channels while I undressed. On the local news, some sort of government official in a decorated military uniform was speaking at a lectern. Flags and banners hung behind him. Cameras panned through the crowd and showed a mix of soldiers and civilians in the audience. The topic was "the opposition." In fact, the entire speech seemed to be little more than a series of metaphors about their inconsequentiality. The nation was a gigantic ship, he said, and the opposition was but a single rat scurrying about its hull. To illustrate, he stuck out his front teeth and made little rat paws of his hands.

A knock sounded at my door. In boxer shorts and undershirt, I stood and opened it just a crack. Raven.

"Can I talk to you for a second?" she asked.

"Is it important?" I opened up the rest of the way.

"I think so." She carried her notebook and a pen. "I need to ask you how they make these genetically modified crops in the first place. Wow, this is a nice room."

I lay down across the bed and stared at the television screen. "I don't work with those things, okay? It's not my job."

"You have no idea how it's done?"

"Most of the time they use the gene gun."

"The gene gun?" She grimaced. "Is that a metaphor?"

"No, it's literal. Basically, they take the genes that they want to add, put them into a liquid solution, and let them soak into a bunch of tiny tungsten balls. Then they use a twenty-two shell to fire the balls at high speed toward the cells of the plant."

"An actual twenty-two shell?" she asked.

"Many of the balls pass right through, but some penetrate the cell wall, head on into the nucleus, and incorporate themselves into the DNA of the plant. Boom: a brand-new crop."

"I can't believe that works."

"The gene gun is best for grasses—wheat and corn and so on. For potatoes, they prefer to use agrobacterium."

"Bacteria?" Her scribbling slowed down, as if she was having trouble spelling the term.

"Right. There are certain pathogens in nature that like to break into nuclei and replace plant DNA with little bits of their own DNA. We—well, my colleagues—use enzymes to piggyback on that process and put in the genes that we want."

Raven bore down on her pad and muttered, "Is it any wonder these things have unexpected consequences?"

I rubbed my eyes with my fingers. "Do we really have to do this now? I have a big day tomorrow."

"I'm sorry, Eddie. I don't mean to be a burden on you—the science and the language and all. But I want to get it right. This assignment is a big deal for me too."

"Look, Raven. I hate to be the one to break the news to you, but you won't exactly be breaking any news on this trip."

"Excuse me?"

"This story of yours? There's no story. You might succeed in fueling a little anti-GMO paranoia, which is fair enough. There's a whole canon of Luddite journalism out there—most of it forgotten now—railing against telephones and cameras and penicillin and whatnot. It never holds up to

45

the long sweep of history, but it might sell a few magazines. Or in your case . . . what? Clicks?"

She turned away and stared at the wall, her cheeks flushed pink.

"I plan to get to the bottom of this as quickly as possible," I said. "Put this fire out and head home."

"Okay," she said. "We're both here to find out the truth."

"The truth!" I laughed out loud. "The truth is that some *campesinos* are trying to pull a fast one on my company. The only real mystery is which of Tuberware's enemies put them up to it. So don't start with a bunch of Woodward and Bernstein notions. They chose to send you along for a reason."

"What's that supposed to mean?"

I shrugged. "Well, it's not like your story is in any danger of making the front page of the *New York Times*, now, is it?"

She swallowed, hardened her gaze at me. "You mean that they sent me because I'm not a good journalist?"

"I didn't mean 'good'; I meant more like 'established.' They could've gotten somebody else, you know, had they wanted."

She turned to the wall again. "I see."

I was worried she was about to cry. "Now, don't get so—"

"Good night, Doctor Morales." She slammed the door and left the room.

"Raven!" I called after her, then turned back to the television. "Oh, whatever."

On the screen, the same official used his thumb and forefinger to pinch a tiny piece of air. It sounded as though he were comparing the opposition to a hair on the body of a much larger animal. I wondered if he wasn't some sort of Extended Metaphor Czar. As if on cue, a title came up on-screen, identifying him as Puerto Malogrado's "Vice Minister of the Interior." I watched him compare the opposition to a couple more things, then turned it off. In the dark bedroom, I lay still for a long while, trying to sleep, wondering exactly what I was meant to be doing in this country.

In the morning, an odd combination of roosters and car alarms harassed me out of a deep sleep. Next, a neighbor blasted techno music on a stereo, inexplicably moving the volume up and down. For a few minutes I covered my head with a pillow. Soon enough, I rose from bed and got dressed. I hadn't eaten since the Miami airport, and I looked forward to breakfast.

Doña Ana had a few small tables set up in a courtyard. One other group of guests already sat eating. They were European—German or Swiss—speaking in a language I couldn't follow, wearing hiking boots and sporty hats. Their sunburns spoke of long days already spent in the Andes.

In a far corner, an old woman used a walker to approach a table, where a cup of tea and some toast were set out. Her spine bent forward like a reed in the wind. The legs of her walker clacked hard against the tile floor.

I chose a table with an abandoned copy of the daily paper. On the front page, above the fold, was a picture of the Vice Minister from his speech last night.

Though it had been spoken in my childhood home, I had little experience reading in Spanish—and even less with the dense prose of newspaper writers. But this reporter seemed to find the speech far bolder and more insightful than I did.

Below the fold, there was a shorter article about the nebulous "opposition." In an out-of-focus photo, a scruffy man in a floppy-brimmed hat and a red handkerchief around his lower face—apparently one of the leaders—held his hand toward the lens. The headline said something about cowardice.

Doña Ana surprised me at my table. "Good morning, Don Eduardo!" she said. "Did you sleep well?"

I looked up and saw two teenage girls in tow, both cowering against their mother's sleeves.

"Yes, very well." That was true, until all the racket of the morning.

"These are my daughters, Ermelinda and Natalia."

"*Mucho gusto*," I said.

They didn't respond, just poked their blushing faces out from behind their mother's shoulders.

"And that's my mother over there." Doña Ana pointed to the woman in the corner, now seated at a chair beside her walker. "Say hello, Mama!"

Without looking up from her tea, the old woman waved a hand in our direction.

"Hello," I said.

"Breakfast?" Doña Ana asked.

"Please," I said.

"Do you like eggs? Potatoes?"

"Yes and yes."

She nodded, and the three of them spirited off toward the kitchen.

I did a quick scan of the rest of the newspaper, pleased to see that nothing about a family walking on all fours had made it in. Perhaps the ongoing revolution had given us a break.

One of Doña Ana's daughters reappeared with a cup of coffee. I thanked her as she placed it on the table. She did a sort of embarrassed curtsy, then ran off to the kitchen.

The Germans rose to leave, hoisting their walking sticks and backpacks. I nearly asked what mountain they were off to summit but kept it to myself.

The other daughter brought me a plate heaping with over-easy eggs and pan-fried potatoes. Before I could dig in, Doña Ana delivered a shallow tray full of bright-colored sauces and coarse salt.

The breakfast was amazing. The egg yolks were the color of carrots. The insides of the potatoes were so soft and golden that I wondered if Ana and her daughters hadn't somehow injected butter into them with a syringe. (We tried that technique in the lab once, for a frozen product, but ultimately abandoned it.) The sauces were unnecessary but delicious— one spicy, one creamy and tangy, another that was probably just ketchup. I was hungry and unsure what sort of food I'd find in the countryside. It only took me a few minutes to finish the plate.

"Good morning, Doctor Morales." At the far end of the courtyard, Raven stood by the entrance with wet hair, still looking upset.

I did my best to swallow and wipe the sauce from my chin. "Raven, listen: I'm sorry about last night. What can I say? I'm a scientist. I can be a little harsh when it comes to the facts."

She rolled her eyes.

What was she expecting? For me to praise her journalistic credentials? "You have to try this food. It's amazing."

"Thanks, but I had some granola bars in the room. We should get ready. Oscar will be here any minute."

I checked the time on my phone. She was right.

"Everything I need is in here." I patted my briefcase. "Let me get my lab coat, and we'll be good." I drained the last of my coffee.

"Meet you out front," she said.

oth Raven and Oscar waited outside the gate.

"Good morning, Doctor!" Oscar said. "Ready to leave?"

I looked up and down the street but didn't see his little rickshaw anywhere. "Where's your . . . your vehicle?" I asked.

"Right this way." He led us to an older Toyota sedan with a forest-green paint job that was badly peeling. "We'll take this out to the *pueblo*."

Oscar climbed in behind the wheel. Raven and I were about to do the same when I noticed something up the street. "Wait a second," I said.

About a block away was the same teenage security guard from the night before, ambling about with a weapon much too large for him. But this time he had several other people in tow—walking slowly just two steps behind. A chubby gringo held a video camera at waist level, hunched over and shooting the guard from a low angle. An Asian girl in clunky glasses and thick headphones held a microphone on a pole. And then the third one: another gringo, his thumbs and forefingers held up to make a square, directing the first two with nods and taps. My stomach trembled as I made out his face.

"Kearns?" I shouted. "That better not be you, Kearns."

He turned and saw me. "Eddie? Eddie Morales?"

He'd changed his appearance since I'd last seen him. Now, he had a carefully groomed five o'clock shadow. His hair was close-cropped on the sides, with a big, product-filled poof at the top. His jeans and thin leather jacket were both a size too small.

"I should've known you'd be behind this," I said.

"Behind what? The revolution?" There seemed to be a fake British accent in his voice now. He walked over to join us.

His crew abandoned the guard and followed Kearns. They stayed a step behind him, gear resting on their shoulders.

"It's good to see you, Eddie." He reached out to Raven for a shake: "Hi there. Spencer Kearns. Pleased to meet you."

He put his hand out for me. I considered it for a moment, then shook.

"Don't I know that name from somewhere?" Raven asked.

"You probably do." I let go of his hand. "He's in the entertainment industry. Makes reality television."

"Award-winning feature-length documentaries, actually," Kearns said.

"Sensationalized pseudo-science meant to scare ignorant people," I corrected him.

Kearns cracked a half-smile. "You say 'potato,' eh, Eddie?"

"Oh, yes!" Raven said. "I saw your piece on celiac disease."

"Right," he said. "That was a finalist for the Enduring Progression medal. We were the first researchers to identify the gluten-vaccine connection."

"You're not a researcher," I said. "And there is no such connection."

"What about you, Eddie? Still working for the evil empire?"

"Still feeding the world, you mean? Yes, I am."

"They haven't moved you into pesticides and plastics, then?"

"No," I said. "Still food. Making it safer, making it cheaper."

"So, what are you doing down here?" he asked.

"Same as you, probably," Raven spoke from behind me. "We're here about the kids who—"

"Potatoes!" I cut her off before she could finish. "What else?"

"But now?" Kearns wrinkled up his face. "Things are heating up with this conflict."

"Yes," I said, as if I knew that. "Tuberware wants to ensure the food supply of this nation, come what may politically."

He raised his eyebrows. "Tuberware wants to do that?"

I nodded. "And you? I suppose you're here to make third-world conflict porn. That seems to be trendy at the moment."

He shrugged. "Good work, if you can get it."

From inside the car, Oscar tapped on the horn. "Boss! *Vamos.*"

"Sorry, Kearns," I said. "We have to go."

"Of course," he replied. "We should get together sometime. We're at the hotel on the plaza just back there. Is this where you're staying?"

I said "no" and Raven said "yes" at exactly the same time.

After an awkward pause, Kearns asked, "So, which is it, then?"

I took Raven by the arm and opened the door to the back seat for her. "We're staying here, but we're super-busy. We probably won't have time to get together." I closed the car door behind a confused Raven, then went around to the front seat. "You know how it is, working for a living. Oh, wait. No, I suppose you don't."

"Goodbye, Eddie."

"Goodbye, Kearns."

I slammed my door. "Drive fast, Oscar. And make sure nobody follows us."

"Roger that, boss." He jerked the car out of the spot and onto the main road.

"What the hell was all that about?" Raven poked her head up from the back. "You didn't have to be so rude."

"It all makes sense now," I said. "Kearns is behind this."

"Surely you don't mean that he's behind the hand-walkers?"

"Of course I do! Think about it. A guy like him would have the most to gain. The greenie groups might be able to forward their quasi-agenda based on a scandal like this. But Kearns, he'd actually profit from it. For him, it would have to be something visual, something that translates to film. The guy doesn't have a nuanced mind when it comes to science."

"Eddie, he's a respected filmmaker."

I turned back to face her. "So is Woody Allen. Would you like to put him in charge of the FDA?"

"Do you two have some kind of history?" she asked.

"You could say that," I admitted. "We were in graduate school together, for a while. He had to leave prematurely."

"Eddie." Raven turned serious. "What happened, exactly?"

I sighed. "We were part of the same cohort in the botany doctoral program. The two of us were close. Kearns comes from money. He had a big house there in Gainesville, and he rented me a room for a fair price. The rest of us were broke students, so he was a good guy to know—always buying drinks at the bar, throwing parties, that sort of thing. But I was serious about my studies. Back then, I still hoped to be an academic."

"You wanted to teach?" Raven asked.

I shook my head. "In my field, most professors are full-time researchers. Anyway, it was a lot of pressure. I wanted to do good work, impress my advisers. For Kearns . . . I don't know why Kearns was there. He had some far-fetched notions about becoming a green-energy baron, but his studies seemed more like a way to kill time before he inherited his parents' fortune."

"So what happened?"

"Once we got into the dissertation process, Kearns started to unravel. He couldn't hack the self-directed work. He felt that all the small calculations were beneath him. Without my knowing about it, he took some data from my computer and put it into his own dissertation draft."

"He stole from you?" Raven gasped.

"It was so stupid. My numbers didn't even make sense for what he was doing. He just figured that the committee wouldn't read it. And you know what: he was nearly right about that. It was only because of one professor—a researcher who I greatly admired—that the whole thing was busted."

"Did Kearns get in trouble?"

"We both got in trouble! They thought I'd conspired with him. I was nearly expelled from the program."

"That's awful. Did they kick him out?"

"Not exactly." I shook my head again. Even as a memory, it all seemed so ridiculous to me. "Everybody knew he couldn't finish. But he walked away with a masters' degree and nothing on his record. Somehow, his lawyers got us all to sign a non-disclosure agreement saying that we wouldn't discuss the matter. You believe that? I'm sure his family wrote a huge check to the university. They were already big donors. That's how he got into the program in the first place."

"What a nightmare," Raven said.

"Even though I was about to finish, it effectively ended my academic career. I couldn't get recommendations from my advisers, and I'd become too jaded anyway."

"It's a good thing you found a fit in the private sector."

"Absolutely," I agreed. "Who knows what I would've done without Tuberware?"

"And Kearns got into film?"

"So it seems. That's his revenge on real science." I turned to the rear-view mirror. Nothing.

Oscar must've noticed. "Don't worry, boss. Nobody follows us."

I nodded but wasn't sure it mattered. Surely Kearns knew where we were headed.

From the hotel we turned onto a broad avenue called Boulevard de los Agricultores. A couple of blocks in, we came to a small, shaded plaza. On a high pedestal in its center stood a statue of a man in a big hat, leaning hard on a foot plow, with a seed basket around his waist.

"What is that?" I asked Oscar.

"La Plaza de los Agricultores," he said. The Farmers' Plaza.

"Hey, look, Eddie," Raven said from the back. "That must be the place Kearns was talking about."

She pointed toward the far side of the plaza. Sure enough, there was a fancy-looking hotel there, flags hanging above the entrance.

"It's close to us," she said.

"Too close," I agreed.

"Don't get ahead of yourself," Raven said. "Maybe Kearns truly is here about the revolution."

"No," I said. "There are wars going on all over the world. He's here for a reason."

The ride outside the city was like a journey through time. We left the wealthy neighborhoods—tall cement walls topped with shards of broken glass, men carrying guns in every doorway. We next passed through some sort of market district—a labyrinth of black tarps and corrugated metal—housing merchants of all kinds: ancient herbs and tonics alongside fake designer jeans and sunglasses. Next, an industrial wasteland of factories and concrete blocks. Little clusters of mud shacks and cast-off wood structures clung like wasps' nests to the undersides of overpasses and walls. Small children ran in and out with bare feet and swollen bellies. Raven furiously scribbled notes in her little book.

We left the valley of the capital city and felt the cold of the surrounding ridgeline. The intermittently paved road reached a high point; on both sides of the pass we could see giant mountains topped by glaciers.

"It's beautiful up here," Raven said.

I nodded.

Oscar rattled off some information about the peaks and their religious significance, pointing at one side and then the other.

"What's he saying?" Raven asked.

"He's talking about the Incas, how they worshiped these mountains, considered them gods."

She scribbled that down as well.

The road shed elevation in a hurry, through a series of switchbacks and elevator-shaft declines. I was doubly thankful that we weren't riding in Oscar's three-wheeled cart from the night before. Soon, we came to a river and drove alongside the rushing water.

The green and white of the mountains gave way to shades of gray and brown. We drove past an alpine lake with impossibly blue water, then later past another with a hue like rust.

A small complex of shacks and trailers appeared at a flat stretch to our left. I asked Oscar what it was.

"The mine," he said.

"What are they mining there?" I asked.

"This one is mostly tin. Elsewhere, we get iron, still some silver, natural gas as well."

I translated for Raven.

"That must create a lot of jobs," I said.

"Oh, yes," Oscar nodded. "They're always hiring. So many miners die; they always need new ones. But the pay is shit."

Raven shot me a self-satisfied smirk, as if she understood more Spanish than she let on.

"This one." Oscar pointed to a ragtag complex of corrugated metal and plywood buildings. "They call it the Devil's Basement, for all the collapses and deaths that occur there."

I opted not to translate that part.

We drove on, finally regaining a little of the elevation we'd lost. The landscape grew verdant. Soon, on either side of the road, we found ourselves surrounded by terraced fields. It wasn't quite the lush greenery and grand geometric bulwarks that they put on the postcards. This was functional farmland: dry stone walls topped with loose soil and a few plants. On several of the terraces, men and boys hunched over their hand plows and stabbed seeds into the earth.

"It's amazing, isn't it?" Raven said. "They've been farming like this for how many thousands of years? It's as if nothing's changed."

I wanted to mention that the spuds they plant now have about a hundred times the calories that they used to, but I managed to bite my tongue. "Yes, amazing."

Oscar pointed out a hamlet of houses in the distance.

"There it is," he said. "That's Huanchillo."

I nodded, then turned to Raven: "We're almost there."

Soon, the town blossomed all around us. A humble Catholic church stood at its center, a small courtyard out front with benches and trees.

"Oh. It's cute," Raven said.

A handful of storefronts surrounded the main square. Smaller houses fanned out from the center. In the hills that rose up behind, I could make out more potato crops—most of them planted in stone terraces older than Christianity itself. Oscar turned and slowly drove down one of the side streets.

Raven was charmed by the little town. She leaned her big camera out the window and snapped photos of the goats and llamas walking down the dirt streets. An old woman with long braids and a wool hat turned to stare at us.

"Better not to aim that camera at the people here," Oscar shouted. "They feel that a photograph steals the soul from its subject."

"Raven," I explained. "No pictures of the people, okay?"

She seemed to understand. Oscar brought the car to a stop at a house on the town's rural outskirts. It was a one-story structure with a roof of Spanish tiles. Three strands of barbed wire enclosed a few square meters of grass in the front. On the far side, a separate kitchen coughed out a column of black smoke.

In the front yard, a baby llama sniffed at his mother's butt. A small goat stretched to the end of his tether. Two dogs perked up their heads, as if to consider barking or attacking, but then lay back down.

"This is the house." Oscar cut the engine and opened his door. "This is where the Morales children live."

"Their family name is Morales?" I asked.

"Yes."

"That's my last name," I said.

"Maybe you're related." Raven smiled, again revealing a bit of Spanish comprehension.

"It's a common name," I said.

As Oscar walked up to the front door, the two dogs lay there unbothered. Raven and I followed him into the yard, and suddenly the mother llama came toward us. She pinned back her ears and stuck her head right in my face. Her mouth opened to make a sort of "Mwah!" sound.

"Don Pablo!" Oscar knocked at the wooden door. "Niña Rosa?"

I stomped on the ground to keep the llama at bay, shouting *"Vaya!"* while Raven chuckled from behind. The animal kept its black eyes trained on me and snorted; her lips peeled back to expose big yellow teeth.

The door finally swung open. A middle-aged woman stood there in an apron and a red sweater, her straight hair pulled into one long braid down her back.

"Don Oscar," she said.

Apparently they'd already met.

Oscar shook her hand. "These are the gringos sent by the American company." He spoke slowly and deliberately as he went through the introductions. Finally, he turned to me and whispered, "Spanish is not her first language."

I nodded. The llama pressed its nose against the side of my face.

"This man is a scientist," Oscar said. "He'd like to see your children."

"Yes." She nodded, seeming quite nervous. "My husband is still out in the fields."

"We can wait," I offered, ducking away from the llama's head. "It's not a problem." I saw no reason to upset this woman or to start friction on our first visit.

"Thank you." She smiled. "He won't be long."

Oscar let out a frustrated sigh.

"Don't worry," I said to him. "We'll take a stroll around the town."

I turned to Niña Rosa. "If we come back in one hour, would that be sufficient?"

She nodded and closed the door. The llama backed off.

"Relax, Oscar." I put a hand on his shoulder as we left the doorway. "No reason to start this off on the wrong foot." I wanted this family to trust me. Otherwise, I'd get nowhere fast. My best hope for solving this mess, I realized, was to catch one of them in a lie, maybe force a confession. It was crucial that they be forthcoming with me.

"I'll wait in the car." Oscar climbed in and reclined the driver's seat.

I tapped him on the shoulder before he could pull the door shut. "Oscar," I said. "That gringo from out front of the hotel, the one with the camera?"

"Yes. What about him?"

"Just keep an eye out. If you see him or anybody like him around this house, keep them away. Got it?"

"Sure thing, boss."

I stepped back, and he closed the door.

"What was that all about?" Raven asked.

"The *señora* was reluctant to invite us in without her husband there. I told her we'd come back later."

"That was kind of you."

I nodded. "Shall we have a look around?"

———

We walked back in the direction that we'd come from. A thick layer of clouds clung to the surrounding mountaintops but was broken up intermittently by bright blue sky. In the small square outside the church, schoolchildren in uniforms pointed and whispered at the two of us. We found a "store," which was more like a doorway covered by an iron cage. Merchandise hung from the walls; a couple of wooden benches sat out front.

I asked the storekeeper for two Coca-Colas. He took the glass bottles from his fridge and pried the caps off. I held out my hands, ready to accept. But rather than pass the bottles through, he placed them on a counter and grabbed two clear plastic baggies. One in each hand, he slipped the bags over the necks, then inverted the bottles. The soda bubbled and fizzed its way into the bags. The storekeeper placed a straw in each, then passed the baggies through the bars.

"Here." I handed one to Raven.

"What's all this?" she asked.

I shrugged. "He must want to keep the glass-bottle deposit."

We sat on the benches and studied the mountains behind the church.

"Look at that," Raven pointed to one side of the steeple. "Is that a condor?"

Sure enough, the prehistoric bird gave its wings a couple of flaps and cruised upon the wind. Raven struggled to lift her camera without spilling her soda.

"Careful." A tall, gangly man approached us, a sack slung over his shoulder. He spoke English. "The condor is very much sacred."

"I'm sorry." Raven lowered the camera. "I wasn't trying to steal its soul or anything."

"I'm Arturo." He turned to me. "Are you here about the Morales children?"

"Something like that," I admitted.

"It's sad, their situation." He watched as the condor flew away, its white collar still shining in the distance. Arturo had stringy eyebrows and an unkempt mustache, a face with prematurely deep lines. "They are my . . . how do you say in English . . . my nephews?"

I stole a glance into the sack that he carried over his shoulder. It was full of some sort of long purple potatoes that I'd not seen before.

"How did you learn English?" Raven asked.

Arturo shrugged. "Mostly I taught myself. It's not difficult to find American magazines and films around here."

"Speaking of," I said. "Don Arturo, by any chance have you seen a gringo around here? Not today, but recently? A funny-looking guy with a camera? Fuzzy beard? Clothes that are too tight for him?"

He shook his head. "Not many gringos make it out to this valley."

"Their loss." Raven smiled.

"Where did you get these?" I took one of the potatoes out from the open sack and held it up between the two of us, rotating it with my fingertips, inspecting all the bumps and nodules.

"That? I grew it."

"Where'd you get the seeds?"

He threw his head back and laughed. "I sprouted these. They come from the highest part of my farm, so I cut them from a potato that did well up there."

"It's an heirloom? You didn't buy it?"

"No offense, but I don't buy that American shit," Arturo frowned. "Those big potatoes will make you fat—and lazy. I plant the same kinds my grandfather grew, even if I'm the last farmer in Puerto Malogrado to do so."

"And you say you use different cuttings for the different levels of your farm?"

"*Claro.*" He shrugged. "It would be silly not to. Every terrace has its own soil, its own amount of moisture and sun."

"Doesn't that get . . . complicated?" I asked.

"It's my work," he said. "My livelihood. Is it meant to be simple?"

"Could I keep this?"

"My gift to you." Arturo cocked one eyebrow. "That one is called 'La Vieja.' Very old. Very sacred."

I was barely listening to him, still studying the odd, lumpy texture, the inconsistent coloring. The skin was most similar to the one known as eightyfold, often dated back to 1800 or so. But the shape was far different—more like a sweet potato.

Arturo bought a bag of cooking oil from the store and said goodbye.

"You're really into that potato," Raven said.

"Sorry." I looked up at her. "It's not quite like any varietal I've come across before."

"I thought all the farmers down here were supposed to be using your seeds."

"That's what they think back in Idaho." I took the last sip from my bag of Coke and crumpled it up in my fist. "But it looks like that guy Arturo is holding the line."

I dropped the potato into my pocket. We handed our empty bags to the storekeeper. After we'd taken a few steps away, he tossed them out through the bars and onto the street.

"Well," said Raven. "Shall we see if the father is home yet?"

—

Back at the Morales house, Oscar slept soundly in the driver's seat of the car, his hat pulled over his eyes. So much for keeping watch . We saw no need to wake him and went straight to the front door. The dogs barked from inside. The llama must've been moved to another pen. I knocked at the door and called out Rosa's name.

A big man with a gray mustache answered, his hair a bit more curly than the fine, straight hair of the rest of the locals.

"Don Pablo?" I asked. "I'm the scientist sent from America. Did your wife mention our visit?" I was pleased by how quickly my language skills had returned. The local dialect was slow and clear, much easier to follow than the rushed, nasal accents I'd heard as a kid.

He nodded. "Come in."

The humble earthen walls of the interior were whitewashed. A wall calendar featured the Virgin of Guadalupe and advertisements for auto parts. Portraits of stern-looking ancestors had been altered to look like oil paintings. The two dogs collapsed in a corner, silent.

Don Pablo led us straight through, to the other side of the house. There, a packed-dirt courtyard was enclosed by several small outbuildings: an outdoor kitchen billowing smoke, a pit latrine, and what looked to be a small shed. The llamas and the goat were tied up on the far side of the courtyard. The wind had blown in more clouds; the sky gave off a flat, gray light. "These are my children," he said.

Until I saw the three of them out there, I'd momentarily forgotten my reasons for being in this country.

"Here is Pablito, my oldest." He touched the shoulder of a young boy, who was settled in a low hammock and barely looked up. He had big eyes and lips, a childlike softness to his face that made him appear even younger than twelve.

"Hello," I waved.

"And these are his sisters," Don Pablo said. "Rosita and Carmen."

The two girls sat together on the ground beside a wooden bench, giggling to each other. They were both dressed in the traditional big skirts and sweaters like their mother—both with toothy smiles and bushy eyebrows, long braids down their backs. They barely noticed Raven and me.

Something about the atmosphere within this household touched me. The innocent faces of those children, their humble home, the quiet warmth of the parents—how could anybody manipulate this family into a scam? Was Kearns really capable of turning their lives into a grotesque sideshow? How much could he offer them in return?

"*Hijos!*" came a call from the far end of the courtyard. "*A comer!*" Niña Rosa emerged from the kitchen with her back to us and dropped a steaming dish of food onto a table covered in a red-and-white oilcloth. She turned and saw Raven and me for the first time since our last visit. The color drained from her face.

Pablito swung his upper body out of the hammock and set his fists on the ground. With head and shoulders turned upward and his posterior high in the air, he made his way across the packed-earth courtyard. His straight arms swung outward and made long strides. His hips and feet followed with a motion that was more fluid than anything I would've ever dreamed from that one photograph. There was an undeniable grace to it. It looked . . . well, natural, for lack of a better word. He walked the fifteen feet or so over to the table, all his weight set on his knuckles and the balls of his feet.

The two girls followed suit. They had shorter limbs and thicker trunks than their brother, seemed to waddle more than lope, but the fundamentals of the motion were otherwise the same.

"Oh, my God," Raven said from behind me.

Pablito pulled out a chair and climbed toward his plate. The two girls did the same. Their mother looked embarrassed at the fact that we were witnessing this and stormed back into the kitchen. The father was more stoic, perhaps believing that our presence here would help make sense of it all.

"Eddie," Raven said at my shoulder, "I don't think they're faking it."

I shook my head, eyes still on the now-seated children. "This is way outside of my area."

The children ate their food. Raven stared, incredulous. I squirted hand sanitizer into each of my palms, only because it seemed a vaguely medical thing to do.

"They've been this way since birth?" I asked.

"Well, not since birth," Don Pablo explained. "Only since they began to walk."

"Of course. What happens if they try to walk upright?"

He shrugged. "If there is a wall or a table, something to hold on to, they can get by. Pablito is the best at that. Otherwise, they lose their balance. It's like you or me trying to walk on our hands. Maybe possible for one second, but not natural."

I nodded, trying to summon some more intelligent questions.

Raven approached the children where they ate, smiling and signaling, making them laugh. She took out her digital camera and turned toward me.

"Eddie, would you ask him if it's okay?"

"Don Pablo, would you mind if she takes some pictures, of their hands and whatnot?"

He sighed. "I suppose that would be all right."

I nodded to Raven. She first clicked some snapshots and showed the children their own images on the other side of the camera. This got them all giggling and squealing. She soon moved on to photos of their hands and feet, capturing the swollen knuckles and oddly placed calluses.

The mother emerged from the kitchen and shouted something to Don Pablo in the clipped tones of their indigenous language. He lifted his hands and yelled back at her.

"Raven," I said. "How about you cool it with the pictures."

She nodded, slipped the camera into its bag, then said "I'm sorry" to the mother.

Niña Rosa made a dismissive gesture with her hand and faded back into the kitchen.

"Don Pablo, I'd like to do some simple tests on your children. It shouldn't be intrusive."

He sighed again. "Yes, Doctor. As long as we can keep this as discreet as possible. I'd rather their plight not become a spectacle."

"Believe me," I said, "I feel the exact same way." Niña Rosa brought out a plate of thick-cut homemade potato chips and offered them to us as a snack. Raven and I both accepted. We sat down at the dining table with Don Pablo.

"Thank you," I said. "I'm starving."

"These are great," Raven said.

I turned to Don Pablo. "Are these the DS 400s?"

"*Sí.*" He nodded. "That's all that I grow on my parcel anymore."

He went over to a basket in the corner, took out a potato, and held it out to me.

I took it from him. It was like a piece of art: russet-brown in color, perfectly round, calorie-dense, delicious to humans but unattractive to parasites. And now with the ability to heal itself from bacterial afflictions.

"Is that the one?" Raven asked. "The one with the dog genes?"

I nodded. "It's what you're eating."

She looked down at the rest of the fried potato in her hand.

"Don't worry; it's gluten-free." I smiled and went back for more.

She rolled her eyes at me but then made a small grin—almost a laugh.

"Don Pablo." I reached into my pocket. "Have you ever seen one of these?" I held out the lumpy blue potato that Arturo had given me.

"Of course." Don Pablo took it and rolled it between his fingers. "They call this 'the ancient one.'"

"Do you grow these?" I asked.

"Not anymore." He shook his head. "It doesn't like to share a field with the newer American varieties."

"It doesn't?" I asked.

He shook his head again. "Also, it causes problems with the regime."

"The regime?" I cocked my head to one side. "They tell you which potatoes to plant?"

"In a sense," Pablo sighed. "The American potatoes, they have legal protection."

"A patent?" I was happy that this conversation was occurring in Spanish, and that Raven didn't seem to follow it.

"Something like that. The regime forces us to buy new seeds each year."

"New seeds for the DS 400s, right? Not for the older varieties? Surely they don't have patents on those?"

"Well, they don't claim to own the old ones, but they will still punish those who grow them. The officials say that old potatoes can mix their pollen with the new ones—which is a form of damage to the newer varieties, an infringement on their legal status. It's all in the license that we must sign upon receipt of the seeds."

"Right." I acted as if I knew all this already. "Say, you wouldn't have a copy of that license, by any chance?"

"Of course," Don Pablo said. "In fact, I'll give you the one from last year, and you can take it with you. I'm sure it hasn't changed much."

"That would be helpful."

Don Pablo rose and went to a small shelf. He shuffled through a stack of papers held inside plastic bread bags.

"On our way here," I said, "we met a man named Arturo. He said he grows these old varietals as has been done for centuries."

"Oh, yes." Pablo smiled. "Arturo is my cousin. He does what he likes."

I wasn't shocked by the existence of a licensing agreement. That was increasingly standard practice for a proprietary crop. But the local government's zeal for its enforcement took me by surprise. This struck me as the sort of thing I should've been briefed on before leaving Idaho.

Pablo continued. "Nowadays most farmers grow for export. They've left these old varieties behind. The new ones, from America, they have a better yield, fetch a better price, you know?"

"Oh, yes, I know all about that."

"Of course." He smiled. "You're one of the scientists that helped to create these potatoes, correct?"

"No, no." I shook my head. "I work for the same company, but I don't do that sort of thing."

"It's amazing what they do now, with science. Here, we've been breeding potatoes for thousands of years, but we can't make one like this, probably couldn't even in a million years. Very impressive, your company."

"Yes." I smiled. "It is impressive, isn't it?"

"Here you are." Don Pablo handed me the paperwork from last year's planting. I took it out of the plastic bag and had a look. As expected, the agreement started off with the fact that the farmer was granted rights to this plant only for one season, that saving the seeds and tubers would violate the law. Below that, the print was particularly small and cryptic. It would be a test of my Spanish legalese. "Thanks for this," I said.

The sun was now in the last quarter of the sky. At their mother's urging, the children left the courtyard and went inside. I studied their walk as they disappeared behind the door, hoping in vain to catch one of them standing upright.

"I'd like to come back and do a DNA test," I explained to both parents. "We'll have to find a lab in the capital where they can process that sort of thing."

"The children, they won't suffer?" Niña Rosa asked.

"No! A little swab on the inside of the cheek is all." I demonstrated the motion with my finger.

The parents exchanged glances, then nodded at each other.

"Thank you for your help." Don Pablo extended his hand.

"Thank you." I shook it. "Could I ask one more favor of you?"

"Anything, Doctor."

"Could I take one of those potatoes? The DS 400s?"

"Of course." He went to his sack and fetched a particularly large one for me.

"*Gracias.*" I tried to fit it into my pants pocket like Arturo's blue one, but it was too large. I managed to shove it into the side pocket of my lab coat. Its weight pulled at my shoulder.

Raven and I said our goodbyes, then headed out to the car. Oscar sat behind the wheel, reading the paper.

"Let's go home." I climbed into the passenger seat and put the license into my briefcase.

"Yes, sir." He fired up the engine.

Our trek back to the city began in the late afternoon. We passed by the church and the plaza and the town proper, as the farmers headed for home and the children played in the streets before dinner.

"Oscar," I said, "I need to find a laboratory that can run some basic tests. Could you help me out with that?"

He nodded. "I know the place."

Soon we wound above terraced farming parcels. Both Raven and I pressed our foreheads against the glass and took in the ancient stonework.

"Boss! *Cuidado!*" Oscar suddenly said.

Up ahead, a white pickup truck with POLICIA painted across the side was parked upon the shoulder of the road. Two officers in what looked like riot gear—helmets and bulletproof vests—had another man on his knees.

In the back seat, Raven had taken her camera from its case and pointed it out the window.

"Raven!" I shouted. "Don't even think about it."

She lowered the camera but kept her eyes on the scene. "Eddie, look! It's that guy from the plaza. The one who gave you the potato."

I turned to see. "Arturo?"

Sure enough, it was the same man: his hands in the air now, that familiar potato sack at his feet. One of the policemen held an assault rifle trained on him. The other went to fix handcuffs to his wrists.

"Oscar, stop the car," I said.

"What? Those are the police! You don't want to get mixed up with them."

"Now!" I said.

Oscar pulled off to the shoulder, muttering something about *"gringos locos"* under his breath. I grabbed my briefcase and hopped out the door before we'd come to a complete stop.

A good distance from the police car, I made my way over while the officers cuffed Arturo face down on the ground. The one without the gun held a clipboard and a pen.

"Perdón!" I shouted. "Excuse me, officer!"

The one with the rifle—who, up close, looked to be about sixteen—shifted his aim toward me.

I held my hands up, briefcase dangling from one thumb. "I'm sorry; it's okay. I'm a scientist, from America. This man is an associate of mine."

Both Arturo and the officers looked equally bewildered.

"I think that there may be some confusion here," I said. "If you don't mind, may I ask what this man is in trouble for?"

"Agricultural offenses." The officer with the clipboard seemed to be in charge, and proud of his vocabulary. "It's a serious crime, one that threatens both the nutrition and the security of our great nation."

"Yes, of course," I said. "I think I know what happened. If you would be so kind as to allow me to open this briefcase?"

The two officers exchanged inquisitive looks, then shrugs, then nods.

"Thank you." I put the case on the ground before me, popped open the locks, then took out the letter I'd been given back in Boise, on Tuberware letterhead, along with the potato license that Don Pablo had just lent me.

"I've come to study the agricultural production here in your country."

I handed the letter to the senior officer. "This man did me a favor, you see. I asked him to plant an older, less productive crop—in order to measure the amount of damage it does to the nation's food supply."

The officer in charge furrowed his brow. He looked at my letter, then back at Arturo.

"In fact"—I kept one open hand in the air, reached into my pants pocket with the other—"he gave me this, a sample of the old potatoes he was going to grow for our experiment. As you can tell, I've been sent by the same company that holds the rights to the newer potatoes."

I held the sad blue tuber out toward him. The officer leaned away from it, as though it had a bad smell. After a second of shifting glances between myself, Arturo, the letter, and the potato, he spoke to his subordinate: "Let him go. Let's get out of here, already."

I sighed out loud. As the junior officer shouldered his rifle and set about uncuffing Arturo, I heard a familiar clicking sound from over my shoulder.

Several yards behind me, back toward the car, Raven knelt, snapping photos.

"Cut it out!" I mouthed to her, along with a frantic throat-slitting gesture.

She obliged.

Past her, I saw Oscar in the driver's seat with his hands still on the wheel, perhaps willing to abandon us if things got too hairy.

"Next time," the senior officer said to me, "you should let us know if you come conducting experiments around here. It's a serious matter."

"Yes, sir, absolutely. I apologize. I'm still getting acquainted with some of the laws of your fine nation."

The two officers got into their pickup and headed off toward the capital.

Arturo stared daggers at their bumper as they left. *"Hijos de la gran puta!"* He spat on the ground, then rubbed his wrists.

"Are you okay?" I asked.

"I'm fine, until they come back to interfere once again."

Raven joined us with her ledger notebook out. "They do this just because you're planting a particular type of potato?"

He scoffed. "It's not what I *am* planting; it's what I'm *not* planting."

"You mean the American variety?" I asked.

He nodded. "They claim it's because of the pollen drift and whatnot. But the truth is that they want to sell more imported seeds."

"But why would the regime care about that?" This still made no sense to me.

Arturo rolled his eyes. "Why? Because they're in bed with companies like yours, that's why. This regime, they only know to sell off our resources and our culture to multinational corporations. They are a one-trick donkey that way."

"Pony," I said, mostly to myself. "It's 'one-trick pony.'"

"Listen." Arturo put a hand on my back. "I appreciate your help. I know you mean well. But if you don't see your employer's role in this, then you must remove the scales from your eyes."

I was at a loss for words. Raven, on the other hand, scribbled so fast into her notebook that she looked about to tear the paper.

"If you'll excuse me now," Arturo picked up his sack and put his foot plow over his shoulder. "I have work to do."

He took a crumbling stone staircase up the first tall wall of the terrace, and headed uphill—just as so many of his ancestors had.

"Let's get out of here," I said to Raven.

At the car, Oscar started to scold me for my foolish actions, but I lacked the patience to listen. I leaned my head against the window and watched the landscape roll by.

"Can I ask you something, Eddie?" Raven spoke after several miles. "These GMO crops, are they all designed to fight off infection? Or to withstand poison?"

"Not exactly." I sighed. "Many GMO crops are more nutritious. Like Golden Rice."

"Golden Rice?"

"Yes. It's a kind of rice that uses dandelion genes to produce beta-carotene. It can save children from malnutrition, in places with vitamin A deficiency."

"I see," Raven said. "So everybody must be on board with that, right?"

"You'd think so," I said. "But the environmental groups hate that one too. They tore the plants right out from farmers' fields in the Philippines a few years back."

"Wow." Raven paused for several seconds. "Did you work on something like that, Eddie?"

"Me? No. I've been too busy with the French-fry vending machine."

"Seriously? That's a thing?"

"It's an experimental thing right now. But it will be a reality soon." Sooner still, if I could get myself out of this country.

We drove the rest of the way back in relative silence, night falling like a heavy blanket over the small towns, the fields, the mines, and finally the skyscrapers of the capital.

The next morning, I slept in as late as I could and then had another delicious breakfast in the hotel courtyard.

As I was finishing up, I noticed Doña Ana flipping through the folded pages of a photocopied newsletter. I stole a glance at the section she was reading and saw a photo of one of the guerillas, wearing the red handkerchief around his chin and carrying an assault rifle across his chest. The headline proclaimed: "Victory Imminent in the Mountains."

"What is that?" I asked. "Some kind of newspaper?"

She nodded. "The underground newspaper. The one that the regime does not control." She held it up for me to see. It was called *Voces del Pueblo*.

"Is it accurate?" I asked.

She shrugged. "Not exactly. But between this and the state-run media, one can get some idea of what's going on. The truth hides somewhere in between the two."

I had a closer look. The opposition group called themselves "FURP," or *Frente Unido para la Revolución Permanente*. Their main challenge seemed to be uniting other disparate rebel groups under a single banner. The red handkerchief was the closest they came to a uniform. Ideology aside, it appeared to me that—without air power or any other heavy weapons— they would have a hard time against the current regime and its military.

I went to check on Raven and found her in her bedroom, furiously typing away at a laptop.

"I'm going with Oscar," I said. "To check out that laboratory."

"Great." She looked up and struggled to focus her eyes on me. "We heading back to the village tomorrow?"

"That's the plan," I said. "If things go okay with this lab."

"Cool." She turned back to the computer.

"See you later then."

"Bye, Eddie."

———

Outside, Oscar met me with a motor scooter and an extra helmet. I didn't ask.

"Good morning, Don Doctor!" His smile exposed that one sharp tooth. "Lovely day, no?"

It was overcast. I took the helmet from him and strapped it on. "You know where we're going?"

"To see the laboratory, yes?"

"It's a good one?" I asked.

"Best in the country."

"That will have to do." I climbed on the back. The scooter rambled up and down the hills of the city, straining against the weight of both our bodies. Morning sun broke through the clouds shortly into our trip. Soon, my back was covered in a layer of sweat.

The neighborhood that we ended up in was nicer than where we were staying. When Oscar finally stopped in front of the lab, it turned out to be on the bottom floor of a modern brick building with well-kept shrubbery all around the outside.

I walked in and felt the cool blast of air-conditioning and breathed the harsh scent of sterilizing agents. The atmosphere reminded me of my beloved lab on the second floor of One Potato Way. I took a deep breath, comforted by the promise that some actual science might be taking place here.

"Hello." A beautiful bespectacled woman in a long white lab coat greeted me in English. "Are you Doctor Morales, from Tuberware?"

"Yes." I extended my hand. "And you are?"

"Call me Nora."

We shook.

"Eddie is fine."

"You need to take some DNA samples, is that right?"

"Correct. Nothing too sophisticated. I need to get buccal swabs on three subjects."

"Paternity?" she asked. "What are we matching to?"

"It's not paternity. It's a matter of finding anything abnormal and common to the three of them. Can we check the chromosomal markers for motor skills? Look for extra or missing genes?"

She nodded but looked confused. "We can try."

"They have a rare condition," I attempted to explain without saying too much. "I'm trying to find out if it's genetic or not."

"I'll get you some swabs," she said.

I waited at the counter while Nora put together a packet.

"There you go," she said. "You'll bring these back tomorrow?"

"That's the plan."

"I'll be here," she said. "This is much more exciting than our normal jobs—looking for the cause of diarrhea or helping catch a deadbeat dad."

"Oh, I don't expect that too much will come of this." I stared down at the bag of swabs and tubes that she'd prepared for me. "Listen, could I ask you for one more thing?"

"Of course."

"Could you run a DNA profile on this?" From my pants pocket, I took Arturo's wrinkled blue gift and laid it on the counter.

"It's a potato," she said.

"I know." An awkward chuckle escaped my mouth. "But I have a hunch about it. I work with potatoes, back home. It would be nice if I could get a closer look."

She shrugged. "It's a bit unusual, but I can certainly give you the data."

I smiled. "That would be very helpful."

"Do you have a control? Anything to compare it to?"

"Oh . . ." I extemporized, then patted the pocket of my lab coat. "This. Compare it to this." I took out the DS 400 that Don Pablo had given me.

"Wait here for one second," she said. "I'll take samples and give these back to you. No need to leave the entire thing."

She took the potatoes into the back, then returned with them a moment later. A small gouge, about the size of a pinky nail, had been taken from each tuber's side.

"Perfect," I said. "Thanks."

"Thank you, Doctor Morales." She gave me a shy smile. "See you soon."

———

Outside, Oscar sat on the scooter, grinning. "She was very beautiful, no?"

I strapped on my helmet and nodded to him. "And smart. Let's go."

I was in high spirits on the ride back. With a couple of swabs and a legitimate lab test, I might close this matter. And now I had the whole afternoon to relax, maybe get in touch with Jill or send a message to Warren.

Oscar went to pull up at the hotel, but a big white car was parked right in front of the entrance. It was a long, shining white Cadillac, with darkly tinted windows and a small national flag at each corner of its front hood.

Oscar pulled up alongside it and killed his engine. I climbed off and removed my helmet.

The driver's door opened on the Cadillac. A man in a dark suit and sunglasses stepped out. "Doctor Morales?"

I looked at Oscar. He shrugged.

"That's me," I said.

"The Vice Minister of the Interior would like to meet with you. I've been sent to pick you up."

I leaned toward Oscar and mumbled, "What should I do?"

Oscar raised his eyebrows. "I would go with this man."

I handed Oscar my helmet and climbed into the back of the Cadillac. The leather of its interior was crisp and cold with air-conditioning.

We took off in a direction I'd not been before. The big car went downhill, toward the historic city center—a place I'd only seen from the airplane. Spanish colonial architecture—full of archways and statues, tall iron gates—sprang up on all sides. The people on the streets turned to stare and point at the car as though it carried an actual head of state.

"Do you know what this is all about?" I asked the driver. "Why the Vice Minister wants to see me?"

His sun-glassed eyes found mine in the rearview mirror. "No, sir. I'm just the driver."

We came to a plaza as big as a city block, with a few fountains scattered throughout. A small group of protestors gathered at a corner so far away, it seemed like a whole different city. A massive palace—recently painted pink—ran the length of the plaza on the near side. The driver pulled up in front of it. On an iron plaque beside the entrance, the words MINISTRY OF INTERIOR were written in a blocky script. At the very sight of the car, uniformed guards opened up an iron gate and waved us in.

Within the gates, the Cadillac came to a stop and my door was opened by a young man in a finely tailored suit.

"Doctor Morales, I presume?" His English was perfect.

"Yes," I said. "That's me."

"Very nice to meet you." He shook my hand and then used it to help me out of the car. "I am Alejandro. Could you come with me, please?" I followed Alejandro up the stairs and into the Ministry. The building had a crumbling regal air to it, but I barely had a chance to take it in as I kept up with my young guide. He rushed up several flights of stairs, sometimes taking them two at a stride. By the time we reached the top floor, I was out of breath.

At a tall wooden door with a pair of guards outside, Alejandro knocked, then waited. I put my hands on my knees and leaned over, still trying to catch my breath.

A voice sounded from the chamber within; Alejandro pushed the door open and gestured me inside.

The interior of this office put the rest of the building to shame. It was paneled in carved wood and brassy accents. There were no windows, but instead a series of nineteenth-century paintings—mostly of ships and horses—hung close together in gilded frames.

A massive wooden desk sat at the far end of the room, ornamented with a series of small flags. A uniformed man sat behind it, his back to me. He appeared to be staring up at the triptych of paintings behind the desk. In those pieces, an army of centurions headed over the mountains atop elephants. Many of the elephants reared up on two legs; others slipped off the narrow paths. A few dangled by ropes from the edges of cliffs. A pretty awful scene.

"Doctor Morales." The man's back was still turned toward me.

"Yes, sir," I said.

"It's amazing, isn't it? What these soldiers accomplished."

"Is that Hannibal's army?" The name popped into my head the second I said it. "You know, I think he may have lost the war . . . in the end."

"In those days, one's nation meant something. People were willing to march for it, to die for it. Now? They ask 'What can this government give to me today? And if that's not enough, I'll support another.'"

"Politics isn't my area, sir."

He turned around to face me. It was the man I'd seen making the speech on television, the one I'd jokingly thought of as the Extended Metaphor Czar.

"And what exactly is your area, again?"

I swallowed. "Potatoes, mostly."

"Oh, yes." He shook his head as if just now realizing why I was in his office. "They sent you down to deal with this mess of the children who walk on their hands."

"Their hands and their feet," I corrected him.

"Can you prove that they are faking?" he asked.

"They're not faking, sir," I said.

"That's not what I asked you."

"Oh. I see. Well, no. I don't think I could prove that."

"I'm sure you're aware that my government's position is somewhat fragile at this juncture."

"Really? I was under the impression that the opposition was quite insignificant." I started to pinch together a bit of air with my fingers, as he had done in his speech, but then thought better of it.

"One of the issues that those cowards in the mountains have been using against us is our relationship to American corporations, like the one that you represent."

"By 'cowards in the mountains,' you mean FURP?"

"This scandal—or the way it might play out in the press—would not be helpful. Many lives could be at stake, you see."

"Scandal?" I asked. "What's the scandal?"

He sighed, as though frustrated with me. "That this office allowed some US corporation to sell our people potatoes that turn them into dogs."

"Oh, *that* scandal." I'd never thought of it in quite those terms.

"If you cannot prove that these children are faking, then I'm afraid that Tuberware doesn't have much of a future here. There are plenty of other companies that would be happy to sell us experimental crops."

"Look." I raised my voice, tried to take control of this conversation. "They're not faking it, and I can't make it seem as if they are. However, this has nothing to do with our potatoes. And that's something I can prove."

He sat down in his office chair, leaned back, and stroked his chin. "You're sure about this?"

"I'm sure. I already have a laboratory lined up. I'll get the samples from Huanchillo tomorrow, and we'll have this sorted out within days. What those children are suffering from is a genetic disorder—a mutation of sorts—like extra nipples or vestigial tails. It's not common, but it does happen. It's happened elsewhere, in nations where they don't grow any potatoes at all."

The minister nodded, looking satisfied. "Let's take care of this thing before the press gets involved."

"I'm with you there," I said. "But tell me: Don't *you* run the media?" I hoped that question wasn't overstepping my bounds.

He nodded. "The big papers and TV stations, yes. But with this internet these days, it's very difficult to control."

"Don't worry about those internet writers," I said. "Nobody reads them, and they don't do any actual research. We'll take care of this well before they get wind of it."

He stood and offered me his hand. "If you can resolve this as you describe, I will personally ensure that it's worth your while."

I didn't know what he meant by that. We shook hands and said our goodbyes.

Back at the hotel, I had expected to run into Raven, but she was nowhere to be found. I took a shower and walked out onto the street just before sunset, in search of dinner.

I left the hotel's residential neighborhood and crossed a major avenue into what looked to be more of a business zone. It didn't take long to come across a woman in an apron with a big griddle set up on the sidewalk. She stood over an assortment of fried goodies alongside jars of sauces and spices. I pointed at a couple of things, asked what was what, then took a seat at the long communal table inside the storefront.

I'd brought the license form that Don Pablo had given me, and I studied the finer print at the bottom of it. It was difficult to understand, but it did appear that the seeds were protected from pollen drift and other forms of "unintentional genetic infringement." I supposed those were the grounds for going after farmers who did not plant it, though it still struck me as an odd practice. I was also surprised to see it mentioned that the potatoes themselves were registered as a pesticide.

My reading was interrupted by a sudden squeal of tires. I looked up. Across the street, a black car pulled up and a few police officers hopped out. They knocked on a door and were allowed in.

The woman with the apron slid a plate in front of me, along with a fork. "*Buen provecho,*" she said with a smile.

"*Gracias.*"

I dug in. The food was amazing. She'd served me three football-shaped globs that turned out to be mashed potatoes stuffed with soft cheese. On the side was a pool of spicy, herby sauce and a pile of pickled onions.

A couple of other diners joined me at the long table. I realized that it was probably still early for dinner. The woman in the apron fetched beer bottles from a cooler of ice for the newcomers.

"Would you like a beer?" she asked me.

I must've been staring. "Yes, please."

She placed an amber bottle in front of me. It read "La Dorada" in a Germanish font. Cold, crisp, and watery, it went perfectly with the food.

I finished my meal just as the others were served. I fished out a few of the bills that I'd barely learned the value of from my pocket and drained the last of my beer.

A loud crack sounded across the street. A door burst open, and the same police officers I'd seen earlier carried out a young man in a jean jacket who thrashed in their grip and shouted *cabrones!* at them. They shoved him into the back of their car—which didn't have a cage or a police logo or any sort of official marking. A cop sat on either side of him.

The other diners averted their eyes. The man in the jean jacket shouted once more, then the car left the second his door closed.

After it was gone, I asked the food vendor exactly what had just happened.

"It's the police," she said. "Always looking for revolutionaries."

"Are there a lot of revolutionaries around here?" I asked.

"Psshh. Only by *their* definition. Anyone who tries to find out what's really going on, they get branded as the enemy. That man, my neighbor, he has family in the mountains. He keeps people here updated, that's all."

One of the other patrons interrupted. "They like to see their statistics go up, so they go around making arrests and interrogations. This regime thinks they can get away with anything."

I nodded, not wanting to say the wrong thing. The vendor made change from my bill, and I left some coins on the table for her. I took my phone from my pocket before I left, but I couldn't get any reception. I asked the vendor about an internet café, and she directed me toward a place nearby.

—

On the Boulevard de los Agricultores I found the café she had described. The PCs were all tragically slow, running ancient operating systems, and lacking basic software. My keyboard was beige-colored and had Spanish punctuation—tildes and inverted question marks—taped over the tops of the English keys. I watched the digital hourglass as the machine whizzed and putted its way toward my email account.

Once it finally came up, my inbox was fuller than expected. I read one from Jill first:

> Hola *Eddie! Hope your trip is going* bueno *so far. Things are great back here. Listen to this: they put me in charge of the fry machine project! It's so exciting. I've got some really good leads on pinning down a varnish for the outside layer. (Spoiler alert: It's mostly corn syrup!) And once you get back, we'll basically be equals—which makes everything totally not weird! Take care Eddie!* Hasta luego.
>
> *-XO*

Jill? In charge of the machine fries? That project was *my* baby! Nothing against Jill, but she wasn't qualified to run it. And corn syrup in the French-fry mix? That's such a cop-out. More importantly: What plans did Warren have for me, once this errand was over and done with?

On that note, I scanned my inbox for a message from Warren. There was one sent from his secretary, dated late yesterday:

> *Dr. Morales:*
>
> *We understand you've met with the Vice Minister of the Interior. Stay on his good side. He's the most important figure in that nation.*
>
> *-WS*

That was it? Nothing about the science? I didn't feel up to checking other messages or even responding to those two. There was still plenty of time left on my half hour of internet. I tried to look at some American news sites, but all my favorites were unavailable. A pop-up message repeatedly appeared, saying:

> *For your protection, this subversive website has been blocked on account of dangerous and corruptive content. Failing to abide by this blockage might result in prosecution under the anti-subversion act.*

"Screw this," I said aloud, in English, and left the café with over twenty minutes on the clock.

———

On my way back to the hotel, I noticed a familiar face under the lights of the Boulevard de los Agricultores.

"Raven?" I shouted. "What are you doing here?"

"Oh, hi, Eddie. I'm looking for the internet café."

"It's right over there," I pointed in the direction I'd just come from. "But don't get your hopes up. The state has everything blocked—even the real news. I'm sure your lefty sites will be doubly censored."

She laughed. "That's all right. It's just some personal stuff that I want to do."

"Should I walk you over there?" I asked the question to myself as much as to her. "It's pretty late."

"No!" she scoffed. "You look tired. I'll be fine."

"Okay," I said. "If you insist." I certainly was tired.

"So, tomorrow we head back to the village?"

"That's right," I said. "Apparently, Oscar is picking us up early. I need to take some samples, get to the bottom of this."

She nodded. "Well, I better be off, before they close."

"Good night, Raven."

I went back to the room and immediately collapsed onto the bed, not stirring or dreaming until the twin blares of roosters and car alarms sounded at daybreak. Oscar pounded on my door before I'd even risen.

"Boss! Time to get going."

I climbed out of bed and opened the door just a crack. "Give me a minute, will you?"

"One minute? Okay, boss."

"Also, if you could ask the *señora* for a cup of coffee, that would be great."

He nodded. I shut the door.

I'd already learned a thing or two about this shower. There was neither hot water nor showerhead. Instead, a raw copper pipe projected half a foot from the wall—at about my eye level. The pressure was surprisingly good. In the cool mornings, its quick power-wash served as a vigorous wakeup call.

Back in the bedroom, I clicked on the news as I got dressed. The Vice Minister of the Interior again was holding a press conference. The bright foam of microphone covers blossomed about his chin like a bouquet.

He mentioned the opposition as I put on pants. By the time I buttoned my shirt, I noticed that he was more unnerved than normal. Beads of sweat slid down along his temple. He hadn't shaved since our meeting yesterday.

His speech seemed more encoded than the last. This time, his subject was the media—the "cowardly underground gossip networks who hide in their holes like little burrowing rodents!"

Again, he did his rat impression. I clicked the TV off and put on my lab coat. Those two potatoes were still in my pockets: the DS 400 from Don Pablo and the La Vieja from Arturo. I placed both of them side by side along my windowsill, then grabbed my briefcase.

Out in the courtyard, Doña Ana's mother sat with her tea at her preferred table in the back, her walking frame leaned against the wall. Oscar sat at a larger table with two cups of coffee in front of him.

"Boss. Your coffee."

The state-run daily paper lay untouched on another table. Its headline read: "Government dismisses reports of quadripedal citizens as subversive propaganda." There were no images on the entire front page.

"Uh oh."

In the kitchen, I saw Doña Ana and her daughters looking over one another's shoulders at the underground newspaper. I ran in to join them.

"Pero que barbaro!" The eldest daughter proclaimed.

I shouldered my way over to see. The front page stole my breath like a punch to the stomach. There, above the fold, was a picture of Pablito followed by his two sisters, ambling their way over to the dinner table. It was a photo from our visit two nights ago.

"Fucking Raven," I muttered.

"It's terrible, no?" Doña Ana said to me.

"It's even worse than that." I rubbed my temples.

"Morning, Eddie." Raven entered the courtyard, wearing her floppy hat and hiking boots. "We should get going, huh?"

"Do you have any idea what you've done?"

"Excuse me?"

"The pictures. Whatever you wrote about that family. You've created a massive incident here!" I grabbed the illegal paper from Doña Ana's hand and dropped it alongside the official one.

Raven gasped.

"This all started with you, I presume?"

"Oh, my God," she said. "But . . . but . . . *nobody* reads my blog."

"They do when it covers a story suppressed by their state-run media."

"I'm sorry, Eddie. I had no idea." She pulled the hat from her head and twisted it with her hands. "I only wanted to tell the truth."

"Psshh." I was so frustrated, I had to look away from her. "Not only did you make this family into tabloid freaks, but you may have put them in serious danger. This regime doesn't mess around."

"Hey, boss," Oscar said. "Time to go, yes?"

I tried to compose myself. "We need to swab those kids, take the swabs to the lab, and get this mess over with."

"I'm sorry, Eddie," Raven said again.

"Can I take this?" I lifted the underground newspaper from the table and turned to Doña Ana.

"Of course," she said. "I always burn it in the sink after reading it. You don't want to get caught with that thing."

I folded it up and tucked it under my arm, then followed Oscar out. Raven came along behind us. I didn't quite have the heart to tell her to stay here. Besides, it was best not to let her out of my sight, lest she cause any more trouble.

Once out on the street, Oscar said, "Here we go." He gestured toward a small blue pickup truck with a single bench seat.

"That?" I asked.

"Indeed."

I turned to Raven. "You're sitting in the middle."

As we left the city, I tried to read the underground paper. It wasn't easy; Oscar had to pull the seat far forward so that he could reach the pedals. My knees jammed into the dashboard.

"I can't believe you did this," I muttered.

Raven looked ashamed, her body stuck between the two of us, legs wrapped around the stick shift.

I translated out loud. "'Potato seeds from an American corporation, seeds which are not legal in the US and contain genes from four-legged beasts. The regime has kept all this under wraps, not wanting to damage its valuable relationship to foreign capitalists.' Is that what you wrote?"

"No!" She shook her head. "I mean, not exactly. My language wasn't quite so . . . Marxist. Something must've been lost in the translation."

"Or gained." I sighed. "This is exactly the sort of thing that the parents wanted to avoid."

"Eddie, it's really sweet of you to care about them, but this is bigger than the one family."

"No, it's actually not. This problem is completely contained within the one family. I'll be able to prove that by the day after tomorrow. Hopefully before you or some poor bastard from this paper gets picked up by the security forces." I rubbed at my temples again. How much did Warren know about all this?

"Look alive," Oscar said.

I took my hand away and saw a crowd of people on one side of the road. "What's going on?"

"Miners," Oscar said. "They're going on strike."

I could barely see the ugly monoliths of the mining operation for all the bodies in alpaca-wool coats and hats. Oscar slowed down and lowered his window as we approached a roadblock of trash cans and tree stumps.

"Your business?" one of the striking miners asked. He seemed confused by the sight of gringos inside.

"We're heading through to Huanchillo. Not stopping here." Oscar reached over and pulled the underground newspaper to his lap, straightened it out so the headline was visible.

The miner waved to others, and they moved the metal barrels out of the way. On we went.

"Why now?" I asked Oscar.

He shrugged. "Maybe they think the regime will be busy with this." He lifted the newspaper and put it back in my lap. "Or maybe it's just coincidence."

"Do their strikes get taken seriously?" I asked.

He nodded. "More so than other labor groups, yes."

"Is that because so much of the nation's export economy comes from the mines?" I asked.

"There's that," Oscar said. "Also, the miners have dynamite."

We carried on toward the village as the strikers faded from sight.

The day was less overcast than last time. The bright morning sun did its battle with the chill mountain air. Even at the outskirts of Huanchillo, something seemed amiss. A pack of kids wandered back and forth around the town square, but none of them stopped to stare at us or our vehicle. By the time we reached the Morales household, I understood why.

A huge gaggle of people and cars surrounded the front of the humble family house. There was one international news team—from Argentina, by the sound of their accents—with a van, and a female anchor holding a microphone.

A large group in attendance seemed to be from the evangelical church. The men all wore crisp white-collared shirts with dark trousers, the women somber dresses and head coverings. Their leader—a lean, weathered man with his collar and cuffs cinched tight—spoke through a raspy megaphone, going on and on about Jesus as the cure for physical afflictions. I heard something about evolution—or "backwards evolution"— but it was hard to tell over the tinny speaker.

And there, with a camera in one hand and a megaphone in the other, was Kearns. He had a sizable group behind him, carrying signs and wearing T-shirts with anti-GMO slogans. I scanned the faces of his bunch, and they looked more like ex-pats and wealthy people from the capital, not the local villagers. I didn't know when he'd found Raven's story, but he'd snapped right into action.

Oscar got the truck as close as he could. The three of us stared out the window at the chaos.

"Hope you're happy." I couldn't even look Raven in the eye.

"I told the truth, Eddie. Nothing else." A fault line of insecurity ran through her voice. "That's why they sent me here, after all."

I had the latch to the car door in my hand, and I knew I should just go ahead and open it. But my rage got the better of me.

"They sent you here to be a symbol. They sent you here to fail as a journalist." I leaned in closer to her. "Some unemployed Boise woman with a blog? You think Tuberware expected you'd get to the bottom of this? You were picked for your incompetence. How can you not see that?"

Oscar pretended to look the other way.

Raven wiped at her eyes.

"I've got work to do." I opened the door and stepped out of the truck.

grabbed my swab kit and went straight for Kearns. As soon as he saw me coming, he handed the camera off to his chubby underling.

"Eddie!" he said. "Good to know that Tuberware is living up to its reputation."

"Can't say I'm surprised to see you here, Spencer. You've found your people." I gestured toward the religious protest happening alongside him. "Zealous cult members, denying evolution."

He shrugged. "There's more than one reason to be wary of GMOs, Eddie. The new food movement is a big tent."

"More like a circus," I said.

His assistant held the camera close to the two of us. The woman with the microphone pole leaned in.

"How is it that you can create a protest and simultaneously pretend to document it?" I asked. "Are there no ethics or best practices for this . . . field of yours?"

"You're telling me about ethics? Look at what your company has done to these kids."

"Our potatoes have nothing to do with the condition of the Morales children." I turned toward his cameraman. "You can put that in your stupid film."

I headed toward the house, moving through the crowd with purpose, ready to push anyone down if they got in my way. Raven waited by the gate. I entered the yard, gave the mother llama a threatening stare, and proceeded to the doorstep.

My fist pounded on the wooden door. A puffy-faced Raven stood a few paces behind. Oscar guarded the vehicle.

"Don Pablo? It's me: Doctor Morales. I'm sorry about all this commotion. Could you please let me in? I need to perform the tests we discussed the other day. Hopefully that will settle the matter."

The door cracked open just a hair, to reveal one of Don Pablo's worried eyeballs and part of his nose.

"Doctor Morales?" As he spoke, a flashbulb went off from behind me. "Why is this happening to us?"

"It's her fault." I used my thumb to point toward Raven. "Can we come in for a moment? I only want to straighten this out."

He opened the door a bit wider. Questions, chants, and prayers came from the congregation of weirdos assembled behind me. As we stepped across the threshold, Raven meekly said "I'm sorry" in her best Spanish.

Niña Rosa was sitting on an easy chair, gripping a set of rosary beads. The children seemed completely unfazed by the situation. As soon as Pablito saw Raven, he ran over to her—on all fours—and asked to see her camera.

She removed the device from its bag but didn't take any photos. Instead, she set about showing him how to work it properly.

"I'm so sorry about all this trouble," I said. "Please let me take this DNA test, get the results, and hopefully we can quiet down this scandal."

The parents looked at each other, then gave tepid nods. I took out the buccal swab kit, hoping to get started before a debate ensued. The two daughters were sitting on the floor at the far end of the room. I walked over to them and explained the test.

"If you'll open your mouth just a little, like so." I demonstrated.

Rosita opened up. She giggled as I inserted the swab and ran it up and down along the inside of her cheek. I'd never had any reason to test DNA in a human before, but it seemed simple enough.

After a few seconds, I put the swab into one of the sterile tubes from Nora's lab.

Rosita giggled and covered her mouth, as though this were all part of a game.

I turned to Carmen. "You're next."

She opened her mouth and let me do the same thing.

"Doctor Morales?" The mother spoke up as I collected the second swab. "Is it true what that preacher says, about backwards evolution?"

"No. It's nonsense," I said. "That preacher, he's from the evangelical church, correct?"

"Yes," Niña Rosa concurred.

"So neither he nor his congregation believes in evolution to begin with. Now they want to say that it's happening in reverse? That's beyond ridiculous."

Don Pablo nodded and said "exactly," as if to reassure his wife.

I put the second swab into the corresponding tube. "Evolution doesn't go forward and backward. Organisms never return to their former states; that's Dollo's law."

I moved on to Pablito. As I approached, he held up Raven's camera. The flash temporarily blinded me. I covered my eyes. Pablito looked at the screen on the back and exploded with laughter. He turned the machine around so I could see.

I suppose it was a funny image: me with the swab in hand, squinting my eyes against the light. He showed Raven, and she laughed out loud— clearly pleased that she could bring at least a small measure of joy to this family today.

"Okay, Pablito. I'm going to stick this in your mouth, like I did with your sisters. It won't hurt a bit. Open wide."

He did as he was told. I rubbed the swab up and down along the inside of his cheek, then sealed it inside my last tube. "That's it."

Pablito rubbed his face.

Don Pablo rose and spoke in my ear. "So, tell me, Doctor: what do my children have?"

I let out a long exhale. "Your children have a genetic abnormality: a mutation, it's sometimes called. It's affecting whichever part of the brain helps us to balance and walk upright. It's something that has occurred before, in other children, but it's very rare."

"Like the X-Men?" Pablito asked.

"What?" I said.

"Mutants, like the X-Men."

"I suppose that's true, Pablito. A bit like the X-Men."

"What should we do about all these people outside?" Niña Rosa asked.

I shrugged. "I would keep doing what you're doing. Stay indoors, wait for it to pass. Don't talk to any reporters. Don't sign anything."

They nodded. Raven hung her head.

"I'll try to get the scientific aspect straightened out as soon as I can. That should silence at least a few of the groups outside. Perhaps the others will lose interest."

The parents nodded. They obviously had some faith in my words and my little bag of DNA samples. I took a step toward the door.

"Doctor, wait. Would you please join us?" Don Pablo asked. "For some tea?"

"Tea?" I glanced at my watch, eager to get on the road. But this family's trust was one of the few advantages I still possessed. Perhaps Warren had been right in that estimation, if in nothing else. "Of course."

I turned to Raven: "We're staying for tea."

Niña Rosa dusted off a chair and presented it to me. I sat. She then went and set up cups and saucers, poured them full of a steamy, herby liquid.

"Tell me something, Don Pablo." I turned to the *paterfamilias*. "That potato I showed you the other day?"

"Oh, yes." He joined us at the table. "La Vieja."

"Exactly. Is that common around here? Do other farmers grow that variety?"

He laughed. "When I was a boy, almost everyone grew those, or something like them. It was the preferred crop of my grandfather's generation. Very good for making *chuño*."

I vaguely recognized the term for a high-altitude method of freeze-drying potatoes.

"But those are all disappearing," he went on. "Nobody wants them for export. They turn an ugly gray color when cooked."

"I see."

"Also, it looks similar to another variety of potato, one which is very toxic. The old men, they know how to tell the difference. But fewer and fewer have that knowledge now."

"That would make them hard to sell," I admitted.

"This tea is nice," Raven said to me, then *"muy rico"* to Niña Rosa. "What is this, Eddie? Some kind of green tea?"

"It's coca leaves," I said, then took a long slurp.

"Oh." The color drained from Raven's face. "Are we going to get high here?"

"No more than with your average double latte," I said.

Don Pablo continued, "I can get you some more of those *viejas*, if you like, Doctor Morales. There is a man in town who still makes very good *chuño*."

"I would love to try that," I said.

"When are you coming back this way?"

"As soon as the lab can finish the results," I said. "Maybe the day after tomorrow?"

He nodded. "We will eat *chuño* then, God willing. May all these crazy people outside find something better to do before then."

"I look forward to that." In one hot gulp, I finished my tea. "Now, speaking of the lab, we should be on our way."

We said our goodbyes. Raven offered her Spanish apologies several more times.

As we approached the door, I turned back and said, "Remember: don't talk to reporters. This should all settle down soon."

We opened the door and suffered the camera flashes of the news crew, a volley of their stupid questions, and glares from the confused evangelicals. Through his microphone, the preacher hurled at us some spittle-spiked accusation about reversing evolution.

Before I could get into the car, Kearns had materialized with a microphone, his cameraman just a few paces behind.

"Doctor Morales," he shouted in a formal, for-camera voice. "What does Tuberware have against nature? Against sustainable agriculture?"

I threw my briefcase into the pickup's cab and turned to Kearns. Something—perhaps the coca leaves—had raised my pulse and loosened my tongue.

"You know something, Spencer? You ought to spend some more time out here in this village, with these hardworking *campesinos*. Ask them how they like living hand to mouth, trying to convince consumers to eat blue potatoes rather than yellow ones. Ask them what it's like in a bad drought year. Or a year with too much rain. Let me know if subsistence farming turns out to be the idyllic pastoral life you seem to think it is. It's true that this government has done some unfortunate things. It's true that my employer doesn't always behave like a charity or the UN. But at the end of the day, GMO potatoes have helped people here. Have helped people all over the developing world. If you're going to deny that, based on some squeamish notions about nature versus technology, then your outlook is dangerously simple."

I started to enter the car but decided I wasn't quite finished. "And don't you dare take the moral high ground when it comes to this family." I pointed toward their house. "You're the one—one of many—using their plight to advance your own agenda. But that's no surprise; you've only ever cared about yourself."

With that, I climbed into the car and slammed my door.

Oscar had no bones about driving straight through the crowd. The second we were aboard, he got us out onto the main road. His trick seemed to be never yielding, even as reporters flung themselves in front of his hood and protestors clung to the tailgate.

On the way through town, we saw Arturo walking along the side of the road with his foot plow, the only person in Huanchillo with no interest in the circus back at the Morales home. We exchanged a wave through the window.

"Oscar," I said. "Stop the car."

He sighed. "If you say so, boss." He pulled the pickup over to the curb.

"Arturo!" I shouted, excited to see him.

"Doctor Morales." He turned around. "How are you?"

"I've been better, to be honest. I guess you've heard about the excitement over your nieces and nephew."

"I was there earlier today," he said. "It's best not to engage with those sorts of people. They come looking for confrontation, so why give it to them?"

"That's very decent of you," I said.

He shrugged. "Decency is free. That's why poor people have it in abundance."

Raven climbed out from her middle seat and greeted Arturo. Oscar stayed behind the wheel.

"I'm heading up to my parcel now." He lifted the foot plow to demonstrate. "Would you like to come with me? It's a bit of a walk, but very beautiful."

Raven and I exchanged a glance.

"I would love to see where you grow your potatoes," I said honestly.

"*Vamos.*" Arturo motioned for us to follow him.

I took off the lab coat and stowed it in the pickup. Oscar looked frustrated, but he agreed to wait for us there. Raven was excited: at last, an activity that suited her wardrobe. Both of us were still feeling invigorated by the tea.

We followed Arturo through the main square of the town, past the church, and up a side street. The street soon narrowed to something like a tight alleyway between houses—the intricate stonework of the foundations visible on either side. Our path then morphed into a set of stone stairs headed straight up the mountain. Not long into the climb, I found myself huffing and puffing, the effects of the elevation pressing hard against my lungs.

"Doing all right, Eddie?" Raven asked from behind.

"Yeah," I managed. "Just not as acclimated as I thought."

Arturo continued at a brisk pace.

"It's nice up here, isn't it?" Raven asked.

"Very much so." I turned back toward Huanchillo. From this vantage, we could see how the oldest part of the town was wedged between the mountains. The shadow of the ridge we stood on stretched far out, past the plaza and over to the houses on the outskirts.

"The difficult part is almost over," Arturo shouted from above.

"Shall we?" Raven asked.

"After you." I gestured for her to go ahead.

For the next few minutes, I leaned into each of my steps, pushing down upon my knees, my eyes on the steep stone stairs—each of them probably eight hundred years old.

As promised, we soon reached the top, where Arturo waited, and were rewarded with a blast of afternoon sunlight. The air was as rich and thin as a supermodel.

"It's quite a view, no?" Arturo said.

We stood at the beginning of a long, narrow ridgeline. On either side of the mountain's spine, the hillsides were terraced to hold crops. The effect was something like a 3D topo map—colored in with the brilliant greens of the foliage and the inky black of the stone.

ONE POTATO

"It's amazing." Indeed, I could think of few vistas that combined the awe of nature with the marvels of human ingenuity in such equal measure.

"Shall we continue?" Foot plow over his shoulder, Arturo kept walking along the ridgeline. We passed a father-and-son farming team on their way home, a heavy sack over the boy's shoulder.

"There aren't many people up here today," I said.

"No," Arturo concurred. "For those who plant the American potatoes, it's a slow time of year. If you've sprayed for bugs and weeds, you have nothing to do right now. It's only people like me—the stubborn ones—who are busy these days."

"Look!" Raven pointed skyward. "Is that another condor?"

I followed her index finger and saw the giant bird, the shock of white at its collar, the blood-red face. The flaps of its pterodactyl wings seemed a half step too late, as if it were in danger of falling from the sky at any second.

"Ah, yes," Arturo said. "That one, she is here often."

We watched for another second. The bird then dropped and made an arcing turn toward the next valley.

"Now, this way." Arturo led us down one side of the ridgeline. We started on a narrow path, then took a flying staircase: a set of long stones that extended out from the front of the terrace walls.

"This is so cool." Raven admired the design.

"Very clever, no?" Arturo said. "My ancestors were excellent masons. They thought of everything."

We walked along the walls of a high terrace, winding around a curve in the hillside. We took one more flying staircase, covered a little more distance, then stopped.

"This is my parcel," Arturo announced. "These three rows, from here to the end."

It didn't strike me as the best spot in the area: tucked tight up against the hillside, mostly in the shade of an adjacent mountain. The terraces here were narrower than the others we'd passed—perhaps that was why he had all three levels to himself. I imagined he must do a fair amount of schlepping up and down while working this spot.

Straightaway, I could tell that he planted differently than the others. His crops were well tended, but smaller and less uniform, without the saturated green we'd passed elsewhere.

"It's very nice," I said. "You must have challenges with the sunlight. Don't you get more at that end"—I pointed back to the way we'd come—"than over here?"

Arturo grinned and tapped his temple. "You're very observant, Doctor. These," he bent down and touched the leaves at his feet, "they like the shadows. It's a wild potato that grows deep in valleys, along riverbeds. They do well in this spot. Those"—he pointed to the other end—"they like the sun."

"Wait," I said. "You plant two different varieties in this one row?"

"Two?" He laughed. "More than that, Doctor. Look closely. These here, they're a cross between the two varieties I just described. This one? It's very tasty, so I give it the best spot."

I bent over and studied the leaves. Sure enough, they were quite different from one another—in their shape, their size, and their hue. I couldn't believe it; I'd rarely seen such a diverse array of potatoes, even in gardens specifically designed for the purpose.

"Up here, they are different, of course." Arturo walked up a staircase to the next level of his farm. "You'd be surprised, Doctor, by just how much a small change in elevation affects the plants. On this level, I mostly put La Vieja—with which you are familiar. That one, it will grow anywhere. Some years, I don't even plant it again; it just shows up."

"A volunteer," Raven said.

"I've never seen anything like this," I said. "So much variety."

"Psshh." Arturo was dismissive. "This is just my little parcel. If we went farther down the valley, I could show you some others—some that like a lot of water."

"Are any of them ready to harvest?" I asked.

Arturo grinned. "Why else would we be here?" He led us up to the highest of his terraces. Raven and I watched as he stuck his foot plow in beside one of the plants. Without looking at it, he moved the tool around a little—like he was picking a lock—then stepped down on the blade with his foot. He pried upward, and the stalk abruptly keeled to one side.

"There we are."

Without removing the plant, he then walked around the patch and chose the next one. He performed the same move half a dozen times—loosening the plants without fully harvesting them—then threw the plow to the ground.

"Let's see what we have, shall we?" He bent over the nearest loose plant, reached under the leaves, and pulled upward. With a few shakes and a twist, the roots gave way, and he pulled the whole thing out. As he brushed the dirt away, I saw that the potatoes were bright yellow and round as Ping-Pong balls—visually the opposite of La Vieja.

"These are very tasty—buttery flesh with a little sweetness—but fussy to grow."

Raven went to the next loose plant. She did her best to emulate Arturo's motion, but the stem tore on her and she ended up using her hands to dig the spuds out. I rushed over to help her brush the dirt off. These were a dark red color. Against my fingers, the texture was rough and barky.

"We mostly put that one in soup," Arturo explained. "Not much flavor, but they will store for ages."

I ran over to the next one and pulled it up myself. It had been a while since I'd done such a thing. In my haste, I nearly broke the stem right off. My second try was more gentle. This time, it gave a satisfying release and came right out. I brushed the soil away and saw that the spuds had a rosy pink skin. Each one was long and skinny, with tapered ends like little sausage links.

"Doctor." Arturo pointed at his nose and then at the potatoes in my hand.

I lifted them up and gave a good sniff. They had a powerful herby smell that burned in my sinuses.

"Onion?" I said. "What causes that?"

Arturo shrugged. "Nature, I suppose. It's good for keeping the bugs away. Some people plant those around the perimeter."

By the time our small harvest was finished, we had a greater variety of potatoes than I'd ever seen in one place. Pink, brown, lemon yellow, carrot orange, bright purple. They were long, narrow, short, round, with every kind of texture. All were smaller than you'd find back in Idaho, but this little parcel of land was shockingly productive.

Arturo asked us to wait while he pulled a few weeds farther down. Raven and I sat with our feet dangling over the edge of the terrace wall. I held one of the yellow Ping-Pong potatoes in my hand, rolling it against my palm.

"Listen, Raven, I apologize for what I said earlier, about you being sent here to fail. That was cruel."

She sighed. "Thanks. But at least you were honest. I mean, why else would they have sent me?"

"Well, if it means anything, they were wrong. You did get the story out there—around the censors and everything else."

"Yeah, I guess I did."

"For better or for worse," I added.

"And I'm sorry about that, Eddie. I know you wanted to protect that family's privacy." She shook her head. "When nobody reads your stuff for so many years, it gets hard to imagine all the implications."

I nodded. We sat there and enjoyed the view for a minute.

"What a spot," Raven said.

"I feel like Vavilov when he found Alma-Ata."

"Who?"

"Nikolai Vavilov," I explained. "The Russian botanist. He found the birthplace of the apple in Kazakhstan—the spot where wild strains were first domesticated by humans. It was like here: a dazzling array of biodiversity. So many different varieties. All the genes you'd ever want. Most of them were barely edible, but they crossbred with more palatable strains. It was a massive discovery, a breakthrough in his work on centers of origin." I rotated the potato in my fingers, wondering just how many steps it might be from its wild ancestor—if any.

"So this Vavilov guy," Raven said. "He must've become a big deal after finding all that."

"He starved to death in prison, back in the forties."

"Prison?" Raven was shocked. "Why?"

I shrugged. "Stalin came out against the genetic manipulation of plants."

"Stalin?" She grimaced. "Really?"

"Yep. Him and Kearns have that in common."

O kay!" Arturo rose up to join us. "Let's pack these up and get going." He pulled a burlap sack from his back pocket and unrolled it. We stuffed it full of the potatoes we'd picked. I offered to carry the half-full sack, but Arturo wouldn't hear of it.

"There is another path down that leads to the main road," he explained. "That's where you saw me the other day, with the police. I use that when I have a heavy load. But I prefer this way. It's more scenic."

We climbed back up to the ridgeline, then caught our breath on a flat stretch. Soon we rose again to a mid-ridge peak. Once there, Arturo stopped abruptly and held his hand in the air. Raven and I halted.

"Listen," he said. "Can you hear that?"

Apart from the wind, the only detectable sound was a tiny buzzing, easily mistaken for an insect.

"Is that . . . a plane?" I asked.

Arturo stretched his arm out and pointed at a spot far on the horizon. "There."

Raven and I turned and made it out: a tiny little thing with fixed wheels and a single propeller. It bounced and wobbled along the horizon. Suddenly it descended into one of the distant valleys.

"It's here for the . . . how do you say . . . eradication?"

"What?" I was shocked. "It's spraying coca plants?"

"Sí," Arturo grunted. "Part of the government's agreement with your country."

"They're spraying herbicide?" Raven asked.

Then the plane rose into view again, and we saw the mist coming out of its wings. It banked into a hard turn and descended for another pass through the valley.

Arturo shook his head. "We, Andean people, we have these powerful plants, and for centuries we've cultivated them responsibly. You gringos, you get your hands on them and it gets out of control. You take a sacred leaf and you turn it into poison. You take the potatoes and you get too fat with them. And then you come back here to destroy the crops." He turned around to face me. "It's a little crazy, don't you think?"

"It's very crazy." For the first time in my life, I nearly insisted that I wasn't a gringo.

"To keep cocaine from the gringo's nose, they would rip the lungs right out of South America," Arturo said.

"Do they ever come over this way?" Raven held a hand near her mouth, as if worried about breathing the poison.

"No." Arturo shook his head. "This valley isn't good for coca. This is potato country."

"If they did," I said, "they would only kill off the native varieties."

Arturo turned to me with a furrowed brow. "How's that, Doctor?"

"Surely, the herbicide they use is glyphosate," I explained. "The DS 400s would survive—according to their licensing agreement, at least. Potatoes are a little more resilient than coca, but your native spuds would probably die." I pointed at the sack on his shoulder. "If that plane made a wrong turn, you'd lose all those ancient varieties."

We all three paused and let the notion settle.

"It's not a *wrong* turn that concerns me," Arturo said.

We continued back toward town, our mood much more somber than on the way up.

—

Oscar was asleep in the driver's seat when we arrived at the truck. Raven and I thanked Arturo profusely, then climbed aboard. By the time we reached the main road, the daylight had given way to dusk.

"Eddie, can I ask you something?" Raven said. "Why are you so taken by that purple potato that Arturo gave you?"

"It's hard to explain," I said. "And a little nerdy."

"Try me."

"Basically, it seems to be very old."

"You mean, like, overripe?" she asked.

"I mean 'old' in an evolutionary sense. The variety looks like it could be a distant ancestor of the potato we eat now."

"But people here, they still eat it, right?"

"Sure. That's not what I mean. I think it could be important, in terms of the potato's family tree. It seems to have never changed to suit other climates or elevations. It's trapped in time up here, in this isolated valley."

Raven still looked confused.

"Think about dogs," I went on. "We have all these specialized breeds now. Potatoes are similar. What we grow in America these days are like standard poodles or great Danes—specially bred for certain characteristics, some functional and some aesthetic."

"Is that what you guys used? Poodle genes?"

"No. It's just a metaphor. We could be talking about any specialized pure-breed. The important thing—in terms of evolution—is that at some point, all dogs started out as wolves, a wild species. There was some moment of crossover."

"Okay. . . ."

"So with this potato, I think we might be looking at one of the first cases of straddling that line, between dog and wolf."

"Like a husky?"

I rolled my eyes. "More like a missing link."

"Oh. Okay."

"It's curious; most of my colleagues place the potato's first domestication in southern Peru."

"So they could be wrong about that? Puerto Malogrado could be the real birthplace?"

"Maybe. Or there might've been more than one point of origin. In which case, the cultivars they have around here could be doubly valuable for cross-breeding."

"Interesting," Raven said.

"To people like me, it is interesting."

"Can I ask you one more thing, Eddie?"

"Sure." I prepared myself for the worst.

"How did you become so fascinated with potatoes, generally?"

"I don't know." I shrugged. "I guess . . . I identify with them a bit. They're humble, practical, resilient."

Raven cocked her head. "Seriously? That's the reason?"

"Well, yes," I said, defensively. "Also, when I was a kid, I had this one friend, from a wealthy WASP family, in the nice part of town. They'd have me over to their house for dinner. On Sundays, it was always a big roast of lamb or beef. And on the side they served potatoes: mashed, au gratin, scalloped. In my house, we always ate rice and beans, sometimes plantains. Nothing like the potato dishes in their house. I always thought of it as a noble starch, ever since childhood."

"That's so funny!" Raven laughed out loud.

"Funny?" I thought I'd been forthcoming.

"Yeah. If you grow up Irish Catholic, like I did, you think of potatoes as peasant food."

"Well, not for me," I said. "As a child, at least, I was attracted to all the cultural associations: the wholesome meat-and-potatoes thing, Sunday roasts, Thanksgiving, the changing of seasons, all that."

Raven puckered. "But that's all bullshit, right? I mean, the potato's origins are here, in Latin America. It was basically colonized by the West, wasn't it?"

I sighed. "Sure, okay. But I'm talking about the visceral reaction I had as a kid."

Though I didn't say it aloud, I couldn't help but wonder if this wasn't another part of the potato's appeal to me: that its Latin origins had been all but eclipsed by its Middle-American connotations.

We passed by the striking miners as the sun set. They were gathered around a series of fires, hunkering down for a cold night. Nobody bothered to stop us.

"They're staying out here all night?" Raven asked Oscar in broken Spanish.

"Yes," he answered. "Otherwise, the owners bring in the scabs."

I leaned my head back against the headrest, but that pickup cab felt all the bumps. Rest was not an option.

As we entered the outskirts of the city, I stirred and said to Oscar: "I need to get these to the lab tonight."

"Lab's already closed, boss."

I sighed. "First thing in the morning, then."

Oscar clicked on the radio as we turned onto the Boulevard de los Agricultores. The station played what sounded like Bollywood music. I was about to ask, when the radio was drowned out by a deafening roar from above.

"Jesus!" Raven craned her neck to see.

It sounded like an airplane about to land on top of us. After a few seconds, the roar faded to a distant rumble.

"What was that?" Raven asked the question in English.

"Some kind of aircraft," I guessed.

"It's a bomber," Oscar said. "They're sending it up to the mountains."

"Why?" I asked.

"There was a big offensive today. The regime is very worried."

"They're using air power?"

He sighed. "For them, it's much better than the infantry. Their soldiers are not so good at fighting."

"Are they any better at flying planes?" I asked.

"More or less," Oscar answered. "In the air, nobody shoots back."

"Who are they bombing?"

Oscar shrugged. "The opposition."

Another plane took off without quite as much noise. Already, it felt less shocking than the last.

Oscar pulled up in front of the hotel, but left the motor running.

"First thing tomorrow, we go to the lab, okay?" I said to him.

He nodded. "I'll be here early in the morning."

oña Ana let us in, looking concerned. "There you are. Thank God."

I took out my phone and tried to get a signal. No luck. I needed to reach Warren, or anyone high up at Tuberware, and let them know what was going on. I wasn't sure if this was safe anymore. Would the PR issue be of any consequence if this civil war continued to intensify?

"You must be starving," Doña Ana said—of all things.

"Uh . . . yes, actually. We haven't eaten dinner." I was hungry, but it seemed a lot to ask, given the circumstances.

"Have a seat," she said. "I'll have it right out for you."

Raven and I did as we were told.

"I'm beat," she said.

"Me too," I sighed. "The buzz we got from the coca leaves is finally crashing."

"It made an impression on me today," Raven said. "Seeing you in that potato patch."

"Me?" I was shocked. "How do you mean?"

"The way that you have a passion, something that you're so good at—and that happens to be your career."

I nodded. "I'm lucky that way. I do love my work."

"I envy that. My dad, he was in sales—a slick, fast-talking type of guy. I never wanted a life like his—the hustle and the deals all the time. With him, it was all about confidence and opportunism."

Doña Ana slid two plates in front of us: a cold potato dish, and a hamburger patty on the side, covered in red sauce.

"Oh, sorry, Doña Ana," I said. "This looks great, but she doesn't eat meat."

"No?" Doña Ana raised her eyebrows.

"Eddie," Raven started. "It's—"

Doña Ana grabbed Raven's plate and headed back into the kitchen.

"Sorry," I said. "I should've mentioned it earlier. You were saying?"

"Just that with that shucker-and-jiver for a father, I always thought I'd do something more substantial—honest work."

Doña Ana reappeared with a new plate for Raven. This time, it was a chicken breast in place of the hamburger steak.

"No," I said. "Meat. She doesn't eat meat of any kind."

Doña Ana cocked her head and went off to the kitchen again.

"So you went into journalism?" I asked Raven.

"If only," she said. "No, first I was an English major. I wanted to be a writer—novels and poems and things. And I was dumb enough to borrow money to go to grad school for that. But it turns out that people don't read novels anymore—don't pay for them, at least. Then I get the bright idea to try my hand at magazines and newspapers."

"And now nobody wants to read those either," I said.

Doña Ana came back with another plate: the exact same piece of chicken, now chopped up into small pieces.

I opened my mouth, but Raven beat me to the punch.

"Eddie, it's fine." She smiled at Doña Ana. "*Muchas gracias.*"

We both took a bite.

"So here I am," Raven said. "A blogger. Waiting for everybody to decide they don't want to read those anymore."

"I think they'll still read them." I cut a piece of meat. "They just won't pay for them."

"You're lucky you work with food. People still want that."

"Want it more than ever," I said. "Though they don't like to pay much for it either."

"Still," Raven said. "It's a living."

"So far." I nodded. "Is your dad retired now?"

"Who knows? He left my mom when I was in grade school. He visits occasionally, but it's impossible to get a straight answer out of him. His fortunes seem to fluctuate—judging by the cars he drives and the sorts of vacations he takes."

"So your mom raised you?" I asked.

"Along with my grandmother and my aunts. It's a big Irish-American family." Raven swallowed a mouthful of food. "Mom never had much of a career. Odd jobs: restaurants, offices, and such. Several marriages. We were always moving in and out of Grandma's, in and out of a new boyfriend's place. Mom's finally with a decent guy now, a doctor. They have a nice house in the foothills, and another spread in Sun Valley. I've stayed with them a lot in the past few years."

"Not too shabby." I raised my eyebrows.

"She landed on her feet in the end," Raven admitted. "But I never wanted her life either: always depending on the goodwill of a boss or a husband."

"What *did* you want, Raven?"

"Good question." She leaned back in her chair. "I wanted work that was fulfilling and that paid the bills—something I was passionate about."

I nodded. "That can be hard to find."

"And I wanted to see the world a little, get out of Boise. When I was a kid, I swore up and down I'd leave Idaho. This trip is the farthest I've ever been from home."

"Puerto Malogrado is pretty far."

"I meant Miami too."

"We were only in the airport for an hour."

"It still counts!" Raven said, in earnest.

"Okay."

"Anyway." She looked down at her plate and shook her head. "Getting this assignment was a step in the right direction. But now I've screwed that up as well."

I took a few more bites in silence. Then, from far away, we heard a series of bombs go off in the surrounding hills. They might've been mistaken for thunder, if not for the frequency. After a second, it stopped.

Doña Ana came in from the other room. "Sounds like it's time to go to bed."

I wolfed down one last bite before she cleared the table.

———

Raven followed me into my room. I turned on the TV. Again, the Vice Minister of the Interior was behind a lectern, proclaiming that the resistance was a grave threat, but also a bunch of incapable cowards.

"What's he saying?" Raven asked.

"Same old thing," I said.

The Vice Minister went on to explain that he'd been forced to take extreme measures in order to keep the country safe for its hard-working citizens.

Raven changed the channel to another news program. They interviewed a woman in the *campo*, in front of an adobe house that looked ruined and battle-scarred. Her interview was edited, apparently with a razor blade and splicing tape. Her face jumped around the frame as she spoke single words: "The regime . . . has helped . . . the freedom fighters . . . will die before . . . the government."

Every once in a while the editors would miss something. She'd utter an adjective or an expletive that betrayed her allegiance. I understood what Oscar meant about reading between the lines. It wasn't hard.

The TV flickered off and then all the lights abruptly went dead. Another explosion sounded, this time louder and with more light through the window.

"Well," I said. "I guess it's bedtime after all."

"Eddie." Though I couldn't see Raven, I detected the quiver in her voice. "Do you think we're in danger?"

"Us? No." I did my best to sound confident. "Revolutions are like a tradition down here. They throw them every year, like baseball season." Warren's line didn't sound funny anymore; I felt foolish for ever having fallen for it.

Raven said nothing.

"Anyway," I went on. "There's nothing we can do now."

"Eddie, do you think that my article—my blog, whatever—about the Morales kids, do you think that affected this situation?"

I sighed. "Who knows? The notion that the regime had some hand in turning poor children into doglike creatures might have galvanized a few folks. But there's a lot more history to consider. Any country that's just one blog post away from a civil war is already in deep trouble." I wondered about her question, as well as about my answer. If she'd helped cause this offensive, would I have said as much? Would I have allowed her to take the credit or the blame?

"It's pretty ridiculous, isn't it?" she said.

"How's that?"

"All the actual atrocities this regime has committed, and the thing that's got everyone upset is pure speculation."

"Not to mention false," I added.

She shrugged. "I suppose oppression is old news."

"The oldest."

"Good night, Eddie."

"Good night, Raven."

The next morning, breakfast at the hotel was way below its normal standards. My potatoes and eggs had become only potatoes—and these were simply boiled. I asked Doña Ana about it.

She shrugged. "The conflict. They're rationing the groceries again."

"Oh," I said. "So they can send food to the soldiers?"

"Pfftt." She rolled her eyes. "To make us lose patience with the freedom fighters, to get us to hate their offensives as much as the regime does."

I nodded, grateful that there was still coffee.

"Don't worry." Doña Ana smiled. "My sister has some hens. I'll send the girls there this afternoon."

I picked at the plain breakfast. In the corner, Doña Ana's mother sat at her normal table with a cup of tea, her walker leaning against the wall. She gave me a sly grin, then looked away. For some reason, she seemed to be enjoying my disappointment over the meal. Oscar arrived right on schedule, this time with a full-size motorcycle.

"Good morning, boss."

"Morning, Oscar."

"Where to today?" he asked.

"The lab, of course."

—

We arrived just as the place was opening. The same beautiful young attendant was behind the counter.

"Good morning, Doctor Morales."

"Morning . . . Nora, correct?"

She nodded. "We have the results from your potatoes."

"Excellent! I have the buccal swabs we spoke about as well." I took out the bag with my swabs and their tubes.

She handed me an envelope with the words "Potato Profiles, Morales" written on the front. I opened it up and had a look, but it didn't mean much to me. I'd need to get access to our potato-gene database in order to make any sense of it.

"How soon do you think those swabs could be done?" I asked Nora.

"It shouldn't take long," she said. "They'll be finished by this time tomorrow."

I nodded. "See you then."

———

I walked outside and saw Oscar where he'd parked on the far side of the street. As I stepped off the curb to go meet him, an older model sedan pulled up between us.

"Doctor Morales." The driver stepped out of the still-idling car. "We would very much like a moment of your time." He wasn't in a uniform, so much as a mechanic's jumper.

"And you are?" I asked.

"We represent a group of workers—farmers and laborers and blue-collar people. We have concerns about the future of this country. We'd like to hear about your research."

I looked over to Oscar. He shrugged.

"It won't take long, Doctor," the driver said. "We'll give you a lift back to your hotel and have our chat along the way."

The driver seemed nice enough. I couldn't help but think of the people who had been thrown into that black car while I ate dinner. But it was clear that this was not the police. And, more than anything, I was intrigued. There were obviously more forces at work in this country than I understood. Perhaps this group could shed a little light on the situation.

"Very well," I said. "Let's take a ride."

Oscar kick-started his motorcycle and took off down the street without so much as a goodbye.

The back door to the sedan popped open. From within, a man's voice said, "Step inside, Don Doctor."

I bent over and climbed in. The man in the back was dressed in camouflage fatigues and combat boots. It was no ceremonial uniform, no polished medals or starched creases. This one had seen a good deal of use; it was worn at the knees and elbows, full of holes and stains.

I did as I was told and climbed inside the car. We shook hands.

"Pleased to make your acquaintance." He had a salt-and-pepper beard, round bags beneath his eyes, and a deep baritone voice.

"You're, um . . ." I cleared my throat. "You're from FURP?"

"I've been a member of many organizations over the years and gone by many names."

As evasive as his words were, his delivery all but confirmed it. At some point, the car had begun moving.

"What can I do for you?" I discreetly slipped my hand behind my belt buckle, felt around for the panic button.

"Within our organization, there's been considerable interest in your work."

"My work?" It was useless. That stupid button was impossible to press unless I turned the whole buckle around.

"This situation with the potatoes and the quadrupedal children."

"Oh, that work." I let go of the belt.

"There are some within my organization who'd like to exploit this scandal's potential."

"Its potential?" I said. "I don't understand."

"The potential for galvanizing the populace against the regime.

It grabs the attention, you must admit: the idea that the government conspired with foreign capitalists to turn its own citizens into doglike creatures which walk on all fours."

"That's one way to look at it," I said.

"Personally, I am more cautious." He shifted in his seat, had a look out the window. "Sensationalism is a double-edged sword."

"As is fear-mongering."

"Indeed. However, we can't trust anything said by either the administration or the mainstream press, so it's difficult to know what's truly going on." He turned to face me. "Which is why the two of us find ourselves meeting this way. I'd like to hear it from the expert."

"I see." Though I wasn't truly an expert, it was impressive that somebody in this country finally gave a fig about the truth behind the Morales kids and their condition. This man—this guerilla or revolutionary or whatever he was—had already earned a measure of my respect.

"Tell me, Doctor. What is going on with these children? Is their condition real?"

"It is real," I explained. "They're not faking. However, it has nothing to do with potatoes or anything else in their diet. Their problem is a genetic aberration, a very rare mutation."

"Mutation?" His head popped back as though punched. "Like the X-Men?"

"Well . . . in a sense."

"This is worse than I thought."

"Not really," I said. "It's similar to humans born with extra nipples or small tails. Very rare, but it does happen. It might be some old gene that's expressing itself, but more likely it's a deficiency of some kind—important genetic material that they were born without."

"And you can prove this?" he asked.

I sighed. "I'm working on it."

He nodded. "I think I understand."

"Sorry," I said. "Not exactly fuel for a revolution, I know."

"Not in my opinion." He shrugged. "But others in my organization may disagree. I keep telling them that honesty and transparency are the only high ground that we hold over this regime. If we lose that, then we lose everything."

"That's very noble," I admitted.

"Noble perhaps, but not necessarily pragmatic. Some of my colleagues, they see no harm in stretching the truth, if it furthers our cause—even in the short term."

"They think the ends justify the means."

"Exactly." He raised his eyebrows. "The starting point of all moral dilemmas."

"Your hotel, Doctor." The driver spoke from the front seat. We had arrived outside La Posada.

"So," I turned to my mysterious new friend. "As far as your cause. Are there any actions, well . . . forthcoming?"

He held my gaze then offered a subtle, decisive nod.

"Is Huanchillo . . . will it be safe there?"

He grinned, almost laughed. "That valley is good for growing pota-toes, but it has no strategic value."

"I see."

"Thanks for your time, Doctor."

"My pleasure." I climbed out of the car.

As they drove away, I felt foolish for not asking more about their next attack. Huanchillo might be spared, but what about this hotel?

———

By the time I got inside La Posada, I'd grown paranoid. I pulled out my phone and promptly kicked myself for not having checked for a signal while in the nicer, hillier parts of town. Now there was nothing.

"Doña Ana!" I called.

She emerged from the kitchen with a broom in her hand. "Doctor?"

"Where can I make a phone call around here?"

"There's a *locutorio* on Los Agricultores." She pointed over her shoulder.

I nodded and looked around the room. No sign of Raven.

T he *locutorio* turned out to be a series of plywood stalls with beige touch-tone phones inside them. A man behind the counter quoted me a rate for a five-minute call to the US, then demanded payment up front. He took the number for Tuberware, then sent me to the first of the plywood stalls.

I didn't know Warren's extension—if he even had one—so I waited through the call tree for a human being. Instead, a robotic voice asked for the nature of my inquiry.

"This is Doctor Morales, from Processed Foods. I'm calling from Puerto Malogrado. I need to speak to Warren at once."

"Hold, please."

I let the phone slide down around my shoulder, and had a look at the man behind the counter. He glanced at his watch, then straightened out his newspaper.

"Doctor Morales?" A human voice came over the phone.

"Yes?"

"Warren isn't available at the moment."

I silently mouthed the word "shit!," but into the receiver I said, "That's unfortunate. Could you possibly connect me with Jill Kimball? She's in Processed Foods also."

More waiting. The company's banjo music played on through the earpiece. I wondered what I might find for lunch around here.

"Eddie?" A new voice sounded in the earpiece.

"Jill! Is that you?"

"Of course. It's so good to hear your voice. How are you?"

"I've been better," I admitted.

"And the project?"

"Well, I get along with the family well enough. But otherwise this country is completely nuts. I've got these government ministers on my back, guerilla leaders following me around, miners with dynamite, this asshole filmmaker. And the state-controlled media, that's a whole other story."

"Oh, my God, Eddie. That sounds terrible!"

"I know. But I'm okay. The food is delicious, anyway."

"Is it real? The hand-walking?" she asked.

I sighed. "They're not faking it, if that's what you mean. But it has nothing to do with our potatoes. It's just a rare mutation."

"Can you prove that?"

"That's why I'm calling, actually. I have DNA profiles for the hand-walkers, but I need something to compare them to. Could you send me the genetic information for our main potato varietals?"

"I guess so." A keyboard clicked in the background of the call. "I'll just go into our database, make copies, and send them to you."

"Through email, preferably," I said.

"Look at you." Jill continued to punch away at the keys. "Turning into a genetics expert down there."

"Not quite," I chuckled. "Hopefully there won't be much more to it than holding one profile up against another."

"*Tiempo!*" The man behind the counter tapped his watch with a fat finger.

I nodded and held up an open hand, hoping to placate him. "Jill, I have to go. I prepaid for this call; my time's about to run out."

"I'll send this off as soon as I can."

"Thank you," I said.

"I miss you, Eddie."

"I miss you too." I realized how true it was as I said it.

"Be safe down there."

"I'll do my best."

The signal cut off. Only a dial tone now sounded from the earpiece. I had another look at the proprietor. His wicked smile suggested that he took pleasure in cutting off long-distance calls. I walked out of his shop and onto the Boulevard.

A few doors down, I found a clean-looking *comedor* and ordered a two-course fixed-price lunch. The soup came out right away. Bright yellow potatoes floated alongside a slow-cooked animal joint. The fat and connective tissue melted into a delicious broth.

A man with a long coat came in and waved around a stack of papers. "The news!" he cried. "Who wants to read news?"

A couple seated in the corner raised their hands. He dropped one paper on their table; they gave him a coin.

"The truth, my friends. It's a small price to pay for the truth."

When he passed my table, I bought one as well.

The large woman serving the food handed the paperboy a foil-wrapped plate. He gave her several papers, thanked her, then headed out.

On the front page was a picture of the evangelical preacher from Huanchillo, along with the caption "Evolution in Reverse?"

Great. Even the underground press had it wrong. But most of the issue was dedicated to the rebel offensive. I tried to take the paper's coverage with a grain of salt, but from the photos alone it seemed indisputable that they were gaining ground.

The images showed men and women with red handkerchiefs over their faces, marching into villages in the mountains above the capital. In almost all cases, the villagers hung from doorways and windows, waving red clothes back at them.

One poor-quality photo caught my attention: two rebels knelt beside a downed airplane. They carried only assault rifles, and there was no caption. When I looked more closely, it became obvious that the men had been cut out and pasted over the picture of the plane. Immediately, I felt silly for having bought the paper. If one of the sides learned Photoshop, this war might be over by now.

In the final pages, there were more earnest pictures of the citizens who'd been arrested for collaboration. The paper listed names if it had them, the whens and the wheres of the disappearances, any other known details. I scanned for an account of the apartment raid I'd witnessed a few days earlier, but I wasn't even sure of the address.

The server returned with my main dish: a small fish, coated in egg batter and covered in red sauce. On the side were pale beans topped with a creamy, crumbly cheese. Apparently, the rationing hadn't affected this business.

I was about to take the first bite when one of my fellow customers screamed, "*Policia!*"

Everyone stuffed their newspapers under the table. I followed suit.

Two uniformed officers approached the door, deep in conversation. One of them held the door open for the other. The first one shrugged, then shook his head. The second one pointed up the street. The door was released and closed again. The officers moved along. Inside the *comedor*, the entire room exhaled.

I moved the paper to a seat beside mine and was too afraid to touch it for the duration of my meal.

———

After lunch, I walked straight to the internet café from the other night— still a bit paranoid about being watched or snatched up by the police.

Once I found my terminal and paid for my time, I was glad to see that Jill's email had made it through without any trouble from government censors. I opened the file, gave it a quick scan, and asked the clerk about printing. After several blank pages, the shop's slow printer chugged out the information I wanted. Once it was over, the clerk was kind enough to give me a manila folder to carry everything.

By the time I left the café, I felt like an actual scientist again. A small collection of data under my arm, some samples undergoing analysis at the lab—perhaps I still had some small scrap of control over this situation.

———

Back at the hotel, I spread out the materials Jill had sent me across the bed, scanning them for anything of interest. In the dozen or so Tuberware varieties, the bulk of their genes were identical. I had to look hard to find any variation at all. And presumably, most of those deviations had been carefully engineered by our scientists. Out of curiosity, I took out the results of Nora's test on La Vieja. The comparison was surprising. La Vieja was radically different; its genes only bore a passing similarity to the others. Had I only seen the comparison—and not known the source of the oddball DNA—I wouldn't have guessed it came from a potato.

I looked up from the papers on the bed and turned toward the windowsill, where the two spuds sat side by side. From the eyes of La Vieja, pink and green sprouts had already begun poking their way out. Beside it, the DS 400 showed no signs of reproduction. I picked it up and turned it over: nothing. Our engineers must've found a way to delay the sprouts. Smart. It would ship and display so much better this way.

"Eddie!" A knock sounded at my door. "Can I come in?"

I went to answer it. Raven stepped inside, eating an apple.

"Hey, Raven. How are you?" I found that I was grateful for a bit of human contact after all this staring at plant data.

"I'm fine. Just a little confused." She took a seat on the bed and held the apple in front of her teeth. "I've been looking at some of the things Kearns has up online. He's big on the risks of monoculture. Can you tell me what he means by that?"

"Monoculture?" I shrugged. "That just means growing a vast quantity of one single crop."

"You don't think it's such a big deal?"

"Actually, I do think it's bad practice, but I can't understand how it's become so synonymous with GMO foods. We've been planting monocultures for centuries. I assume you've heard of the Irish Potato Famine?"

"Heard of it?" She raised her voice. "It's the reason my family came to America. My grandparents called it, The Great Hunger,"

"Do you know the cause?"

"Yeah, the British," she said.

I laughed. "How's that?"

"With their laws against Catholic land ownership and the steep rents they charged to farmers—even if they had no harvest."

"Okay," I said. "In my world, we blame it on a type of alga called *phytophthora infestus*. It arrived on trading ships, probably from America or Mexico, and spread like wildfire across the Irish countryside."

"The blight." Raven nodded.

"That's correct. The thing about Ireland in the mid-1800s is that they only used one potato: the Lumper. The farmers cloned it—"

"Cloned it?" she interrupted. "They could clone plants back then?"

"Potatoes have always cloned themselves. After they sprout, farmers cut off the eyes and plant them. Like this." I took La Vieja from the windowsill and used my finger to demonstrate where the cuts might happen. "What results is lateral propagation, a clone of the original. So they were genetically identical. They all had the same immune system, so to speak. Or lack thereof. When one got sick, they all got sick."

"They turned into a stinking black mush, is what they did." She took another bite of her apple.

"That's right," I said. "So there you have it: the dangers of monoculture. No GMOs necessary."

"Well." Raven covered her mouth and swallowed. "If my grandmother were here, she'd be happy to explain to you that Ireland was still exporting food throughout the famine. That starving farmers watched boatloads of butter and meat and grain being shipped off to market. The wealthy people didn't go hungry." She threw her apple core into the wastebasket next to the wall. "I'm not saying you're wrong, Eddie. But if you think there's not a cultural and economic element to that famine, you're being naïve. It's never as simple as a lack of food. It's food not made available to poor people."

I shrugged. "I don't doubt it. But I'm a scientist. Issues of class and such, that's not—"

"Not your area, I know."

I smiled. We were silent for a second.

"Raven?" I asked. "Can I tell you something?"

She shifted to face me. "Of course, Eddie."

I swallowed, turned away from her eyes. "There's more history between me and Kearns than I initially let on."

"What do you mean?"

"Remember when I told you about the rich kid I was friends with growing up?"

"The one whose family served scalloped potatoes?"

"That's right."

"That was Kearns?"

"Correct."

"So you didn't just know him from grad school?"

"No, I knew him before. We planned to study together. His parents bought him a house near campus—an 'investment,' they called it—and I got to live there for free."

"That was generous."

I sighed. "In a sense. The trouble is that there turned out to be strings attached."

"How do you mean?"

"That story I told you, about him cheating, then getting caught?"

"The thing that ended your academic career?"

"That's right."

"What about it?"

"I was complicit."

"Eddie!" she gasped.

"It was the biggest mistake of my life," I admitted. "But what could I do? This guy had basically given me food and shelter since I was a child. He came to me in the eleventh hour and needed my help."

"You should've refused!" Raven insisted.

"I realize that now." I shrugged. "But back then I was still under his spell. What can I say? I'd never said 'no' to him before."

Raven saw how upset I was. She put a hand on my shoulder.

"Up to that point, I'd spent my whole life in awe of Kearns and his WASP family. I wanted to be one of them. It's a good thing he didn't have a sister, or I probably would've stalked her and begged her to marry me."

Raven grimaced. "Who says you know nothing about class issues?"

"Anyway. Our relationship is more complicated than I admitted at first."

"It's okay," Raven said. "I can see why you didn't want to go there right away."

I rubbed my temples. "You know how long I've been running from Kearns and that mistake? I went all the way to Boise to get away from it."

"And then you two found each other here, in Puerto Malogrado." She grinned and stood up off the bed. "Don't worry about it too much, Eddie. If that's the worst mistake you've ever made, you're ahead of the curve."

"Thanks." That did make me feel better, oddly.

"I'll see you in the morning."

"Good night, Raven."

I lay down on the bed amidst my papers. Tomorrow I could go to the lab and pick up the results for the children. And what exactly did I think I'd do with them? Hold them side by side with another child's and look for a variation? Without a full genetic mapping—and somebody who knew how to read it—this process would only get me so far.

Finally, I cleared the papers, took off my clothes, and went to bed.

I n the morning, I was woken by the now-unfamiliar sound of my cell phone ringing. I blinked the sleep from my eyes and looked around the room until I found the device on the floor by the bed.

"Hello?" I said, unsure how I'd finally gotten a connection.

"Eddie? Is that you?"

"Who is this?"

"It's Jill. Are you okay?"

"I'm just waking up, is all. Why? What's the matter?"

"The video of you. It's on the internet. Did they force you to say those things?"

"What video? What are you talking about?"

"Morales!" Another voice came on the line. "Is there a gun at your head? Are you being blackmailed?"

"Warren? I mean, Mister Shepherd? No, I'm fine. What's the matter?"

"You're all over the computer blaming Tuberware for this hand-walking mess. That's what's the matter!"

Fucking Kearns, I thought to myself.

"'We don't behave like a charity or the UN' . . . you're on tape saying that."

"Well, that's true, isn't it? We're neither of those things. We're a for-profit company. What's wrong with that?"

"You're meant to be protecting our interests down there, Morales. Whose side are you on, anyway?"

"I'm on your side! I'm just really bad at this! What do I know about speaking on camera? I mentioned this several times back in Boise."

Finally, some silence from the other line. I went on.

"Look, whatever you think I said—"

"*Saw* you say," Warren interrupted.

"I'm sure it was taken out of context."

"You also suggested that the government had let its people down."

"Well, that's not exactly untrue, either."

"Morales, listen to me. You're doing good work down there. I understand that you've established a rapport with the family in question."

"Yes," I defended myself. "We get along."

"Good. Now make that Vice Minister happy, and keep the press at bay."

"It's not the real press that's the problem, sir. That Kearns guy is just a self-styled filmmaker idiot."

"He's an idiot with a camera and a million YouTube followers. That's much worse than actual press. Now, remind me: Where are we on the science?"

"Due to get some results back from the lab today. I'm hoping we're in the home stretch."

"Make this work, Morales. We're all counting on you."

"Thank you, sir. That means a lot." Even if it wasn't entirely believable. "Could I speak to Jill privately, please?"

Some clicking and shifting came through the line.

"Eddie? Are you there?"

"Jill? I just wanted to hear your voice again."

"It's not the same without you here, Eddie. Lord knows I could use your help. I'm dealing with Engineering right now. Those guys don't have a knack for nuance."

So the fry machine was already with Engineering? That seemed fast to me.

"No kidding," I said. "Listen, Jill, I've thought a lot about the last time I saw you. About our last night together—"

"Eddie," she cut me off. "I've been meaning to get in touch with you about that."

"Oh?"

"I'm sorry," she said.

"Sorry?"

"About that night. That wasn't very professional of me. I know you were trying to keep our relationship collegial. It was my fault, not yours."

I was at a loss for words. That night had kept me going since arriving here. That night encapsulated my hopes for the future as much as anything. And Jill regretted it? I'd have given anything to see her face-to-face, to talk this out over a plate of stuffed potato skins at our favorite after-work spot.

"Don't be sorry," I said—which was sincere. And then: "It's not that big a deal,"—which was the opposite of sincerity.

"No, I suppose it's not," Jill agreed. "Sounds like you have more pressing matters to deal with anyway. It's been so amazing working closely with Warren these past few days. I've learned so much about leadership and ambition. He's an incredible man."

Why on earth was she spending so much time with Warren all of a sudden? He hadn't even known about the fry machine when I left Idaho.

"I'll talk to you soon, Eddie."

By the time I said goodbye, there was nobody on the line to hear it.

I hung up, then turned toward the potatoes on the windowsill. The DS 400 was still smooth and uniform. A lonely specimen, that spud: trying so hard to feed the world and having to do it all alone, with a flurry of accusations in place of gratitude.

——

Out in the dining area, Raven had her laptop open and was entertaining Doña Ana and her daughters. They gathered around the screen, giggling and covering their mouths at some sort of silly rap song.

Once they saw me, all of them turned and pointed, breaking out into even greater laughter.

"There he is!" Raven said. "The latest viral video sensation."

"Excuse me?" I asked.

She turned her computer around so that the screen faced me.

I gasped. There was my image—red-eyed and too close to the camera. A robotic version of my voice sang: "We're not a charity, or the UN!" (The "not" was in a ridiculously high range.)

That same line played over and over a few times, jump-cutting to the beginning, my body jerking around like some perverse dancer.

"What the hell is this?" I asked. "That's totally altered."

"That's the idea, Eddie," Raven said.

The children still giggled, but their mother sent them off toward the kitchen.

"It's DJ Green Eggs. He does environmentally relevant mash-up videos. Usually he goes after politicians or news anchors. But you made his special GMO song."

"Is there any footage of the children in there?" I asked sternly.

"No." Raven shook her head. "He only has whatever your buddy shot."

"Kearns is *not* my buddy."

One of the daughters came back from the kitchen and placed a cup of coffee in front of me.

"Do you think he knows DJ Green Eggs?" Raven asked. "I would kill to get an interview with that guy."

I rolled my eyes and went after the coffee.

"Buck up, Eddie. Some people spend their whole lives trying to get the kind of exposure you're getting right now."

"Let's hope the Vice Minister doesn't feel that I'm overly exposed."

Doña Ana's other daughter slid a plate with a baked empanada in front of me. The dough was hand-kneaded along the seam, a dusting of powdered sugar on the top. I took a bite and tasted meat, onion, even some chopped egg.

"Boss!" Oscar walked in. "The lab is open. We can pick up your results."

"Great." I held a hand over my mouth. "Can you give me a minute?" I pointed toward my breakfast.

"No problem," he said. "I'll wait outside."

"Big moment for your tests, huh?" Raven asked.

I shrugged. "Yes and no. If I can find something out of the ordinary, that would be a huge help. But this sort of test . . . it only scratches the surface of the human genome. To get to the bottom of what's wrong with the Morales children, they'd need a full genetic mapping—which is both rare and expensive."

"Hmm." Raven closed her laptop. "That's a pickle. Everybody's expecting you to find the answers."

"Tell me about it." I sighed. The conversation with Jill still had me shell-shocked. What was I doing here, after all? What would I have to go back to, once my so-called work was done? But I kept these thoughts to myself; little could be gained by self-pity.

"What do you have planned for today?" I asked Raven.

"Not much," she said. "Hopefully talk to somebody about the conflict, see what people have to say about the regime and FURP."

"Good luck with that." I raised my eyebrows. "Folks in this country have mastered the art of non-incriminating statements."

She cocked her head toward her laptop. "You could learn a thing or two from them."

I couldn't help but smile at that one. "Maybe you're right."

From outside, a high-pitched horn honked. "Boss!" Oscar shouted. "*Vamos!*"

"See you later, Raven. Stay out of trouble."

"Same to you," she said.

———

Oscar waited for me atop an off-road motorcycle with plastic fenders and knobby tires.

"Is this thing street-legal?" I asked.

"More or less." He gestured for me to climb aboard.

checked my teeth in the side-view mirror, then stepped off the curb. At the entrance to the lab, I pushed the door open, closed my eyes, and breathed in the ordered scientific atmosphere. In a country full of chaos and inexplicability, this was my happy place.

I soon caught sight of the lovely Nora standing near the back: her crisp white lab coat, the clunky glasses, her short haircut showing the caramel-colored skin of her neck. That vision allowed me to momentarily forget all about Jill. Perhaps there was more than one possible future out there for me—more fish in the sea.

She kicked her head back in laughter. I turned my eyeballs only a few degrees to see what had caused it. In that instant, my pulse rate doubled and bile rose from my throat: Kearns.

"Hey . . . hey!" I shouted and made my way toward the back. "Nora, do not show this man anything! Do not speak to him about my tests." I inserted myself between their two bodies, facing Nora.

"Doctor Morales?" She was surprised, and spoke in English. "Do you already know Doctor—"

"He's not a doctor." I cut her off, in Spanish now. "He's a fraud. A trickster. You may want to call security and have him removed."

"Eddie!" Kearns called. "What are *you* doing here, mate?"

I turned around to face him. "Don't call me 'mate' or 'buddy' or any other term that might indicate friendship! You got that?"

"Relax, Eddie. What's gotten into you?" Kearns asked.

"What's gotten into *me*?" I stuck a finger to his chest. "Your stupid pranks, those dumbass online videos. That stuff has consequences, you understand? And not just for me. There's a poor family with young children involved. Children that you and the rest of the media want to exploit."

"Eddie, please understand." Kearns spoke in a voice much calmer than my own, still with that stupid half-baked British accent. "I didn't doctor up that online video. I released a little footage. What the internet does with it is out of my hands."

"You're pathetic, you know that?" I was a bit surprised by my own volume. "You never accept any responsibility for anything. You're still just a spoiled brat."

"Doctor Morales." Nora put an index finger up in front of her lips. "Please keep your voice down."

I suddenly felt embarrassed. Once again, Kearns had managed to make *me* look like the crazy person.

"I'll tell you what." Kearns held his palms up in a pacifying gesture. "Why don't I just step outside, let the two of you get on with your work."

"That would be so kind of you," I said sarcastically.

He kept his palms up like that—as though trying to calm a skittish horse—and backed his way out of the lab. "Goodbye, Nora," he said at the door.

I let go of a long exhale as soon as he was gone. "Well, it's a good thing that's over, huh?" I turned to Nora.

She'd retreated to the back of the lab and furiously stuffed documents into a large manila folder.

"Nora, I know that he can be charming, but that man is bad news."

"Here you are, Doctor." She handed me the folder full of documents and a plastic bag with the samples.

"Thank you," I said. "Look, let me explain. Kearns is a—"

"Doctor Morales," she interrupted. "If there's nothing else that I can do for you today, I think it might be best if you just leave."

Outside, Kearns stood waiting for me.

I met his eyes, then continued toward Oscar's motorcycle.

Walking alongside me, Kearns said, "Do you ever think about our parents' generation, Eduardo? Driving around in those big-ass cars, listening to rock-and-roll, filling up the tank with the spare change from between the seat cushions? That's where we are now with food. We don't pay anything for it, so we take it for granted. Once these oil wars end, the next round of global conflicts will be fought over calories."

"First of all, in case you've forgotten: my parents are Cuban exiles. So they never drove around in big cars with your parents. Second, if food wars do begin, you'll be thanking Tuberware for coming up with drought- and blight-resistant strains of potatoes."

"And if one of those strains fails? You're steering us toward mono-culture, Eddie. It's unsustainable."

"As opposed to what? Sharecropping? A plantation system? Hunting and gathering? What is this Golden Age of Agriculture that you greenies seem so nostalgic for? Fact is, tilling the earth has always been a miserable life. Companies like mine have made it slightly less so. If you can't under-stand that, you have a warped sense of history."

"Can't you admit that it's all too centralized? Too much power in the hands of one company. What if your seeds fail?"

"What if they fail?" I threw up my hands. "What if fossil fuels run out? What if the internet stops working? What if the dollar collapses? All these things might happen. At least with Tuberware, we're working our asses off to prevent it."

"Is that how you see it?" Kearns asked.

"That's how it is! And in return for my hard work, I get to be the butt of jokes."

"Oh, come on, Eddie. Don't be so. . . ."

"What? Don't be so what?" I wouldn't allow him to answer. "Maybe this stuff is all fun and games to you. You don't have a career to look after.

You can sit back and throw stones at those of us who actually have to roll up our sleeves and get elbow-deep in the murky, messy, unsightly activity of earning a paycheck. For people like me, it *is* a big deal. My boss saw your stupid videos. So now I'm fighting for a job that I'm great at, that I've spent my whole life working toward."

"Eddie, don't be ridiculous. You don't have to worry about losing your job."

"What are you talking about? My boss called me this morning, half-cocked."

"Who? Warren?" Kearns took a cell phone out of his pocket. "Do you want me to make a call?"

"You can't call Warren," I said.

Kearns shrugged. "Not Warren; my father. The two of them were part of the same fraternity, way back when. You didn't know that?"

"Fraternity?" I felt light-headed. Once again, lights flickered at the sides of my eyes.

"Eddie, how do you think you got hired at Tuberware in the first place?" Kearns shrugged. "Dad felt terrible about that mess with the dissertations. He made some calls on your behalf. I thought you knew."

I shook my head, unwilling to accept what he was saying. "No," I managed.

"Don't worry about it, Eddie. That's just how the world works."

I was so frustrated that I stopped talking and shook my head furiously. "Just, goodbye, okay?" Unable to even look Kearns in the eye, I hopped onto the back of Oscar's motorcycle. We left Kearns there on the curb.

B ack at the hotel, Raven was nowhere to be found. I spread the results from the DNA tests out across the bed but soon grew frustrated. These tests were basic—the kind of thing that might tell if the kids were related or what race they were, but nothing deeper than that. And even if these tests could reveal more, I wasn't qualified to read anything complex into human genetic data.

In truth, I couldn't even look at these results. Kearns's revelation about why I'd been hired by Tuberware had shaken me to my core. Although I didn't enjoy thinking about my past, I was most proud of the fact that I'd made a fresh start, a new, better life in Idaho. I hated the notion that the Kearns family had continued to pull strings in my life and might still have a back-channel way of controlling my career. But most of all, I detested the idea that I hadn't earned it on my own merit.

I figured that a walk—and maybe some lunch—might clear my head. I left the room and went out the front gate and onto the street.

I made it about a block from the hotel. A teenager with a gun was about to shuffle past me. From behind came a horn tap and a screech of tires. I turned around to find the Vice Minister's Cadillac there.

"Doctor Morales." Alejandro, the young man from the palace, stepped out of the back.

"Yes?"

"Our mutual friend would like an audience with you."

"You mean, the Vice—"

"Shh!" Alejandro put a finger up before his lips. "We're trying to be discreet about his comings and goings at the moment."

"This big white Cadillac with flags on the hood probably isn't much help in that department."

"I suppose not," Alejandro admitted. "Would you care to step inside?"

I turned to the kid with the gun, who looked puzzled by all of this. He shrugged.

"All right," I climbed into the car and sat upon the crisp leather seats. "Are we headed to the Ministry?"

"No," Alejandro said. "It's not safe there. We'll go to the Vice Minister's country estate. It's close by and very pleasant."

The car turned into a valley and then drove up a road so steep, it felt like we were in a plane taking off. Through the tinted windows, the city fell away before our eyes. First we rose above the crowded apartments and multi-family homes, then passed through pricier houses with tall outer walls. For the next stratum, we had to cross through a security stall—manned by an older guard in a proper uniform—then continued on to even more extravagant homes. The change in elevation pressed heavily against my head.

Finally, the road hit a plateau and flattened out. Thick pine trees lined either side, not a house in sight. The road grew tighter and narrower, all the sounds muffled by the foliage, the leaves and pine needles crunching beneath the tires.

My palms were sweating profusely. I hoped there was indeed something at the end of this road—and not a cliff or a shallow grave.

"Where exactly are we heading?" I asked Alejandro again.

"It's the Vice Minister's country house," he said again. "A bit like your president's Camp David, no?"

"Okay."

"It's not much farther."

Just when my paranoia was about to get the best of me, we came to a closed gate. The driver stopped the car, got out, and undid the chain.

Once on the other side, I felt immediate relief. The grounds were well maintained, gardens and little outbuildings off to the sides of the drive-way. We drove on toward a Spanish colonial-style villa atop a round hill.

The car stopped short of the main house. Alejandro led me to a covered terrace off to one side.

"It's nice up here," I said.

Below us was a tennis court with a tall fence. A single putting green sat further below that.

"*Estimado* Vice Minister," Alejandro announced. "May I present Doctor Morales?"

We turned the corner, and I saw the man's back. Instead of a uniform, he wore a sort of cruise-wear ensemble: tennis shorts and boat shoes, with a baby-blue *guayabera*.

"So nice to see you again, sir," I said. "This is a lovely place you have here."

Back still to me, he tossed small coins at a piece of furniture in the corner. I craned my neck and saw that it resembled a wooden chest of drawers. On the top sat a big brass frog with a gaping mouth. It appeared to be a parlor game of some kind.

"Doctor Morales," he said. "I thought we had an understanding, you and I."

His coins clicked against the sides of the brass frog.

"What do you mean, sir?"

"'Unfortunate things,' isn't that the term that you used? The phrase that you shouted across the entire internet, as an accusation toward my government?"

Not that stupid video again. "Oh, that," I said. "That's just silly. Some punk with a camera took what I said out of context. I wasn't implicating you or your government at all: I was *defending* you. That part they used was just a—you know, a concession argument."

"A concession!" He turned around to face me for the first time. His eyes looked bloodshot and sleepless. "There is no room for concession here, Morales! I'm doing everything in my power to hold this country together."

"I understand, sir. Trust me, we have a common goal, as far as those children are concerned."

With a loud sigh, he finally seemed to soften. He dropped the rest of his coins down beside the brass frog. "Come this way. Let's have a drink."

I followed him around to yet another side of the terrace. This one had an incredible view of the city below: the skyscrapers, the cathedrals, the colonial plazas, and that dusty old stadium. Further in the distance, snow-capped peaks made it all look insignificant.

"It's beautiful," I said.

"One of the perks of my position." He grinned.

We took a seat at a small table. Alejandro brought over a pitcher and two glasses of ice. As he poured, I tried to identify the beverage. The color was like lemonade, but with a darker layer at the bottom and flecks of red and black throughout.

"*Salud.*" The Vice Minister raised his glass to me.

"*Salud.*" I took a sip and had to suppress a cough. It was some sort of beer cocktail—full of pepper and lime.

"So, tell me." The Vice Minister's eyes were on the vista of the city below. "How goes the science?"

"Not bad," I said tentatively. "The results came back from the lab only a few hours ago. I haven't had time to study them closely."

"But you're confident they will show that the children's affliction has no connection to the potatoes in question?"

I let out a sigh. "I'm one hundred percent confident that the results will *not* demonstrate any connection." Somehow, with all the wild accusations being thrown about, the burden of proof had fallen on my shoulders. "Is more expected of me? There's no genetic overlap. What else could I do?"

The Vice Minister put down his drink and crossed his arms in front of his chest. "Isn't that obvious? You must find the true cause of their affliction."

"I *what*?" My words were louder than intended. "Sir, with all due respect, that's way outside of my area. I'm not a medical doctor; I don't know the first thing about humans."

He raised his eyebrows. "That's become quite clear."

My head fell into my hands. What was I thinking? That I could disprove a ridiculous rumor with actual science? This was truly a fool's errand.

The Vice Minister drained the rest of his cocktail. "Come with me a moment. I'd like to show you something."

I looked up and nodded, resolved to stay composed—at least as long as I was in this man's presence. He rose to his feet, and I did the same. Once he began walking, I drained the rest of my drink and then followed.

"You see, Doctor Morales, your employer is not the only company to take an interest in Puerto Malogrado. I'm often approached by your competitors."

"Is that right?"

We walked down the hill, then took a stone path to a large greenhouse. Once we arrived at the door, he grabbed the latch and waited for me to catch up.

"Do you mind my asking, sir, why Puerto Malogrado? What is it about your nation that appeals to these companies?"

He smiled broadly. "There are various reasons. We are located in the tropics, but with high elevation; this makes it possible to isolate certain variables: latitude, temperature, shade, and so on."

I nodded. "That would be helpful."

"But also, there is a certain political advantage."

"Oh?" I asked. "How's that?"

"In your country, you elect the president. But you also have the legislature, all the state governments." He sucked on his teeth. "Very inefficient, no?"

"That's true."

"Here, the system is more streamlined. We get things done much faster." The Vice Minister began to lift the latch, then turned back to me a final time. "And, as you know, I'm a pleasure to work with."

We entered the greenhouse: a long structure with ribs of stainless steel covered over in transparent plastic sheeting. Between the heat and the odd lighting, I grew dizzy. The static started at the sides of my eyes again, and I was reminded of the incident at the clinic back in Boise.

"Doctor!" A stiff hand materialized at the small of my back. "Doctor, are you all right?" The Vice Minister rushed over to support me. "You looked like you were about to keel over."

Beads of sweat broke out on my forehead, and a wave of relief came along with them. My senses returned, and I stood up under my own power.

"Sorry, sir," I said. "I think the altitude must've gotten the best of me. I'm fine now."

"Very well." He nodded. "Shall we continue?"

"Please," I said.

"Look around." He spread his arms like a game-show hostess, demonstrating the wares of this greenhouse.

It was quite a sight: orderly rows of various plants—most in pots or boxes, but some planted directly into the soil. At the rear was a hydroponic setup: wispy roots dangling into a tank, some breed of catfish slinking about among them. I recognized the near wall as all potatoes—though their leaves bore a variety of shapes and sizes.

I leaned over for a closer look. "These are . . . are these from Tuberware?"

"No." He shook his head. "My contract with your employer, it's an exclusive arrangement. In spite of all other offers, I've always respected that. But when I'm courted by your competitors, they often share their most curious specimens." He touched the leaf of the plant I was studying. "These are from a Canadian firm. Apparently, the potato they produce absorbs less fat when fried." He removed his hand. "They assure me there is a market for such a thing, in your country."

"I imagine there is."

"This one here." He moved down the line. "It has the genes from a flounder. It can survive a frost."

"I've heard about that," I said.

"And this one," he continued. "This has the measles vaccine already inside it. You could feed it to children, and they would be inoculated."

"Wow!" I was genuinely impressed. "We should come up with one that carries insulin. You could cause and cure diabetes with the same French fries."

The Vice Minister turned to face me. "That's a good idea."

Already, I was unsure myself whether or not I'd meant it as a joke.

"But this," he continued, "this is my favorite." We came to the last plant in the row. "Doctor, why don't you go ahead and harvest this one." He found a trowel on the ground and held it toward me. "Go on. It's mature."

I took the tool from him and rolled up my sleeves. For the second time this week, I'd pull potatoes from the soil. But the same act felt much more stressful now than in Arturo's parcel just days ago. I was overwhelmed with something like stage fright. With one hand, I reached underneath the leaves and took the plant by the stem. With the other, I gently pushed the trowel's blade into the loose earth of the planter, allowing enough room to clear the tubers below. I pried on the handle a couple of times. Once sure it was below the roots, I pulled on the plant and lifted with the trowel. First, a moment of tension as the roots stubbornly clung to the soil. Then that pleasing moment of release.

The Vice Minister and I smiled at each other. I dropped the trowel and used both hands to free the potatoes from the soil.

At the first sight of their skin, a sound like "whaa!" escaped my mouth. I let go of the plant and took a step back. The Vice Minister laughed. My eyes were trained on the potatoes. Now mostly exposed, their skins were glowing: an eerie green incandescence that was plainly visible even in the flat light of the hothouse.

"Genes from fireflies." The Vice Minister picked up the plant and brushed dirt off the tubers. Once clean, they were even brighter.

Mouth still agape, I said only, "Why?"

He shrugged, dropped the plant, and wiped his hands against each other. "Because they can, I suppose. There isn't much use for them—apart from the curiosity. And they taste terrible."

I couldn't stop staring. Something about those glowing potato skins made me wonder if I hadn't been wrong all along. All my life, I'd thought of myself and my fellow scientists as careful stewards of knowledge and technology. Was that truly the case? Or was my industry hastily slapping together whichever oddities we could dream up? Firing off our gene guns and asking questions later?

The Vice Minister must've sensed my ambivalence. "Let's go back to the terrace, shall we?"

———

We took our seats at the table again. Alejandro rejoined us and refreshed our drinks. The beer cocktail was welcome, after the heat of the greenhouse and the sight of all those odd plants.

"I'm glad you could make it up here today, Doctor Morales." The Vice Minister smiled. "I fear that our relationship has been all business, no? Tell me, how have you enjoyed your stay in Puerto Malogrado?"

"Well." I thought about the question. "I've been so busy. And traveling was never a hobby of mine. But I like the place. The food is delicious."

"This is true." He took a dainty sip from his glass. "It's odd how the most innovative cuisine often comes from the poorest and most desperate cultures."

"Necessity, I suppose."

"Indeed."

"To be honest," I said, "my visit has been stressful. I'm concerned about this situation with these children, and not just from a public-relations standpoint; I'd like to offer the family some answers. Now this idiot with a camera is sticking his nose in, making a fool of me at every turn." My teeth clenched up at my mention of Kearns.

"This filmmaker?" The Vice Minister took an interest, leaned toward me. "He causes trouble for you?"

"A lot of trouble," I nodded.

"Do you know his name?"

"Sure," I said. "It's Spencer Kearns."

The Vice Minister snapped his fingers and made a gesture like writing. Alejandro dashed over with a pad of paper and a pen.

"Please, repeat the name," Alejandro said.

"Spencer Kearns," I said again.

"And do you know where he stays?"

"Yes," I admitted. "It's just off the Plaza de los Agricultores, beside the statue of the farmer."

Alejandro and the Vice Minister exchanged a nod.

"Hey," I said. "What's this about? You're not going to do anything . . . untoward to him, are you? I didn't mean to suggest. . . ."

"Not to worry, Doctor." The Vice Minister held a flattened hand out toward me, palm down. "We'll ensure that he gives you some peace in which to work. We can be very subtle."

"Well. That does sound helpful," I admitted.

"Now, if you'll excuse me, I have some issues that demand my attention. Alejandro can see you to the car."

———

The ride down the hill was silent. Alejandro stared at his phone while I squirted my hands with sanitizer—paranoid that one of those freak potatoes was going to infect me.

"Can I ask you something?" I finally said, once we were back in the city.

He looked up. "What's that, Doctor?"

"Are people worried about this rebellion? The Vice Minister didn't even bring it up today."

He squinted with one side of his face, then the other. "It's a complicated situation. It is true that the fighting has grown more intense. But the opposition, they lack consensus. The common people know that FURP could never rule the country. Their coalition is too loose. When push comes to shove, their differences always break them apart."

"Why is that?"

Alejandro shrugged. "It's the nature of idealism."

"Idealism? And that's not a problem for the current government?"

Alejandro smiled, glanced in the driver's direction, then back to me. "This regime is nothing if not pragmatic."

I nodded, impressed by his turn of phrase.

"But you are correct: the fighting is serious. And the Vice Minister is concerned. But he must keep up a brave face. Appearances are important in this country. There's little to be gained by looking worried."

"Right," I said. "One more question: Is there a reason he's only the Vice Minister of the Interior? I mean, he is the one running the country, correct?"

"That's a long story." Alejandro sighed. "The Minister of the Interior is an old man now—definitely senile, possibly dead. His last real decision was to paint the Ministry that hideous pink color. He was quite popular once, so it would be bad politics to replace him. And what would be the point? Power is power; titles are just words."

"I see. So, how did the Ministry of the Interior become the branch that runs the country?"

"That's simple," Alejandro smiled. "The military reports to it."

Ask a stupid question, I thought to myself.

We pulled up at the hotel, and they let me out. The teenager with the gun stopped his pacing; the two of us stared at the Cadillac as it drove off.

It was well past lunchtime, and I hadn't eaten since breakfast. Instead of entering the hotel, I headed off in search of food.

Luckily, I came across a woman with a wheeled cart and a flat-topped grill. A sign above her head read "Incaburger."

"Yes?" she said as I approached.

"Eh . . . one." I held up my index finger.

With a plastic squeeze bottle, she squirted oil onto the flat top and then added a handful of chopped onions and another of diced potatoes. While they sizzled away, she found an egg and two pieces of crusty bread underneath the counter. She placed the bread face-down against the grill and let it brown—one piece on either side of the onions and potatoes. With a metal spatula, she gave the vegetables a flip, then cracked the egg right on top of them.

My stomach rumbled in anticipation.

The pieces of bread kept most of the running egg in place. The rest of it she corralled with the spatula. With one swift strike, she split the yolk. From below, she produced a couple of slices of ham and cheese and put them atop the pile. One piece of bread was removed, squirted with a pink sauce from another squeeze bottle, and placed atop the pile. She flipped the other piece over. With the spatula below and a finger on top, she lifted the whole thing off the grill and then landed it atop the other piece of bread.

I repressed the urge to clap and cheer.

She added a little more oil and gave the top and bottom of the sandwich a chance to brown, cheese now running down the sides. She wrapped the whole thing up in white paper with an almost violent motion, and charged me the equivalent of about fifty American cents.

"Thank you," I said as I received the sandwich and practically ran back to the hotel.

———

I ate in my room, while poring over the data from the Morales children and their DNA test. It was as I had anticipated: nothing that demonstrated a connection to the DS 400, but nothing to offer any alternative explanation either.

The sandwich was delicious, but I could hardly enjoy it for the sinking feeling in my gut. My options were limited. If the Vice Minister was expecting me to come up with the real reason for the children's ambulatory problem, then he would be disappointed. If that were also what Warren was expecting, then I'd let him down as well.

The Morales kids would need a full genetic profile to get to the root of this—something they surely couldn't afford and which wouldn't lead to a cure so much as a better understanding of the condition. Perhaps some full-time geneticists or neurologists might be interested in studying them? If their case did reach the international press, that might be one good thing to come out of it: attention from experts.

At dusk, the government's air force planes took off again. Explosions echoed in the mountains. I unplugged my laptop from the wall, as if it were thunder and lightning outside.

More than anything, I wanted to find a satisfying explanation for the family—not just a scientific washing of our hands. I spread all the children's profiles out in front of me, along with a sample group that Jill had emailed to me.

Suddenly I noticed something I'd not seen before. There was a sort of misspelling in their genetic code—even in the cursory version that I'd gotten from the lab. It was the exact same for all three of the children. This could be the mutation I'd been looking for. It was possible that biologists already knew whether this gene was related to balance or motor skills.

From outside my bedroom, I heard a door slam and then a sound like sobbing. A familiar voice shouted: "Eddie! Eddie!"

I dropped the papers and went out into the main room of the hotel.

"*Tranquila*," Doña Ana said.

Raven stood there, looking like a wreck. She sobbed in the middle of the room, hands held up to her face. "Oh, my God, Eddie. It was awful."

"What happened?"

She ran over and buried her face into my shirt. "It's Kearns."

"Kearns?" I almost pushed her away. What had that asshole done now? "You were hanging around with Kearns?"

She lifted her head and wiped at the sides of her eyes. "I ran into him, and we had lunch. We decided to compare notes."

"You *what*?"

"Strictly about the revolution. I told him that I couldn't talk about the Morales kids. Anyways, we went around the city a little; he introduced me to a couple of his sources, and then we decided to go back to his hotel for a drink."

"You don't say."

Behind Raven's back, Doña Ana's mother was watching television, her walker set in front of her. She flipped channels at full volume: one second of intense, incoherent sound after another.

"Eddie, it was horrible."

"What happened, exactly?"

"We took a cab to the hotel and started to head in, but before we got to the door, this black car full of policemen pulled up. They just grabbed him and shoved him into the back. I kept screaming that he was a journalist and a foreign national, and what was he being arrested for? They said something ridiculous about 'audio-visual crimes.'"

"Oh, my God." I took a step backward. My head felt drained of blood. They'd done it. They'd freaking dragged him off to jail. For my sake. On my accidental orders.

"Eddie?" Raven cocked her head. "Are you okay?"

"Me? Sure. I'm just a little shocked. Did you get hurt?"

"No. I'm fine. It just rattled me, seeing what they can do to journalists."

"Right." I wasn't sure what to tell her. That it was my fault? That it was all a big misunderstanding between me and the repressive dictator I'd been having drinks with? "Listen: it's terrible. But don't worry about Kearns too much. He's got resources. He'll be okay. This regime knows better than to go after a wealthy fake journalist with the kind of platform he has."

"Do nothing? Are you sure? I actually got some footage of those police thugs, on my phone."

"No! Don't post that!" I said it too sternly. I had to backpedal. "I don't mean do nothing, not exactly. The best thing we can do is to get to the bottom of this matter with the Morales kids. If we can close that case, then Kearns won't be a thorn in their side."

She nodded, seeming to like the semblance of a plan. "How's that going?"

"Good, actually. I may have found something. There's an anomaly in their genetic code."

"Could that be behind their hand-walking?"

"It's possible," I said. "It might be an atavism of some kind."

"A what?"

"Atavism. A sort of evolutionary throwback. The appearance of an ancestral genotype."

"Really?"

"It's possible." I shrugged. "Or it might have been caused by environmental factors. Something in the air or water while they were in the womb."

"Maybe from the poisons they spray from the airplanes?"

"The herbicides?" I hadn't thought of that. "I guess it's possible."

"So . . . can it be fixed?" she asked.

I shrugged. "They do have some exotic drugs and gene therapies nowadays. But they're almost all experimental."

"Like your French-fry machine."

"That's right, like my French-fry machine."

A loud explosion sounded from the north. She ran back and clutched me again—head against my chest. I held on to her as the shock waves rumbled, then stopped. The television went silent and the lights cut off. After a second, it became awkward and we released each other.

"Did you find out anything interesting?" I asked. "About the conflict?"

She rolled her eyes. "People are so cagey about it. No one would go on the record."

"Can you blame them?" I asked. "They've got the police to worry about. You print anybody's name or picture on that blog of yours, and they could end up being snatched in broad daylight."

"That's the problem, although there are some folks who want to get the world's eyes on this, want the international community to know what's going on. A few of them gave me quotes."

The lights and the television came back on. Doña Ana left the kitchen and joined her mother on the couch. On screen, the Vice Minister now stood at his normal lectern. But this time his face looked shiny and severe, like they'd forgotten to do his makeup. His voice sounded thin and panicked.

"I repeat," he said. "Our nation is under grave threat from these cowardly insurgents. I call to all young Malogradeños to report to their recruiting stations at once!"

"What's he saying?" Raven asked.

"He's begging people to enlist in his army."

"He looks worried," she said.

"Things must be going poorly in the mountains." Much worse than even a few hours ago, I thought to myself.

An enormous explosion went off. I couldn't tell whether it was on television or in real life. Then I realized it was a mix of both: we could hear it from outside and also through the speakers.

The television and the lights both flickered a couple of times and then went out again.

"*Híjole*," muttered Doña Ana.

Raven and I stood in the darkened silence.

"The rebels must be getting close," I said.

"So, what happens now?" Raven asked.

"Try and get some sleep, I suppose."

"And tomorrow?"

"Back to Huanchillo. I've got to share this stuff with the Morales family. I'm hoping to convince some real research teams, with grants and whatnot, to take this on. I'll be more good to them in Boise than I will be here."

"Is it safe, to travel there tomorrow?"

"I think so. All the fighting is in the north. I'm sure Oscar will know if there's any problem." Also, I'd been assured by a big cheese in FURP that Huanchillo would be safe.

Another distant explosion on one of the hillsides flooded the windows with yellowish light. For a brief second, I could see the outline of Raven's hair and face.

"Okay, Eddie," she said. "I guess this is good night."

"Good night, Raven."

n the morning, I was woken by the roosters and car alarms. The lights came on when I tried them. So far, this new day had a welcome air of normality to it.

In the courtyard, Doña Ana and her daughters had a delicious breakfast prepared—loaded with both eggs and potatoes this time. The three of them seemed oddly happy as they served me coffee and a full plate. The grandmother was in the other room; her walker clicked against the tile floor.

"Morning, Doña Ana," I said. "Where's the newspaper?"

She held up empty palms. "Hasn't arrived yet."

I wished I'd thought to turn on the TV and check the latest fake news.

Raven emerged from the bedroom in her usual yoga safari clothes, carrying her Moleskine notebook.

"Morning, Eddie!" She too seemed in better spirits.

"Good morning," I said between bites. "The breakfast is great."

"So I guess the fighting must've settled down since last night."

"I guess so," I said. "There's no paper yet, so it's hard to say."

"Huh." She took a sip of her coffee.

One of Doña Ana's daughters dropped a plate of breakfast before her. As usual, it looked smaller and less delicious than mine.

"So, after this we head out to Huanchillo?"

"As long as Oscar shows up."

"Speak of the devil," Raven said, looking over my shoulder.

"*Buenos días*, boss!" Oscar gave me a pat on the back.

"Morning," I said.

"We should get on the road soon, no?" he asked.

"Give me one second." I pushed my plate of food out of the way and put my briefcase on the table. I popped it open, double-checked my papers, then re-closed it. "Great. Let's go."

———

Raven and I followed Oscar out to the street. We were both surprised to see a small SUV waiting there. He unlocked the doors with a click of the remote car key.

"Where have you been hiding this thing?" I asked.

Oscar shrugged. "It just came available."

"Shotgun," I called, and went to the front seat. Raven climbed in behind Oscar.

It was hard to tell that there had been any kind of rebel offensive just a few hours ago. Once we ascended out of the capital's deep valley, we could make out the scars of minor landslides and some smoldering craters on the peaks to the north. But on our journey, things were basically normal—if not a bit sunnier and quieter.

In fact, once we'd passed the silver mine, it looked as if all the strikers had gone home. Nobody appeared to be working, but nobody stood around blocking traffic either.

Huanchillo itself was slightly more alive. Farmers walked past with sacks of Tuberware potatoes in tow, their children carrying smaller sacks. I thought I caught a glimpse of Arturo but wasn't sure it was him.

At the Morales house, a pair of evangelicals stood outside, looking exhausted. But there were no reporters or onlookers. No sign of Kearns, of course. Oscar parked right out front and stayed with the car. Raven followed me to the door.

"Don Pablo," I said as it creaked open. "I have good news."

"Ah, Doctor Morales." Again, he seemed happy to see me. "Come in."

Raven and I entered. We had a seat around that same wooden table. Rosa and the children were nowhere to be seen.

"I've got some of the *chuño* that you asked about." On the table was a dish of some sort of small roll or dumpling, along with a shallow plastic bucket. He pushed the bucket toward me. "This is the more traditional black *chuño*. It isn't washed after the preservation process."

I looked inside and saw the shrunken potatoes. They looked like a cross between dirt clods and dry prunes. Don Pablo picked one up and handed it to me.

I rolled it around in my fingers. "There's no moisture in this at all."

He grinned. "That's the idea. Here, in the *altiplano*, you leave them on the ground for three days or so—expose them to the freezing nights as well as to the sun. Then trample upon them to remove the skins and the moisture."

Raven reached between us and took one out of the bucket.

"Once dry," Don Pablo went on, "these will last for years. When the Spanish ran this country, it's all they fed to the miners. It's not very exciting, but you can add it to soups or make flour. It will keep you from starving." He moved the bucket away and pushed the dish forward. "This is my favorite way to eat it." He picked up one of the little rolls.

I followed suit. It had a dark purple-gray color to it, and an odd smell. I took a tentative bite.

"This is delicious," I said.

Don Pablo nodded.

There was something in the consistency that intrigued me—more dense and starchy than I'd expected. I wondered if we could add some of this flour to the mixture in our fry machine and come up with a firmer product—without turning it purple.

While Raven helped herself to one of the dumplings, I decided it was time to get to the point.

"Don Pablo, I think I may have found the gene responsible for your children's problem."

He turned to me with a fresh intensity in his eyes. "And you know how to remedy it?"

"What?" I was caught off guard. "Well, no. I'm not that kind of doctor."

He stared at me for a second and then gave a slow nod.

"Still, Don Pablo, this is exciting news." I took the papers out from my bag. "At the moment, you see, mapping a human's entire genome is a million-dollar project that takes years and years. Only a few dozen people on earth have actually had such a thing done."

Raven interrupted me. "But, Eddie, aren't people testing DNA online now? I have friends who've done it for a hundred bucks." She seemed to be following the Spanish fairly well.

I sighed. "Those tests are rough approximations. They do matches to find paternity and things like that. It's broad strokes, not a full mapping." I turned to Pablo and switched back to Spanish. "It was a quick and cheap test that I did in the lab over the past few days. It might have found nothing, but I stumbled across this abnormality. . . ."

I spread the profiles out on the floor and found the spot I'd highlighted on each of the children's charts. "It's a T that ought to be a C. Look." I pointed to the control sheet. "That's the mutation. It must affect balance or walking."

Both Raven and Pablo leaned in for a closer look, but they didn't share my enthusiasm.

"Now, the best thing would be to get the attention of a crackerjack genetics team. For all we know, this could be a watershed moment for understanding human evolution, walking upright and so on."

"These other scientists you speak of . . ." Don Pablo looked confused. "They will study my kids but not necessarily heal them?"

I shrugged. "I couldn't say, to be honest. It isn't really a medical issue."

He turned back to the papers with a sullen glare. Raven took a step back.

"This is big news." But I could barely muster the sincerity.

"Well done, Eddie," Raven said half-heartedly.

"I don't mean to seem ungrateful, Doctor." Don Pablo kept staring at the papers. "It's just that—well, I'm not quite sure how all this would help."

Suddenly, being a lone research scientist among potato farmers seemed about as useful as being a lone poet among them—less so, perhaps. "Where are the kids?" I asked. "Out back?" I gestured toward the rear courtyard.

"No, I'm afraid not," Don Pablo said. "Their mother has taken them to a place outside of town."

"Oh?" I didn't like the sound of that. "Are you sure that's wise? Those journalists, they might film them or something."

He let go of a long sigh. "It wasn't my idea, I can assure you. But my wife has lost patience with this situation. She left early this morning, before even the evangelicals had a chance to arrive and molest us."

"Don Pablo." I moved my face an inch closer to his. "Where did your wife take your children?"

He averted my gaze. "To a local healer, someone who works with herbs and things."

"To a *brujo*?" I asked. A witch doctor.

"In a manner of speaking," he admitted.

"Don Pablo!" I shouted. "This is a terrible idea. We're trying to keep this in the realm of science, not superstitious hocus-pocus!"

"Hocus-pocus!" He raised his voice to match mine. "What do you call these things that you bring me? Some cryptic letters and numbers on a confusing set of documents? The promise of more complex letters and numbers to come? I don't care about the history of human beings walking upright. I care about my children! I won't live forever. How will they provide for themselves once I'm gone? With all this nonsense?" He poked a callused finger at my stack of papers. "Will this put potatoes in their bellies?"

Our argument was interrupted by a commotion from outside. The three of us ran to the door and saw the rest of the family on the street. They were being mobbed by a crew of reporters with cameras and microphones. From further back, the evangelicals hurled holy water at them. Niña Rosa waved an umbrella at those closest to her and shouted *"Bestia! Animales! Dejame en paz!"*

Behind her, Pablito and his two sisters dodged the advances of the cameramen as best they could, gathering behind their mother in their fastest four-limbed gait.

Raven was the first to run out to their aid. The father and I followed close behind. I threw myself between the reporters and the children, covering a wide camera lens with one of my palms.

"That's enough! *Basta!* Let's leave this poor family alone!" I shouted.

The others led the children through the front door, while I brought up the rear. Just as I was about to duck inside the house myself, I took a direct hit of holy water from one stiff-collared evangelical. It was the wrinkled preacher. We made angry eye contact with each other. I couldn't summon words to contain his hypocrisy, so I swallowed my rage and went indoors.

With everyone inside the house and the door shut tight, our troubles were far from over. Each of the children had thick bandages wrapped around both their heels.

"Niña Rosa," I said. "Please tell me you didn't get them a bone-setting." I remember hearing about how the breaking and realigning of bones had once been a popular folk medicine service—a voodoo brand of chiropractics.

"Ay, no." She rolled her eyes. "They're just herbs." She loosened one of the bandage wraps from her daughter's ankle to demonstrate.

I was relieved but still frustrated. "Niña Rosa, please don't visit any more of these witch doctors." The girls were frightened—first by the evangelicals, and now by my admonishing tone. "It's important that we stick to science, keep the black magic out of this. Otherwise, you'll rein-force everything those idiots are saying about you and your family."

"With all due respect, Doctor Morales." Don Pablo's voice rose to match mine. "I'm not a supporter of *brujería* either. But my wife's patience wears thin. We don't care about making some scientist famous; we want our children to have a decent life." He again pointed toward my stack of papers, of which I'd so recently been proud.

"Calm down," Raven said in passable Spanish, her open hands push-ing some invisible force toward the ground. "Why don't we all settle down a little?"

"Fair enough." I conceded the father's point. "Perhaps the bigger problem, at the moment, is the footage those reporters took."

An unsettling minute of silence ensued, nobody sure what to say or do. Pablito and his sisters sat on the floor, pulling at their herb-packed bandages.

"Who would like some tea?" Niña Rosa asked.

Raven and I both nodded. Rosa went off to the small kitchen in the courtyard.

"Please." Don Pablo motioned toward the table. "Have a seat."

We both settled into chairs.

"I'm sorry," I said. "I shouldn't have raised my voice."

Don Pablo smiled warmly. "This is frustrating, no? This situation."

I laughed out loud. "That's an understatement."

Don Pablo picked up the plate of *chuño* rolls, carried it across the room, and offered them to his children. Each of them took one.

"Can I ask you something, Don Pablo?" I recalled the conversation I'd had with Raven in the hotel, about possible environmental exposures. "Where did you get your drinking water during the time that your wife was carrying the children?"

"Same place that we get it now. From the spring in town."

"Could I go there and get a sample?"

He shrugged. "I don't see why not."

"I'd need a clean and dry container, something that seals, preferably made of glass."

"Let me see what I can do." Don Pablo went into the kitchen. He returned a minute later with a baby-food jar and a dry rag.

"That's perfect." I took them from him and set about sterilizing the jar with my hand sanitizer.

Before I finished, an aggressive knock sounded from the front door.

"*Hijole*," Don Pablo rolled his eyes. "What do these bastards want now?"

Raven and I exchanged a glance.

"Listen up, *cabrónes!*" Don Pablo shouted as he approached the door. "I'm fed up with you bothering my family." He swung the door open.

"I'm so sorry, Don Pablo." It was Oscar. "I must speak with Doctor Morales."

"Oscar?" I stood up. "What's the matter?" The crowd outside had completely dispersed.

"Something has happened." He was pale and frightened—a look I'd not seen on him before. "I heard it over the car radio and then confirmed it with my cell phone."

"What's going on, Oscar?"

"We can't go back to the city. We'll have to stay here. It's too dangerous—for foreign nationals in particular."

Raven gasped.

"Oscar, what happened?"

"The rebels are approaching the capital. They've seized control of several surrounding towns. The army is struggling to keep them at bay."

I turned to Don Pablo. "Did you know about this?"

"No." He shook his head. "I've been here all day."

"It just happened," Oscar insisted. "Nobody knew. The guerillas forged some sort of coalition, which includes the striking miners. The regime refused to report anything about it, of course."

"Let's have a look," Don Pablo said. He pulled a dusty piece of cheese-cloth off the old television set in the corner.

A couple of the channels were suddenly out of service. Don Pablo paused for a second at each one. Finally, we landed on some jumpy handheld camera footage of the city streets. Along the Boulevard de los Agricultores, men and women in makeshift fatigues and bright wool hats walked along with an assortment of weapons, those red bandannas covering their faces, or now only hanging loosely around their necks. The civilians on the street and in their houses waved red cloths of all kinds at them. From two windows hung red and yellow flags with the rebel group's acronym: "FURP." I couldn't tell whether the whole city had been waiting for this revolution to happen, or if everyone had quickly jumped aboard the bandwagon after it started rolling.

Niña Rosa walked in from the kitchen and placed the tea service on the table. "What's all this?" she asked.

"It's true," Don Pablo said softly. "They might finally take the capital."

Rosa crossed herself.

"Eddie?" Raven had lost the thread of all the Spanish conversation. "What exactly is happening?"

"A revolution, I suppose."

We all continued to stare at the television, trying to make sense of the images. I wasn't sure how such raw footage could even find its way onto the airwaves. Perhaps the propagandists had fled, and some frustrated underlings were able to show the unfiltered news—for once.

"Does this not happen . . . often?" I asked the question mostly of Oscar.

"Never." He shook his head. "Never even close to the city."

Some of the crowd threw coca leaves into the air, at the feet of the guerillas. Apparently this was a show of support from the highland communities that were so well represented by FURP.

Don Pablo put a hand on my shoulder. "You'll stay with us tonight, Doctor Morales. We'll make you as comfortable as we can." An hour passed, and we all did our best to stay calm. Somebody must've told the news to the evangelicals out front. They departed, presumably to pray over more urgent matters. Another hour passed, and the news grew repetitive.

"Well," I said, "if we've got all night, I may as well go get this water sample. Where's the spring, exactly?"

"Keep going past the church." Don Pablo pointed toward town. "Then just follow the women with *cantarros*. You can't miss it."

"Can I come with you, Eddie?" Raven asked.

"Sure. Let's go."

Raven and I took our clean jar and set out for the heart of Huanchillo.

—

Just as Don Pablo had said, it was easy to find the spring. Women came and went with large plastic jugs and buckets atop their heads, often with small children in tow. When we came to the spring itself, we found a line five women long, all waiting to fill their vessels. I craned my neck to see. The spring was a small crack in the rocks, dribbling down into a tiny stream below.

"This is where they get their water?" Raven asked.

"So it seems," I said.

"And you think it might have been contaminated somehow, with something that caused the children's condition?"

I shrugged. "It's a long shot. Environmental factors only account for about ten percent of all birth defects. And I have no idea what the contaminant might be. Even for an industrial pesticide, this would be a stretch."

"*Perdón*, Don Doctor?" One of the women ahead of us turned back to me.

"Yes?" I asked.

"Why don't you go ahead? You only have that small *jarra*. No need to wait."

"Thank you." I stepped forward, nodding at the other women.

At the spring, my jar filled in an instant. The water was clear and cool, and I had to resist the urge to take a sip. Without touching the rim or the inside, I sealed the lid. We thanked the women in line once again and made our way back.

———

The sun was setting as we passed the central plaza, the top of the cathedral lit dramatically by pink light. I thought I saw another condor beyond the spire.

"It's beautiful here," Raven said.

"At this time of day, in particular."

"Hey! Doctor Morales?" A familiar voice sounded from behind.

I turned to see. It was Arturo.

"Come, join us!" One of his hands held a clay mug. With the other, he gestured toward the open door of what looked to be a bustling, makeshift cantina. "We are discussing the future of our nation."

I turned to Raven. She nodded.

"Come on!" Arturo insisted. "I'll buy you each a *pisco*."

Inside, the cantina was dark with a low-slung ceiling. A pool table stood in the center but was being used for leaning or setting drinks upon rather than playing.

"*Colega!*" Arturo called to the bartender. "*Dos piscos.*"

"Wow!" Raven was excited. "That's the brandy from Chile, isn't it?"

"Chile? No." Arturo corrected her. "Peru and Chile both claim it, but it was invented in this country." He passed us each a small cup of spirits. "Like so many things from the Andes, we started it and larger nations have taken it from us."

"Including potatoes, possibly," I said.

"I'll drink to that." Arturo raised his mug and touched it to our cups.

Raven and I each took small, cautious sips. I placed my water jar on the table.

"Wow," Raven said. "This is delicious."

It was good—aromatic and not too strong.

Arturo was pleased that we liked it. "So, what do you make of the situation?"

"With the children?" I asked.

"With the revolution!" he said. "It's exciting, no? So many years, they've been fighting in the mountains without success. Now, at last, a near victory."

"Yes!" Raven had already finished half her *pisco*. "Very exciting!"

"Very sudden, is how I would describe it." I took another sip. "Tell me, Arturo: Were you surprised?"

"There were rumors." He nodded. "It's been said that the regime had overextended itself. The news never admits anything like that, you know. But some people whispered that a big offensive was on its way, that the key rebel groups finally had a workable alliance." He took a sip from his mug and shrugged his shoulders. "But then again, there are always rumors."

"So, what was the turning point?" I asked. "Who exactly made this alliance?"

"Well. . . ." he sighed. "This is all a bit speculative. But it sounds as though it was mostly a matter of FURP finally getting along with some fringe groups. Groups that are smaller, well funded, but . . . less ideological."

"You mean drug traffickers," I said.

He grinned. "Among other things."

Raven and I exchanged a glance.

"They've been trying to reach some sort of agreement for years: FURP, the labor groups, the *narcotraficantes*." Arturo went on. "But each faction was always fearful of ceding control over their cause. I guess their hatred for the regime finally overcame their squabbles with each other." None of this seemed to bother Arturo.

"So," I said. "The unions have the people, the drug cartels have the guns and money, and FURP has the political ideology."

Arturo grinned again. "A good match, no?"

"Are you not concerned," I asked, "about Puerto Malogrado becoming a narco-state? That the next government might be just as corrupt—or even more so—than the old regime?"

"It's possible." Arturo nodded. "But I'll take my chances. We were going nowhere with the old regime. That's the thing about revolution: it's guaranteed to be something new."

"I'll drink to that!" Raven raised her glass.

"Another round." Arturo motioned to the bartender.

"As for being a narco-state," Arturo went on. "I think it's more complicated than that. The coca leaves are part of our culture. To stop their cultivation—as the old regime constantly tries to do—it's like stopping the French from growing grapes for their wine."

"Well," I said. "Cocaine's international reputation is slightly different from that of French wine."

"Unfortunately true," he said. "Still, a natural resource is a natural resource. Poor nations can't afford to be picky about that. Also, I'll tell you one thing I've learned about the drug trade: there is nothing that's worse than a power vacuum in that industry. The real tragedies occur when rival factions are competing. Perhaps now—with the biggest cartel and the national government being one and the same—we'll have some stability at least."

"Have I mentioned how much I love *pisco*?" Raven dropped another three glasses on our table.

I reached for one, and a firecracker sounded from the front of the cantina. A sulfurous, burning smell filled the room. All the talking stopped abruptly. Some people jumped behind the bar. The rest of us crouched in place. A small chunk of plaster fell down from the ceiling and clunked against the floor.

"In the afterlife!" A shrill voice sounded from the front entrance.

I looked up and saw the evangelical preacher—the one who'd espoused his theory of reverse evolution, and who had hit me with the holy water just hours ago—holding an antique-looking revolver up in the air.

"You will all repent for having so loved this life, for your liquor and your vice!" He waved the gun around the room, aiming from one person to another in quick succession. People raised their hands as the barrel came toward them.

"Your whores!" He put the gun on Raven, who sat at the far side of the table from me.

Not thinking, not knowing why, I stood up—empty hands raised—and put my body between Raven's and the red-eyed preacher.

"Why don't you move along, sir?" For the first time, I found myself using the slow, clear pronunciation typical of Puertomalogradeño Spanish. The barrel was a couple of feet from my chest. "I may not be an expert on God, but I'm quite sure He doesn't support shooting at strangers. Correct?"

His hand twitched as he finally lowered the gun. "You're wrong!" he shouted, raising his other hand. "These godless communists cannot save you!"

"Please." I tried to look him in the eye, but he wouldn't hold my stare. "Move along. Leave the justice to God."

His lips parted as if about to speak, but no words came. He turned to look at the gun and seemed surprised to find it there. With a nervous twitch of the head, he backed out of the cantina and disappeared up the street.

Immediately, the rest of the patrons stopped cowering and stood up to their full height, shouting curses at the departing preacher.

I was bought a bevy of drinks and clapped on the back. Raven looked pale and frightened in the corner. She threw back more of the *pisco* and leaned against her chair, speechless. Over the next few seconds, I realized what had just happened—how close I'd come to being shot in a bar by a crazy person.

"Well done, Doctor Morales." Arturo helped himself to one of my congratulatory drinks. "The evangelicals, they all supported the regime, you see."

"But wasn't the regime officially Catholic?" I asked.

"Everything here is officially Catholic," Arturo said. "Even the communists. But this isn't the fifteenth century anymore. Catholicism has become very flexible. There's a spectrum of religiosity to it."

"Not to mention morality." I finally took one of the offered shots.

"Eddie." Raven put a hand on my other forearm. "Thank you. I mean that."

Her fingers were cold and clammy.

"You're welcome," I said.

"Believe me: we've been lucky so far," Arturo went on. "There's likely to be plenty of violence throughout the small towns and villages in the wake of this revolution. Many people have fought for the regime. Many have suffered at the hands of the rebels as well—especially back before they formed this alliance." He took another sip and grimaced. "This will be worse elsewhere than it is in this town."

"You wouldn't know there was much discord, looking around here." I gestured around the crowded bar, where everyone still seemed to be toasting the impending revolution, discussing the positions they might be offered in a new administration, the public works that were long overdue.

"This may be a representative of the majority, in this village at least. But there are other rooms—perhaps less public than this one—where they are cursing FURP, and planning its demise."

"Eddie." Raven leaned toward me. "Maybe we should think about going back to the house. It's getting late."

"That sounds like a good idea." I figured there'd only be more drunks and more crazy preachers as the night wore on. I grabbed my water jar, and we headed out.

Arturo insisted on accompanying us back to the Morales compound. After the events of the past few hours, it was hard to say no.

Fortunately, the walk home was cold but otherwise uneventful. We bundled up in the coats we'd barely needed until now. At the doorstep, Arturo knocked gently. Don Pablo opened up. Arturo said goodbye. Don Pablo showed us to the little casita they'd prepared out back.

The effects of the booze and of the adrenalin finally seemed to be canceling each other out. I started to feel like I could, in fact, get a good night's sleep.

"I'm sorry we don't have a finer room to offer you." Don Pablo opened the door to the outbuilding. "But you'll be safe here, and warm." When we looked inside and saw the two twin beds, I let out an audible sigh of relief.

"This will do just fine," I assured him.

Raven said, "*Gracias.*"

"Consider this your home," Don Pablo said. "Have a good night."

Once he'd closed the door, I put my jar on the table and sat on the longer of the two beds. "Do you mind if I take this one? I'm not sure I would fit in the other one. It's probably best if we skip the teeth-brushing and whatnot. Wouldn't want to wake the children."

"Eddie." Raven sat down beside me, put a hand on my knee. "Thank you for what you did in the bar tonight." Her eyes were so big and ghostly, it was as if a gun was still pointed at her. "No one's ever done anything like that for me."

"You're welcome. Honestly, I didn't even think about it. It just happened. I'm not sure what came over me."

She kept the hand on my knee and leaned a little closer. "Courage. That's what came over you."

"I suppose so," I said.

"And it didn't appear out of nowhere. It was inside you all along." She closed the distance between our two faces and kissed me.

At first, I figured it was just a quick peck of thanks, but soon, the kiss became much more. Raven's mouth was moist and warm, alternately hard and soft, smashing up against mine at all angles. I hesitated at first, thinking this an error of some kind, that she must've mistaken me for somebody else. A series of images flashed through my mind, like a sort of mental checklist: Jill's face, my condo in Boise, then that greenhouse of the Vice Minister's with those glowing potatoes.

And in the next second, I realized that there was no error. It was everything else—the ambitions and the rigid expectations—that had been flawed. Just because I hadn't seen this coming, just because it wasn't part of some silly life plan, that didn't mean it was a bad thing. Just the opposite, in fact. So I committed to the kiss, pushed back against Raven's tongue with my own. My arm around her back, I turned her toward the bed and gained the high ground. Perhaps it wasn't courage that had caused me to step between Raven and the preacher; perhaps it was something more like affection. Her hand ran up and down my back, reached up under my shirt. I put my feet on the floor; and before I'd fully stood up, Raven had started to undo my fly.

"Wait!" I said.

"What?" she asked. "Too fast?"

"No, it's not that. This stupid belt." I gingerly unbuckled it. "I don't want to set off the panic button."

Raven undid her top. "What happens if it goes off?"

"Who knows?" I carefully laid the belt on the other bed. "It sends out a homing beacon, calls the police or something."

She chuckled. "I'd rather *they* not show up right now."

"The thing probably doesn't even work. Doesn't hold pants up, that's for sure." I yanked my shirt off over my head.

In another second, we'd pulled off our clothes and thrown them about the room. Soon we were making love on the longer of the two little beds. Raven was no Mormon or jack-Mormon, that was for sure. We screwed like it was our very last night on earth, like bombs and bullets were whizzing by us on all sides. We fucked like the food-obsessed four-limbed creatures that we were.

———

Once it was over, the two of us lay entangled upon a mattress that wasn't even big enough for one of us alone. For the first time since I'd arrived in this country, I felt like I was doing exactly the right thing.

"Raven," I said. "There's something I have to tell you."

"What's that?"

"I was partly responsible for Kearns getting hauled off to prison."

"What?" She lifted her head up and turned to me. "You? How?"

I sighed. "The Vice Minister, he asked about my progress. I mentioned that Kearns was causing me problems with his stupid online videos. Next thing I know, you see him get snatched up. I was ashamed, so I didn't mention it."

"Wow."

"I know. I'm sorry I didn't say anything sooner."

"Why are you telling me now?"

I shook my head. "I don't know. It feels right. You mentioned my courage, but frankly I've been feeling more like a coward lately."

She nodded. "Do you think he's all right?"

"Kearns? Oh, totally. I bet he wasn't in there for an hour. With his wealth and his connections, I'm sure the regime wouldn't want anything to do with him."

"You're probably right," she admitted.

"Trust me," I said, "that guy always lands on his feet. Right now, I'm more concerned about the way I kept it from you. Do you forgive me?"

She nodded. "I forgive you. Now let's try to get some sleep."

Our heavy breathing abated, and the night air sent a chill across my skin. I reached down to the foot of the bed and covered us in blankets as best I could.

"Good night, Eddie."

"Good night, Raven."

woke around sunrise, to roosters crowing but thankfully no car alarms. Raven snored softly at my side. One of my arms was asleep underneath her head. I tried to free it without waking her, but she stirred.

"Eddie?" she said. "Are you getting up?"

"No," I whispered. "Just getting comfortable." I kissed her on the forehead.

"Mmm." She smiled, pulled the blankets more tightly around us. I couldn't help but smile myself. "Can I ask you something?" she whispered.

"Sure." I lay on my back and felt the blood rush back into my numb arm.

"About the Irish Potato Famine."

I laughed out loud. "That's what you're thinking about right now?"

She grinned, eyes still closed. "How did they stop it, the scientists?"

"Actually, they came here, to the Andes, and found a potato that was resistant to the blight: the Garnet Chile. It was this region's biodiversity that ended it."

"Really?" she said. "So, if they plant all Tuberware potatoes around here, we'll be screwed during the next big potato famine."

"Well, technically the Tuberware potatoes are already resistant to that alga."

"What about some other alga we've never seen before?" she mumbled. "Something totally different, the way the blight was?"

"Let's hope it never comes to that." I moved my fingers, felt the tingling of the returning sensation.

"Let's hope," she said. "Soon, there may not be a great big gene pool to come back and borrow from."

"Wait." My eyes opened wide, my mind now spinning. "Say that again."

"What? Nothing. It's just: if there were only one potato, then there would be way fewer genes, and way more problems, right? Or at least fewer places to find solutions."

"I need to get up." I popped out of bed and started gathering my clothes from where they lay throughout the room.

"You okay, Eddie?"

"Yes. You stay in bed as long as you want. Something just occurred to me, regarding the kids. I have to check it out."

—

I shut the door behind me. Outside the casita, the chill of the high-altitude air came as a shock. I tucked my hands deep into my pockets and headed for the main house.

"*Buenos días*," Pablito called to me from the floor of the courtyard, where he sat cracking eggs into a bowl.

"Morning, Pablito." I squinted in the early morning sunlight and caught a whiff of fresh coffee.

Across the courtyard, the baby and mother llama stood silent, necks extended and nostrils flaring, as if they were sniffing the wind.

Thick black smoke churned out from the adobe kitchen. Niña Rosa emerged with a rag in her hands. "Morning, Doctor. I hope you like coffee."

"More than anything," I said. "Is Don Pablo up?"

"Inside," she nodded. "I have some beans from my sister's parcel. The girls are grinding the first batch already."

"Excellent." I smiled. Whatever else this revolution had in store, at least I'd get a good breakfast out of it.

I asked to use the latrine; by the time I returned, the coffee was ready. Niña Rosa served it inside the house. My first cup was nutty and delicious. Seated in one of the plastic chairs, I drank half of it in a second.

"Morning, Doctor Morales." Don Pablo showed up and poured himself a cup. "Did you enjoy last night?"

I nearly choked on my next sip, but then I realized that he meant the cantina, not the sex. "Mostly, yes. It was interesting to hear everyone's thoughts on FURP and their progress. There was one incident, though, with the evangelical preacher. That was . . . unpleasant."

"That man." Don Pablo shook his head. "He has a talent for unpleasantness."

"So it seems."

"And the *señorita*?"

"Still asleep." I tilted my head toward our casita. "Don Pablo, I have something to ask you: Do you think I could look at any available birth documents for the children? I'd like to see how they line up with environmental records. Perhaps there was something going on with the mining or the crop eradication while they were in the womb." It was a white lie but justified.

He nodded slowly, considering an answer. "Okay, Doctor." He stood and went to a small shelf on the other side of the room. It held a couple of framed photos, an old soccer trophy, and a plastic statue of the Virgin Mary. From below that, he removed a large photo-album-type book and blew a cloud of dust off its top.

"Their mother puts that sort of information in here." He handed it to me. "She's very good with old papers and things."

I set the book on my lap and opened it up. Right away, I could see what he meant. Plenty of documents were tucked inside. Not just birth and marriage certificates, but land deeds and wills as well. The papers weren't showing me what I hoped, however, so I turned to the family photos. I looked over the pictures from Pablo and Rosa's wedding: everyone somber in the Catholic church, other couples lined up behind them, as if they were all being married on the same day.

I noticed a tall silver-haired man in the back of the wedding pictures.

He stood regally above everyone else, with his thick frost of hair, caramel skin, and an old scar below his eye. He was in the photo on their mantelpiece as well.

"Who is this man?" I asked Don Pablo.

"Grandfather," he said. "Don Serafín."

I kept flipping pages and saw other shots of him at the wedding. He was in several without Pablo. I spotted a younger version of Arturo, with long, shaggy hair.

"Is this Arturo?" I asked.

"Yes." Don Pablo laughed out loud. "Looks like a child, no?" In the photo, he too was with the bride and her mother, no groom.

"Is Arturo your cousin or your wife's?" I asked.

"Well. . . ." Don Pablo bounced his head from side to side. "Both, I suppose. It's a small town."

"Right." I forced a smile. Some unidentified organ dropped several inches lower inside my chest.

"And Don Serafín?" I tried my best to make no judgment. "Is he a grandfather to both you and your wife?"

Don Pablo exhaled. "Only technically. My wife's father, you see, was a bastard—not accepted by his birth parents, raised by a family in another village. It's not as if my father-in-law was ever part of the family. It wasn't even discussed openly until after Serafín's death. That was the first I heard about it."

I nodded slowly, drawing out the family tree in my mind. "But . . . your mother-in-law . . . she isn't?" I pointed to a photo of Rosa's mother with the bridal party and immediately saw a resemblance to Pablo's side.

"Well, yes. She's my father's sister. That's not so strange, is it?"

My jaw hung slack. "It wouldn't be but for the fact that they were already half-siblings, whether they knew it or not." I shut the book and leaned in toward him. "Don Pablo, you and your wife are technically double first cousins."

He wrinkled his brows. "Marriages between cousins aren't so uncommon. Not around here. Besides, the kings and queens of Europe do that all the time."

"I realize that. But this is different than normal cousins. You and your wife share something like twenty-five percent of the same DNA." There was that small gene pool—the thing that Raven feared might produce future famines.

"And that's bad?" he asked.

The sound of chopping came from the kitchen. How had I not considered this before? It was perhaps the oldest and most reliable way to increase the expression of deleterious genes: inbreeding.

"Don Pablo, might I ask: Did you two have any children that didn't survive?" I couldn't remember the Spanish word for miscarriage.

He blinked twice, his eyes suddenly full of tears. "Oh, yes." He wiped at his face with his shirtsleeve. "Several. It's something I'd never wish on any parent. That's why we felt doubly blessed to have the little *baroncito*." He tilted his head in Pablito's direction. "He and his sisters are a gift from God in our eyes, no matter what."

"Of course." At that moment, my insides were seized by a mix of emotions. I'd essentially solved this case, found the origin of the children's condition: a birth defect due to inbreeding. Something even a dilettante could understand. Had I thought of this on my first day in the country, I might've closed this matter up in the tidy fashion I'd hoped for. I could've been back in Boise the next day, with Jill and my fry machine—and perhaps even a promotion.

Now, everything was more complex. I felt horrible for Don Pablo. This was already a huge burden for him. And now all I could offer was more blame? And dash his hopes for a cure?

As a scientist, I understood that most of our ideas regarding cousin marriages were simply cultural taboos. Darwin married his cousin, for crying out loud. As had Einstein and all the European royal families.

However, if this was a double-first-cousin situation, then the coefficient of relationship and the likelihood of genetic effects were exponentially greater.

As much as I wanted to shake Raven awake and tell her, or to get a call in to One Potato Way, I couldn't handle the thought of being insensitive to this poor man.

Niña Rosa came in and refilled our coffees. "Who has hunger?" she asked.

"I'm getting there," I admitted.

She nodded and left the room.

"Don Pablo," I leaned toward him and used my gentlest voice. "I have to tell you: the close genetic relationship between you and your wife, this is the source of your children's problem. Inbreeding. . . ." I swallowed, wishing there was a more delicate word. "It increases the likelihood that a deleterious or a recessive gene—a mutation from the past, for example—will be expressed."

He stared into his coffee cup and nodded.

"The good news is that it might put the media circus to rest."

"It's unlikely to be treated, then, is that correct?"

I shrugged. "It isn't really an illness. I still think that some neuroscientists might be interested in taking a closer look, in order to understand what parts of the brain are responsible for what. It's possible that they might stumble upon some solutions."

"I see." He nodded stoically. "Then this is indeed our lot in life. What God wants."

I took a gulp of coffee. A cavern in my stomach opened up. I was suddenly ravenously hungry. "I don't think God would object to your consulting more experts, gathering as much information as possible."

"So be it," he said.

And there it was, I thought to myself. The case of the dog-gene potatoes was closed—without a single drop of the satisfaction I'd hoped for.

Nothing more to do now but eat breakfast, wake Raven up, and have Oscar take us to the airport before the fighting got any worse.

I decided to change the subject. "By the way, is there any news on the revolution?"

"Oh, yes." He stood and walked over to the television. "The regime has regained the upper hand."

"Really?"

He turned the TV on. Once again, there were shots of the streets, but now they were quiet. The camera took special interest in discarded red FURP bandannas strewn about the pavement.

"Indeed," Don Pablo explained. "The military was relentless during the night. They sent the rebels running."

"Is this a good thing, or a bad thing?" I asked him.

He shrugged.

A hard knock sounded at the door.

"Don Pablo!" came a voice through the wood.

I figured it was Oscar and felt bad for not inviting him inside.

"Please open up at once!" It definitely wasn't Oscar.

Pablo went to answer. "Who is it?"

I stood up from the table and followed a few steps behind. Rosa came in from the kitchen.

Pablo swung the door open. Standing there in the threshold were three policemen, wearing the same riot gear as the ones who'd harassed Arturo days earlier, each of them carrying an assault rifle.

The children gasped. Niña Rosa crossed herself. Pablo did his best to ask them what they were doing in his home, but they weren't listening. One of the armed men took a step inside.

"*Perdón.*" Pablo touched him gently on the shoulder and suddenly found himself on the business end of the rifle.

Some hushed shouting went back and forth between the guerillas. The barrels of their weapons circled the room. Two of the officers fanned out through the house; the third stayed in the living room. The little girls screamed in their bedroom—awakened by the terrifying sight of strangers sticking guns in their faces. The cops moved on to the courtyard. The two girls crawled in and hugged their father.

"It's okay; it's okay. Calm down, everyone," I said. Then, to Don Pablo: "They must know about a meeting I had with the FURP leader. We'll sort it out. I'll be fine."

"Get your damn hands off me!" Raven was dragged in from the yard, wearing only the sheet off our bed. The two cops pulled her forward by the upper arms.

"Raven!" I cried. "Leave her alone!"

Don Pablo stood in the middle of the room, his wife and three children gathered behind him.

"I'll go with them," I said. "It's only me they want."

One of the policemen produced a pair of handcuffs and dangled them from his fingers.

"*Tranquilo*. I'm going with you." I held my wrists together, out toward him. "I won't be any trouble."

"We don't care about you, asshole." The one with the handcuffs ignored my bared wrists. "We're here for the girl."

He walked right past me and over to Raven, who hastily tried to tuck herself into that bedsheet as best she could. Once the head officer reached her, he seized her wrist, cuffed it, then went after the second one as she thrashed in his grip.

"But that makes no sense," I said, bewildered. "She didn't do anything."

One of the other men stepped in front of me and put his open palm to my chest. The third went to help the first guy with Raven. She was in tears by the time they had her fully cuffed. I thought of the night before in the cantina, how she'd thought me so brave for staring down one crazy preacher with a rusty revolver. Before three men with assault rifles, I was now paralyzed. The size and shape of my courage had been well mapped in the past twelve hours, and it wasn't as vast as I'd hoped.

"Help me, Eddie!" Raven shouted as they led her out the door. One of her breasts broke free from the makeshift toga and she looked momentarily like that Roman figure that represents peace . . . or was it tyranny?

"I'll sort this out, Raven. I promise." I followed them to an unmarked black car and demanded that the soldiers tell me her crime.

They ignored me and shoved her into the back.

Again, I insisted that they tell me why she was being taken. She'd done nothing, was no fighter, wasn't even from here.

Just before he climbed into the driver's seat, the leader turned to me. "Her crime? I have it somewhere around here." He reached into his back pocket and pulled out a piece of paper. "She is wanted for libelous and slanderous comments against the government and its heroic leaders." He stopped and looked up at me with a grin. I couldn't tell if he was impressed by the grandeur of the charge, or simply pleased by his own verbosity.

"That can't be right."

"She's a journalist, is she not? It sounds right to me."

"She's not really a journalist; she's just a blogger."

He shrugged. "Perhaps she's a good one." With that, he climbed inside the car and drove off.

"Oscar!" I screamed and walked toward our own vehicle. "Oscar!" I shouted again.

He poked his head up above the window on the driver's side. "You all right, boss? I saw them arrive and kept low. Shall I drive you to the airport? There's a roundabout way."

"We're not going to the fucking airport." I pointed up the road. "Follow that car."

"The police car?" he asked, incredulous.

"Of course. They have Raven."

Oscar gulped, swallowing the fact that I meant business, that I wouldn't take no for an answer. Then, finally, he said "*Vamos.*"

I said a quick goodbye to the family.

"Be careful, Doctor Morales!" Pablo insisted. "These men are dangerous."

Rosa continued to guard her children, her arms spread wide as if to protect them from shrapnel.

"I have to get her back," I said.

Oscar set off at a high speed, not slowing through town, and soon got us within eyeshot of the car. I took my stupid belt off and squeezed away at the panic button, squashing it between my thumb and forefinger like a rosary bead. The word SENDING flashed on the tiny digital readout, but nothing else happened.

"Don't follow too close," I said.

"*Claro.*" Oscar hung back and let them cross the horizon line.

We continued at a safe distance as we went past the mine, and then a few small towns on the outskirts of the capital. On the street, people glared at the police vehicle. Though it was unmarked, they seemed to know exactly what sort of errand that black sedan was used for.

———

In the labyrinthine downtown of the capital, the police car got away from us. Oscar sped up, made a series of purposeful rights and lefts, but after a while we could both see that it was pointless.

"I think they lost us, boss," he admitted. "But it seems to me that they were headed for the government buildings. We could try the Ministry of Interior. Perhaps they'd let you in."

"That's worth a shot." I wasn't exactly sure what I'd do at the entrance. Perhaps Alejandro would be around and might recognize me.

Oscar slowly wove his way between the government buildings until we reached the ugly pink monstrosity. At one corner of the Ministry proper, he pointed to a utility entrance. "You see that, boss?"

There, behind an iron gate, was the black car that had abducted

Raven. The back door was open, and the bedsheet that we'd shared the night before was draped from the seat down to the pavement. It was all I could do to keep from breaking down in tears.

"That's it," I said. "I'm going in to get her."

Oscar came to a stop. "Good luck."

I nodded, checked my teeth in the side-view mirror, and climbed out. Crossing the plaza, I straightened the sleeves of my lab coat and practiced what I would say to the guards: "Good morning. My name is Doctor Eduardo Morales, from America. I'd like an audience with the Vice Minister right away. He knows who I am. If he's not available, then his assistant Alejandro will have to do. No, it cannot wait."

I'd covered about half the distance between the truck and the uniformed guards. A bead of sweat started down my forehead; I wiped it away and practiced my speech again: "Good morning, my name is. . . ."

The first sound was a single pop. It was so loud that I jumped to one side. I looked around the plaza, hoping to find a car backfiring. A series of similar pops followed; one of the two palace guards fell to his knees.

"Jesus!" I shouted.

Across the plaza, a handful of armed men scurried toward the gate. They wore ragged fatigues and carried mismatched rifles. All wore the familiar red bandannas over their faces.

The other palace guard finally freed his weapon. With a deafening series of *rat-a-tat-tats*, he let go a spray of bullets.

Screams came from bystanders. Car alarms went off. A horn beeped incessantly from behind, and I made out Oscar's voice. "Boss! Over here, boss!"

I turned back toward the pickup, where my passenger door was already open. As I ran for it, another half-dozen guerillas came from the opposite direction. One of them stopped and set fire to a Molotov cocktail, then hurled it over the iron gate of the Ministry.

Oscar continued to scream for me.

I reached the truck, dove in next to Oscar, and slammed the door shut. "*Vamos!*"

He popped the clutch and punched the gas. We jerked our way down the street.

"What happened?" I kept my head as low as I could.

"Looks like the *Frente* isn't finished with their offensive quite yet."

"What about Raven?" I asked.

Oscar shrugged. "Hard to say, boss."

Now that we heard no more bullets, I summoned the courage to turn around and have a look at the Ministry of Interior.

"You have any more ideas?"

"No," I admitted, feeling powerless and stupid, like I might get somebody else in trouble if I weren't more careful. "I need to regroup." I stared out the window at all the people on the street—the bystanders checking out the gunfire. Many had FURP scarves at the ready, but few were waving them around. I wish I'd learned to be half as wily as they were.

Suddenly, the smartphone that had barely gotten a signal during this entire trip started to ring. I picked it up.

"Hello?" I said.

"Eduardo! Is that you?"

"'Eddie' is fine. Wait! Warren? I mean, Mister Shepherd?"

"We just got the beacon from your belt."

"That thing actually worked?"

"Listen up, Morales: Potato One will fly through the night and land in Puerto Malogrado first thing in the morning. You'll be back in Boise by tomorrow afternoon. The wheels are coming off that country. I'm pulling the plug on this whole mess."

"I can't go, sir."

"Excuse me?"

"Not now. They've got Raven."

"Raven? Did you adopt a pet down there or something?"

"No, sir. Raven's the reporter you sent along with me. She's been abducted by the regime, and now they're under siege by the guerillas. Sir, I understand that you—or your people—probably chose her for her incompetence. But she's actually proven quite skilled at spreading the word about what's going on down here. Too good, perhaps."

"So what the hell are you going to do about it? Did you turn into some sort of commando all of a sudden?"

"I've got to do *something,* sir. I had several meetings with the Ministry of Interior. That might make me an asset, help me get my foot in the door. I always told the truth to the Vice Minister—about the children, about our prototypes. I must have some kind of credibility." And if the government should fall to FURP, then I secretly hoped they'd free all the prisoners—on the old "the enemy of my enemy is my friend" principle.

"Eduardo, have you lost your damn mind? You really think these guys care about your credibility?"

"I have to do something, sir."

"Just come home. Stay out of trouble. She's a faux journalist; that'll cause a small outcry in the media. Maybe it will merit some back-channel diplomacy. That's more than you'll be able to do on your own."

It was, I realized, almost exactly the same advice I'd given Raven after Kearns was abducted.

There was some jostling around on his end. I heard a woman's voice: "Let me talk to him." Then a thump and a crackle.

"Eddie, is that you?"

"Jill?"

"Eddie, I have something to tell you. Something that you don't want to hear."

"What are you doing there . . . with Warren?"

"You know how you just described that woman, the journalist?" She said the last word sarcastically. "How she was sent along with you because of her incompetence?"

I thought about it for a second. "I suppose I did say that. But she's actually been a great journalist. She broke this story wide open, in a sense."

"Well," Jill exhaled. "You weren't wrong. But you see, that assumption could apply more or less to the entire operation, it turns out."

I heard my own breath echo through the earpiece. After a second, I managed to ask: "You mean me?"

"Well, obviously they were wrong about you. And you shouldn't blame Warren for this. Those sorts of decisions are not happening at his level."

"Get to the point, Jill."

"Okay. Yes, you were sent there partly because you were considered expendable."

In the background, I heard a gravelly voice say: "Sweetheart, let me talk to him."

The phone was wrestled around again. Warren's voice came back on. "We knew about this revolution, Eduardo. We were in talks with those FURP guys, had some arrangements. But they've turned out to be about as trustworthy as a damn Indian treaty. The whole thing's gone tits-up now."

"I think I'm going to hang up," I said.

"Now just a moment, son!" Warren swallowed. "It's not as bad as it sounds. It's simply a matter of thinking a few moves ahead. If things went smooth down there, then fine. But if anything unforeseen came up, well, then, we needed somebody we could throw under the bus, somebody we could discredit and then start over. That's where the expendability came in. For God's sake, Eduardo, you're not even a geneticist!"

I pulled the phone away from my ear and pressed the hang-up button.

"Where to now, boss?" Oscar asked.

"I'm not sure," I admitted. Everything in the world seemed to have been taken from me in a matter of the past few hours. "Could you find me a place with a real, uncensored internet connection?"

"Have you got money?" Oscar rubbed his thumb and forefinger together in the international sign for cash.

I put my hand on the too-big belt around my waist and remembered the hundreds hidden there for emergencies. "Yes," I said. "Yes, I do."

Before we arrived at the black-market internet place, I freed one of the Benjamins from inside my belt. Oscar parked and led me up to the door of what looked like a garden-variety internet café: a slim room lined with late-model PCs on old furniture, full of teenagers playing video games.

We approached a man in the back, seated at his own computer. Oscar put a hand to the man's shoulder and whispered into his ear. He said something about money and pointed at me. As discreetly as I could, I flashed the C-note from the bottom of my hand. The man rose and led me through a locked door to another room in the back, this one with only two computers.

"Here you go." The clerk gestured toward one of the machines. "No restrictions."

"Thanks." I handed him the bill, sat down, and opened a browser.

The second I was online, the screen was bombarded by pop-up ads.

"Hey!" I stopped the clerk on his way out of the room. "What's all this?"

He shrugged. "One of the prices of freedom."

He had a point. Soon, I'd carved enough space from the porn sites and prescription medication ads to find what I was after. Raven had posted several articles, at least two of which had been picked up by other news outlets. One of them was very critical of the regime. She'd managed to get some strong quotes from sources—none of whom would give their full names—about the Ministry's crop-eradication program, as well as their heavy-handed military actions in the small towns where FURP was rumored to be active.

I couldn't understand how Raven had found the time to do all this. I'd only let her out of my sight for a day or two. It looked as though her initial article—about the Morales kids and Tuberware's hybrid prototypes—had gone viral as well.

I made an online alias and left comments on all her pieces, both on her blog and on the websites that reposted and quoted her work. My comments explained that she'd been picked up by the police and imprisoned by the government. It seemed a somewhat futile gesture, but I wasn't sure what else to do. Hopefully, if FURP won this battle, they'd see her as a political prisoner and let her go. If the regime held on, then maybe they'd consider her too much of a liability to keep locked up.

I started to rise from my chair but then had one more thought: what about the other cases of hand-walkers, similar to the Morales children? This might be my only chance to research them without restriction. A quick search produced the family with the same affliction from rural Turkey. I found the names of the scientists who studied them and published on the topic. The lead geneticist was a British researcher; his email address was available at his university's website. I sent a brief message about the situation, omitting only the inbreeding. I left every bit of contact information I could think of, including the phone number at La Posada, and begged him to get in touch with me.

After that, I nearly stood up and went on my way. But a small, morbid curiosity had festered inside me for several days, and this was my first chance to indulge it. I took a deep breath, typed the names of my boss and of Spencer Kearns's father into the same search pane, and hit enter.

Right away, I saw an image of the two men together, taken years ago. They were wearing matching blazers with some kind of burgundy seal on the breast. Both smiled widely. I didn't bother reading any of the text.

Feeling defeated, I walked out into the main room of the café.

"Done already, boss?" Oscar asked.

"Yes," I said. "Can you take me to La Posada?"

"Get inside!" Doña Ana pulled us in through the front door as soon as we rang the buzzer.

The lights were turned down low, but the television was on at high volume.

"They've done it." She pointed toward the screen. "They've finally done it!"

Oscar and I came all the way in and stood in front of the television. The Vice Minister of Interior was standing at his normal lectern. All the medals and decorations had been ripped from his uniform, leaving torn holes across its chest area. A lone epaulet dangled sadly from one shoulder. One of his eyes was blackened. His lower lip was split. The toupee I hadn't realized he wore was now missing. Two FURP members—still in their red handkerchiefs—stood at either side of him. His hands looked to be bound behind his back.

In a trembling, pathetic voice, the Vice Minister read a statement. His eyes squinted, as though struggling to read the words off a teleprompter. "I hereby acknowledge that my oppressive army has been soundly defeated by the glorious miracle of the people's permanent revolution, and that no longer will the citizens of Puerto Malogrado needlessly suffer from this corrupt and petty regime." He swallowed. "I retract all the lies I've told from this very spot and hereby ask for mercy from FURP and their brave leaders."

"Again!" shouted a voice from off camera.

"Again?" The Vice Minister's face contorted as though weeping. "Can't you just replay it?"

A figure in green stepped into the picture and brained him, but obviously not *too* hard, with a rifle butt to the back of the head. The Vice Minister groaned and then resumed reading.

"*Dios mio!*" Oscar said.

"Tell me about it." I turned to him. "I met with that guy two days ago; he didn't seem worried then."

"Thank goodness you weren't with him when the rebels showed up," Doña Ana said. She turned off the television and crossed herself.

"When did this happen?" I asked.

"Very recently," Doña Ana went on. "In this morning's paper, they were still talking about you and your hand-walkers." She took out a copy of the underground newspaper. There, on the cover, was a photo of the Morales children on their way back from the *brujo's*—bandages full of herbs at each of their ankles. I could see a part of my elbow as I rushed in to cover up the lens.

With the television off, the clicks from the old lady's walker against the tile floor rang out from a back room.

"I'm confused." I looked back and forth between Oscar and Doña Ana. "Is this a good thing, or a bad thing?"

Oscar raised one hand, palm down, and tilted it back and forth. "It's not so simple. The Vice Minister's regime was corrupt; there's no doubt about that. But installing a new government can be a messy process. It's not like just flipping a switch."

"And now?" Doña Ana wrung one hand within another. "With my mother not well, I can't handle much more fighting. *Ojalá* these FURP guys know what they're doing."

It was an interesting moment for me: to see how much these citizens favored stability over ideology. But I had another aspect on my mind. "Oscar, can you take me back to the Ministry? With FURP in power, I could get them to release Raven. She was imprisoned by their enemies; surely the new guys will let her out."

"Not tonight!" Doña Ana was adamant. "It's not safe. Listen."

In the distance, several shots went off, followed by whoops and hollers.

"More fighting?" I asked.

"It's probably just celebration. But still," Oscar said. "It's best if we wait until morning. The first night of a revolution, there's always a lot of drinking and stray bullets. We'll go early tomorrow, while the young men are sleeping it off."

"Is Raven going to be okay?"

Oscar shrugged. "She's locked up, no? At least she won't get caught in the crossfire."

———

Oscar went home to his family. Doña Ana was visibly upset. She offered me dinner, but I couldn't summon an appetite. Instead, I went to my room and lay in bed. Outside, more gunshots, as well as breaking glass, screams and shouts, barking dogs. I couldn't stop thinking about Raven, imagining her in some cell while her captors were overthrown, surrounded by teenagers with guns, all the while begging for clothes. It made sense to wait until morning, but it didn't feel right. Not even twenty-four hours ago, things were finally starting to make sense. Now, it was more chaotic than ever.

The next morning was, oddly, the quietest I'd yet experienced in this city. Perhaps the revolution had exhausted itself the night before. I rose and showered at first light. Oscar waited for me in the kitchen, sipping a coffee that Doña Ana had made for him.

"Are you ready, boss?"

I shrugged. "As ready as I'm ever going to be."

———

"If it's all the same to you," Oscar said as we approached the Ministry, "I'd rather just drop you off out front. It's not a place where I want to sit around waiting and watching, in days like these."

"That's no problem, Oscar. I understand."

He let me off in the plaza where we'd witnessed the fighting just yesterday. On the far side, two young members of FURP—with their fatigues and their red bandannas—were trying to lower the previous regime's flag from a tall pole. They had a red one in their hands that they were clearly hoping to raise, but they couldn't seem to get the old one to descend. Frustrated, one of them tried to push the other out of the way and have a go at the chains. The first one shoved back. Their FURP flag fell to the pavement, and a scuffle ensued.

Many other guerillas, in ragtag versions of uniforms, were simply hanging around: playing cards, drinking Cokes from plastic bags, showing their weapons off to one another. A slightly more organized bunch guarded the front gate.

"Excuse me?" I approached the most responsible-looking of them. "I have some important information regarding a prisoner who was brought in here by the old regime."

"Get lost." The guard pulled a small apple from his pocket and took a bite. He had to lower the bandanna from around his mouth to get his teeth into it.

"She's a journalist. An American. Locked up by the old regime. Don't you think that's something your bosses might be interested in?"

He shrugged. "What about me?" He wasn't shy about showing the half-chewed fruit in his mouth. "Have you got anything *I* might be interested in?"

I nodded, then turned around so that my back was to him, and fished another of those hundred-dollar bills from my oversized belt.

"Would this interest you?" I spun on my heel and showed him the money. He stood up at once and looked from side to side, as if checking to make sure none of his comrades had noticed the cash.

He wrapped his fist around the bill and said, "Let's go."

I followed him inside, where the entire building had turned into a sort of clubhouse. Bottles and cans were all over the place. Sleeping guerillas were wrapped up in blankets in the corners. The antique furniture had been ransacked: lamps lying on their sides, drawers upturned and left on the floor. Little white piles of cocaine spotted several of the polished wood surfaces. Cigarette butts lay everywhere.

"Doctor Morales!" A voice called out to me from down the hall. "What a surprise."

My jaw dropped as I made out the speaker: Alejandro, the Vice Minister's sharply dressed aide.

"He's got a question about an American reporter," my young guide explained. "Can you deal with him?"

"Of course." Alejandro shook my hand. "So nice to see you again, Doctor."

"What are you doing here?" I asked. "Didn't you get . . . ousted?"

"I saw the way the wind was blowing and positioned myself for a lateral move."

"You're with FURP now? How'd you pull that off?"

Alejandro grinned. "I have an indispensable skill set."

"Which is what?" I asked.

"Communications, mostly. Let's talk to my new superior, shall we?" Alejandro led me up a flight of stairs. "*Maciso!*" He knocked on a door that was ajar. "Doctor Morales would like to speak with you."

I didn't notice it at first, but I'd been led to the same room where I'd first met with the Vice Minister. The horse paintings had all been vandalized, given Pegasus wings, unicorn horns, explosive fart clouds, and gigantic penises dripping with ejaculate.

New things had been added to the walls: the FURP flag, a poster of Che Guevara, another high-contrast portrait labeled as Karl Marx but which I believed was actually Jerry Garcia.

Behind the desk, I immediately recognized the middle-aged man in fatigues and military cap. We'd shared a conversation in the back of a car, several days earlier. In this light, I could more clearly see his forward-slumping posture, the deep, round bags under his eyes, and the salt-and-pepper beard. His skin was scarred and wrinkled, as though he had indeed spent many years in the mountains, fighting against the forces of an oppressive government.

An unruly stack of maps and documents occupied the desk in front of him. In a fancy glass ashtray, the last half of a loosely wrapped cigar emitted a thin ribbon of blue smoke. The nameplate on the desk was covered by a piece of notebook paper that read "Subcomandante Fernandez."

A couple of other men stood at the walls behind his chair.

"Doctor Morales," the Subcomandante said. "So nice to see you again."

"Pleasure's all mine, sir," I said. "And congratulations on your victory."

He nodded, looking more exhausted than victorious. "What can I do for you?"

"I'm a friend of the journalist—the American woman—who was brought here yesterday, by the old regime. I'd like to take her with me, if that's okay."

"Is that right?" The Subcomandante stared at me without blinking, as if considering my person more so than my request.

"Well, yes." I cleared my throat. "I'm sure you're aware that her fellow journalists and the human-rights organizations will make a big deal out of a detained reporter. It's very bad press, for a new government."

Alejandro dashed over and whispered into the Subcomandante's ear.

The Subcomandante's eyebrows rose.

Alejandro dashed away again.

"Those children, in the campo, they excited the populace, did they not?" the Subcomandante asked.

"For better or for worse," I admitted.

"Here's what I'd like from you."

Alejandro came over again, did a bit more whispering, then backed off.

"A scientific statement detailing how this hand-walking thing was the result of unsanctioned experiments by the old regime, in collusion with large American corporations."

"But that's not true," I said.

He shrugged. "It happened on their watch, did it not? Surely they bear some responsibility? Are we going to split rabbits?"

"It's hairs." I said the last word in English. "Not rabbits."

"Whatever. It's a small thing that we ask of you. Then you can take your wife and go on your way."

"She's not my—" I started to say.

"Alejandro here will give you the details. We'll call the media together tomorrow at noon."

"Tomorrow?" I asked. "You want me to address the media tomorrow?"

The Subcomandante looked at his watch. "Could be a long night for you, eh? Don't worry, *colega*. Here, in the city, we have electric lights. One can work all night without a problem."

"I hadn't thought of it that way," I admitted.

Alejandro approached me. "If you'll follow me, Doctor."

"Wait one second. If I'm doing this speech—a speech that will likely ruin my career as a scientist—then I want to see her first."

"The journalist?" the Subcomandante asked. "Sure. Why not?" He nodded to Alejandro. "We're not like the old regime, Doctor. We're not heartless."

I stared into his eyes but couldn't quite judge his level of sincerity.

"One more thing, Doctor."

"Yes?" I replied meekly.

"You're a plant scientist, correct? There's one crop we'd be very interested in improving the yield of."

"What? Coca?" I asked.

He leaned back in his chair. "All the labor necessary, it creates too many security risks. Do you have any ideas? Some sort of genetic alteration, perhaps?"

"Sorry." I shrugged. "I only do potatoes."

"That's a shame," the Subcomandante said. "There's no money in potatoes."

"I'll mention that to my employer," I said. "But seriously: do you think it's a wise move, this alliance with the drug traffickers?"

He sighed. "That's a matter of the enemy of my enemy being my friend. And also an economic necessity."

"You don't feel that it compromises your cause—in the eyes of the international community?"

"Perhaps," he admitted. "But at the moment I'm more concerned about local eyes. Trust me: our handling of the narcotics issue is far more realistic than the old regime's."

I couldn't argue with that.

"Goodbye, Doctor."

Alejandro touched my arm. "Right this way. I can fill you in with all the details."

We left the executive office and headed down the palace halls.

———

"So." Alejandro led me to a staircase. "What we need from you is a sort of science-based appeal to the hearts and minds of this country. There are areas where the Vice Minister still enjoys support. We'd like to extinguish that sympathy as quickly as possible."

"And these sympathizers," I said. "They're willing to take up arms?"

Alejandro shrugged. "That depends on several factors, including the quality of your speech tomorrow."

I laughed out loud. "I'm not that kind of speaker. I'm a scientist. I don't do pathos. And I'm certainly not going to get up there and lie to everyone."

Alejandro stopped walking and turned to me. "Doctor Morales, there are people in the mountains who are dying over this conflict. All you're being asked to do is talk about potatoes for twenty minutes—"

"To lie about potatoes," I interrupted. "That's what you're asking of me, correct?"

He cocked his head to one side. "Is your field really so black and white, Doctor, that you cannot possibly come up with a set of remarks that accomplish our goals without offending your lofty sense of truth? Is there no ambiguity, no gray area there, in which you could work comfortably?" He resumed walking. "If that's the case, I envy your work. I can assure you that my field is rarely so cut-and-dried."

He didn't seem interested in answers to those rhetorical questions. Silently, to myself, I now wondered whether my career had ever been as simple as I'd believed it to be.

Alejandro led me to a small door, which opened on a dark staircase. "Right this way."

We descended into what appeared to be a Spanish-Inquisition–era dungeon underneath this old building: unfinished stone walls, dark and moist, with a stench of mildew. Immediately, I was terrified for Raven. We walked along a low hallway—I had to crouch forward—lit by a series of lone light bulbs hanging from their wires, until we reached a door guarded by a FURP guerilla. She was a thick and intimidating woman, puffs of hair sticking out from under her cap, bluish tattoos on her face, one dim gold tooth.

"What do you want?" she said to Alejandro.

"We're here to see the *gringa*."

The guard squinted her eyes in disbelief.

"The Subcomandante sent us," he insisted. "This man needs to speak with her for a moment, that's all."

There was a pause. The guard took a long breath, then turned around. "Follow me."

She opened up the door behind her and walked through it. I gave Alejandro a curious look. He held a hand out toward the open threshold. I followed the guard in. We walked down a long hallway with bars along one side. Behind them were windowless cells, nothing but canvas cots and cowering prisoners within. I willed my eyes away from them and stared forward.

"*Guapisima!*" the guard called out in a sing-songy voice. "You have a visitor."

"Eddie! Eddie, is that you?"

I saw a flash of ginger hair up in front. "Raven!"

We came to the very last cell in the hall, and the guard took a step back. It looked like a medieval catacomb, with a lone window high along the back wall. A cot and a wooden chair were all the furniture inside. Raven stood and wrapped her hands around the iron bars. Seeing her in such a state was like a punch to the stomach, but I knew I couldn't break down.

"Are you okay?" I put my hands over hers. "Nobody has hurt you or anything?" I wasn't sure what to ask.

"No. I'm fine. Deanna's taken a special interest in me." Raven tilted her head toward the guard. "She was a political prisoner under the old regime, so she takes pride in being fair. The ride in was the worst part. FURP is much better than the cops who grabbed me."

"They got you some clothes, at least?" Raven wore a set of the ragtag fatigues common among the FURP ranks.

"That's right." She chuckled. "It's my paramilitary look." She moved her hands to the top of mine.

"The whole government was overthrown the second you got here. Oscar and I tried to come after you, and we wound up in the middle of a gunfight."

"I know that—now." Raven shook her head. "In a sense, I'm thankful that they managed to lock me up before the shooting started. I might've been caught in the crossfire."

Was I the only person who didn't take any comfort in that fact? "I'm going to get you out of here tomorrow," I said.

"How, Eddie?"

"I've cut a deal with the FURP guys. They want me to give a little talk to the media, about the old regime and whatnot."

"Will it be . . . true?" she asked.

I shrugged. "I haven't written it yet. Is there any chance I could get into your computer, to use some of your photos as slides and whatnot?"

"Sure," she said. "It should be in my bedroom. Just look for the most recent picture files, and you'll find everything."

I nodded. An awkward pause passed between us, a moment of doubt in my plan for her release.

"Are you okay with this?" she asked me.

"You mean okay with telling a lie for the right reasons? Sure. What choice do I have?"

"So," Raven swallowed, "the ends justify the means?"

"That's right," I said. "The starting point of all moral quandaries."

We stopped talking, squeezed each other's hands more tightly through the bars. In that moment, all the ideologies, all the creeds and dogmas that had torn apart all these assorted Americas for so long seemed so utterly ridiculous. Didn't everyone want to be safe and to be free? Was it so impossible to have both at once?

"That's it," Deanna grunted. "Time's up." She tapped my shoulder.

"I'll see you tomorrow, Raven." I walked backward away from the cell.

"Goodbye, Eddie . . ." Something seemed to trip Raven up. "Be careful."

—

I followed Deanna to the end of the hall, where she searched her ring of keys to find one for the heavy final door.

"Eddie?" A weak voice sounded from an adjacent cell. "Eddie, is that you?" it asked in English.

I had to crane my neck a little; the light bulb within was dim and flickering. The face was unrecognizable at first: a scraggly beard, unkempt hair, bloodshot eyes.

"Kearns?"

"You've got to get me out of here!" He stuck his face between the bars.

"What happened to you?" I asked.

"The police. They came for me at my hotel and dragged me off." His breath smelled foul, even from a foot away. That fake accent of his had disappeared. "I've been here for days."

"What?" I was genuinely shocked. "You've been locked up this whole time?"

"No lawyers. No phone calls. Nothing. It's unbelievable!"

"Well." I shrugged. "You were poking a bear. This is an autocracy—or was. They don't play games."

"So what am I supposed to do? Just rot away in here?" His voice rose and hit a whiny note. "They can't treat me like this!"

For the past several days, I'd had a knot in my chest: guilt about the small, unintentional part I'd played in getting Kearns picked up. Now I suddenly lost all sympathy for him. He probably would've been imprisoned by the regime anyway—with or without me. I was surprised it hadn't happened sooner.

"There's been a coup," I explained. "A change of government. Just yesterday. The new guys will probably let you go, once the dust settles."

"I don't even speak the language, Eddie. These people . . . it's like they don't even care who I am. It's not fair."

"Let me ask you something." I took a half step closer to the bars. "You see all of these Puertomalogradeños out here biting their tongues about their government, being cautious about what they say, in front of whom. Do you think they're cowards or something? You think they're just dumber than you? No, they know how to be careful. They know that if they want to speak out against the regime, they'd better be willing to carry a weapon and risk their lives over it. Why should you be immune to all of that? Why should you be able to say whatever you want and get out of jail free? Because of your American passport? Because of your white skin? Your YouTube followers? Your family money?" I shook my head. "You're not in Kansas anymore, Spencer. You're in a repressive third-world dictatorship. You don't get your phone call; you don't get your court-appointed attorney; you don't get the Bill of Rights or anything else. So stop acting so entitled."

"I'm begging you, Eddie! You've got to help me. This isn't fair!"

You'd think this experience might've humbled him. But somehow Kearns's ego had survived his imprisonment fully intact. "Kearns, this conflict's been going on for decades. They're not fighting it for your benefit, so that you can become some famous filmmaker. Or grow your damn platform. It's war; it's never fair." But in another way, his imprisonment seemed to me the most just thing in the world. His chickens had finally come home to roost. I started toward the door.

"I've got leverage over you, Morales. You know that."

"How's that?" I turned back to him.

"That job you love so much? I could end that with one phone call."

"Is that right?"

"You bet it is. And I have information that would ruin you for any other job: academic dishonesty, cheating, falsifying information. I could expose you, end your career—with Tuberware or anybody else."

I took a step closer. Kearns's face was more familiar now. He never looked so much like himself as when defining the difference between his options and mine.

"You know," I said, "you're not making a very good case for me to get you out of here."

"I've been a friend to you so far, Eddie. All our lives I've been your friend—whether you realize it or not. Don't make me into an enemy. Not now."

Suddenly impatient, Deanna swung the door all the way open, so that it banged against the wall. "*Basta!*" she said.

"Sorry, Spencer. I have to go."

O n the way back to La Posada, neither Oscar nor I had much to say. Perhaps he'd expected me to leave the Ministry with Raven; perhaps I'd expected the same thing.

Once at the gate, I finally turned to him and asked, "Will you take me back to the Ministry tomorrow, for this ridiculous speech?"

He nodded slowly. "Of course."

———

Doña Ana let me into Raven's room to get her laptop. I took it back to my own room and plugged it in. From the solarium, I dragged in the little table and chair and set them up. Though she found it an odd request, Doña Ana agreed to brew me a pot of coffee.

All these preparations made, I sat down and set out to produce—for the first time in my life—fake science.

It wasn't as easy as I'd hoped. Every claim had some sort of relationship to another claim. Every made-up fact demanded an air of credibility. Perhaps Kearns could've been helpful for this part, if nothing else. Indeed, I started to feel that this was more like a style of writing or speaking than an actual act of deception: a language I'd never learned.

A knock sounded at my door. "Don Doctor?"

I rose, my eyes struggling to focus once they'd left the computer screen, and swung the door open. "Doña Ana."

"Some dinner for you." She held out a large plate that held unfamiliar food.

"Thank you." The late hour had sneaked up on me. I took the plate from her and brought it close to my face. It appeared to be a large sausage. "What is this?"

"*La Mentira.* It's an old Malogrado recipe."

"*Mentira?*" I asked. It was the Spanish word for "lie."

"Yes," she nodded. "They say it dates back to colonial times. The indigenous people were starving, but the viceroys always demanded meat. The farmers invented this dish to give to their exploiters, told them it was sausage. It's a normal casing, but the filling is potatoes—with spices and bits of organs and entrails for flavor."

"Did the viceroys fall for it?" I asked.

She shrugged. "I suppose some of them did. Others probably just liked the taste. That's the thing about lies: it's not their content, it's how they are delivered."

"That's ingenious," I said. "A revelation."

"Pshh." She waved her hand dismissively. "It's survival, is all. Good night, Doctor." She closed the door and left.

I pushed the computer aside and ate my dinner. It was delicious, starchy and rich like Thanksgiving stuffing. Inventive and obvious all at once, it tasted like the product of a resilient, resourceful people. I would base my speech around this: not so much a falsehood, but a cunning bit of innovation. Not quite what was expected, but palatable to my audience anyway—with little bits of their demands sprinkled throughout, for flavor.

woke to a determined knocking at the door, sunlight already seeping in through the window. I'd fallen asleep in my clothes, curled up around the laptop, my notes and pens scattered across the bed.

"You in there?" Another series of knocks.

I dragged myself off the mattress and answered the door.

"Oscar." I squinted to make out his face. "What are you doing here so early? The speech isn't until this afternoon."

"There's been a change of plans, boss. You're needed elsewhere."

"Can I get dressed?"

He nodded. "Quickly."

I got myself organized as best I could. My only guess was that they wanted me at the Ministry earlier than planned. I put my remarks and the laptop into my briefcase. With no time for a shower, I brushed my teeth and dressed in my cleanest shirt and slacks—as well as the white lab coat.

Doña Ana asked about coffee as we made our way out of the hotel. Oscar assured her there wasn't time.

———

Once again, we made no small talk on the drive. Oscar seemed particularly somber. He was driving the small SUV again; it was comfortable enough for me to nod off during the ride.

"Boss." A light tapping on my knee. "We arrive."

I opened my eyes. We were nowhere near the Ministry. Instead, I stared out at a long stretch of asphalt. The thick layer of clouds gave the feel of a giant ceiling. Soon, it became clear to me that this was the airport we'd flown into, a place I'd not been to since the night of our arrival.

"Oscar," I said, "what are we doing here?"

"This way." Oscar opened the door and climbed out.

Before I could protest, he was out of earshot. I followed him. "Oscar! I don't have time for this."

He pointed to the far end of the sky. I followed his finger with my eyes, then watched as a small plane burst through the cloud layer and began its descent toward the airstrip.

There was something hypnotic about watching a lone aircraft negotiate the sky and the ground like that. For a second I lost myself in the grace of the pilot's work. Only once the wheels squeaked against the tarmac did I turn toward Oscar and say: "That's Potato One."

He nodded and kept watching.

Now fully landed, the plane taxied in our direction. Indeed, it seemed to head right for us—the jets blowing back the tails of my white coat.

It came to a full stop just a few yards from where we stood. The engines shut down, and the door popped open. Its little staircase inched toward the ground.

Much to my surprise, Jill's face was the first to emerge.

"Eddie!" she shouted. As soon as the stairs were deployed, she ran down and wrapped me up in a hug. "Eddie, we've been so worried about you."

Totally perplexed by this entire situation, I stood there in my white coat holding my briefcase, allowing myself to be embraced. Her hand grabbed my shoulder. On her finger was an engagement ring with the biggest diamond I'd ever seen.

"Score!" The next person out of the plane was Mitch, the doughy blond International Strategist who'd filled me full of vaccines back at One Potato Way. "That panic button actually works! You believe that?"

"I thought Potato One couldn't make a trip this far."

Mitch snickered and shook my free hand. "It's a damn jet, dude. It'll go anywhere as long as there's fuel in it."

"So." Jill exhaled. "Let's go. Let's get out of here."

"What?" I turned to her. "I can't go now. They've got Raven."

"Good Christ, Eduardo." A new voice boomed out of the fuselage. "Again with this Raven business." Warren emerged in the threshold of the aircraft door—blue suit in place and silver hair shining. He took the stairs one at a time, holding tight to the railing.

"I'm on my way to get her out," I said. "If you can wait a few hours, I'll come back, and we'll all leave together."

Warren completed his descent. "Listen here, Eduardo." He put a hand on my shoulder. "I realize that this mission didn't quite work out the way you expected. But believe me: there are bigger factors at play. I can't reveal much, but suffice it to say that time is of the essence. If we don't get out now, we may never get out. Between us, air travel to and from this country won't be possible much longer."

"I don't believe you," I said.

"Eddie! Hush!" Jill stage-whispered.

"How's that, Morales?" Warren cocked his head.

"You lied about what I was doing here. You lied about this whole scandal. Why should I trust you now?"

"Eddie!" Jill said again.

"You're right, Morales." Warren nodded thoughtfully. "We haven't been fully forthright with you. I hope you can see—now or in the future— that it was justified. That it wasn't in your best interest to know all the details, that it would've only put you in greater danger."

"What about this?" I pulled a potato out of my pocket: the DS 400 that had sat in my windowsill for days.

"What about it?" Warren asked. "It's a potato."

"It ought to look like *this* by now." I took La Vieja from my other pocket. It was covered in long, serpentine sprouts from each of its many eyes.

"Gross," Mitch said.

Warren grinned and nodded at me.

"Not one sprout, in all the time I've been here," I said.

"Once again, Eduardo, it seems we've underestimated you."

"It isn't about bacterial infection, is it? It's about reproduction."

Warren chuckled. He turned toward the capital city and took in the view. "It's an amazing plant, the potato," he said. "Every day, I'm more impressed by them. Their ability to basically clone themselves—laterally—from a few cuttings . . . that's a greater genetic achievement than anything we'll ever come up with in our fancy laboratories."

He was right about that.

"But think about this from a business perspective, Eduardo. What if you built a shoe factory, and your shoes were so good that not only did they stay in style forever, they had the ability to spontaneously give birth to brand-new shoes once your customers got them home? You'd do a brisk trade for a while, but then nobody would buy from you ever again. Hell, you might come out with a better shoe, but what fool would go back to the store and buy more?" He raised his hands out at his sides. "How on earth would you stay in business like that?"

"So." I swallowed. "This has only ever been about selling a few more potatoes?"

"Eddie." Warren exhaled. "My whole *life* has only ever been about selling a few more potatoes."

"They buy seeds from you for spuds that can't propagate vegetatively. Then they'll have to buy them from you again every year."

Warren nodded. "In principle, it's no different than what our competitors do with corn and soybeans. But they do it via lawyers: sell the rights to a patented crop for a year. If the farmers save the seeds, then they sue them. That's a bit ham-fisted. We're going to sell them seeds that only work once. Take the paperwork and the lawyers out of the picture. It's a more elegant solution, don't you think?"

"How will you get the farmers to buy it?"

"Same way we always have: higher yield, more demand, better blight resistance."

"And if they don't want it? If they'd rather save some potatoes for replanting, the way all potato farmers have for centuries?"

Warren shrugged. "I suppose we could lower the price dramatically for a short while, if it came to that. Force their hand. So far, demand hasn't been a problem."

"But this would be the mother of all monocultures: one variety of potato that can't even reproduce? Imagine if it came down with any sort of disease. There'd be no adaptation, no hybrid vigor . . . the entire world could potentially have a potato famine like the one that starved the Irish."

Warren puckered his face. "Doomsday scenarios, that's all that is. I've never understood the monoculture argument. Why not have the best possible version of a product, rather than many lesser versions?" He lifted his hand and waved the idea away, as though it were a pesky insect.

"The whole 'DS' thing?" I said.

"'Doesn't Sprout,'" Warren admitted. "It started just as an abbreviation on the prototypes, and pretty soon it stuck. A bit silly, I know."

"Are there even any dog genes in the potato?"

He shrugged again. "I don't know. Maybe? There are lots of genes in it. But let's be serious, Eduardo: bacteria resistance is pretty basic stuff. No need to scour the animal kingdom for it."

"But you sent us here. You had us study those children. Why not just ignore it? You knew it was all bullshit."

"Well, you must admit: nobody's talking about the fact that those spuds can't sprout, are they?"

I stared back at him, incredulous.

"We both knew it was bullshit, Eduardo. You said as much in my office. And none of this is breaking news. Patents on living things is settled case law. We're not doing anything wrong. We're just getting really good at playing by the rules."

I looked at Jill and at Mitch. Both of them seemed lost by all this.

"Now get on the damn plane already." Warren turned to each of us. "Let's get out of here while we still can."

"Roger that." Mitch ran up the stairs.

"C'mon, Eddie." Jill put a hand on my shoulder.

I didn't move.

"Listen, Morales." Warren spoke to me in a more measured tone. "As I said, you've exceeded everyone's expectations—on all fronts. Your future is brighter now than ever. We've got plans for you at One Potato Way. No more frying and seasoning."

"No," I said.

"No?" Jill and Warren asked in unison. And I realized it was probably the first time I'd ever said that word to either of them.

"I'm not leaving. I have to go get somebody out of prison."

"Morales, if you don't get on this airplane right now, you're finished at Tuberware. That I can assure you."

I looked Warren in the eye. For so many years, I'd done whatever had been asked of me by this man or his underlings. All I'd ever wanted was the opportunity to do more, to obey even more of his orders. But everything in my life had been turned on its ear in the last hour, in the past week. Everything I'd thought I believed in, that I trusted, was now suspect. The air in this country suddenly felt even thinner than it was, and I said: "I quit."

"Eddie!" Jill shouted.

"You *what*?" Warren asked.

"You heard me. Have a nice trip back. I've got work to do."

Warren went inside the plane. Jill climbed the stairs but continued to call my name even as the engines started up and the doors closed.

I ignored her and turned to Oscar. "Look," I said. "I know you're technically not on the payroll anymore. But would you be so kind as to take me to the Ministry?"

He grinned, that one sharpened tooth looking sinister. "For you, this one time, I'll do it as a personal favor."

Once inside the car, I checked the clock. "And, Oscar," I said, "if we could get there quickly."

"You got it, boss."

O scar took us on a white-knuckle tour of the city. I removed La Vieja from my pocket, pulled off all the sprouts, and chucked them out the window. Lots of people were roaming the street—odd for this time of day. Perhaps the concern over the revolution—and potential counterrevolution— was finally abating. The plaza in front of the Ministry was packed with media and onlookers.

"I'm going to have to drop you off in front again," Oscar said. "No place to wait around here."

"Understood." I tucked the laptop and other papers into my briefcase and scanned the front of the building.

"There!" I pointed to a person standing near a smaller entrance on the ground level. "That's the man I need to meet."

By the curb, Alejandro stood in one of his typically well-tailored suits, this time with a FURP scarf draped around his neck. Oscar squeaked his tires to a stop just in front of him. I swung open the door.

"Doctor Morales." Alejandro helped me out of the car. "You're late."

"Sorry." I switched grips with the briefcase and shook his hand. "Been a rough morning already."

I leaned into the car once more. "Thanks, Oscar."

"Good luck today, boss." Oscar gave me a sort of salute. "And goodbye."

"Goodbye." I shut the door and waved to him.

"Right this way, Doctor." Alejandro gestured toward the building.

—

Once inside, I was taken to a hair and makeup room. A woman rushed to cover my face with thick brown foundation. Another brushed at my white coat with a lint roller.

"You're on in two minutes, Doctor." Alejandro looked at his gold watch. "You'll give your speech in English, and we'll have a simultaneous interpreter dubbing the broadcast for state television. This man can wire your computer up for the projector."

I pointed toward my briefcase.

A smiling technician took out the laptop and carried it out the main door.

"Two minutes?" I fumbled through my notes, my face pulled upward by the makeup artist.

Alejandro inserted himself into my field of vision and smiled. "I'll be out there, along with the Subcomandante. Don't let us down, Morales. The revolution is at stake."

Nobody else seemed to find anything ironic about a revolutionary wearing a gold watch and an expensive suit, so I didn't bring it up.

"Good luck, Doctor."

I nodded.

He left the room.

—

When they finally led me out to the press room, it had either been protected from the vandalism of the rest of the palace, or else already restored. Perhaps that was one of Alejandro's ideas.

The room was packed. Reporters from all over the world stood in khaki vests. Their flashbulbs burst in my face. I squinted and slowly made my way toward the lectern, suddenly afraid that I might pass out under the lights. It was a great relief to finally get my hands on either side of the lectern—if only to keep from falling over.

Once anchored to the lectern, I checked Raven's laptop; it seemed to be working. I took my notes out of my coat pocket. Straightaway, the perspiration started. In my back pocket, I found a handkerchief and dabbed at my forehead. When I looked out at the room, I could hardly see anyone for the array of microphones. The former Vice Minister, I realized, must have stood on some sort of box when he came out here to give those speeches.

"Good afternoon," I finally managed. "I'd like to thank all of you for coming, especially our friends from the foreign press, who've recently shown such a great interest in Puerto Malogrado." I took a sip from a glass of water that sat on a shelf below the top of the lectern.

"I'm an American scientist, an expert on potatoes. I was sent here to investigate the situation in a small town to the south, called Huanchillo. What I found there has caused quite a bit of alarm: three children who don't walk upright on two legs, as the rest of us do, but instead walk with their hands and feet."

I pressed a button, and the first slide was displayed on the screen. It was the photograph I'd seen on Warren's desk back in Boise—at that very moment where my life began to unravel. A wave of gasps went through the crowd, along with a volley of flashbulbs.

"I was sent here to investigate whether or not this condition has anything to do with a strain of genetically modified potatoes, produced by my employer, Tuberware, and which apparently contains certain genes from dogs."

For whatever reason, the faces on the reporters all went blank. I suddenly asked myself how much they knew—or believed—about this situation. In the back, by a pair of giant ancient video cameras bearing the logo of the state-run television station, stood Alejandro and the unkempt Subcomandante. Alejandro spun a finger in the air, urging me to get on with it already.

"I came here with the impression that these children were faking it.

The assumption throughout my company was that this was probably a ruse, a stunt cooked up by one of the many special-interest groups that spread rumors and scares about GMO foods."

Alejandro whispered into the Subcomandante's ear—perhaps translating my speech on the fly.

"Well, after several weeks of careful study, I can assure you that they are most certainly not faking."

Another volley of flashbulbs. A couple of reporters lowered their notebooks in order to cross themselves.

"Who am I kidding?" I went on. "I could tell they were genuine within two minutes of seeing them—anyone could've, scientist or not. I can also tell you that, without any doubt, the former government is guilty of irreparable damage to this country, and to its agrarian population in particular. They used the countryside of this great nation as a Petri dish: a place to test new technologies that hadn't been approved in the United States."

The reporters all earnestly took to their notebooks. Alejandro grinned wide and patted the Subcomandante on the back.

"However," I swallowed, "I must tell you that GMO potatoes had absolutely nothing to do with the condition of these children."

Gasps from the reporters. I didn't allow myself to look up. My greatest fear was that FURP would pull the plug on this, shut it all down. I needed to say my piece before that happened. Eyes on my notes, I continued.

"Those children have a genetic anomaly, a very rare mutation. This is partly due to a genetic anomaly in their family line, though even more is due to plain old bad luck. As far as I can tell, this happens very rarely, a couple of times a century—perhaps even less. This case is simply higher-profile than the others because of certain . . . interested parties."

My eyes finally rose and met Alejandro's. He held his pointer finger up to his throat, slowly drawing it across. I held up my open palm, urging him to wait.

"However," I cleared my throat. This was it, one silly connective word that signaled the point of no return. Things might already be irreparable with Tuberware, but up to here I might still have some sort of future in the industry, with one of their competitors. To read beyond this point was to leave behind the life I knew and step into something else, something strange, a life I'd spent no time preparing for.

"However," I said it again. "The things that Tuberware—my former employer—has been doing to this nation are much more serious and much more damaging."

Alejandro lowered his hand, gave me a half nod.

"Most of the crops they test here would be considered genetically modified organisms. I want to be clear on this point: GMOs are not bad technology. It's very possible that they will and should be a part of our agricultural future. Their increased yields, drought resistance, and supplemental nutrition could be game-changing advantages—particularly for developing nations. But frankly, much of the work that's been done in this area has only forced crops to handle more herbicides—so that the same chemical companies that make the seeds can sell more of their chemicals to farmers."

The foreign journalists were eating it up. Alejandro looked confused. For all I knew, he might be cooking up a deal with one of Tuberware's competitors. That was part of my plan; if they were going to use me to gain some moral high ground over the old regime, the least I could do was make sure they stayed up there.

"More specifically," I went on, "in the case of my former employer, the damage that's been done in the rural areas of Puerto Malogrado is not so much biological as it is legal, economic, and cultural."

Alejandro turned and whispered in the Subcomandante's ear. The old man scratched his beard, interested.

I put up a slide from Raven's memory card, of Arturo handcuffed on the ground beside his sack of blue potatoes.

"This man, for example, is being arrested by the police for growing this." From my pocket, I took out the now-sproutless La Vieja. "This is a staple of the traditional Andean diet, something that the indigenous people of this country have been growing for centuries. In fact, it's quite possible that this is the very first edible variety: Potato One, as it were."

Cameramen rose from their seats to photograph it.

"These native potatoes are not just a historical curiosity. The many varieties found in this part of the world provide us with a wealth of genes. These genes help combat insects or diseases that might come along in the future. Genetic diversity has always been our best defense against blight and famine. At the moment, we're narrowing the crop's gene pool down to almost nothing." I pinched a small column of air between my fingers. "It's flirting with disaster." Not so unlike human inbreeding, I thought, but I kept that to myself.

"The old regime effectively made it a crime to grow these traditional varieties. Because the release form for the American potatoes prohibits even accidental crossbreeding, the police could harass farmers simply for growing their ancestral crops.

"It's true that most of the farmers here have switched to the foreign varietals without protest. They offer better returns. But can you imagine if all the cheese-makers of Parma gave up on their traditional methods, because of a foreign method that was slightly more profitable? Can you imagine if the grape-growers in Bordeaux tore up their vines to make way for a more drought-resistant variety developed in an American lab? If the coffee-farmers in Kona were to. . . ." I looked up and saw that I'd made my point. "You get the picture. These proprietary seed rights are, I believe, one of the most egregious threats to traditional agriculture that have come from GMO crops."

I put away La Vieja and removed the DS 400 from my other pocket.

"This American potato received a lot of media attention recently, for the notion that it contained canine genes—an idea which seems to captivate our imagination. But based on my research, I've come to believe that the true purpose behind this variety—and the true threat—is its inability to reproduce."

I hit another button on the laptop and put up a picture of the two potatoes side by side on my windowsill. "As many of you may know, one of the great advantages of potato cultivation is potatoes' ability to clone themselves, to sprout from their eyes, without the necessity of seeds. This is how commercial growers have functioned for many years. But, as you can see here, this American potato doesn't sprout from its eyes."

The audience looked a little lost, and I resolved to dumb it down for them.

"Sprout-inhibiting technology has been around for a while. Mostly, it's a matter of chemicals sprayed on the tuber before it's shipped—so that it looks nice in the supermarket. But Tuberware has somehow managed to make this potato produce its own sprout inhibitor. And this isn't for aesthetic purposes; it's economic.

"The truth is, it's a redundancy. They already have the farmers sign away their rights to save seeds or replant sprouts—just as their competitors do with corn and soybeans, in the US as well as abroad. But that's an enforcement nightmare, even if you're lucky enough to have a puppet dictator in your pocket. Now they can force the farmers to buy new seeds after every harvest. No paperwork necessary."

The reporters scribbled furiously. Alejandro and the Subcomandante were rapt. This seemed to be news to everybody but Warren and the farmers.

"Look, I'm not an economist or a politician. I'm not here to debate the merits of capitalism or free markets or any of that. I'm a scientist, an expert on food. Imagine, if you will, a crisis of some kind. Imagine difficulty in shipping these seeds. Imagine a fire at the facility that processes them. Imagine a major strike or a natural disaster. Imagine, even, a very greedy individual at the helm of the company that produces all the world's potato seeds. Millions would starve, without the ability to plant new crops."

I paused for effect. Alejandro grinned wide, then leaned into the

Subcomandante's ear. I stared right at them. No more trying to please those two, I thought to myself. I've got the room now; I've got the leverage. They should be ashamed for keeping Raven as long as they have.

"The old regime played fast and loose with the laws of nature—as did my former employer. It's my sincere hope that this new government acts much more responsibly, that it regards Puerto Malogrado's potato farmers as the cultural treasure that they are. While there have been some encouraging signs, I must say that I've already been disappointed—particularly by their treatment of the press."

Both Alejandro and the Subcomandante stiffened. I didn't back down.

"Again," I exhaled, "allow me to reiterate that the condition of the Morales children has absolutely nothing to do with GMO crops. Nobody—not consumers and not farmers—is at any risk of developing a similar condition. Let us leave them alone, and let them grow up to have as normal a life as they possibly can. Thank you. I won't be taking any questions."

I pulled the cord out of the computer and walked back to the green room, a flurry of shouted comments and bursting flashes as I went. I found a bottle of water back there, took a long swallow, and rubbed my eyes.

"What the hell was that?" Alejandro had materialized right beside me.

"That was the truth, Alejandro. It might not be exactly what you wanted, but it's what I gave you."

He met my gaze, unblinking, unsure whether to thank or to scold me.

I took a half step closer to him. "Get Raven out of that fucking cell. Now," I said. "Unless you want me to call another press conference. In case you hadn't noticed, I'm the most credible man in this country."

The Subcomandante walked in, looking much more collected. "Well done, Doctor," he said.

"Thank you, sir." I turned back to Alejandro and silently mouthed the word "now."

He dashed through a side door.

The Subcomandante extended his hand, and we shook.

"This was very interesting for me. I had no idea of the sorts of agendas these American capitalists have."

I nodded. "Those are among the many difficult things you're going to have to navigate, sir. It won't be easy, running this country."

"No," he agreed. "I'm starting to think it will be more difficult than fighting a revolution."

"Well. Good luck to you," I said.

He raised his eyebrows. "I'll need it, especially in the coming days."

"Is that right?" I figured things would be slowing down for him.

"Indeed. The sympathizers are mobilizing."

"Sympathizers? You mean those sympathetic to the old regime?"

He nodded. "And to the Vice Minister."

"But . . ." I was confused. "Don't you have the Vice Minister in custody? Last time I saw him, he was giving a concession speech at gunpoint."

"You haven't heard? There was an escape: an inside job, it seems. He's absconded to the east, with several loyal squadrons from the military."

"The military's been split up? So now both sides have planes and bombs?"

"That's correct, Doctor." He turned to me. "The fighting could get much worse."

"Eddie!" Raven burst in from the side door, alongside Alejandro. By the time I recognized her, she'd already wrapped me up in a tight embrace.

"Raven, are you all right?"

"I'll live." She kissed me on the mouth. "Alejandro told me what you did. You're my hero."

"We've got to get out of here," I said.

"Thanks again, Doctor," the Subcomandante said. "Is there anything else I can do for you?"

"Yes, actually." I decided I liked him. His curiosity, his willingness to consider other ideas—that was an attitude I hadn't seen in this building before. "We could use a ride. First to our hotel, and then to the airport."

"Consider it done." He snapped his fingers and waved at somebody.

"Also . . ." I paused, beset by indecision.

Raven and the Subcomandante both glared at me.

"Also, I need you to release that other gringo. The idiot filmmaker."

Outside the palace, all the young men were suddenly—finally—being rousted from their naps. I found myself surprised—impressed, almost—that they were capable of snapping into action. Senior officers barked orders and dispatched the teenage guerillas to their errands. Makeshift military vehicles lined up. I held Raven by the hand, unwilling to let her out of my sight again.

Kearns still had the same long beard and filthy clothes as the day before. He shielded his eyes from the daylight with both hands. "What's happening?" he asked.

"They're getting ready," I said. "The old regime is likely to strike back."

"Fuckers," Kearns muttered.

I wasn't sure if he meant FURP or the old regime—or both.

"Is Oscar waiting out here?" Raven asked.

"No," I admitted. "Oscar is no longer at our service."

A pickup truck painted in FURP colors pulled up in front of us, piloted by a guerilla that looked to be about eleven years old. Alejandro crouched in the back. Once it came to a complete stop, he jumped to the curb and shot his cuffs. "Here you are, Doctor. He will drive you to your hotel."

I insisted that Raven take the front seat; Kearns and I loaded into the bed. Alejandro gave the driver directions.

Off we went, retracing the route I'd seen so many times from the back of Oscar's motorbikes or through the tinted windows of the Vice Minister's limousine. I kept my eyes peeled for taxis or buses, but there were none to be found.

Other FURP vehicles roamed the streets, right through stoplights and signs, effectively shutting down certain roads. I couldn't tell if they'd actually declared martial law, or if most of the residents simply had the good judgment to stay indoors. The shopkeepers appeared to take it in stride, doing a good business in batteries and canned goods. It looked as if many of the FURP banners had been taken down—in anticipation of yet another government, perhaps.

Kearns was quiet the whole way, still squinting against the light. We pulled up at his hotel, and he froze.

"Go on, Kearns," I said. "Get your things, and then we'll go to the airport and get out of here."

Raven came out of the truck's cab to help me.

"Go on!" I said again.

He covered up his eyes with his hands now. A tremble took over his body.

"Eddie." Raven touched my arm. "This is where he got picked up."

"Oh, right." I turned to her. "He has to go in there. He'll need his documents, at least."

She nodded, then approached Kearns where he sat in the far corner of the pickup bed. "Spencer? It's okay." She put a hand on his back. "Those people who put us in jail, they're not in power anymore. We're all here. Nothing is going to happen to you now. But we have to get your passport and things out of your room. I'll go with you. You'll be fine."

After a second, he removed his hands from his eyes, nodded vigorously, and allowed Raven to lead him into the hotel.

The driver stayed behind the wheel of the pickup. I waited in the bed. Only a few minutes passed before Raven and Kearns emerged again, with a couple of bags in their hands.

"Well done, Spencer," I said.

He hopped into the back. "Nothing to it."

———

We pulled off the Boulevard de los Agricultores and approached La Posada. The teenaged guard took one look at our FURP truck, dropped his shotgun to the ground, and took off running in the opposite direction.

Once we reached the hotel, my heart sank. The windows were all boarded up, and the gate was locked tight. We rang the bell and banged on the outer fence.

"Maybe Doña Ana shut it up and got out of the city?" Raven suggested.

I looked around for some way we might break in. Raven gave the door a couple more rings. Our teenaged driver honked his horn.

"Go away!" A muffled voice from inside. "The hotel's closed!"

"Doña Ana!" Raven and I shouted in unison. "It's us!" I said in Spanish. "The Americans! Please, let us in to get our things."

"You two!" Doña Ana burst out of the door and immediately began admonishing us. "Haven't you heard about the fighting that's anticipated? I sent my daughters and my mother away to stay with my sister in the *colonia*. Get inside!" She swung the gate open.

"We only need to grab our things, and then we're off to the airport," I explained.

Kearns stayed in the still-running truck.

Raven and I each went off to our separate rooms to pack. I shoved clothes into my rolling suitcase even more quickly than I had back in Boise. I pulled the two potatoes from my pocket and dropped them into the bag as well.

Raven and I met back in the main room.

"Ready?" I asked her.

She nodded. "Here goes nothing."

"Doña Ana," I called to her in the kitchen. "We're about to leave."

The landline right next to us let out a ring so loud, it made me flinch.

Doña Ana emerged from the kitchen and held an index finger at us. She picked up the phone. *"Diga?"* She looked surprised, put a hand over the mouthpiece, and turned to me. "It's for you."

"Me?"

She nodded, held the receiver out.

I took the phone from her and said, *"Sí?"*

"Doctor Morales?" The voice on the other line spoke English with a British accent.

"Speaking," I said.

"This is Doctor Mears—from the Turkish study. You reached out to me, via email?"

"Oh, right!" I suddenly remembered the other case of hand-walking children and the message I'd sent. "Thanks for getting back to me. Listen, I need to come clean about something: that family—it turns out there was a high coefficient of relationship." Again, I used the fancy scientific term for "inbreeding."

"Yes." He didn't sound surprised. "That was also the case in our subjects, though it doesn't make your discovery any less significant, from a genetic perspective."

"Is that right?" I was pleasantly surprised. "Do you think there's any chance of a real, comprehensive study?"

He cleared his throat. "Do you mean apart from your own work, Doctor? I assumed that you plan to publish on this."

"Oh, no." The suggestion struck me as funny. "My work here has been a bit of a farce, I'm afraid. It was a public relations exercise, undertaken on behalf of a corporation I no longer work for. I'm not an actual geneticist; I'm more of a fry cook, it turns out."

"I see." An awkward pause. "Do you mean that no scientists are currently studying these children?"

"None," I said. "Your team would be most welcome."

Outside, an explosion sounded much closer than the last. The phone line crackled.

"But I should probably warn you: there's a bit of a revolution—or counterrevolution now—taking place here."

"Yes," he said. "I saw that on the news. It certainly does complicate things. Still, this is something we ought to look into."

"I agree," I said.

Our driver honked, and Kearns shouted my name. Raven hoisted her backpack and took it out to the truck.

"And I'd of course like to help you in any way I can," I went on. "But it might be difficult, logistically. What I really need to do right now is get out of this country."

"Roger that, Doctor Morales. Perhaps we can communicate over email then."

"That should work." Outside, there was a sound like a bottle rocket blasting off and then whizzing from one side of the sky to another. "Though I may be unavailable for the next couple of days."

"All right, then, we'll keep in touch. I can't tell you how much I appreciate your contacting me."

Raven came back in for my bag. She picked it up and carried it outside.

"It's my pleasure, Doctor Mears," I said. "But can I ask you one more thing?"

"Of course."

"Did you ever find a way to help those Turkish children? To improve their mobility or to make them more comfortable?"

He laughed out loud. "It's funny you should mention that. After so much fuss over the origins of their condition, that rather slipped through the cracks. But there was indeed one simple idea that seemed to help . . . something one of the graduate students came up with toward the end of our trip. It's not scientific at all, I'm afraid, just a bit of common sense."

My stomach dropped a few inches within my chest cavity. I turned my head and found myself staring into the vacated bedroom of Doña Ana's old mother.

"Go on," I said.

hung up the phone. Our driver kept honking.

"Come on, Eddie!" Raven yelled from the passenger seat.

I walked outside, feeling like I might keel over once again, the way I had at the Vice Minister's country house.

"All right!" Kearns brightened up at the sight of me, became himself again. "Let's get the fuck out of this shithole already."

I went around to the passenger side.

"What's wrong, Eddie?" Raven asked. "You look like you've seen a ghost. Get in the truck. We may not have much time."

"Raven, I can't leave just yet." I realized it was true only when the words came out of my mouth.

"What?" she asked. "You know that planes might not even take off from here much longer, right?"

"I have to go back to Huanchillo," I said. "There's something I can do to help the Morales kids. It's a small thing, but it might work. It worked for another family with their same problem."

She stared into my eyes, trying to see if this was a joke or a mistake, good news or bad. "I'm going with you." Her door swung open.

"*Hijo de la gran . . .*" the driver muttered.

Raven went to the pickup bed and pulled her backpack out. I grabbed my rolling suitcase and did the same.

"What the hell is this now?" Kearns asked.

"We can't leave today. We have to stay and tie up some loose ends," I explained. "You can have the front seat."

Kearns didn't hesitate to take me up on it.

By the time I came around to the driver, he had his forehead rested against the steering wheel in frustration.

"*Oye*," I said. "It's just him now. Thanks for your help."

He nodded, confused.

I walked around to the passenger side, where Kearns had just settled in. "Have a safe trip."

"Hey, Eddie," he said. "Thanks. Thanks for getting me out of that cell."

"It was nothing," I admitted.

"I knew you could do it. As soon as I saw you in there, I was sure you'd be the one to bust me out. You're too good of a person not to."

I laughed out loud. "Actually, I'm not." I took a breath. "Spencer, I was partly responsible for your being in there in the first place."

"How's that?" He squinted his eyes even tighter.

"It wasn't intentional, but I mentioned to the Vice Minister that you'd caused trouble for my work. He decided to handle it in his own way—unbeknownst to me."

"You fucker!" Finally, he got angry. "It was a stupid online video. I could've died in that cell!"

"I never meant for that to happen," I said.

"Well, you didn't exactly rush out and do anything about it either! I'm your oldest friend, for crying out loud."

"You're right. I screwed up. I'm sorry."

He scowled at me, unsatisfied.

"Look, I don't work for Tuberware anymore, so there's no need to have me fired. You can go public with our cheating scandal if you want, ruin my professional life—that's all within your power. But I would ask one thing."

"What's that?" He still scowled.

"Just wait a few weeks," I pleaded. "If I get exposed as a fraud—who cheated his way through school and found a career through his rich friend's daddy—then those Morales children might be in jeopardy. I'm trying to get some real researchers to come in and study them. If I'm publicly discredited, the scientists might not show up. Give it a little time before you say anything. For the kids' sake, if not for mine."

Kearns's expression betrayed nothing. He turned to his driver. "Airport."

They took off down the street, and I shouted "good luck!" even though they couldn't hear.

Raven dropped our bags inside the entrance to La Posada. "We should probably wait until tomorrow to make the trip out there, don't you think?"

"You're right." It was already late.

"Doña Ana!" I shouted. "Can we stay one more night?"

She emerged from the kitchen with a rag in her hands. "I suppose you'll be wanting dinner then?"

I grinned. "If it's no trouble."

"I don't have much food."

"Here." I opened my bag and pulled out the two potatoes I'd used during my speech. "I can contribute these."

She cracked a smile, took them from my hands, then said, "Shh." She looked up toward the ceiling. "Listen."

I heard a distant crack like thunder: the first bomb of a new battle, landing somewhere within earshot.

"Are we safe here?" I asked.

She shrugged. "We're safe until we're not."

———

The three of us sat down to dinner at a table that had been dragged in from the patio. Doña Ana fried thin slices of those two very different potatoes in a pan with onion, then cracked a couple of eggs into the mix. Once the potatoes were brown and crisp, she served them alongside some chicken livers sautéed with tomatoes.

We ate around the patio table, listening to the faint sounds of revolution carrying in from the outside.

"This is excellent," I told Doña Ana. "One of the best meals I've ever had."

She smiled.

"*Sí*," said Raven. "*Delicioso.*"

I turned to Raven and asked in English: "You know there's chicken in there, right?"

She shrugged. "There are no vegetarians in foxholes."

I laughed out loud.

After the meal, Raven carried her things into my bedroom. Doña Ana gathered up the dishes; I followed her into the kitchen.

"*Mira*, Doña Ana, I wanted to settle up for all that you've done for us."

"No need," she said. "Your employer took care of your bill already."

"Are you sure?" I asked.

"Oh yes. I got the money up front. There's no credit here, not for strange foreign corporations." She began scrubbing out the pan.

I rotated the belt around my waist, fished out one of my remaining hundred-dollar bills. "Let me give you this anyway, for all the other things that you've done. For all your help."

"Absolutely not!" She held up a soapy palm and shook her head.

"No?" I hadn't expected a refusal.

"If we start taking money just for being decent to one another in difficult times, where will that leave us?"

"You're sure?"

"*Ba.*" She nodded. "That's the fast road to hell: collecting payment for one's Christian duty. Keep your money; you'll need it, if you make it out of here."

"Well, thanks," I said. "Sincerely. For everything. Especially the food."

"Any time," she smiled.

"Sleep well, Doña Ana," I said.

"Same to you."

———

We kept our bags packed. The windows to the solarium were already boarded up. The television was gone. My same sheets were still on the bed.

We lay down, in our clothes, and held each other close.

"I thought I'd lost you for good," I admitted. "Once you were dragged into that building, then the building itself was under fire . . . it was the worst feeling ever. Total helplessness."

"But you got me out. I knew you would." She pressed her cheek into my chest. "You did it with your tact, your patience, and your courage."

"It didn't feel like my plan was working at the time, I can promise you that."

She rubbed a circle into my belly. "Let's don't worry too much about that part. We've got bigger problems now. How are we going to make it out there, to Huanchillo?"

"We have to try," I said. "I think we'll be okay, once we get out of the city. There never seems to be any fighting down in that valley."

"Maybe they know better than to bomb their breadbasket."

Another explosion in the distance: this one too far to be felt, only heard. We held each other even more tightly.

"Well." Raven bent to take off her shoes. "Let's try to get some sleep anyway."

"You go ahead," I said. "I need to pack up one more thing. Be right back."

I left the bedroom and softly closed the door.

n the morning, I awoke wrapped up in Raven's arms. The city was oddly quiet. For a dreamy moment, it felt as though our troubles were over, that we'd succeeded. But as full wakefulness crept over me, I remembered that our troubles were only just beginning.

While Raven slept in, I slipped out of bed and went into the main room. Doña Ana sat on the couch, watching television with a younger man I'd not seen before. The news played silently, showing footage of a few blown-up buildings.

"Morning." I took a stance behind the couch.

"Morning, Doctor," Doña Ana said. "The fighting stayed on the outskirts of the city, praise God. Most of it is in the east, where the Vice Minister is believed to be staying."

"That's good news, I guess."

"Mmm." She nodded. "If they get him, it should end. This is my nephew, Quique. He brought me some groceries."

"*Mucho gusto.*" I shook the young man's hand. "I'm Doctor Morales."

"Of course." He smiled. "I watched you on television yesterday."

I nodded. "Speaking of that, what channel is this?"

"It's the state-run television," Doña Ana said. "The same station that you were on."

"But now it's . . . accurate?"

She shrugged. "Seems to be, since the FURP takeover. Perhaps they're more honest. Or they haven't learned how to manipulate the truth as well as the old regime."

The three of us stared at the footage of the destruction for a few more seconds.

"*Bueno, Tía.*" Quique stretched his arms over his head. "I should get a move on. Let me know if you need anything else." He leaned over and kissed her on the cheek, then took a ring of keys from his pocket.

"I'll be fine." She waved the notion off with a hand. "Take care of yourself."

"Doctor." Quique rose to his feet. "It's been a pleasure."

"Wait!" I said. "You have a car? Do you think you could drive me someplace? I can pay."

Quique and Doña Ana exchanged a glance.

He turned back to me. "As long as it's not too far."

In the bedroom, I shook Raven awake. "Wake up," I whispered. "We need to go."

"Huh?" She blinked her eyes. "What's going on, Eddie?"

"Doña Ana's nephew is here. He's got a car. He offered us a ride."

"To Huanchillo?"

"We didn't get into specifics. But let's hurry." Back in the main room, Quique was anxious to get going. We loaded our luggage into his pickup truck, climbed into the cab, then set off, the three of us waving hard and saying farewell to Doña Ana.

"Okay," Quique said. "Where to, then?"

"Actually, Quique," I said, "we need to go to Huanchillo."

"Huanchillo?" he shouted. "Out in the campo? Don't be ridiculous."

"One hundred dollars," I said. "American."

"Even for a hundred dollars, that's way too far."

"All right." I sighed. "Can you take us in that direction? Get us out of the city at least? To someplace where we might be able to hitch another ride?"

He stared out the windshield, shaking his head and sighing.

"Please," I said.

"I can take you to the *desvio*," Quique said. "But that's as far as I go."

"That will be fine," I said. "We'll make do from there."

The city was eerily quiet. Many of the main arteries had makeshift roadblocks; it was impossible to tell which were official and which had been put up by the citizens. Finally we made our way onto the small but familiar road Oscar had used to get us out of town.

We carried on, Raven and I silent, hoping that Quique might keep going. Alas, once we reached the turnout, he pulled off and said, "This is it."

"Thank you." I fidgeted with my stupid belt.

Quique looked on, confused, while I got it loosened. Perhaps he feared that I was about to urinate in his vehicle.

Raven stepped out of the truck and unloaded our luggage.

Finally, I freed one crumpled bill and handed it to him.

"This is too much money," he said. "For this little ride."

"I don't have anything smaller. Do something nice for your aunt, if you like."

"Much obliged." He straightened the bill out, then folded it. "May you go with God."

"Same to you," I said.

As he drove off, leaving Raven and me at the side of the empty road in this war-torn country, I had to wonder what on earth we were thinking.

"Well," she said. "Now what?"

There was no sign of vehicles. My ideas about hitchhiking or finding some semblance of public transport looked dead on arrival.

"I guess we start walking."

"Great!" Raven was excited by the prospect. "It'll be nice to finally get some exercise on this trip." She shouldered her big backpack, cinched up a series of straps, and started walking uphill, shoulders tilted toward the climb like an oxen to a yoke.

I struggled to keep up with Raven's long, confident strides. My wheeled suitcase bounced up and down on the rutted asphalt of the narrow road. My shoes pinched at my feet. The altitude pressed against my skull. I watched as Raven's well-supported ankles pounded out a rhythm against the steep and empty road.

"You doing all right back there?" she asked.

"For the first time," I wheezed, "I don't find your choice of wardrobe or luggage completely ridiculous."

She laughed but didn't stop walking. "It's all about function, Eddie. I'm surprised you don't know that, being a scientist."

She finally indulged me with a break and offered a sip from the bottle of water she'd had the foresight to bring along. I panted hard, but she barely seemed out of breath.

"The elevation must be getting to me," I said.

"It's beautiful up here," she observed.

I turned around. Indeed, we'd climbed high enough to get a good view of the city—both the newer skyscrapers and the old colonial churches and plazas. A thin cloud of smog hung down below us.

"It seems quiet around here," Raven said. "Let's hope all the fighting happens elsewhere."

"So far, that seems to be the case. At least the Vice Minister was kind enough to set up his lair in another part of the country."

"How far do you think we are from the village?"

"I'm not sure," I admitted. "What did it take . . . a little over an hour to get there with Oscar?"

"Something like that. But there was some traffic involved."

I sighed. "If we don't get a ride, it's going to be a while."

Raven kept right on ascending. She was good at this. Besides the equipment advantage, she had strong legs.

I, on the other hand, felt like an idiot in my lab coat and dress shoes, dragging a ridiculous rolling bag behind me.

"How are you holding up?" Raven asked again over her shoulder.

"I've been better," I admitted.

"Let this be a lesson to you." She smirked. "Always bring comfortable footwear."

We finally reached the top of the first hill and again paused to look back at the city. Sucking air, I put my hands on my knees and hung my head between my legs.

"I did not anticipate a hike like this."

"Buck up," Raven said. "Look on the bright side: at least you were born with the gene that allows you to walk upright." She handed me her water bottle.

"Feels more like a curse than a blessing at the moment." I stood up and took a sip.

"I don't see any fighting going on," Raven said. "Everything looks normal."

I did a quick survey of the skyline. "There," I said. "To the east."

We watched what looked to be a thinning dust cloud. Underneath it was a small crater of sorts. I recognized the site from the television news back at La Posada.

"They dropped something big over there, from the looks of it."

"God." Raven covered her mouth with a hand. "What was there before?"

"Who knows?" I said. "Hopefully nothing residential. I'd expect the counterrevolution to try to be precise. Honestly, I'm not sure what they can blow up. You'd think they'd want to take the military back intact. And they need the citizenry on their side. There just aren't a lot of targets that make strategic sense."

"Do you think Doña Ana is okay?"

I nodded. "She's all the way over there, across town."

The next stretch was relatively flat, which would've been nice, but the road went from rutted asphalt to gravel, and there was no hope of rolling my stupid suitcase. It was close to noon, and the sun had chased off the early morning chill. I stuffed my white coat into the front of my suitcase, and then hoisted it up on one shoulder.

"It's a beautiful day, at least," Raven said.

"There is that."

From far away, we heard a rumbling engine and got to the side of the road.

"It's heading in our direction," she said.

I nodded. "Stick your thumb out."

We both made the international hitchhiking sign as a rusted flatbed truck came around the bend. Through the dusty window of the suicide cab, the driver ignored us and kept on going. In the back, three chickens were tied up inside a basket strapped to the bed.

We watched as he disappeared into the other side of the horizon, only the chickens willing to make eye contact with us.

"No dice," I said.

"You ought to show a little more leg next time."

"I wish one of those chickens had fallen out. I'm starving."

"Oh, yeah?" Raven reached into her cargo pocket and pulled out a packaged energy bar. "I still have a few of these left."

"Thanks." I opened it up and had a bite. As I chewed, I turned to the ingredients list. "This is interesting."

"You like it?"

"It tastes fine. But it's all corn and soy. Tuberware hasn't made much of a foray into this market. I bet a potato-based energy bar would have a nice texture—and some natural sweetness. We could compete with these."

"Eddie." Raven put a hand on my shoulder. "You don't work for that company anymore."

I met her gaze and swallowed the rest of the bar. "Right." I nodded. "Sorry. I'm just having a little trouble letting go of my old life, I guess."

"It's okay. It happens."

I nodded and mumbled an agreement. I didn't regret quitting my job at Tuberware. There had been no other choice. But I'd been an expert on potato-based processed foods for so long, it formed a large part of my identity. What was I now? I had no idea.

"Look!" Raven pointed up ahead. "The mine. It looks deserted."

Without the crowds of strikers around, it seemed a bit spooky.

"Where are all the workers?" Raven asked.

I shrugged. "The minerals are nationalized. Maybe they're waiting to find out who their new bosses are." In that sense, I could relate to them.

"I guess you're right," Raven said. "I sure as hell wouldn't go down there without a paycheck."

We passed by those multicolored mountain lakes without seeing another soul—on foot, or behind the wheel. The sun grew stronger. To keep from getting burned, I wrapped the lab coat around my head like a turban. I tried carrying the suitcase every which way: by the handle, under my arm, out in front, up on one shoulder, even atop my head like the local women did with jugs of water and sacks of potatoes. Whenever my arm got too sore, I'd give the wheels another try—only to once again grow frustrated by the potholes of the dirt road. It was even more difficult once we began descending into the valley.

After another hour or so, we finally caught sight of some terraced farmland—not terribly far from where the police had harassed Arturo. I wondered if the new government would do a better job on this front, if my speech had at all helped to keep them honest.

The sun disappeared behind a cloud, and the air suddenly went cold again. The sweat-soaked skin of my back felt a chill.

"Let's take a break, shall we?" I asked Raven.

"Sure."

We stepped off the road. Raven de-shouldered her big backpack, then took a seat along the stones. We were both panting now, me much more than her.

She took out her bottle and swallowed some water. "How are we going to get out of this country, Eddie?"

"I have no idea." I suddenly remembered the Harley-Davidson stamp on my passport and wondered how much longer it was valid for, if the current government would even know what it meant. "Maybe the airport will reopen soon, if . . . if some sort of a victor prevails."

"Which side are you rooting for?" Raven asked.

I shrugged. "With the Vice Minister, we know he's corrupt and autocratic. He's got a proven track record of censorship and repression."

"Don't forget that he damn near ruined the country's agricultural base—a system that had worked for decades."

"More like centuries," I agreed. "And he locked you up."

"Locked up several journalists who didn't play his tune," Raven added.

"So for those reasons alone, I'd stick with FURP. As far as I could tell, the Subcomandante believes in a cause—unlike the old regime. Perhaps he'll steal a little less."

"I agree," Raven said. "Even with all the chaos and the questionable alliances, FURP fought for a better country, at a high price. It's not just a cash cow to them."

"*Amigo!*" We heard a voice yell from farther uphill.

Raven and I both turned to see. There, with a foot plow in one hand and a sack at his feet, stood Arturo—waving at us with his free arm.

"Arturo!" Raven stood up. "It's so good to see you!"

He nodded, gathered his things, and made his way toward us.

My spirits immediately lifted just by knowing that we'd made it this close to Huanchillo.

"How did you two get here?" Arturo asked. "Where's your driver?"

"No driver," I explained. "He disappeared once the counterrevolution began."

"You came here on foot?"

"From the capital," Raven beamed. "Almost all the way."

"Oh, my!" Arturo laughed and clapped his hands. "Just like the old days!"

"And now I know what it was like to lug a potato sack the entire way." I kicked at the side of the suitcase with my foot.

"How are things here?" Raven asked. "Are the children okay?"

"Oh, yes," Arturo said. "Never better." He turned to me. "We watched your speech on the television, Doctor. Everyone was very impressed."

"Is that right?" I smiled. Already that speech seemed like years ago. It filled me with pride to think that my improvised strategy might've worked.

"Now, with the counterrevolution, nobody has time to bother them. Look." He raised his sack. "I can grow my old potatoes, without trouble from the police."

"So there's no danger of the fighting spreading to this area?" Raven asked.

"Not much," Arturo said. "This valley is not very strategic. Our biggest fear is that our young men might be impressed into service. Several *muchachos* have already fled."

"I see." That was an aspect of the conflict that hadn't occurred to me.

"Well, come on, then." Arturo grinned. "You two must be hungry and tired. Let's get you to my uncle's house, so you can rest."

"Sounds good to me." Raven re-shouldered her pack.

Arturo offered to take my suitcase, but I wouldn't allow it. The three of us made our way into the main street of Huanchillo. Seeing it on foot, after such a long journey, the place looked more charming than ever.

At the Morales home, we were given our warmest welcome thus far. Even the mother llama seemed happy to see me. She turned her head up to have a look as I entered, then went back to grazing.

Niña Rosa gave me a huge hug and patted my shoulder. Don Pablo shook my hand with both of his.

"We saw your speech on the television," he said. "Thank you for that."

I shrugged. "It was only the truth, that's all."

"Sometimes that can be the hardest thing."

I nodded.

Straightaway, Raven was down on her knees, playing with the children. She seemed reluctant to bring the camera out, but Pablito was so insistent that she finally took it from her bag.

His mother looked a little bothered by this, but she stopped herself short of saying anything. Pablito truly loved playing with the device, taking shots of his sisters from different angles. The girls giggled with delight at the sight of their own faces on the built-in screen.

I told Don Pablo that I had something important to discuss with him. He, Arturo, and I sat around their dining table. Niña Rosa fetched mugs of coca tea and then joined us.

"The big news," I began, "is that I've been in contact with a group of British scientists. They are, I suppose, the world's leading experts in your children's condition."

"Experts?" Arturo asked. "I thought this was the only case."

"The group in question, they worked with a family in Turkey that has a similar ailment, about twenty years ago. They spent months with them, scanned their DNA, took images of their brains, everything. The lead researcher is very interested in visiting you—once the political situation cools down, of course."

The three adults looked around, gauging each other's enthusiasm.

"Doctor Morales," Don Pablo swallowed. "I know I've asked you this before, and I hope you'll forgive my narrow vision. But my concern is this: Would the foreign experts have any interest in healing my children, or simply in studying them?"

I sighed. "The thing is, in a case like this, there is no cure. All science can really do is learn everything we can about the situation, to study and document it all meticulously. If, in those findings, a remedy presents itself, then so be it. But there's no promise. These would be researchers, not medical doctors."

Niña Rosa looked particularly worried. Don Pablo squeezed her hand. Arturo leaned back in his chair and folded his arms across his chest.

"However," I cleared my throat, "in my initial conversations with these scientists, I asked them about this very issue. As it happens, they did stumble upon one potential solution and were kind enough to share it."

All three adults straightened their backs and leaned toward me.

"Yes?" Don Pablo asked.

We all gathered in the courtyard, around my battered wheeled suitcase. I zipped it open and removed the item that had brought me back here to Huanchillo. After a few folds, extensions, and locks, it was soon set up in the middle of our circle.

"That?" asked Arturo.

"*Sí*," I said.

"Eddie?" Raven whispered to me. "That's a walking frame . . . like for old people."

"I'm aware of that," I said. "Specifically, it's the one that belonged to Doña Ana's mother. This is exactly what those British scientists recommended."

"*Que gringo más loco!*" Niña Rosa said to her husband.

"This isn't a joke." I waved to the children. "Pablito, come and see this."

I stood behind the walker, took it in my hands, and pressed all my weight down. With legs still sore from our long walk, it wasn't hard to lean in. I demonstrated for a confused Pablito: moving the frame, then taking a step behind it, then another. "You see?" I asked the boy.

"*Aye Dios mio.*" His mother stormed off toward the kitchen.

"Pablito. Just like this, understand?" I held his gaze, demonstrated one more step. "*Dále.*"

He crawled over and took my hand. Raven came to spot him on the other side. The two of us helped him rise up and lean on the frame.

Once his hands were on it, something in his face immediately changed. The perspective was new to him: to see from this height, without a wall or a door to obscure the view. He had the widened eyes of a climber who'd just reached a summit.

"That's it, Pablito," I said. "Now, when you're ready: carefully, slowly, try taking a step."

Both Don Pablo and Arturo watched in suspense.

Pablito's first step was the simplest: he shuffled his back foot forward to meet his front. Then he tried the harder part, moving the frame itself. His arms trembled, and his face twisted up with concentration. But, steadily, he pivoted the frame up on one corner, planted the other, and then, with relative ease, took the two steps forward to meet it.

"Yes! That's it!" Raven clapped her hands.

"Rosa!" Don Pablo called to his wife. "Come back here."

She rushed out, drying her hands on a rag.

Pablito made another move. Again, planting the walker was the most difficult part, but his confidence had already grown. Once he had the legs set, he relished stepping forward with ease. His grin widened as he caught up to the frame.

Arturo clapped me on the back. Niña Rosa prayed to the Virgin. The little girls squealed with delight.

"You're a genius!" Don Pablo exclaimed. "A genius!"

Raven took my hand and squeezed. "Well done, Eddie!" She kissed me on the cheek.

I shrugged. "It's just a thirty-dollar walking frame." Despite the dismissal, I felt the beginnings of tears sprouting from my eyes.

The eight of us stayed out in the courtyard until it was cold and dark. Pablito was not eager to give up the walker but was finally persuaded to share it with his sisters. They struggled slightly more than their brother, but with his encouragement they picked it up soon enough.

"Had I known this would work so well," I told Don Pablo, "I would've found a couple more."

He was transfixed by the sight of his children. Though they weren't fully walking—and perhaps they never would—there was something about the progress, the promise, the fact that they were getting around on their own, in a way that would not be mocked by the world.

"It occurred to me that I might be able to build something similar," he said. "Not with steel, of course, and perhaps not as adjustable as that one, but a simple version made from wood."

"Absolutely," I agreed. "It's not a complicated design." Soon, it grew so dark that I could barely see the shiny rails of the walker. Niña Rosa called us all inside for dinner. We sat around the fire and ate a delicious stew: some stringy, long-simmering cut of meat, cooked until all the connective tissue had melted down into the broth. Several types of potatoes and sweet potatoes swam there as well, along with green herbs I couldn't identify. Raven abandoned her vegetarianism entirely and chewed the meat right off the bone. As soon as the meal was finished, Niña Rosa collected our dishes. Don Pablo passed out shot glasses. He poured Raven, Arturo, and me each a small dram of *pisco* from an unlabeled bottle.

We raised our drinks.

"To simple solutions!" Arturo said.

I had a small sip and let the hot alcohol evaporate inside my mouth.

"So," Don Pablo asked, "what will you two do next?"

An impatient Pablito had sneaked the walker into the house. He and his sisters took turns going the length of the living room—already dressed for bed.

"We need to find a way out of the country," I said. "I hoped there might be some news regarding the airport."

"Oh, it's closed to commercial traffic," Don Pablo said. "The outlook is grim, so far as that goes. Even before all the trouble, only one airline made stops in Puerto Malogrado. Many of the pilots and crew members have disappeared. They stayed on in Miami after FURP's victory. Depending on who wins, they may seek refugee status."

I sighed. "That is grim."

The mother returned from the kitchen and found the children using the walker inside the house. "Stop this at once!" she shouted. "It's too late. Clean your teeth and off to bed already."

"Yes, mama," they all said in unison, then went out to the cistern.

Raven touched my knee. "Can you tell them thanks, for their hospitality?"

I relayed her message to Don Pablo.

He smiled at us. "It's I who ought to be thanking you. Not only did you put an end to all the madness with 'reverse evolution' and whatnot, but you also found a way to help my children walk."

"That was nothing, Don Pablo," I admitted. "We should've thought of it sooner. I'm hopeful that this British team will bring you even more answers."

"If they can ever get a flight in!" Arturo chuckled and lifted the bottle. "Another?"

I looked at Raven, who shook her head.

"I think we'll turn in," I said. "It was a long day of walking, you know."

"Yes," Don Pablo said. "For you as well as for the children."

—

We excused ourselves and went out to our one-room casita in the backyard. It was a beautiful night, the stars even more brilliant at this elevation. It seemed hard to imagine that a small but deadly war was going on not so far away from here—within walking distance, almost.

My legs and back ached, and it felt amazing to finally lie beside Raven on the larger of the two little beds. On the table was the worthless water sample we'd taken days ago.

"You did a great job today, Eddie." She put a hand flat against my chest.

"You did great too." I stroked her ginger hair. "I don't think I'd have made it past the mine if not for you." After a minute of quiet, I admitted: "I have no idea how we're going to get to the States."

Raven smiled. "Would it be the worst thing in the world, staying in this little valley?"

I chuckled. "I don't have a job to return to, I suppose. Not sure how much need there is in Huanchillo for our skill sets: an investigative reporter and a washed-up food scientist."

"You'd have to learn how to actually grow some of those potatoes. With dirt and sunlight, rather than Petri dishes."

I laughed but couldn't stop myself from picturing it: an acre or two of our own, up here in this tiny village, a parcel among the ancient stone terraces, under these brilliant stars. How much equity did I have in my stupid Boise condo? If I cashed in my Tuberware stock and my retirement plan, how far would that go?

"Good night, Eddie," Raven said.

"Good night."

The two of us slept soundly in that cold little bed. Even the roosters had a hard time waking me. My eyelids were sticky once I finally pried them open. Through the adobe walls, I could hear the tick-tacking of the walker's legs against the hard-packed ground, the shuffle of strengthening steps behind it. It was barely dawn and the children were already practicing. Raven was still asleep. I untwisted my limbs from hers and got dressed to meet the day.

Outside, Don Pablo stood with a cup of coffee, watching as Pablito did laps around the yard.

"The second he woke up," the father said. "He wanted to come out here and start again."

"He's a tenacious little boy; that's for sure." I pulled up the collar on my lab coat, still fighting off the morning chill.

"Did you sleep well?" Don Pablo asked.

"Very well," I said. Fortunately, the memory of having Raven ripped away after our last night in the casita had not haunted my slumber.

"That's good news. I believe I've found a way for you to get out of here."

"Really?"

"Yes." He kept staring at his son's methodical paces. "But it's going to involve a long night."

"Oh?" I asked.

"And a fair bit of cash."

"Are we going to be smuggled?"

"That's one word for it," he admitted. "The young men from the surrounding villages, they've gotten together and found a coyote. They don't want to be impressed into service, for either side."

"I see."

"It would take you across the border, into Peru. The *muchachos* plan to stay only a short while, until the conflict is over, then come back. But there's no reason you couldn't continue on to a Peruvian airport."

I nodded. "And they're leaving tonight?"

He turned to face me at last. "I think you could each get a spot for one hundred dollars, American. Cash only, of course."

I nodded again. That would exhaust the funds from my hollow belt.

Raven emerged from our little casita, bundled in her warmest clothes. She smiled at the sight of Pablito with his walker.

"*Buenos dias!*" She joined Don Pablo and me, then immediately picked up on the gravity of our conversation. "What's going on?"

"A coyote leaves tonight," I said. "We're going to be smuggled out of Puerto Malogrado."

———

Don Pablo began building wooden walkers for the kids. The children were annoyed to give up their new toy—if only for the time it took to take measurements. Raven did her best to entertain them. Once again, her camera proved her most effective toy. Pablito had boundless energy for composing shots, then studying them on the screen.

We did our best to pack lightly, culling anything unnecessary, in preparation for what would be our most uncomfortable journey thus far.

"Are you sure about this, Eddie?" Raven asked over the open luggage.

"What do you mean?"

"Should we be leaving right now? With this country in such a state?"

I shrugged. "What choice do we have?"

"It just feels awful, using our American-ness to flee, while all the people here have to ride out the conflict."

"Look." I touched her arm. "This town is out of harm's way. It's not strategic, for either side. And nobody will expect the Morales kids to head off into the fight."

"You're right, of course," she said. "It's not just that. I feel bad for the entire country."

"Well." I sighed. "Unless you know a way to discredit the former Vice Minister and his counterrevolution, then that's all beyond us." I almost said that it was outside of my area, but I didn't truly have an area anymore.

At that, Raven's head cocked to one side. "It's true. If we shamed him enough, the fighting might stop."

"That wasn't actual advice, Raven. That was like a rhetorical thing."

"Pablito?" She opened the casita door and took a step out. "I need my camera, okay?"

Outside, the girls had gotten their original walker back, and one of the homemade ones was nearly finished. Pablito handed Raven her camera. She sat down on the bed and spent the next hour scrolling through the viewfinder and making notes in her notebook.

In the middle of the day, Raven and I took a walk up to the town center. Our purpose was ostensibly to buy nails for the wooden walker construction, but we also wanted to say a proper goodbye to the place.

In the heart of Huanchillo, it was impossible to tell that so much fighting was going on nearby. We bought the nails at the little store behind the iron gate, then ordered a Coke in a bag and sat drinking it on the bench in the square.

Raven held her camera out at arm's length and took a self-portrait of the two of us. I realized I still had on my lab coat—now covered in stains and filth—and felt duly ridiculous. She turned the screen around and showed me the shot.

"Don't we look happy?" she said. "There's a lot to be said for staying in a place like this."

"Is that what you want?" I handed her the bag of Coca-Cola. "Should I call off our smuggler? I haven't paid him yet."

"No." She sighed. "You're right: we should go. Who knows if we'll get another chance."

"Do you hear that?" I asked. A very faint—but somehow familiar—buzzing sound was barely detectable in the distance.

Raven stopped slurping up the last of the soda from a corner of the bag. "Is that? Oh, no."

"Come on." I stood up off the bench, leaving the box of nails.

The buzzing sound increased as I ran up the alley, alongside the church, and found the ancient stone staircase up which we'd followed Arturo just a few days prior. Without turning around, I could feel Raven's presence at my back, only a couple of steps behind.

"Eddie!" she shouted over the now-loud sound of engines. "Look!"

I turned and saw her finger pointed upward. My eyes followed its trajectory up to the small plane banking into a turn at the end of the valley.

"It's true," I said aloud. "The bastard is spraying the potatoes."

Raven already had her camera out. She snapped off several hasty photos of the plane, then tried to compose one that would show its proximity to town.

I continued upward. At the top of the ridge, a pair of farmers scurried in the opposite direction, hands over their mouths. Raven snapped their picture as well.

"Arturo?" I asked them. "Where is Arturo?"

One of them pointed back the way they'd come, but didn't stop heading downward.

My eyes and nostrils stung, and I coughed repeatedly. Still running along the ridgeline, I pulled off my lab coat and wrapped it around my face. Raven continued to track the plane with her camera. It was far in the distance now, sprayers off, as though setting up for another pass.

"Arturo!" I saw him up ahead, foot plow in his hand. We'd managed to run the ridgeline in a fraction of the time it had taken before. He looked up at me, and for once he didn't have a smile or a kind word. A pile of the world's rarest potatoes was gathered at his feet.

Raven and I ran down to him in seconds.

"Let's save whatever we can," I said. "Any of your varietals that are even close to harvest, we should take. Those that aren't, we'll replant elsewhere."

Arturo's face was full of tears, and I wasn't sure whether it was from the sorrow or the poison or some mix of both.

"Eddie." Raven's shutter stopped clicking. "Incoming!"

I looked up and saw the little plane heading toward us. With a veil of white mist trailing from each of its wings, it resembled some unholy aluminum angel.

"Get down!" I shouted.

The three of us huddled against the wall of the terrace. I spread the white lab coat over us like a crude lean-to. Arturo lay there, despondent, his hands in his ancestral dirt, and allowed himself to be covered. Raven held her camera out from under the cloth and snapped off photos without aiming. We all coughed and rubbed our eyes until the buzzing abated.

I finally lifted the coat and emerged, the crop-sprayer nowhere to be seen.

"That son of a whore." Arturo finally spoke.

"Who did this?" I asked. "The Vice Minister?"

"Who else?" Arturo went about gathering his potatoes. "It wasn't FURP. They don't eradicate crops of any kind."

"But why?" I believed him but couldn't find the logic behind it.

"Spite, perhaps." Arturo shrugged. "Or a desperate appeal to the US entities that conspired with him in the war on drugs. Don't spend too much effort looking for sense in it, Doctor. These are the kicks of a drowning man."

With my soiled lab coat, we made a bundle to help carry Arturo's potatoes. We walked back to town, shirts pulled up over our noses, without speaking. Along the ridgeline, we passed by rows of DS 400s—leaves still green and stiff, unaffected by the herbicide.

We spent the next few somber hours at the Morales house, washing and storing Arturo's rescued potatoes. We lined them all up on an outdoor table. Again, I was taken by their incredible variety: purple, brown, pink, long, round, smooth, rough. They represented a wealth of agricultural potential, a treasure trove of tastes, textures, and growing abilities. A fortune in genetic diversity. Which is all to say: they were worthless in the eyes of the twenty-first-century food system.

Arturo asked me again if the potatoes would survive, but I didn't have an answer for him. It was mainly a question of how much exposure they'd had. There was nothing to do but wait—and hope they sprouted.

Niña Rosa asked if we'd be staying for dinner, and I said that I thought so. Any self-respecting smuggler surely wouldn't operate until after dark, right?

She nodded, then pried the little girls away from their walker so they could peel potatoes. Niña Rosa called us all in to eat as the sun was setting. The sky turned its glorious mix of pinks and blues against the Andes, showing them off like sequential rows of teeth.

"*Ven!*" Pablito, exhausted from so many hours on the walker, waved his hand and urged us to come along.

When I first saw the table, I thought it was some kind of joke. At each setting was a plate of French fries.

Don Pablo and Arturo were already sitting, eating from theirs. Raven and I took our seats.

"Yum." Raven bit into the first fry. "*Muy rico!*" she told Niña Rosa.

"*Gracias.*" Niña Rosa dropped a small dish of what looked to be homemade mayonnaise on the table.

"How did you make these?" I picked one up and studied it. It was long and symmetrical, perfectly browned on each side.

She shrugged. "A sharp knife. New oil. A hot pan. It takes time, but it's not difficult."

I took a slow bite and savored the flavor and texture. Chewing minimally, I let the rest dissolve inside my mouth. The perfection of this dish was overwhelming: the richness of oil and salt paired with the wholesome plainness of the potato flesh. The tuber's irregular form married to such a sleek, geometric shape. With my eyes closed, I let the experience sink in for a second, then went back for another—this time with mayonnaise.

"Are you okay, Eddie?" Raven chuckled. "You look like you're taking communion over there."

I smiled, still in awe. "You know something, Raven? I spent the prime productive years of my life trying to replicate this." I held up the most aesthetically perfect of the fries. "To make simulations of this thing. Whether it was frozen or reconstituted or dehydrated or made from a mix or whatever. In many ways, lesser imitations of this miracle food form the foundation of Tuberware's whole empire."

"I never thought of it that way," Raven said.

"Me neither, until now." I kept staring at the fry, vaguely aware that our conversation was getting awkward.

"*Oye*?" Don Pablo asked. "Is everything okay with the food?"

"It's incredible," I turned to him, nodded, and bit that perfect fry in half. With one hand over my mouth, I said, "It's a life-changing meal."

"Oh, my goodness." Niña Rosa chuckled, embarrassed.

"*Hijole*, Doctor." Arturo grinned. "Around here, we call it *papas fritas*."

I turned back to Raven. "This is how it was meant to be: special. Infused with hours of hard work, by cooks who know what they're doing. Why were we always trying to take that away, to make it ubiquitous—into a food that anybody could eat anywhere at any time?"

"To make money, Eddie." She patted me on the shoulder. "Welcome to America."

I nodded and couldn't help but feel a bit silly. At least Niña Rosa was flattered. The second course was a tasty soup—also delicious, but less mind-blowing than the fries.

"Careful about taking on too many fluids," I warned Raven. "Who knows what sort of journey we'll have tonight? There may not be any bathroom breaks."

"Good point."

Once the meal was over, we asked if we could help clean up. As per usual, Niña Rosa was having none of it. The two girls followed their mother to the kitchen, while the rest of us went out to the main room.

Raven and I fetched our packed bags from the casita, while Don Pablo got a fire going.

Arturo waited out front for any sign of our coyote.

Both Raven and I still felt self-conscious about the size of our bags and made last-minute attempts to pare down our loads. I gave Don Pablo a dress shirt and a pair of wool socks—for which he was quite grateful. I also left him my half-empty bottle of hand sanitizer, but he seemed indifferent to that.

Raven shifted her camera bag within her larger backpack, then had a look over at Pablito where he sat tending the fire. She turned back at her camera, changed out the memory card, then took the machine over to the boy.

"Pablito," she said, "would you like to keep this?"

Though he didn't understand, his eyes brightened as she held it in his direction.

"Eddie?" she asked. "What's the word for. . . ."

"*Regalo*," I said. "*Regalo* means gift."

"*Regalo*," she said, holding the camera out toward him.

Pablito turned to his father, who turned to me. I only shrugged and smiled. Don Pablo nodded reluctantly, and the boy reached out to take the gift from her hands.

"Is she sure about this?" Don Pablo asked me.

"I think so," I said. "She can get another one. Pablito seems to have a talent for photography. Perhaps it might become a useful skill for him." Though I had no clear idea what he would do with the digital images once they were taken.

"*Buso!*" called Arturo from the doorway. "Coyote is here!"

We grabbed our now-leaner bags and headed to the front door. Niña Rosa grew teary and gave us hugs. Don Pablo shook our hands. We all turned back to the children, seated near the hearth.

They looked up with entertained confusion—only now understanding that this time we were leaving for good.

"Take care of yourselves, *niños*," I said.

"*Adios*." The three of them grinned. "Thank you."

From chest level, Pablito snapped a parting photograph of us. The flash of light sent him and his sisters into a giggling fit.

Outside, an idling flatbed truck waited, loaded with sacks of potatoes. Arturo spoke to our smuggler, who sat behind the wheel.

"He wants the money up front," Arturo said.

"Right." I fished the last two bills from my pocket.

The smuggler reached his hand out through the window and said, "You'll need to get in the back."

The voice sounded familiar to me. As I held out the cash, I cocked my head. "Oscar? Oscar, is that you?"

"Doctor Morales?" He jumped out of the cab and gave me a quick hug. He then took the cash from my hand and stuffed it into his pocket.

Raven came over to join us and kissed him on the cheek.

"I'm so glad you're both all right," he said.

"What happened to you?" I asked.

He shrugged. "The situation in the city got complicated."

I nodded. "How did you end up in the smuggling business?"

"Work's work," he said. "It's not so different from my old job: drive people around, avoid men in uniform."

"Is this going to be dangerous?" I asked.

"Don't you worry, boss." Oscar shook his head. "Where we cross is a very tiny border. Most of the time, nobody watches it."

That sounded just fine by me. "Shall we go?"

Raven and I were each given two empty potato sacks—one for our lower halves and one for our uppers. The top one had little holes cut in for our eyes. After a lifetime of forcing potatoes to imitate other things, I would now be forced to imitate potatoes.

Our two pieces of luggage were also stuffed inside potato sacks. The other refugees were already wrapped up—two young men from Huanchillo, both fleeing the country in order to avoid being impressed into combat.

Once Oscar had us disguised to his satisfaction, he arranged the actual potato sacks to help hide us.

"*Ya listo!*" he said at last.

The four of us grunted.

For the next several hours, we endured the worst ride that Oscar had yet subjected us to. The road was bumpy and winding. My hips took blows from the hard planks of the truck's bed, while my ribcage absorbed the same from the neighboring sacks. Raven and I tried to keep our bodies close together—to keep something softer and gentler to at least one side of us. But we skittered apart at every pothole or speed bump.

I couldn't help but think of all those Mexicans and Central Americans who endure much longer and more expensive smuggling trips in order to reach our ultimate destination. I thought of the members of my own family who'd been through wetter, hotter versions of this same journey, on their way to the United States.

———

For so many hours, I tried to keep my eyes closed and my body limp, hoping that a sleep-like state might overtake me—even for a minute. But once the far corners of the sky finally did brighten, I felt as if I'd watched every minute of the long Andean night.

As the sun began to rise, all the passengers grew antsy. One of the youngsters even took off his sack hood and had a look around. Raven and I glared at him through our eye-holes. He ignored us, stood, and leaned upon the cab, then immediately jumped down.

"*Buso*!" He grabbed his hood and hastily covered himself up.

"Be ready," I whispered to Raven.

We felt the truck's brakes grind toward a stop. All of us froze, doing our best potato impressions. Raven even closed her eyes.

Over the still-idling engine, I could hear Oscar explaining to somebody that he was simply delivering a load of *papas* to a buyer in Peru.

The official mentioned concern over what he called "deserters" fleeing Puerto Malogrado.

I wondered which side these border officials were on. Had they started taking orders from FURP, or were they still loyal to the Vice Minister? Perhaps—like so many folks in this country—they were hedging their bets.

My heart sank as the engine shut off. The official asked Oscar to get out of the cab. From my hiding spot, I could see the shiny buckle of his belt, the crease of his synthetic pant leg.

He did a pass along the driver's side, poking and prodding at random sacks with his baton. One of his jabs sent a potato right into my kidney, but I managed to keep quiet. He went around to the other side of the truck, and I felt a wave of relief.

"All right," the official finally said. "This looks good."

I then heard three hard whacks from the baton and an audible groan from inside the truck bed.

"What the hell?" The official whistled. Another set of footsteps came toward us.

He grabbed one of the young Huanchillo men under the arms and pulled him from the bed. The refugee kicked at the air, twisting and turning. The second official arrived and pulled the sack off his head.

Oscar feigned surprise, saying that the guy must have snuck aboard during the night. The two officials had their hands full. I risked turning my head and stole a glance at the border: no other uniforms, no dogs or vehicles.

"Raven," I whispered. "Grab your bag."

"What do you mean, Eddie?"

Just then, the second official found the other Huanchillo man and began pulling him from the truck.

"I mean . . . run!"

We popped up on our side of the truck's bed—to the shock of the border guards. I pulled off my crude potato hood, then yanked off Raven's. She chucked our luggage over the side while I struggled out of my potato-sack bottoms. The first guard started climbing into the truck bed, but I pushed a full sack of potatoes at him. The top of it came untied, and the spuds rained on his head.

"Come on, Eddie!" Raven hopped out of the truck and stood by our luggage on the border side.

I jumped down and joined her and grabbed a bag, and we took off.

With her long legs and quality boots, Raven soon overtook me. I stole a glance over my shoulder. One of the guards was coming after us, while the other stayed with the two who'd been caught.

"*Pare!*" he yelled. "*Alto!*"

But we kept right on running.

Up ahead, there was another checkpoint, this one with a swinging gate and fencing on either side.

"What do we do, Eddie?" Raven asked.

I turned back to our pursuer. He'd gained a little ground on me, waving that same baton he'd used to whack at the potato sacks. I looked up at the guard station on the Peruvian side. There didn't seem to be anyone manning it. Perhaps they started at a later hour.

"Just go on through it!" I yelled to Raven.

The guard giving chase discovered his whistle at some point and blew it.

At a full gallop, Raven undid a series of buckles on her pack and held it out in front of her. She reached the gate, dove, and rolled underneath. On the other side, she strapped her bag on again and resumed running.

Once at the gate, I attempted the same move but lost my nerve at the last second. I settled for crawling underneath the swinging arm on my hands and knees.

On the Peruvian side, I rose to my feet, reached back for my bag, and was surprised by a smack across my upper knuckles. The guard stood there scowling—whistle still in his mouth, his baton cocked back for another blow.

"Ouch!" I screamed, my hand throbbing in pain.

Still on the far side of the barrier, he grabbed my hurt hand by the wrist.

"Hey!" I tried to pry myself away, but the hand he was holding was too tender. I clenched my teeth and prepared to block the blow with my good arm.

"Fucker!" was the next sound I heard.

Raven used the butt end of her backpack as a battering ram against the torso of the guard, sending him to the ground. From under the barrier, she gave him a kick to the ribs.

I held my hurt wrist in my good hand.

She grabbed both bags and said, "C'mon!"

We ran awkwardly for the next half mile, until the border disappeared from our view. The guards must have given up on us.

"That was a close one." Raven put down the bags and had a look at my hand. "Why were there no officials on the Peruvian side?"

I shrugged. "Maybe they don't have to worry about anybody sneaking into Puerto Malogrado. Or maybe they just sleep in later."

"Do you think it's broken?" she gestured toward my wrist.

"I doubt it. Probably just a bruise."

She took out a gauze bandage and some medical tape and did a hasty wrap job.

"Thanks, Raven," I said.

"I'm not sure it'll do much."

"No, I mean thanks for your help back there. Thanks for coming back to get me."

She looked up from the tape. "Don't mention it." She tore the end off and stowed the role of tape. "So, what do we do now?"

I looked around the horizon. "Find a town? Find some transport? Maybe make our way to an airport, and then go home."

Raven nodded. "Why don't you take my bag? You don't want to be holding this one." She helped hoist her backpack up onto my shoulders.

"Wow," I stood up straight, felt the weight rest against my spine. "This is comfortable."

"You don't say." Raven extended the handle and rolled my suitcase as best she could.

We were on a dusty dirt road in a strange nation, not far from a forgotten border. I had no reason to expect to find a town or anything else around here. Peru was a huge country, after all, with large tracts of jungle, desert, and mountain wilderness. Much of its land was not only uninhabited but uninhabitable. We pressed on, in the absence of a better idea, mostly on the notion that this road had to lead somewhere.

"What do you think happened to the others, back at the border?" Raven asked.

"Who knows?" I said. "I'm not even sure which government those border agents are working for."

"Do you think they'll have to go and fight—on either side?"

"It's possible," I admitted. "But let's hope they just confiscate the money and the potatoes and send them all on their way."

"Everyone would be so much better off if the fighting just stopped already."

"Apart from the losing side, you mean?"

"Them too—whoever it ends up being. The sooner the healing starts, the better for all parties." Raven said it so earnestly, you'd have thought our opinions had some bearing on the future of the little country we'd just fled.

"Hey," I pointed ahead with my good hand. "What's that?"

A short distance down the road, a crude stone terrace emerged from the hillside, in what I immediately recognized as a potato field ready for harvest.

"What?" Raven asked.

"It's a little parcel of land. There must be somebody living nearby, a farmhouse at least."

We quickened our pace to a lopsided jog. Raven picked my bag up off the ground and carried it on her hip.

Sure enough, we soon caught sight of an adobe house with a clay-tile roof. It looked a hundred years old.

"*Hola*?" we yelled. "*Por favor? Auxilio?*"

Finally, a woman emerged in a colorful wool dress, carrying a baby wrapped in a cloth. A couple of llamas made their way to the edge of the yard, and I immediately flinched at them.

"Excuse me," I asked in my slowest, most deliberate Spanish. "We need to find transportation. Is there anyone nearby with a vehicle?" She shook her head and spoke laboriously: "*Yo, Castellano . . . no mucho.*"

"What's the matter?" Raven asked.

"She doesn't speak Spanish," I said.

To the woman, I said, "Um . . . *Pueblo*?" I raised my hands inquisitively. "*Sí, sí.*" She nodded and pointed in the direction we were heading.

We thanked her and continued on with a greater skip to our step. Soon, we did indeed come to the outskirts of a town. Raven took out the torn pages from her guidebook and located us on a small map.

In the town's main square, a pickup truck with tall steel rails sat parked, its driver shouting like a carnival barker and loading people inside. I asked where he was going and how much. Raven looked at her map and nodded. We searched our pockets and found just enough change for the fare.

Soon we were crammed shoulder to shoulder with dozens of other passengers, standing upright in the pickup bed and all trying desperately to get a few fingers around the rails along the sides. It was a top-heavy, high-speed ride through the hills—which nobody seemed to mind, other than me. I couldn't manage with only one good hand. The local men were kind enough to allow Raven a nice grip. By the end, I was hugging her torso to keep from falling down with every curve and brake.

By suppertime, we'd made our way to a bigger city, one with a four-story hotel that took credit cards. We wasted no time booking a room. My legs were exhausted, and I was ecstatic to lie down upon the bed and watch bad Peruvian game shows. Raven, on the other hand, riffled through her bag the second we checked in, and then took out some notes and documents.

"I'm going to the internet café down in the lobby," she said.

"Now?" I was shocked that she had the energy. "We just got here. Let's relax, regroup. They must have an airport here. We'll catch a flight to Lima tomorrow, then get back to the US. This adventure is over for us already, Raven."

"I know." She sat down on the bed and put a hand on my aching thigh. "There's a couple of loose ends I want to tie up first. I won't be able to relax until I do. Don't worry. See you soon." She kissed me on the forehead and left the room.

fter Raven left, I took off my shoes and socks and stared at the television: some ridiculous family competition show. Fathers crawled along greased telephone poles suspended over pools of ice water. Mothers sat bound to chairs while their children smothered them with condiments. The crowd went crazy. None of it made any sense to me. For a moment, I felt a pang of nostalgia for Puerto Malogrado's television programming, where at least the agendas were always clear.

After that show ended, they broke in with the news. The conflict in Puerto Malogrado was at the top of the segment. Apparently, the Vice Minister and his loyal forces were in the middle of a major air offensive on the capital. My heart sank as I watched images of bombed-out buildings—many of them familiar. The dusty stadium we'd seen from the air was in flames. Why? Only a few kids with half-inflated balls ever played there.

The Peruvian newscasters spoke about FURP as though they were a passing threat. They didn't interview any actual citizens of Puerto Malogrado. Instead, they had a panel of talking heads in the studio—political-science professors and former diplomats. One of them referred to FURP as a terrorist group. All thought they would be vanquished within days and the Vice Minister restored.

I couldn't take any more of it and clicked the television off.

After an hour or so, a legion of dark clouds invaded the sky. From our hotel window, I watched the storm take shape. It was more dramatic than anything on TV. I stood up from the bed and witnessed the gathering thunderheads. Soon, the sun was blocked completely, and the streets took on a flat, monochromatic hue. Then the rain came down. The drops were soft at first, little sprays that soaked into the hot concrete. But within seconds they'd become fat as water balloons, exploding against the glass of my window. People scurried out of storefronts and hastily opened their umbrellas. Motorbike drivers went extra fast—their tires spraying tall fins of dirty water—as though they might outrun the storm. Across the street, a broad Peruvian flag adorned a government building. Now soaking wet, the flag hung limp and heavy, dripping a long rope of water from its corner down to the sidewalk.

I thought about Spencer Kearns and what his next move might be. For once, he had a right to be angry with me. How much public embarrassment would he heap upon me now? And would he wait a while, like I had asked him to, so it didn't prevent the British researchers from going to Huanchillo?

I was still watching the storm when Raven returned. She carried a six-pack of beer and a white paper bag.

"Dinner in bed?" She held both items up to shoulder level.

"You read my mind," I said. "I was afraid we'd have to go out in this."

"There's a little *tienda* right next door. The front desk changed some money for me."

"Perfect."

"That's the good news." Raven held a beer bottle against the TV stand. She whacked the shoulder of the bottle with her open hand and the cap popped off.

"And the bad news?" I accepted the beer from her.

"There's no airport here."

"Shit." I took a sip.

"Apparently they have some long-distance buses to Lima. But the schedule and the different classes—it was over my head."

"No worries." I reached into the bakery bag and found a small empanada dusted in powdered sugar. "I'll look into it in the morning. Let's just rest tonight."

"Fine by me." She went into the paper bag after me.

We both bit into our empanadas. They were full of finely chopped beef and were now at room temperature. But under the circumstances, they were delicious.

Night fell, and the storm settled down. The last few days finally caught up to both of us, and we fell asleep before we'd even finished the beers.

slept as deeply as I had in weeks. When I finally began to awaken, there was a puddle of drool on my pillow and crust over my eyes. I heard a tick-tacking sound not far away. My first thought: that another rainstorm was starting, that these were the first few drops against the window.

But the little clicks grew faster, more sporadic, somehow familiar. I rolled over in bed and saw that it was Raven, sitting on the one tiny chair in the room, already typing away at her laptop.

"Morning, sleepyhead!" Her eyes didn't leave her screen. "I was starting to wonder if you'd ever get up."

"I must've needed the rest." My back suddenly felt so stiff and tight, I couldn't lie still any longer.

"So, let me ask you this, Eddie: Is it safe to say that by spraying those potatoes, the Vice Minister committed a crime against biodiversity?"

"It's safer to say it now that we're outside Puerto Malogrado."

"You know what I mean." She finally turned to look at me. "Is it accurate?"

"We don't know for sure that it was the Vice Minister, for one thing."

"I know." Raven nodded. "I'm making that clear."

"And secondly—for better or for worse—there is no such thing as a 'crime against biodiversity.' If there were, a whole lot of folks would be guilty of it."

She put her hands up to her own forehead, frustrated. "How would you describe it?"

I groaned. It was too early in the morning for this. "Those potatoes, they're a gold mine—botanically speaking. If you look at all the potato species as a mile-wide spectrum, what we grow and eat represents a couple

279

of inches. Arturo had varieties I'd never seen or heard about. He kept them going despite all the economic pressures against him. No matter your position on GMOs, you have to respect the amount of genetic uniqueness there."

Raven resumed typing, this time more furiously.

"Sorry," I said. "Not exactly a sound bite."

"No, Eddie, it's very helpful. Thanks."

"What are you working on, anyway?" I asked.

"My blog. I really want to make a difference this time, to turn the tide against the Vice Minister."

I nodded. "That's noble of you." It was also a bit quixotic. But I'd learned not to underestimate Raven and her writing.

"Something doesn't seem right," she went on. "I know it's only been ten hours or so, but my post from last night hasn't gotten much traction. And here I can post to all the social media sites that were blocked in Malogrado."

"What was your post about?" I asked.

"The crop-spraying, of course."

I nodded. "Raven, I've got some bad news for you."

"What's that?" She paused her typing.

"The crimes of the Vice Minister—as grievous as they are—they're unlikely to get as much attention as the other stories you've broken lately."

"Why do you say that?"

I sighed, searching for the right words. "There's no nice way to put it: people like freak shows." I thought of that day at the Vice Minister's country estate, the science experiments gone wrong that he collected. "Kids walking on their hands, that draws eyes. I see it all the time in my field—my former field. Why do you think strawberries with flounder genes get so much more attention than Golden Rice? Or the fact that all the legal or economic implications of GMOs always play second fiddle to a good 'Frankenfood' horror story?"

She nodded her head, narrowed her eyes. "I understand."

"I think it's great what you're doing, Raven." Was it possible that I was still belittling her career—now accidentally? "But I know how people are. Oppressive third-world dictators are a dime a dozen. That's not what goes viral."

She squinted at her copy, as if trying to read it from a great distance.

"Why don't I go get us some coffee and look for a bus schedule?" I rose from the bed, put on my pants.

"Eddie? Can I quote what you said? About Arturo's potatoes and whatnot?"

I shrugged. "Fine by me. But I don't know what you'd call me. 'Unemployed food scientist' doesn't sound so impressive."

She laughed. "How about 'potato expert Eduardo Morales'?"

"That's nice." I grinned. "'*Internationally renowned* potato expert' would be even better."

She resumed typing. "International sex symbol and potato hobbyist Eddie Morales. . . ."

I couldn't bring myself to laugh. "Seriously, though, Raven, you don't want to trade too heavily on my name."

"What are you talking about?" She turned to me once again.

"I came clean with Kearns, about my role in his abduction. He wasn't happy. While he was in prison, he threatened me, said he would expose me as being a cheater and a hack scientist."

"Could he do that?"

I shrugged. "He has the cheating incident in college. Apparently his dad helped me get hired at Tuberware. He's got a lot of dirt, and he'd control the story."

"Why hasn't he done anything yet?"

"I begged him to wait a little while, until that British team has a chance to help the Morales kids. Maybe he's cooperating with that part, at least."

Raven turned back to her screen. "You really think he's capable of something like this?"

"I don't know," I admitted. "He was pretty good at humiliating me for no reason. I'm scared of what he might do, now that I deserve it." I opened up the door. "I'll be back soon."

"See you," Raven said.

—

An urn of coffee and a stack of cups sat on a table by the front desk. I helped myself. The young man at the desk offered me directions to the bus station: a series of rights and lefts along unfamiliar streets.

After all the rest, it felt good to be on my feet again, the sun on my face. This objective—to get the two of us from here to the Lima airport—was cut-and-dried, clear and unambiguous. It was the most straightforward task I'd been charged with since the French-fry machine.

I had to ask a couple of people on the street, but I found the bus station soon enough.

Inside, I waited in line while others bought their tickets. Above the counter hung a cryptic list of arrival and departure times, but I couldn't make sense of it. The customer ahead of me had a local paper, and I struggled to read the headlines over his shoulder. Above the fold, there was a picture of the Peruvian president and a quote that expressed his support for Puerto Malogrado's Vice Minister. I turned away.

Once at the front of the line, I was shocked to hear how long the trip to Lima would take: at least twenty hours. I dropped my head into my hands and massaged my temples, worried that I was about to break out in tears in front of everyone.

The attendant spoke in soothing tones. "I do have some spots available in premier class, for the bus that leaves at two this afternoon. It's our most comfortable service, and you'll probably be asleep most of the time. Wi-Fi and entertainment are included."

"Wi-Fi?" I asked. Raven would like that, at least.

"*Sí.*" He nodded.

"Very well," I said. "I'll take two. The best seats you have available." I handed over my credit card, without asking the cost.

"We'll see you this afternoon." The attendant smiled and gave me the tickets. "Thank you for traveling with us."

I took my card and the tickets and headed back to the hotel.

———

Raven was already down in the lobby's little business center, uploading her latest work to the internet.

"I've got bad news," I said. "The bus is going to take over twenty hours to get to Lima."

"I figured as much." Her eyes stayed on the screen. "Like you said, it's a huge country."

"We're in premier class. It has free Wi-Fi, apparently."

"Great!" she said. "When do we leave?"

"Two this afternoon."

"Got it. I should finish up soon."

"How's it going?" I asked. "With your blog?"

"Good." She nodded. "Your advice was helpful."

———

Soon enough, we had our bags repacked and once again hauled them along the street.

"How's that bag holding up?" Raven asked, leaning into her sternum strap.

"This will be its last voyage," I said.

At some point during yesterday's ordeal, one of the wheels had come off my rolling suitcase. My only options now were either to carry it or to drag it along the ground—one corner sliding against concrete. At least my injured hand was feeling better.

We found a little lunch place right across from the bus depot and settled in to have a bite before the trip began.

"This is fun," Raven said. "I've always wanted to try Peruvian food."

The menu was full of items I didn't recognize—regional specialties with Andean names. I warned Raven that it would be a guessing game. She was undeterred. We ordered the three-course, prix fixe lunch. The first turned out to be some kind of cold potato salad, covered in slices of boiled egg and a creamy yellow sauce. Raven's main was duck with seasoned rice, a dish that resembled paella. Mine was a red pepper stuffed with chopped beef.

"This looks great!" Raven said.

"*Buen provecho*," I said. "I'm starving."

I took one bite and immediately felt off. A tingling sensation began in the back of my mouth—at first metallic, then burning. Beads of sweat broke out on my forehead.

"Eddie? Are you okay?" Raven asked.

"Spicy," I uttered through a still-full mouth. "Very spicy."

Then the worst part: a cloud of searing vapor worked its way up from the back of my throat through my sinuses. My vision grew grainy, as it had during my two recent fainting spells. I stood up off my chair and braced myself against the table.

Raven jumped out of her seat. From the corner of my eye I saw her open a cooler along the restaurant's wall. She pulled out a liter of beer. Using the same move as the night before, she popped the cap off on the tabletop and handed me the amber bottle. I took a long swallow of cold beer, which seemed to make things worse at first, then better.

Finally, I sat down and regained my composure. The waitress came over with two empty glasses and filled each of them from the open bottle.

"*Pica*, no?" She pointed at my plate and suppressed a laugh.

I nodded and took another sip.

"So." Raven managed to contain her laughter. "That's not a sweet pepper, I guess."

I shook my head. "Hard to believe they're in the same genus."

She grinned and switched our two plates. With her knife, she cut the stuffed pepper into tiny pieces, while I tucked into the duck and rice.

"Wow, this *is* hot," she said. "Why did peppers evolve their spiciness, anyway?"

I shrugged. "There are several small advantages. The spice chemical resists fungus. Hot peppers are often eaten by birds, rather than by terrestrial animals; that spreads their seeds farther. Some think that humans started eating them because they increase salivation, which can be helpful in cultures with simple, bland diets—all rice or potatoes."

"Huh." Raven nodded. "Not a problem for us today."

With the help of the beer, we made it through the rest of the meal and were given a dessert of rice pudding.

I found a clock on the wall. "We should get going."

Raven pulled out some Peruvian bills and laid them on the counter.

I felt a little tipsy as we crossed the street to the bus depot. At the front counter, an attendant tagged our luggage. We followed him out to the garage.

"Okay," he said. "Two passengers. Premier class. Destination: Lima. Go ahead and board."

"There must be some mistake." I stared at the monstrosity before us. It was a mid-century bus, with the textured silver siding and the split level. The body was covered with patches of Bondo and primer, though the old Greyhound logo was still visible. A massive medallion of the Virgen de Guadalupe took up half the windshield.

"This is premier class?" I asked.

"Yes, sir," the attendant said. "Our finest service."

"What's your *least* fine service?" I asked.

He pointed to the other side of the depot. There, an ancient school bus—an even older model—sat idling. It was painted baby blue with psychedelic drawings of pyramids, condors, and shooting stars. The phrase "*Dios Me Bendiga*" stretched across the near side.

"Economy class," the attendant explained. "Would you like to switch?"

"We're good," Raven assured him. "Come on, Eddie. This will be fine."

The attendant ripped our tickets and showed us to the bus door.

"Whoa." Raven climbed the stairs, her laptop tucked under her arm. "Look at this. It's like a time machine."

The interior was far better maintained. The seats all had two-tone leather upholstery. The panels were a vintage avocado green. Blue curtains lined the rounded windows.

"Looks like we're upstairs." Raven held our tickets and pointed the way.

I followed her to the upper deck.

"Look!" she said.

"Well, this isn't bad," I said. Without realizing it, I'd reserved two seats at the very front of the top deck, meaning we had a panoramic view from above the driver. "Maybe premier class will work out after all."

"It's perfect," Raven said. "Do you mind if I take the window seat?"

"Be my guest." It wasn't like there was any lack of a view.

Raven opened up her laptop. I closed my eyes while the other passengers boarded—silently hoping that nobody would sit behind us, so that I might recline my seat with abandon.

Minutes later, the bus fired up and we lurched our way out of the depot. The driver wound through the tight urban streets until we finally arrived at an open road and gained speed. Raven closed her computer and enjoyed the view.

We seemed to be heading through a broad valley—farms and ranches on either side. We saw pastures full of sheep, cows, and llamas. I recognized some fields of potatoes, others that looked like corn or possibly sorghum. The sky was blue and cloudless, framed on every side by snow-capped Andean peaks in the distance.

After a while, we passed by a small village not unlike Huanchillo. The *campesinos* stood in their traditional garb, babies swaddled in bright wool blankets, women with long braided hair and tall hats, a fuzzy alpaca in tow. Raven was rapt. I almost asked if she regretted giving away her camera.

Now that we were essentially out of danger and on our way home, I couldn't help but worry about the Morales family and the rest of Puerto Malogrado. I'd been so focused on getting us out of there in one piece. Now I shared Raven's concerns and felt bad for having left in such a hurry.

"Raven?" I asked. "How's the blogging going?"

She turned away from her window and opened up her computer for the first time since we'd left the station. "I thought about what you said, about what it takes to get traction online. I certainly don't want to go back to the well with the Morales kids."

"Of course not."

"So I did a sort of first-person thing about my time in the jail. Ramped up the drama a little bit. Made it feel longer than it actually was, made FURP out to be a little more heroic than they were."

"Good thinking," I said. "How'd it work out?"

"Got a few reposts, last time I checked." She tapped a few keys and stared at the screen. "I can't find any sort of signal now."

"I'll handle this." I stood up and walked down to the bus driver.

"Excuse me, sir?" I said politely. "The Wi-Fi doesn't seem to be working."

"The what?" he said.

Through his windshield, the well-paved two-lane highway stretched out toward the horizon.

"The internet?"

"Oh, right." He opened a cabinet underneath the dash and exposed a pile of cables and boxes, dimly glowing with green LED lights.

"Let's try this." Without taking his foot off the gas, he then abandoned the wheel completely and reached into the cabinet. "Sometimes you just have to turn it off and then turn it back on again."

My mouth hung open as I stared at the highway. A flatbed truck came at us in the opposite lane. Our bus veered across the yellow line. I could see the trucker's eyes. He grimaced and pulled down his horn.

"*Cuidado!*" I screamed.

The bus driver rose back up and took the wheel. He inched back into our lane just as we passed.

"Ha!" he said. "Don't worry yourself. I could drive this road in my sleep."

"Please don't try that tonight," I insisted.

"Eddie!" Raven called down from the upper deck. "It's working now."

I considered scolding the driver for his recklessness but knew there was no point. Instead, I said, "*Gracias*" and went back to my seat.

"How's it going?" I asked Raven.

"Good." Her eyes were glued to the screen. "It looks like my piece has gotten some attention since this morning. I'm trying to figure out why. Somebody must have shared it. I need to see the pingbacks."

"Wait," I said. "Let's check the news about Puerto Malogrado first, see if the needle's moving against the Vice Minister at all."

"Good thinking." Raven entered some search terms.

I watched over her shoulder as the pages struggled to load. "Look!" I pointed at one of the headlines: *Inter-American Commission on Human Rights Denounces Vice Minister.*

"And they're calling him the 'former' Vice Minister in all the global papers."

"Click through to that one," I said, curious as to what had prompted the IACHR's denouncement.

The article came up slowly, along with several frozen online ads. I saw something about the Vice Minister's "fledgling counterrevolution" before the whole browser crashed.

"What happened?"

Raven shrugged. "The Wi-Fi went down again." She tapped her track-pad but got nothing. "Do you want to speak to the driver?"

"No!" I said. "We'll wait until we're stopped. What did you catch from that article?"

"Something about the 'rights of journalists' caught my eye."

"Your post must've gotten out there, don't you think?"

Raven shrugged. "I'm not sure how. Something must've happened."

"We'll figure it out at our next stop." I patted her knee. "This is good news." Silently, I worried over when I might have the nerve to search for my own name and see what sort of vengeance Kearns had cooked up for me.

Nobody was sitting behind us, so I reclined my seat as far as it would go and took in the scenery. Soon, the straight valley road that we'd been traveling on for so long wound up into the mountains. Raven and I turned from left to right, catching glimpses of multi-colored lakes and tall snow-capped peaks. Around dinnertime, we came to a small town, and the driver pulled to a stop.

Raven leaned into my ear. "Are you going to ask him about the internet?"

"Yes. Give me a second."

The door swung open, and a small army of food vendors climbed aboard—baskets and buckets suspended on their heads and at their hips. They shouted out the names of their wares: dumplings, meat pies, roasted corn, fried yucca, pickled fruit, banana chips, even skewers with charred chickens' feet.

"We better get some food, Eddie," Raven suggested. "There might not be another stop tonight."

"You're right." With the vendors now crowding the aisle, I couldn't get up to find the driver anyway.

We pointed at a few of the offerings—but stayed away from the chickens' feet—and ended up with a good spread of *ahumadas*, *pasteles*, and chips. The vendors did a brisk trade with the other passengers. Once they began to file out, I made my way downward behind them to the driver's seat.

"Excuse me," I said. "We don't seem to have Wi-Fi anymore."

Just then, a new crop of passengers started to board the bus. They pushed their way around me as I stood awkwardly in their path. Each of them handed a few folded-up bills to the driver as they boarded.

"Let's see." The driver popped open that same compartment and flipped the power switch back and forth once again. I looked up to Raven, but she shook her head.

He tried unplugging and re-plugging a few cords, then finally threw up his hands. "Sorry, sir. Up here in the mountains, we often get no service at all."

"Speaking of service," I said. "I believe the tickets we bought were for direct service to Lima, were they not?"

"What?" He shrugged. "You didn't want a little dinner?"

"I'm okay with a little dinner," I said. "It's the boarding of new people that I'm not okay with."

He laughed out loud. "Why don't you go around and tell your fellow passengers that they need to freeze on this platform tonight, because you don't want their company." He shook his head, tucked the wad of bills into his front pocket, and then turned on the bus's ignition.

After a half-second, I decided it would be best if I just went back to my seat.

The new passengers had filled in all the empty spots on our upper deck—and probably at a far lower price than what we'd paid. Somebody had restored my seat to its upright position, and now a bony set of knees poked right through the ancient upholstery into the small of my back.

"Any luck?" Raven asked between bites of banana chip.

"He thinks there's no signal up here in the mountains." I shook my head.

"Oh, well." Raven passed me the bag of chips. "Let's have some food, get some sleep, and deal with it in the morning."

"Fair enough." I wondered where the eye mask I'd brought from Idaho had gone. Surely it had been lost in one of the luggage purges we'd gone through over the past days.

———

The next leg of our journey made the first feel like a short jaunt in a private jet. We headed straight up into the Andes, on a series of narrow switchbacks and blind corners. The roads themselves looked barely wide enough for a motorcycle; this seventy-year-old triple-axle bus had absolutely no business on them.

Our seats in the upper deck went from blessing to curse, as the bus lurched and leaned through every bend. Though it was technically a beautiful sunset—a brilliant collage of purple and orange—it filled me with terror: I could hardly imagine how we'd continue on this road after dark.

Raven somehow fell asleep before night had even fallen. From all around me came a chorus of snoring Peruvians. I kept worrying that some of the snores might be coming from the driver himself, but so far he'd managed to crank the wheel at every corner.

Soon, all I could see was the moon up above and a dim glow from the headlights below me. The bus swayed like a ship at sea. Indeed, we could've been traveling on the ocean, or through space, for all I could tell. For the remainder of the sleepless night, unsure of which way was up, I clutched my armrests as if that alone might keep the bus on the road.

A t some point, I must've managed to fall asleep. A beam of morning sunlight rose between mountain peaks and flickered into the bus. The light reached my eyes in intermittent bursts and coaxed me awake.

It was dawn, and we were rolling along a smooth, flat road. The hills to our right were dry and brown—more like southern Idaho than the lush green peaks of Puerto Malogrado. To our left was an inky dark ocean, which I hoped was the Pacific.

"Morning, Eddie," Raven whispered. Her computer sat, closed, on her lap. "How'd you sleep?"

"Hardly at all," I said. "That midnight pass was more than I'd bargained for."

"I slept through the whole thing," Raven said.

"Lucky you. Any internet?"

"None. I figure we'll have to wait until we get to Lima."

I nodded. "It's not like the civil war is going anywhere."

"Right."

For a while I was able to enjoy the stillness of the morning and the smoothness of the freeway. Soon, however, we came to a stretch of blacktop poured right on top of a tremendous sand dune running along the sea.

Out Raven's window was a massive drop-off—several stories high— all the way down to the dark ocean. I willed myself to look away. The road ahead had no shoulder and no pilings or foundation of any kind. Just sand. A couple of times, I thought I recognized marks where other vehicles had gone tumbling off.

Other passengers began to wake up. Many made their way to the bathroom. A baby cried near the back. Once the urban landscape of Lima finally sprang up in the distance, it came as a great relief. Half-built brick houses, lots full of concrete sculptures, smoking roadside barbeques, secondhand tire stores, hillside slums—I never thought I'd be so happy to see a filthy third-world megalopolis.

"We must be getting close," Raven said.

"Thank goodness."

———

The bus depot turned out to be in a neighborhood where we didn't want to spend a lot of time. I looked forward to gathering our things, finding a cab, getting to the airport, and buying passage back to the States.

I waited in line for our bags while Raven found a seat and tried to connect to the web. A uniformed handler took luggage out from the bus and placed the pieces on a stainless steel table. With each new item, a half-dozen hands went out to grab it—as if it were their own. The handler had to fend them off until he saw the correct claim ticket.

It didn't make much sense to me. Were my fellow passengers hoping to walk off with better luggage than they'd traveled with? Or double their haul? At any rate, I had to be vigilant.

Raven's backpack came up early and was popular with false claims. I boxed out several others on my way up to the table. The handler studied my ticket closely, then handed it over. I strapped the backpack on and waited for my suitcase. Raven was engrossed in her laptop; she must've found a signal.

Finally, my formerly rolling bag was placed on the table. This time, nobody went for it. I looked around at the other passengers, offended by their low opinion of it. The handler only gave a half-hearted glance at my ticket, then let me have the bag.

"Okay." I joined Raven where she sat. "Let's find a cab and get the hell out of here already."

"Eddie." Raven stared at her screen. "You're not going to believe this."

"What?" I dropped the suitcase onto an adjacent chair. "Your blog is getting legs?"

"It's Kearns." She looked up at me. "Kearns is the one who's been sharing it, been pushing it out there to all his followers."

"Say what?" I unclipped her backpack, dropped it to the floor, and sat down beside her.

"Check it out. First, he put my post about the incarceration up on his site and wrote about how he'd gone through the same thing."

"Typical Kearns," I said. "Always making it about him."

"Social media blew up with it. Then he went back and did the same thing with my post about the crop-spraying. Now he just posted a video of your speech at the Ministry."

"He mentioned my speech?"

She held the screen closer to me. There was a brief note about how we hadn't always seen eye to eye, but that in this video I'd gotten everything right.

"He called it 'a master class on agro-colonialism,'" Raven explained.

"I don't know what that means," I admitted.

She shrugged. "You should figure it out. You're the master of it."

I looked away from the screen, put my fingers up to my temples.

"This is crazy," Raven went on. "He's making Puerto Malogrado his cause célèbre. All the greenie groups are running with it. Look at all these American kids posting pictures of themselves with the FURP bandanna. There's going to be a benefit concert in Central Park. Kearns is doing the talk-show circuit as we speak."

"What about in the country?" I asked. "Has the Vice Minister lost any actual ground in the conflict?"

Raven punched in some new terms but couldn't quite get what she wanted. "All the big Western leaders have denounced him, said it's time for him to go. It's hard to tell how the military part is doing."

She typed in a new search and scanned the headlines. "It looks like he's on the run. I don't see any new attacks. Public opinion sure has lined up against him."

"That's promising."

She looked up and turned to me. "It's a matter of finding whatever hole he's in and bringing him to justice."

I nodded. "Let's hope they find him soon. And that he doesn't do anything desperate in the meantime, doesn't take anyone else down with him."

Raven shut her computer. "Should we go get a cab?"

—

We gathered our things and went out to the taxi stand—an only slightly more organized version of the one in Puerto Malogrado. A kind-faced driver was the next in line, and he helped pile our bags into the trunk of his rusting yellow cab. Raven brought her laptop with her to the back seat.

I did my best to take in the scenery of this famous city I'd never seen. But Lima wasn't meeting me halfway. The neighborhood was mostly garages and warehouses. The sky was covered in a gray layer that was either fog or pollution or some mixture of both. No sign of the mountains or the coastline for which this country was famous. The driver spoke into his cell phone, some cryptic code involving the airport. Raven clicked away at her keyboard. I heard a plane landing nearby and figured we were getting close.

At a corner, the cab driver abruptly veered toward the curb where a man in a jean jacket and matching jeans stood waving one hand. Our cab pulled right up to him. I thought the driver was about to ask directions, but instead he opened up the passenger-side door.

"Eddie." Raven looked up. "What's going on?"

I sighed. "He's probably just trying to pick up an extra fare."

"*Oye!*" I shouted to the driver.

The denim-clad man hopped into the front seat and shut the door.

"No, *hombre!*" I barked. "We're paying full fare. This isn't a *collectivo.*"

The driver pulled away from the curb with a squeak of the tires. The man in the jean jacket turned toward Raven and me in the back seat, pointing a small handgun in our direction.

"Money," he said. "Now."

stared down the barrel of this stranger's pistol, squinting my eyes as though it were a keyhole and an explanation lay on the other side. I almost asked who had sent him: the Vice Minister? Tuberware? Some malcontent within FURP? It wasn't until Raven reached into her wallet and took out the last of her Peruvian bills that I understood that this man was just a common thief. It was almost too simple.

Raven handed over the little cash that we had. I did the same—though mine was much less, and in Puerto Malogrado's nearly worthless currency.

The gunman grimaced at the sight of it. "The computer," he grunted at Raven.

She hugged her beloved machine a little tighter.

My mouth opened as if to say something, but what? Tell this thief how much that laptop meant to her? That it was her livelihood, much as that pistol was his?

Fortunately, Raven surrendered it a half-second later.

The gunman was still frustrated by the size of the haul. "*Poquito*," he whispered to the driver.

Only then did I put together that the two of them were in cahoots.

The driver shrugged. "Express?" he said.

"Oh, shit," I said aloud, in English.

"Take out your wallets," the gunman said.

"Eddie, what's going on?" Raven asked.

"This is going to get worse before it gets better, Raven. But be cool and we'll get through it."

After a few quick turns, we pulled up in front of an empty bank branch. Outside of it stood an ATM within a small glassed-in booth. The gunman came around to my side of the car and opened up my door.

"*Amigo.*" He held the gun under his jacket. "*Vamos.*"

"I'll be right back," I said to Raven.

Once I was standing, the gunman walked behind me, pushed me toward the glass cell with the cash machine.

"Your card," he said.

I took out my debit card and swiped it along the door's reader. It showed a green light. Together, we walked inside. A blast of cool air-conditioning met us there, helped slow the sweat now covering my body. I turned back to check on Raven. She nodded at me.

The gunman gave me an impatient shove from behind. I felt the metal of his pistol against my back and lurched forward.

"The machine," he shouted. "*Ya!*"

I put my card into the slot. There was a small electric eye above the screen. I mouthed the word "*ladrón*" but didn't expect anything to come of it.

The limit for a cash withdrawal was three hundred dollars, converted to the local currency. I took it out, handed it over, and said, "That's all the machine will let me take."

He eyed me suspiciously.

I might've gotten a cash advance from my Visa card, but those rates were robbery. These assholes weren't going to ruin my credit along with everything else.

"Wallet," he said.

"What?"

"Your wallet." He pointed the gun at me. The two of us stood alone inside that glass box.

I handed it over to him.

"Go get the girl." He put the pistol inside his jacket once again.

I stepped out of the box, wishing that the police or at least a teenaged security guard might pass by. A man in coveralls was walking on the opposite side of the street but seemed to be purposefully averting his eyes, as though he'd seen this all before.

"Raven," I opened the door to the cab.

"Yeah, Eddie?"

"Let's get this over with. They just need some cash from your debit card, and we'll be done."

She nodded and climbed out of the seat.

"Sorry, *amigo*." The cab driver lifted his palms. "You know what they say: some rob you with a pistol, and some rob you with a pen and paper."

That struck me as a phenomenally stupid comment. "Nice people don't rob anyone at all."

The gunman held open the glass door for us.

"You can wait outside." He put a hand up to my chest.

"She doesn't speak any Spanish," I explained.

"We'll improvise." He pulled Raven away from me and took her inside the glass cubicle.

As the door swung shut, I couldn't help but remember that terrible morning when Raven had first been taken from me—that time by the Vice Minister's henchmen. I'd sworn never to let it happen again.

Just before the door fully shut, I slipped my toe in to catch it.

"Hey!" the cabbie called from behind the driver's seat.

Raven retrieved the cash, gave it to the gunman.

He looked at the money suspiciously, as though he wasn't satisfied.

Raven shrugged.

The cab driver set the parking brake and got out of the car.

"I have a lower cash limit, is all," Raven said.

The gunman shouted in Spanish at Raven—much too fast for her to understand.

I pushed the door open and stepped inside.

Shocked to see me standing there, the gunman wheeled toward me, his pistol once again aimed in my direction. The glass door clicked behind me, leaving the driver stuck alone out on the curb.

"It's okay." I held my hands up in front of my chest. "Her bank just has a lower cash limit than mine. It's no big deal."

Still frustrated, the gunman seemed to believe me. He grabbed Raven's purse right off her shoulder and pulled her card from the machine's slot. "*Vamos*," he said. "Let's go to the next one already."

"The next one?" I asked.

"The next bank, *pendejo!*" He went to the door. "I know those limits are for a single withdrawal." He grinned. "We're going to make lots of withdrawals, the three of us."

Raven and I exchanged a glance, her face whiter than normal.

"A little help?" the gunman said. Between his pistol, my wallet, and Raven's purse, his hands were full.

I stepped over and pulled the door inward for him.

"Fucking gringos," he said. "Letting somebody else tell you how much of your own money you can have at a time." He laughed. "Aye, to suffer from those sorts of problems."

Once his first step went across the threshold, I put all of my body weight against the door and rammed it into his back.

He was pushed so hard, he fell forward. The contents of his arms skittered across the pavement—purse, wallet, debit cards, gun—as he went to break his fall.

I kept pushing against the door until it clicked shut.

Raven gasped.

The gunman got back up to his feet and turned toward me. Teeth clenched, eyes trembling, he pounded the bottoms of his fists against the glass door and shouted something inaudible. Raven and I both took a step backward. In another second, he was literally foaming at the mouth, spittle spraying the glass door.

The driver picked the spilled items up off the sidewalk. The jean-jacket man turned and took one of our cards from him, then went to swipe it.

I hadn't thought of this. Right away, I leaned against the door and tried to hold it still with my body.

"Eddie, look!" Raven knelt at my feet. She spotted a deadbolt that went into the floor and immediately engaged it.

I cringed as the gunman got the green light from the door latch and pushed. His body bounced right off the glass. The door didn't budge at all.

I let out a long breath. Raven put a hand up over her heart.

The man in the jean jacket was even more furious now. He got his pistol from the driver and took a shooting stance right there on the street.

Raven and I backed away from the door. I reached out and took her by the hand. If this stranger wanted to shoot us both out of anger, there was little we could do to stop him. I looked into his cold, angry eyes, and prepared for whatever was to come next.

The gunman flinched before I heard anything. Some ancient-sounding siren pierced the thickness of the glass and the hum of the air conditioner. Our two assailants jumped into their cab and drove off at top speed. Raven and I stood there in the glass box, confused. Finally, a Peruvian police car drove past us—maybe in pursuit, maybe after something else nearby. At any rate, Raven and I shrugged at each other and figured it was safe enough to step outside.

We stood on the sidewalk with mouths agape. It felt as though we should be doing something, speaking to some sort of official.

"What now, Eddie?" Raven asked.

"I don't know," I admitted. "I guess we go to the airport?" I could still see the planes landing up ahead. "It seems as good a place as any."

"Do you have any way to pay for a ticket?" she asked.

"No," I said. "You?"

"No."

"We'll have to improvise."

Once again, we were walking. This time, at least, there was no luggage—nothing in my pockets, even—to weigh me down.

The Lima airport was not designed for pedestrian traffic. Approaching it on foot was a matter of weaving below underpasses and through parking lots, to walk onward with the glass terminals and towers as your only guide.

"Thanks for what you did back there, Eddie."

"Thanks?" I nearly had to scream it over the sound of a descending airplane.

"For standing up to those robbers, for putting a stop to that . . . whatever that was."

"It's called 'express kidnapping.' I read about it in the security briefing. They drive around and make people withdraw money until their accounts are empty. I read some horror stories about embassy employees who were held for hours. It can get pretty traumatic."

Raven cringed. "Why don't they just take the cards and the codes?"

I shrugged. "Maybe they don't want the victims to freeze the accounts."

"Well, thanks—at any rate."

We were nearing the terminal now and had to walk through a cluster of taxis—their drivers sitting on the hoods or reclining in the seats. They all seemed confused by the sight of us, the angle of our approach. We kept our eyes focused forward, trying not to assume that they, too, were kidnappers in disguise.

Finally we passed through the glass doors and entered the terminal proper. The bright yellow signage and the fluorescent lights made me feel as though I were inside a backwater Nevada casino.

"Well," I said to Raven. "Is there anybody you can call?"

"My mom's with her husband in Europe. I don't even know my dad's number."

"Right." Somehow, throughout our entire walk, there was a small part of me that already knew exactly what I had to do next. "I'll handle this."

"Look." Raven pointed down a hallway in the corner. "There's a phone."

"I wonder what it's like to get an international collect call placed from here."

"Look on the bright side: At least we got robbed in a country that still has pay phones."

—

After a long series of recorded messages, cryptic country codes, and two living operators, I finally heard my mother's voice, accepting the charges on the other line.

"*Mijo!*" she shouted. "*Gracias a Dios.* I've been praying that you would call me. We saw you on the television, and I was so worried."

I could hear my father in the background shouting questions and instructions. My mother kept going on with the narrative of the last few days: seeing me on the news, hearing about the revolution, wondering if I was okay. I couldn't even get a word in edgewise.

"*Oye, mama*," I shouted. "Listen: this is very important. I need your help."

My father finally had the wherewithal to pick up the extension. "What can we do for you, Guayo?"

"Listen, I had to flee Puerto Malogrado. I'm in the Lima airport, in Peru. I've just been robbed. I have no money, no credit cards, nothing. You need to call LAN airlines and buy two tickets from Lima to Boise as soon as possible. I'm stuck here."

My father repeated the salient points of what I'd just said: Lima, LAN airlines. I could picture him writing it all down in the little pad he relied on—relied on increasingly, as he grew older.

"Thank you, Papa. I can't tell you how much I appreciate it."

"One thing, son," he said calmly. "In whose name is the second ticket?"

Raven stood beside me, excited that things were going well, unable to hear the whole conversation—most of which was in heavily accented Spanish.

"Raven Callahan."

I spelled the whole name out for my father, while he wrote it down in his slow, methodical script—repeating each letter aloud.

"She's my girlfriend," I said once he'd finished.

My mother gasped audibly. Raven's eyes widened where she stood at my side. There was a pause over the line.

"Please call the airline as soon as you can," I said. "There may not be many more flights out today, particularly all the way to Boise. I should go. This call is costing you a fortune."

"We love you, *hijo*. Goodbye."

I hung up the phone.

Raven gave me a big hug as soon as the receiver was out of my hand. "Good work," she mumbled into my shoulder.

"We should give them a minute," I said. "I'll use the bathroom, in the meantime."

"Me too." Raven released me, took a step back. "Hey, Eddie," she said. "Thanks for calling me your girlfriend."

"You're welcome?" It didn't seem like the right response, but was the best I could come up with, under the circumstances.

"I'm happy to be that," she said.

"I'm happy about it too," I sputtered.

———

As it turned out, there was a long line at the LAN counter; waiting for my parents to make the purchase was the least of our worries. In fact, as I strained my eyes to see the schedule of departures, I worried that we might miss whichever flight they booked us on.

Once we finally got to the front of the line, the clerk was suspicious of our story.

"We were robbed," I explained. "We don't have any money and we need to get home. My parents bought us tickets—within the last hour—from here to Boise."

"What were those names again?" He was a slender Peruvian guy with a short-sleeved shirt and a knit tie.

I spelled out both of our names as slowly as I could.

The clerk stared into his screen, biting his lower lip in concentration. "This must be your reservation," he finally said.

"Great! Let's get those boarding passes then."

"But it's not going to Boise."

"What?" I asked.

"I have two one-way coach tickets on the direct flight to Miami."

"*Coño!*" I muttered.

"What's the matter, Eddie?" Raven hadn't followed the exchange.

"My idiot parents bought us tickets to Miami, not Boise." I put my fingers to my temples. "This is so typical of them."

"Maybe they want to meet your new girlfriend." Raven laughed. "Come on, Eddie. It's practically on the way."

I turned to the clerk. "We'll take them."

He hit a button. "You'll need to hurry through security. The flight takes off in less than an hour."

We did as he said and rushed off.

———

By the security line, a Plexiglas amnesty box offered passengers a final chance to drop in anything they couldn't carry on. In addition to all the small knives, there was an array of handmade Amazonian weapons: blowguns, poison darts, bows and arrows.

"Ever seen anything like that?" Raven chuckled.

"Who would think they could just take a blowgun on a plane these days?" I asked.

Raven shrugged. "Tourists."

"Your passports, please?" A female immigration official spoke to us. I hadn't even noticed that we'd reached the front of the line.

Raven pulled up her pants leg and exposed a sort of hidden pocket inside her sock. She took out her passport and handed it to the officer.

I stood there, frozen.

"Where's your passport?" Raven asked.

"In my wallet," I said. "The robbers got it." How had I not considered this until now?

"What?"

"Sir?" The officer asked again. "Your identification?"

"Sorry," I explained. "I was robbed earlier today. All my documents were stolen. I'm trying to get back to the United States."

"You don't look like you're from the United States," she said. "Or sound like it either." She hit a button on her radio and uttered a numerical code into it.

"Wait, wait. I have this." I pulled my belt out through the loops and unzipped the compartment. From inside, I removed the last remaining item: a Xerox of the first page of my passport. By the time the officer unfolded it, a colleague had joined her. They both looked it over while I stood there, making my most pathetic face.

"Okay, let him through," the colleague said.

"Thank you!"

Raven and I went forward. Without any luggage, it was just a matter of putting our shoes through the X-ray.

"I have to admit," I said as we headed for our gate, "that belt has been pretty handy."

"Eddie, look!"

At first I thought she'd found our plane; but, instead, she was pointing at a television inside a terminal bar. On screen, we could see the rumpled, unshaven face of the Vice Minister as he was led inside his old pink Ministry by FURP soldiers. His hands were cuffed behind his back.

"What are they saying?" Raven asked.

I could barely hear the TV over the sounds of the terminal and the other customers. We took a few steps closer. The picture switched to a shot of the Subcomandante speaking before the press corps. He said that he was grateful to the international community for the pressure they had applied. He thanked the media for exposing the abuses of the old regime. And—above all else—he was grateful for a new era of peace in Puerto Malogrado.

"The war is over," I told Raven. "You did it! He specifically cited pressure from the media and the international community."

Raven was at a loss for words.

"Excuse me," I turned to a waitress who was busing a nearby table. "Do you know how they caught the Vice Minister?"

"The what?"

I pointed toward the television. "The former leader of Puerto Malogrado."

"Oh, that." She put her tray down. "After all the scandals—the farmers and the reporters and all—some of his sympathizers finally betrayed him and turned him in."

"Incredible," I said.

"It will be incredible"—she shrugged—"if that little country finally stops blowing itself up, sending its refugees over to us all the time."

I fought off the urge to tell her how much I admired that "little country," that so far it had impressed me much more than her own, and that she should thank Puerto Malogrado for giving her people the potato—among other things. Instead, I only nodded.

"Eddie, look." Raven grabbed my arm. "It's Kearns."

I turned back to the screen. Sure enough, there he was—the main talking head on a three-expert panel. His words dubbed into Spanish, he expressed his enthusiasm for the latest developments.

Kearns went out of his way to mention that it was a good day for journalistic freedom and then expressed concern for Raven Callahan, who had last been seen in Puerto Malogrado, just before the worst of the fighting.

"He's wondering if you're okay," I said.

"Me?"

"When you posted those stories from this side of the border, did you mention that you were in Peru?"

She shook her head. "I thought about it. But I figured it might diminish the urgency."

I smiled. "Fair enough. But once we get to the States, you should reveal yourself. The press will want to talk to you."

"This is all so crazy," she said.

"It's not that crazy. It was your idea; it just worked even better than you anticipated."

"With a little help from Kearns."

"Kearns is an opportunist. He can see which way the wind's blowing, is all. You started this."

"Can I bring you two anything to drink?" The same waitress returned with an empty tray and a pad, looking slightly annoyed that we were standing in her floor, not ordering.

A crackling voice then came over the loudspeaker. I could barely understand it, but it seemed to be a final boarding call.

"No, thanks," I said to the waitress.

"Eddie," Raven said. "I think that's our flight they're talking about."

We ran through the terminal—which was much longer than I expected. Both of us were panting by the time we reached the gate. Everyone had boarded, and they were about to close the jetway.

"Wait!" I shouted. "We're supposed to be on that plane."

A flight attendant in heavy eye makeup and a neck scarf stood behind the desk. I handed her the boarding passes.

"We called for you several times," she said.

"These are our seats." I pointed toward the numbers on the passes.

"We had stand-by passengers. Your seats are taken already."

"What?" I was furious. "We just bought these tickets an hour ago. We need to get home."

"One second."

Again I found myself at the mercy of a LAN employee's furious keystrokes.

Raven reached out and squeezed my hand. "We'll be okay. Whatever happens, we can handle it."

"Okay," the attendant sighed. "I have two spots in first class. We'll have to put you in those."

"We'll take it!" I shouted. My grin grew so wide so fast, it almost hurt my face muscles. I turned to Raven. "That's something we can handle."

I tried to control my enthusiasm over our first-class upgrade, tried to remind myself that it really was a small triumph—especially in light of how Raven had just deposed a corrupt dictator and ended a civil war via a series of dodgy internet connections. But I couldn't help it. After that miserable bus ride in to Lima, after that awful taxi ordeal, this was just what I needed.

Raven, on the other hand, barely seemed to care. Had she still owned any sort of connected device, I'm sure she would've been glued to that, following the story. In the absence of her laptop, she didn't know what to do with her hands.

As soon as we were settled, I caught the eye of a flight attendant carrying a tray of champagne flutes. I held up two fingers and she brought them over.

"Here you go, Raven." By the time I handed the glass to her, the plane was already taxiing.

"Thanks, Eddie." She started to take a sip, but I stopped her.

"No, wait," I said. "First, a toast." I lifted my glass. "To Raven. You were sent down to South America in bad faith, and you were underestimated by everyone you met there—including me. But without any major network affiliation, and without any well of money, you did something incredible, something that the finest journalists and diplomats had all failed to do."

Raven's face turned beet-red. I wasn't quite sure where this sincerity had come from. But in the past few days she had consistently blown my mind.

"You're amazing, is all I'm trying to say. Cheers."

We clinked glasses, and each took a sip.

"That was beautiful." She teared up. "That may be the nicest thing anyone's ever said to me. Thank you."

"Try and remember this moment when we're with my parents and they're driving us both crazy." I took a gulp.

She laughed. "I'll bank it for you."

The plane sped up, and suddenly we were on the brink of takeoff. Raven had no calming drugs or trinkets anymore, but she didn't look worried. I grabbed her hand and held it tight. Her palm was nowhere near as cold and clammy as on our last takeoff together. In fact, this time I felt like it was me who needed my hand held. Maybe not so much for the fear of flight as for the fear of what lay waiting at our destination.

We were airborne now, staring down at the city lights of Lima. Higher and higher we went, farther and farther away from South America, this continent that had given the West so much, and asked for so little in return. This other America—one that the US couldn't find a way to live with, but couldn't live without either.

Soon the lights faded, and we saw the rough outlines of the mighty Andes out of our window. And soon, even those mountaintops gave way to clouds.

S taying in Miami wasn't the result of any resolute decision on our part. Instead, it just happened, slowly and incrementally, one tiny convenience after another, until one day it became obvious. In other words, the exact opposite of the way all my previous life decisions had been made.

Straightaway, my parents were more pleasant than I could've hoped. They made Raven feel welcome but weren't overbearing. So great was their joy over my physical well-being that they didn't fuss about my bungled career or uncertain future. They gave us a spare key to the house and to their car and insisted that we come and go as we please.

The morning after our flight home, I woke inside my childhood bedroom. Raven was already up and speaking to a reporter on the land line. All sorts of media had reached out to her in the hours since she'd lost her computer and phone. That afternoon, she did an interview on local television. From there she was off and running.

In those early days, she played the role of in-studio expert on the revolution in Puerto Malogrado. Once America's attention on that conflict waned, she seamlessly morphed into the network's go-to GMO expert. Many of her earlier blog posts were reconfigured into longer magazine pieces, which led to new assignments. A scathing feature-length look at Tuberware—complete with quotes from yours truly—put her on the map. Within six months, she received an offer for a full-time post as a Latin America correspondent—something we initially thought was a prank. Now Miami is her perfect base of operations—though I wish there weren't so much travel involved.

As for me, I was less eager to get a new career under way. After a few weeks at home, I returned to Boise briefly, just to collect my things and put my condo on the market. By the time I found a buyer and closed the sale, it was past time to get us out of my parents' house. We found a small two-bedroom not so far away from them. With the cash from my condo and my Tuberware stock, and all of Raven's new income, we were able to afford it. My folks were over the moon.

For several months I was kept busy by real-estate matters: selling, buying, moving, repairing, paperwork, and so on. Once that tapered off, my hands were already full helping Raven with her new work. That's mostly been a matter of translation—both from Spanish and from scientific jargon. I find I enjoy it more than I would've thought. I even enrolled in an online Portuguese class to help her with the Brazilian assignments.

I suppose there was an unspoken assumption that, once ready, I'd go back on the job market. Maybe widen the net a little and look into research positions. But every time I checked the openings and opportunities, I immediately lost interest. It felt as though I was looking only because that's what people do after they lose their jobs.

Nothing ever came of Kearns's threats to discredit me. If anything, he's gone out of his way to flatter me in public. Still, during those days of anxiety, something changed. I'd stared down the barrel of a career change for so long that I lost my fear of it. Now, a return to the processed-foods industry—all I'd hoped for during my time in Puerto Malogrado—would be a disappointment.

A lot of interesting possibilities have been tossed around. Several editors have approached Raven about book ideas. She's keen to coauthor something with me. There's talk of a cultural and scientific history of the Irish Potato Famine. That sounds interesting, but with the busy schedule Raven keeps now, I don't consider it imminent.

I also took a meeting with the current principal at my old high school. Apparently, due to a teacher shortage in Dade County, they've opened some loopholes for science teachers who lack official certification. Anyone with a PhD in a relevant field is considered qualified. She was ecstatic about the possibility of hiring me to teach in the fall. There is something attractive about returning to the very classrooms where I fell in love with science—and then subsequently felt that this was something to be ashamed of. Though I have no experience, I suspect that my time in Puerto Malogrado might've left me with some of the relevant skills: thinking outside of my narrow specialty, explaining unfamiliar scientific facts, and simply standing in front of an impatient audience. I told her I'd think about it.

The truth is, I like what I do now. When Raven prepares for a trip, I help with the logistical matters: setting up fixers, transportation, and accommodations. We often do research together, combing through related stories—in both the English and the Spanish press. And when she's here, there's even more work: arranging television appearances, fact-checking stories, tracking down sources, and so on. Plus, I try to look in on my parents a few times a week; they're only going to need more attention in the coming years.

We're doing fine, financially. Raven's job covers my benefits, and her success gives me as much satisfaction as my own career ever did. So what's wrong with being the man behind the important woman? Maybe it was never my plan, but it suits me.

It sounds as if things are going well for the Morales family. Those British researchers arrived shortly after the Vice Minister was apprehended. Don Pablo reported that they were pleasant and respectful. Apparently, they considered the condition of Pablito and his sisters to be less acute than the family they had studied in Turkey. The British team brought more walkers and some special shoes, and they erected a set of parallel bars in the back yard for the children to practice on. I'm told that Pablito can now walk the length of the living room unassisted.

Raven has returned to Puerto Malogrado a couple of times for her work. She's usually quite busy but has managed to visit Huanchillo on one occasion. We've discussed vacationing there if her job ever slows down.

Pablito has also taken to the camera that she left him. Every so often, he finds a way online and manages to send her some images. I don't know anything about photography, but his work is striking. Mostly, he shoots daily life in the Andes: the potato harvest, llamas in the misty morning light, colorful Catholic holidays with echoes of Incan ritual. As one might expect, his work shows an obsession with perspective. Many of the shots are from extreme angles—mostly low, but others from high up. Raven has her favorites printed out and framed. They hang all over our little house.

FURP has gone through a few hiccups since they've been in power, and the American media never hesitates to scrutinize a left-leaning, former guerilla group in Latin America. But I think they've done well, all in all. They've severed all official ties with drug traffickers—though they don't cooperate with the US on crop eradication. The Subcomandante has been adamant about allowing free and fair elections once his term ends, which should silence many of his critics. They've ceased to be a testing ground for agrochemical companies, that's for sure. By all indications, their economy is doing well. After all, it's an area full of natural resources and hardworking people; if the government isn't stealing all the money, it's not so difficult to succeed.

———

Raven has no time for cleaning or shopping, so that all falls on me. I've even taken up cooking lately—something I'd never engaged in outside of a laboratory. In fact, it sometimes feels as if I spend all my time in our local upscale supermarket—the sort of place I once dismissed as pretentious and overpriced—fighting flocks of suburban moms for the latest food trends. What can I say? My trust in the big producers has been shaken, and that's hard to get back. Tuberware and its competitors aren't getting Raven's hard-earned money—at least not on my watch.

Plus, I like the bulk bins. My cooking has so far featured pots of beans boiled for hours, slow-cooked roasts, big batches of soups and stews. It's nice to have something that can sit in the fridge and feed us for days. After all those years perfecting processed foods, I prefer dishes made from scratch, dishes that don't hide the hours of labor that went into them.

In fact, I now go out of my way to roll my eyes at all those prepackaged foods—all that corn and soy molded and reworked into different shapes and sizes, pounded into obedience to one diet or another. All those boxes promising to let us eat like cavemen, like Okinawan fishermen, like Incan peasants. All that preindustrial sustenance that's only a microwave and a few layers of cellophane away.

Maybe it's sour grapes. I'm not proud of this, but I do feel some small measure of satisfaction over the fact that Tuberware hasn't yet managed to roll out their French-fry vending machine. Granted, it's more than likely a problem with the machine itself than with the fry mix. But still, it's nice to think that my absence has affected them, if only a little.

Potatoes don't store particularly well in this climate. They're prone to bugs and fungus if left in our pantry too long. Still, I find myself pausing by their section in my supermarket and can rarely resist putting some into my basket. Besides, Raven's coming home from an assignment today, and I always make a special dinner upon her return. It's become a little tradition for us.

After all this time, after all the ups and downs, I can still feel that original attraction to *Solanum tuberosum*: that dense package of useful calories, growing below a plant that's basically toxic, thriving in all sorts of conditions, in that funny and charming shape.

Maybe it isn't as mythologized as the apple, but who could argue that it hasn't been more significant for human history? What other New World crop has been so thoroughly incorporated into Old World cuisines? Corn does way bigger numbers, of course. But corn has succeeded mostly by becoming something else: flour, animal feed, sugar, and now fuel. Not so the potato. Despite Warren's best efforts, it's kept its basic character intact for thousands of years. And while I often fantasize about the demise of Tuberware, I still silently hope that the spud gets its due in the twenty-first-century food system—whatever that turns out to be.

But I suppose it's not my problem anymore. Now I simply carry my reusable bags out to my car, drive them back to my humble house, and get dinner ready. Raven's flight is on schedule, so she should be home within an hour. I gather my Yukon Golds and put a pot on the stove. While the water's heating, I use our sharpest knife to cut the potatoes into thick wedges. Once they're ready, they all go into the boiling water. I've saved the oil from last time and bring it to temperature in another pot. After a few minutes, the potatoes come out of the water. I don't want to start frying too early, so for now I get the draining rack set up—basically just a baking tray covered in pieces of brown paper bag. Still no text from Raven, so I fetch eggs, vinegar, and oil from the fridge and whip up a batch of homemade mayonnaise. The oil's hot, the potatoes are ready, and I finally get the message saying she's in a cab. I drop in all the fries, jump back to avoid the spatter, and listen to that satisfying crackle.

Preparing a special meal from scratch for someone I love—it's become the best part of my new reality. Why did I spend so many years trying to purge this sort of act from American life? What better things did I believe everybody had to do with their time?

It's been a few minutes, so I grab my wire-mesh skimmer—one of my favorite new toys—and check the fries. Close, but not quite there yet.

I rinse the boiling pot and take out a couple of dinner plates. In the windowsill by our cabinet, I've got a couple of potatoes sprouting in water. Probably not a great idea—because of the fungus—but so far they're thriving.

Another minute and the fries look perfect. I cut the heat and then use my skimmer to spread them out across the brown paper. Ketchup, hot sauce, my mayonnaise, and a couple of napkins all go on the table. I shake the tray to turn the potatoes. There's a sound from the street; I have a look, but it's the neighbors.

I salt the fries while they're still spread across the tray, then plate them. Now I'm ready; Raven should be here any second. I check my work and am struck by the color of the fries: that golden-brown hue I coveted for so long in my Boise lab. Who knew it was this easy? The only secret ingredient is oil, heat, and potatoes.

Between the sights and the smells, I can't quite resist sneaking just one fry before Raven arrives. It's hot to the touch, so I hold it above the plate for a moment, an inch away from my mouth.

This fry might represent an hour's worth of my time, but it also represents a few thousand years of history, of humans wresting a perennial nightshade from the wild and making it domestic, then incrementally improving it through seed-saving and cross-breeding. It's no less an achievement than antibiotics, than heavier-than-air flight, or nuclear fission. And like all those things, it can bring us wealth and convenience—but in the wrong hands, it can bring unspeakable evil. When it comes to food science, I'm still nowhere near as dogmatic as my fellow organic-supermarket shoppers. I'm sure technology has even more to offer us—more ways to fight hunger and improve yields. But I have little faith in the current stewards of that technology, those CEOs and billionaires who stand on the shoulders of generations and generations of hardworking farmers. Hopefully, between the media attention, the good-hearted scientists, and the will of the consumers I walked those aisles with today, we will learn to navigate that fine line between nature and industry.

But, for now, a car door slams outside and it's time to hide the evidence. I pop the clandestine fry into my mouth and chew fast. It's perfect.

ACKNOWLEDGMENTS

I must thank Jemima Harrison and all the other filmmakers, scientists, and producers responsible for the BBC TWO documentary entitled *The Family that Walks on All Fours*. That program was a huge part of the inspiration behind this novel. Had I not happened to stumble across it on PBS one evening, I don't believe *One Potato* would exist. I'm also deeply indebted to Michael Pollan's books—particularly *The Botany of Desire* and *An Omnivore's Dilemma*—for their insights into biotech and food production. John Kelly's *The Graves Are Walking: The Great Famine and the Saga of the Irish People* and Susan Campbell Bartoletti's *Black Potatoes: The Story of the Great Irish Famine, 1845–1850* were wonderful resources on the Irish Potato Famine.

I owe another great debt to Barry and Evan Nagle. Their readings, encouragement, and manaʻo were absolutely invaluable to finishing this project. Thanks to J. Reuben Appelman for bringing his one-of-a-kind eye to this work-in-progress and taking it to the next level.

I'd also like to thank Jaimie Gusman and the members of the Hawaiʻi Salon/Saloon—including Tom Gammarino, Timothy Dyke, Susan Schultz, Janine Oshiro, Dave Scrivner, Julia Wieting, and others—for enduring early versions of this story. It offered me some much-needed confidence at a crucial juncture.

Thanks especially to Stephanie Beard and the rest of the team at Turner Publishing and Keylight Books for bringing this story to the world.

ABOUT THE AUTHOR

Tyler McMahon is the author of the novels *How the Mistakes Were Made*, *Kilometer 99*, *Dream of Another America*, and *One Potato*. Tyler is a Professor of English at Hawai`i Pacific University and the editor of Hawai`i Pacific Review. He lives in Honolulu with his wife, Dabney Gough.